PUSH BACK
CHOSON

An Alternate History

RICHARD S. BROWN

BLACK ROSE
writing™

ISBN: 978-1-61296-733-2
PUBLISHED BY BLACK ROSE WRITING
www.blackrosewriting.com

Printed in the United States of America
Suggested retail price $17.95

Push Back Choson is printed in Book Antiqua

The book is dedicated to my wife Sung Hi.

Korean Peninsula

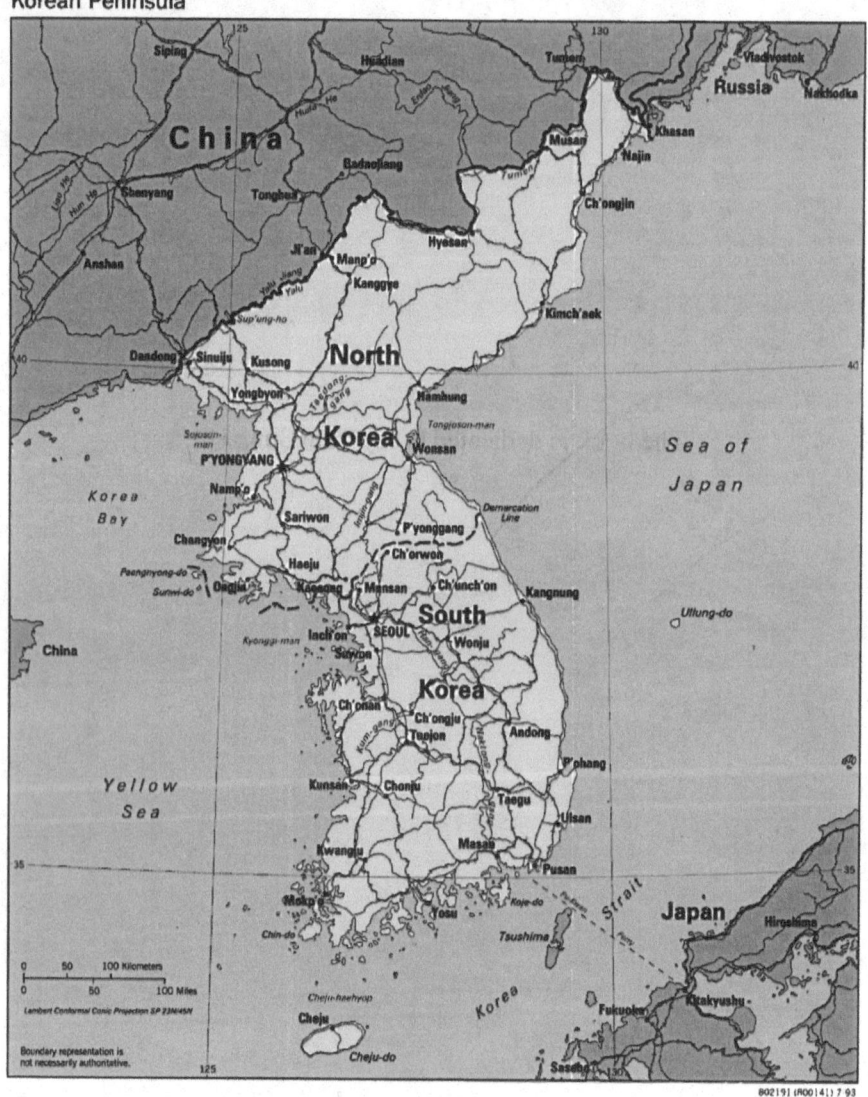

PUSH BACK
CHOSON

PREFACE

Push Back Choson is a work of fiction about a real war. Most of the organizations and places mentioned are real, and many of the events portrayed in this book actually occurred, especially those in the first few chapters. However, the events and actions as depicted in this story are reconstructions based on my own research and are either used fictitiously or are the products of my imagination. The time frames of some historical events have been changed to fit into the fictional story line. Similarly, although many of the characters in this story are real historical figures, the scenes and dialogue are fictional and should not be construed as representing historical fact.

In conducting research for this novel, I made extensive use of the Harry S. Truman Presidential Library which proved to be a gold mine of information on daily activities in the White House during the opening days and weeks of the Korean War. Glenn Paige's carefully documented book, *The Korean Decision*, published in 1968, provided a clear time-line of events, both in Seoul and in Washington, leading up to and immediately following the North Korean invasion and was an excellent cross reference source. The Dwight D. Eisenhower Presidential Library internet site provided similarly useful information about White House activities during the years 1953–57 as well as interesting correspondence concerning relations with Japan, the Soviet Union, and the Chinese People's Republic. The U.S. State Department's publication *U.S. Foreign Relations of the U.S., 1950–60*, accessed through the University of Wisconsin Digital Collection web site, contained a wealth of pertinent historic and legal documents.

Over the past several years I have read a wide range of books and articles related to the subject of modern Korean and Japanese history, the Korean War, and American post-World War II relations with Korea and Japan. These readings provided the background needed to weave real historic events into the fictional story. I have listed those writings that have been of particular use to me in the preparation of this book in a selected bibliography at the end of this book.

The subject matter of this book contains many Korean and Japanese terms unfamiliar to most western readers. Therefore, a word about language use is appropriate. Over the past fifty years the Romanized spelling of words in Japanese, Korean, and Chinese officially recognized by the respective governments has changed, and in different text books the same words are spelled differently. For example Choson, the country name identified in the title, may be written as Choson, Joseon, or Chosun. In this book I have employed a modified version of the older McCune-Reischauer system to spell out Korean words and names, omitting apostrophes and diacritical marks in order to simplify the reading. Where appropriate, I have added end notes on the last page to further define foreign terms, spell out acronyms, and provide supplemental source information.

I used the name Choson to identify Communist Korea, because it is the name the North Koreans use to refer to themselves. The official title of the Democratic People's Republic of Korea (North Korea) in the native Hangul language is _Choson_ _Minjujui Inminkonghwaguk_. Choson is also the name the old Yi Dynasty used prior to its demise in the early twentieth century. Nevertheless, Western nations have used the term Korea to refer to the peninsula for more than a hundred years, and that practice continued after the separation of the country into two sections after World War II, ignoring North Korea's naming preference.

Another aspect of the language differences that I struggled with was the presentation of personal names. The normal order of Korean and Japanese names is for the family name to precede the given personal name. In this book I have compromised by placing the given name first for most of the characters because I believe it is easier for English language readers to relate. I have made some exceptions for certain key historical figures, such as Kim Il Sung where the traditional name order is familiar to most readers.

I would be remiss if I failed to mention the help that I received from members of the Leawood Library Writers Group. Adam Sale, Charlotte Henderson, Joyce Brown, and Mike O'Leary critiqued my early drafts, enabling me to produce an acceptable product. Frank Cook was especially helpful in editing my final draft before publication. Without the encouragement and support of my wife, Sung Hi, this book would never have been written. She not only kept me going when I thought it was hopeless, but she provided invaluable advice and suggestions on Korean cultural practices, foods, and language. Finally I want to thank Black Rose Writing for giving me the opportunity to put this book into print.

INTRODUCTION

One week after American bombers unleashed their atomic bombs on the cities of Hiroshima and Nagasaki, the Japanese emperor announced the surrender of Japan. World War II was over. It was a joyous time for liberated people throughout the world, but it meant something special for people of Korea. It marked the end of thirty-five years as a colony under the yoke of Japan. The streets of Seoul were filled with crowds of people, and shouts of *"Mansei"* could be heard everywhere. A new independent Korea was at hand. A bright new dawn had arrived. But that dawn was to be followed by many dark days, and the Koreans soon found their dream of independence shattered as Soviet and American armies began an occupation to decide Korea's fate.

In July 1945, with Japan's defeat nearing, allied leaders met in Potsdam, Germany to outline final strategy for ending the war in the Far East. In discussions over Korea, American and Soviet staff members agreed that when the fighting ended, the two war-time allies would divide the Korean peninsula into two sectors. The Soviet Union would accept the surrender of Japanese forces north of the 38th parallel, and the United States would handle the surrender south of the line.

Although the war ended on August 15, U.S. forces under the command of Lieutenant General John Hodge didn't arrive in Korea until September 8. By that time, the Soviets were already busy taking control in the north. Prior to the arrival of the Americans Korean nationalists had begun to form local people's committees throughout the country in preparation for the establishment of a unified national Korean government. Korean representatives in the south attempted to meet with General Hodge, but instead of creating a line of communication with these indigenous leaders, Hodge turned them away.

In the northern sector the Soviet Union used the local people's committees, which initially included many non-Communists, as a foundation for handing over local control to Koreans. When the Soviet army entered Korea, they came with a cadre of Korean officers and soldiers who spoke Russian. It didn't take long before these Soviet agents took command of the local people's committees and began organizing the north along Communist lines.

The Americans, under General Hodge, established the U.S. Military Government in Korea (USAMGIK) to exercise control south of the 38th parallel. Without a Korean speaking cadre of his own, Hodge looked to western educated Korean businessmen as well as civil servants and police who had worked under the Japanese colonial government to help him maintain order and administer basic governmental functions. Ordinary Koreans considered most of these appointees to be collaborationists with the enemy, and their retention in positions of authority provided fuel for the growth of pro-Communist sentiment.

With no clear political solution available to the Americans inside Korea, the U.S. Army facilitated the return to Korea of Syngman Rhee who had been living in exile in the United States for twenty-five years. Although he was considered a true patriot by those aware of his early participation in the Korean independence movement, most Koreans had never heard of him before his arrival. Nevertheless, his Christian background, his fluency in English, and his strong anti-Communist stance, gave him a marked influence with USAMGIK, providing him with a decided edge over his Korean rivals in their contest to fill the political vacuum in the south.

In an effort to work out details for the eventual unification of the two Koreas, an American-Soviet Joint Commission was set up in December 1945. The two sides reached an initial agreement to establish a four-year trusteeship under international oversight prior to granting full independence, but conservative political groups in the south refused to go along. They wanted a more rapid transition to full independence. The talks over unification foundered when the Soviet Union insisted on excluding any political group opposing trusteeship from participating in national elections. By early 1947 it was clear that agreement over Korea could not be reached between the two super powers, and the United States took the matter to the United Nations.

In November 1947, the UN General Assembly voted to recognize the Korean claim for immediate independence and authorized a UN supervised election of a national assembly to govern the country. The

United Nations Temporary Commission on Korea (UNTCOK) was established to oversee the elections, but the Soviet Union refused to allow UN representatives into the north to oversee the election process. In the face of Soviet opposition, the United States again submitted the Korean problem to the United Nations for resolution. The United Nations General Assembly subsequently authorized the election to go forward in areas where UN monitoring was permitted. On May 10, 1948, Korean people living in the American administered area below the 38th parallel went to the polls to elect a national assembly. The newly elected legislative body quickly developed a constitution establishing a presidential system of government. Syngman Rhee, head of the largest party represented in the assembly, was elected president by members of the assembly.

Although the newly formed Republic of Korea (ROK) government only controlled territory south of the 38th parallel, it claimed jurisdiction over the entire peninsula. In reaction to this, the North Korean press announced the establishment of the Democratic People's Republic of Korea (DPRK) in territory north of the 38th parallel, naming Kim Il Sung as premier. The Soviet Union quickly recognized the DPRK as the legitimate government of Korea. However, two months later the UN General Assembly passed a resolution recognizing the American backed Republic of Korea as the sole legitimate government of Korea.

By the spring of 1950, both the Soviet Union and the United States had withdrawn their occupation troops from Korea, leaving the political situation unsettled. Neither the Republic of Korea nor the DPRK was satisfied with the country's division at the 38th parallel. Neither considered it permanent. Neither saw compromise as a solution. The clock was wound tight, and the alarm bell was set to go off.

CHAPTER 1

KOREA

June 24–25, 1950

Rain spattered against the office window as Tom cleared his desk, getting ready to leave for the day. *Damn it! Raining again. Another lost Saturday afternoon. I was hoping to get out of the city. Not this weekend.* Junior Foreign Service Officer Tom Crandall had been in Korea for three months, his first assignment after going through orientation classes back in D.C. He thought they'd be sending him to Japan— that's what he'd trained for— but here he was in Seoul. It wasn't that he was unhappy with his assignment. He enjoyed the interaction with the Korean people. He found them a lot different from the Japanese people he'd met—more open and demonstrative. He wanted to learn more about the local culture, but, so far, the press of learning the new job had made that impossible.

He'd been outside Seoul just once—that was on the train to Pusan to deliver a classified packet to the consulate. Now the weather wasn't cooperating. Just as he picked up his briefcase to leave, Miss Baek, the secretary, popped her head in the door. "There's a student outside who says he need to see you. His appointment is tomorrow, but he's been here most of morning."

"Why can't he wait until tomorrow?"

"He didn't say."

Dropping the briefcase unto the floor, he figured his afternoon was already shot. "Okay show him in."

"Do you need me stay?"

"No, Miss Baek, you can go home. Thanks."

A young man wearing dark horn-rimmed glasses, probably in his early twenties, dressed neatly in slacks and a white open necked shirt, appeared at the door. He bowed slightly. "Thank you. Thank you Mr. Crandall for seeing me."

"Not at all. Take a seat," he said pointing to the chair in front of the desk. "Tell me your name and what it is you need."

"My name is Chong Kyu Choe. I am graduate of Yonsei University and I have a student visa request for United States. I received letter from Stanford last week that they accepted my application. Because all is finished, I want to get my visa now. I must leave right away."

Rubbing his chin while considering a response, Tom said, "That's good that you've been accepted at a school in the states. But why the rush? You have an appointment scheduled for tomorrow according to my secretary. You should wait like everyone else, don't you think?"

Choe peered down at his hands. "I'm very sorry to be rude sir. I think something bad might happen, maybe tomorrow."

"Nothing bad is going to happen tomorrow. What makes you say that?"

"I hear from students around Yonsei—students who know things. They say war with Communists can begin any day. And I believe them. If that happens then I can't leave here to go to school in United States."

"You shouldn't worry about that. It's just rumors. I've been here just a few months, and I've seen incidents occurring near the border almost every week. Nothing ever happens. Each side is just testing the other. If something big were to happen, we'd know about it long before. But since you came today, write your name in English on this piece of paper and I'll go look for your folder and see what we have on you."

Tom went to his file cabinet, pulled out a folder, and sat back down at his desk. After skimming through the papers, he looked up and said, "It looks like your application is complete. We've got a copy of your acceptance letter from Stanford, and I don't see anything negative that would hold up your approval. But you still need to go through the interview process before the visa can be signed off. So just relax, come back tomorrow for the interview, and I'm sure in a week you'll have your visa."

Choe nodded his head in reluctant acceptance.

After ushering the young student through the empty lobby to the exit, he turned back to his office to pick up his briefcase. He was surprised to see Soon Hi Chung, one of the office clerks, still working the customer counter. She was cute—pale peach complexion, button nose, heart shaped mouth. Those distinctly Asian eyes reminded him of his mother's Siamese cat. She'd caught his eye the first day he'd arrived at the office. He wanted to get to know her from that day, and thought about asking her on a date, but there were always other people around—no opportunity to talk anything but business. At twenty-five years old, he shouldn't have been shy about asking—but he was. Maybe now was the time when nobody was around.

"Miss Chung, you're still here?"

"Oh, I was in back file room putting away records. Just a few more."

"Can I help you with anything?" he said walking behind the counter.

"No," she said. "I'm finished now."

As she came out of the file room, Tom said, "Miss Chung, I hope I'm not too forward. But I was wondering if you'd like to go out to dinner with me tonight. The Naija restaurant has really good food. I think you'd enjoy it. If you don't have anything else..."

Soon Hi's cheeks began to turn pink as she looked up at him, blinking two or three times to collect her thoughts. "Oh, Mr. Crandall, thank you to invite me. But this weekend I'm going to visit my family near Suwon. I'm sorry."

He swallowed hard, trying not to show his disappointment. "That's all right," he said. "I understand. Maybe another time." He wasn't so sure there'd be another time, but he said it anyway.

She smiled, but didn't respond other than to return the nod. As they walked out the front door of the embassy, she started toward the bus stop. He called out to her as she walked away, "See you next

Monday Miss Chung." She turned and waved. Tom waved back, then opened his umbrella and headed in the opposite direction towards his apartment.

. . .

A window-rattling rumble woke Tom from his dream. He was in a chapel—a wedding chapel. His pal Max was next to him. A Buddhist monk stood to one side of them holding a string of beads and chanting low; a minister in black stood on the other side holding a Bible. Was Max getting married? Or was he? A woman, dressed in flowing Korean dress entered at the rear door and began slowly coming towards them, but her head was bowed and he couldn't see her face. Who was she? She came closer...but then the thunder.

He cursed the thunder for waking him. He got up groggily and groped his way in the early morning half-light to the toilet. He glanced out the window as he took care of his business, then went to the sink to shave. The rain was coming down hard. He got dressed, grabbed his umbrella from the closet, and left the apartment for the Bando Hotel, four blocks away. He knew he could pick up an English version of the *Korea Times* there. It was Sunday morning, and the streets were nearly empty, but the rain didn't bother him. He was getting used to it. Perhaps it would bring cooler weather.

After returning to his apartment, Tom made himself breakfast— two fried eggs, a couple thick slices of spam, and toast— and settled down with the paper in the canvas lawn chair that served as his easy chair. The headlines were about Secretary of Defense Johnson and General Bradley's visit to Korea and Japan. They'd just left Korea for Tokyo yesterday. There was a picture of them with MacArthur on the front page. He read through the article, and it seemed the leaders were pretty positive about what they'd seen. MacArthur was quoted as saying that despite threats of invasion from the north, he was confident that the South Korean forces could stand up to anything the north could throw at them. Colonel Roberts, the outgoing chief of KMAG (Korean Military Advisory Group), was also in Japan at the time and reiterated that view.

As he was browsing through the sports section to see how his Cubs were doing, he was a little irritated when the phone began to ring, upsetting his quiet morning.

"Hello. Who's this? Don't you know it's Sunday morning?"

"Tom? This is Kate. It's almost eleven o'clock. You shouldn't complain. Haven't you heard the artillery pounding north of the city?" Kate Keeler was Tom's counterpart in the consulate section, but she had seven years' experience on him, having served in Europe and the Middle East before coming to Korea a few months before him. When he first arrived, she'd been a big help in teaching him the ropes around the embassy.

"Artillery? I heard some noise this morning, but I thought it was thunder. Is something happening?"

"Better believe it. Looks like the Communists are making a push to start a war. I got a call from Sid a few minutes ago telling me that the North Koreans were attacking at a number of places along the border. I'm on call this weekend, and he told me to start notifying staff that the ambassador has put us on yellow alert. He wants to have a meeting at one o'clock with all the American employees in the main conference room. So be here."

"Are you sure about this attack? We've seen lots of these scares before."

"I'm not sure about anything. All I know is that there's a briefing in two hours. Be here."

Tom hung the phone up, rose from his chair, slipped on his shoes, and was out the door.

It was half past twelve when he got to the embassy gates. Showing his badge to the Marine guard, he was waved through and hurried into the main lobby where several staff members were already congregating and talking among themselves. He saw Kate standing to one side with Phil Crosswaite. Phil was the senior political officer in the embassy. If anyone knew anything it would be him. Before joining the State Department last year, he had been an intelligence officer who'd come to Korea in 1945 with the American occupation forces under General Hodge.

He caught Kate's eye, and she gave a wave. He walked over to the two of them, and Kate greeted him with a smile but with a measured concern in her eyes. Phil, his mouth set tight, greeted Tom with a nod.

"Do you think this is the real thing?" asked Tom. "What've you heard?"

Phil gave him a look that was all business. "Yeah, it looks like more than just a skirmish this time. We've got KMAG advisers with ROK units on the border and the information we've been getting from them is that the north struck several different places along the parallel. They've overrun the ROK garrison on the Ongjin peninsula and may have taken Kaesong by now. I don't know what the situation is elsewhere, but it's not good."

"Jesus! They really know how to pick a time for an attack. What…"

Just as he was about to ask another question, Sidney Croft, the deputy chief of mission walked up to the podium with Nick Hogarth, the security officer, close at his heels. The room quieted.

Sid began, "I know all of you have been anxious to know what exactly is happening on the border, as rumors are spreading fast. This is what we know at the present. The North Koreans initiated a surprise attack at four o'clock this morning on the Ongjin peninsula. They overran the ROK garrison there and the ROKs are evacuating survivors by ship. After that the North Koreans opened up attacks all along the 38th parallel. Based on the latest information we have, they captured Kaesong this morning and have forces moving towards Uijongbu. In the east, Chunchun and Kangnung are also under attack."

Murmurs of concern rolled through the audience as the impact of what he was saying soaked in.

Croft continued, "Even though the situation looks grim, this attack is not totally unexpected and the South Korean forces are initiating counterattacks as I speak. The ROK 2nd Division is moving up to confront the North Koreans north of Uijongbu and we fully expect that they'll stop them and drive them back. In the east, we've received reports that ROK forces have repelled the North Koreans in their effort to take Chunchun."

A curly-haired man brandishing a pad and pencil, apparently a reporter for one of the news services, raised his hand and asked, "What's the ambassador's position on this? Has he notified Washington? What's their reaction?"

Croft replied, "We've notified Washington and they're waiting to see what happens here before they make any move. This was a surprise attack, and the situation is in flux. As I said, ROK Army forces are now moving north of Seoul to confront the Communist aggressors. If they can stop them in their tracks, then this whole thing may blow over. Before coming out here I talked to the ambassador on the phone. He's been in touch with President Rhee, and Rhee assured him that the ROK Army is up to the task and will be able to turn back this attack in short order. The ambassador will be going on our English language radio station in the next hour to make an announcement to the Americans here in Korea urging them to remain calm and stay in their homes."

Kate raised her hand and said, "There are several hundred American civilians in country. Shouldn't we be doing something now to prepare for their possible evacuation?"

"I was just about to get to that. At present the ambassador doesn't want to implement the evacuation plan. He thinks it would send a wrong signal to the Korean people and to the Korean government. But we need to be prepared to put it into effect if that decision is made. We also need to identify and gather up equipment and records that need to be destroyed in the event the Communists succeed in entering Seoul. I'm going to turn this meeting over to Mr. Hogarth to brief you on just what actions you need to be taking now."

As soon as the briefing ended, Tom returned to his office and began sifting through his files, pulling out records that should be destroyed and separating them from those that they would want to transfer should they have to relocate. It was late in the afternoon before he finished emptying his files. He took a last look around the office for anything he'd forgotten. He noticed the file for the student he'd talked to the day before still sitting on his desk. He picked it up and put it in a box of active folders so it wouldn't get lost in the shuffle if things started to go haywire.

On his way out of the office he checked in with his boss, Randall Stickley. "No need to stick around here," said Stickley. "Go home, but stay close to the phone."

Tom exited the embassy grounds, expecting to have to fight to get on a bus or streetcar but it was strangely quiet. He started walking, but then suddenly the roar of low-flying airplanes made him look up. Several prop fighters with what appeared to be red stars under their wings began dropping leaflets like fluttering snowflakes. *Russian fighter planes. Next time it'll be bombs they're dropping.* He picked up one of the leaflets— there was Korean writing that he couldn't translate. But he had no trouble interpreting the picture which showed a jubilant soldier waving a North Korean flag while sticking a bayonet into a prone Syngman Rhee caricature wrapped in an American flag. He saw a streetcar stopped at the next intersection and, throwing the leaflet to the ground, ran to catch it.

CHAPTER 2

WASHINGTON, D.C. AREA

June 24–26, 1950

It was ten o'clock, Saturday night. Secretary of State Dean Acheson, relaxing at his home outside Washington, had just turned his radio dial to catch the late news when the phone rang. He considered ignoring it, but then thought better of it.[i]

"Acheson residence."

"Mr. Secretary. This is Dean Rusk. Sorry to bother you on a Saturday evening, but it looks like we've got a crisis brewing in Korea."

Acheson laid down his pipe and leaned forward in his chair. "Of course, of course. What's happening? I thought things were fairly calm over there right now."

"We got a cable from John Muccio, over in Seoul. He reports that the North Koreans have attacked South Korean forces all along the 38th parallel. It's the ambassador's opinion that this is not just a probing action, but an all-out invasion."

After Rusk read the entire message over the phone, Acheson queried, "What's the reaction of the South Koreans? Are they able to handle it?"

"It's too early to tell," said Rusk. Ambassador Dulles just left South Korea a couple days ago and he said he thought the South Korean army was in good shape and able to defend itself, but these initial reports are not encouraging. I'm here at the office now with John Hickerson and Frank Pace, and we all think we need to make some response to try to nip this thing in the bud."

"Yes, I agree," replied Acheson. "And we need to get the UN involved. They've got a big stake in this. Let me talk to John."

Rusk handed the phone to Hickerson, the Assistant Secretary of State for UN Affairs. Acheson asked, "John, do you think you can reach Secretary General Lie tonight and see if he's aware of this?"

"Yes, I'm pretty sure he's in town this weekend."

"Good, I'd like to get him to call a special session of the Security Council right away. We'll want to get a ceasefire resolution to try and get this stopped before it gets out of hand."

He turned the phone back over to Rusk.

"I think I have what information I need for now," said Acheson. "I'm going to call Truman. I expect he'll be back here tomorrow and will be looking for answers. I want you and your staff to work with the Pentagon brass to get a fuller assessment of what's going on over there. He's going to have some decisions to make."

• • •

The president, at his home in Independence, Missouri for the weekend, was sitting in his living room reading Winston Churchill's new memoir on World War II, when the telephone rang. He laid down the book and answered, "Truman here."

"Mr. President? Dean Acheson. Sorry to call you so late, but we've got a situation brewing in Korea I needed to make you aware of."

After a brief pause to let the words sink in, Truman said, "You wouldn't be calling me now unless you thought it was something bad. Tell me what you've got."

"We've received a message from Ambassador Muccio in Seoul reporting that the North Koreans have crossed the 38th parallel all along the border on a major scale and are threatening Seoul. He thinks it has the makings of an all-out invasion."

"What are the South Koreans doing about it. Are they able to stop them?"

"They were taken by surprise. There's no doubt about it. But they seem to be putting up a fight now. According to announcements put out by President Rhee his army is initiating a counter attack to push them back across the border. But if the Reds are serious about this, they've got an advantage with the tanks and artillery the Soviets gave them."

"You think the Soviets are behind this invasion?"

"I'm pretty sure Kim Il Sung wouldn't have started this without Stalin's okay, but right now he's keeping a low profile. Stalin could be using this to deflect our attention so he could start something somewhere else, such as Formosa. As far as Korea is concerned I've told John Hickerson to get in touch with Trygvie Lie at the UN to try to get a special session of the Security Council together as soon as possible."

"That's exactly what we need. Tell Hickerson to work up a ceasefire resolution for them to act on. If this is a real invasion, it's a direct attack on a United Nations sanctioned government. A resolution like that, if the Soviets don't interfere with it, may be enough to stop things from getting any bigger."

"Yes, sir. It may. Right now the Soviets have been boycotting the UN and haven't been attending any of the sessions."

"Good. That'll make our job that much easier. Is there anything more you need from me right now?"

"No sir. I think we need to see what happens at the UN before we do anything overtly on our own. If the South Koreans can stop them, then nothing more may need to be done immediately."

"I agree. I'll be coming back to Washington tomorrow. I don't want to be caught off guard if this thing mushrooms into something bigger. I hope the South Koreans can handle it, and the Soviets will put their dog back in its cage. But if that doesn't work, I don't intend to just stand aside picking my nose and watch those Red bastards run over a friendly country. Call me tonight or in the morning if anything new develops."

"I will sir."

. . .

Marty Kessinger, deputy White House press secretary — at least that was the title he'd been given when he took the job four months ago — wasn't happy about being called in on a Sunday morning, his one day off. He flashed his gate pass at the guard and used his key to enter the west wing door nearest to his office. *What could be so important to get called back on a Sunday? The president isn't even in town.* The office he shared with two secretaries was empty, but the door to Charlie's office next door was open and he heard him talking loudly on the phone.

Charlie Ross had been White House press secretary since 1945, shortly after President Truman took office. Having worked for a number of years as a Washington correspondent for the St. Louis Post-Dispatch, and even winning a Pulitzer Prize, he was close to the president and was well respected within the Washington press corps. Marty was glad that he had the chance to learn from him. When he got the opportunity for the White House job after working five years as a beat reporter for the Chicago Daily News, Marty felt like he'd gotten the opportunity of a lifetime, and working with Charlie was a bonus. Peggy was excited too until she found out he'd be working twelve hours a day, six days a week. He loved the work, but he just wished Charlie would give him something to get his teeth into, instead of just having him write routine press releases all day. *Maybe something's come up today.*

He peeked into Ross's office, gave a wave, and waited for him to finish his phone conversation. Ross motioned to him to take a seat. When he finished the call, Ross said, "I was just talking with Jim Lay. The president's returning late this afternoon."

"Oh...why's he coming back so soon?" asked Marty. "I didn't see anything special in the paper this morning, other than an article about those Rosenberg's being arrested for spying for the Soviets."

"It's not that. The North Koreans have invaded South Korea. It hasn't hit the papers big yet, but it will. It looks like it's a full scale invasion, and something the South Koreans might not be able to handle on their own. The president's pissed, and he's coming back here to meet with the National Security Council this evening."

"Oh shit! Sure hope it doesn't mean we're going to get involved over there. We just got finished with the last war."

"I hope not too, but that's something outside our control. I'm sure the Washington newspapers are starting to get teletype feeds from Korea now, and they'll have some reporters there at Andrews with questions. So I need to get out there to pacify them if I can."

"So, what did you want me to do? How can I help?"

"I want you to fly up to New York for a couple of days. I talked to Ernie Gross earlier this morning. The UN Security Council is going to meet this afternoon on a ceasefire resolution for Korea. Not sure if the Soviets will be there or not or how long the thing will drag out. I need to be here when the president arrives, and I want you up there to be my eyes and ears. The press can be relentless and I want the president prepared for any questions."

Marty was glad to get an assignment that would put him at the heart of a breaking news story, but Peggy wouldn't be particularly happy. "I'll call to get a ticket right now."

"No need," said Ross. "I already booked you on a flight to LaGuardia. It leaves at 12:10 out of National. You can pick up your ticket at the TWA counter."

When he got to the airport, he called his wife to let her know he wouldn't be home that night or probably the next. He didn't like leaving her alone, especially with her eight months pregnant, but she didn't complain, and he loved her for it. He needed to do something special for her when he got back.

. . .

By the time he got to the UN headquarters at Lake Success on Long Island, the Assembly session had already started. When he entered the auditorium sized hall, he looked around and caught sight of a familiar face in the press gallery, Evan Frantz, East Coast political correspondent for the Chicago Tribune. He went up to the gallery and took a seat next to him.

"What have I missed? Anything?"

Frantz turned, at first not recognizing Marty, then said, "Not much. Just a couple of speeches. Who you working for now?"

"I'm at the White House— deputy press secretary."

"So you've joined the other side have you?" Frantz asked half-jokingly.

"Ah, I don't look at it that way. I think I'll be a better journalist if I know more about the internal workings of government."

"Maybe so. Just don't forget where you came from."

"Have the Soviets spoken up against the resolution?"

"Nope. Malik hasn't shown, and it doesn't look like he will."

"Phew. We shouldn't have any trouble getting the ceasefire resolution through then."

A little after six o'clock, after several more speeches and a round of debates over alternate resolutions, a final resolution was passed, calling the attack of North Korea a breach of the peace and demanding withdrawal of North Korean forces back to the 38th parallel. As soon as the resolution was passed and copies distributed to the press, Marty ran out to the lobby and put a call in to Charlie Ross's answering service. Five minutes later Ross called him back.

"Did they get the resolution through?"

"Yes, the Russians weren't here, and it went pretty smoothly, nine in favor and one abstention from Yugoslavia." He read the full resolution over the phone so Charlie could take it down word for word.

"Good work. This will make the president happy, that's for sure. His plane is supposed to be arriving in about an hour. It'll give him something positive to offer the reporters. After he gets done with them, he's got a meeting set up with his national security team, and I'll need to be in on that. Call me tomorrow morning around ten, and I'll let you know if we need you to stay there any longer."

Marty returned to his hotel room feeling upbeat and called his wife about the day's events. The next morning he was up early and went to the hotel lobby to get a copy of the New York Times. On the lower half of the front page was a headline: *President Shortens Vacation to Deal with Korean Crisis*. There wasn't a whole lot of information other than the North Koreans had crossed the 38th parallel at several points and the U.S. ambassador had begun evacuation of embassy dependents and American civilians in Seoul.

At ten o'clock Marty made his call to Ross's office as he instructed, and Ross picked up the phone immediately, but his voice sounded worn out.

"Any more news on Korea?" asked Marty?"

"Nothing yet, but we need to give it a little time to see how the North Koreans respond. I think you'd better hang around there another day in case we need to go back to the UN for any further action. I'll call you tomorrow morning around eleven."

CHAPTER 3

COLLAPSE

June 26–June 30, 1950

Tom tossed and turned all night, unable to sleep more than an hour at a time because of the nightmares. At four thirty he was awakened by explosive booms. There was no mistaking it. He knew what it was *this* time. It *was* artillery, and it was louder than yesterday. That could only mean one thing — the North Koreans weren't backing off in their attack. He got up quickly, went to the bathroom to piss, then went to the sink and started to lather up his face when the phone rang. It was Kate.

"I didn't wake you this morning did I?"

"No, I'm up. I heard the artillery. What's happening?"

"The North Koreans have broken through the South Korean defenses north of Uijongbu. The ROK Army is still resisting, but it's not looking good. The ambassador issued an order last night to evacuate all dependents and American civilians, and they're starting to assemble here at the embassy grounds now. We're sending around cars to bring in some of the staff to help with the processing. Wait outside your apartment and there'll be a car by to pick you up in a few minutes."

Tom wiped the soap off his face, finished dressing, and hurried outside. The embassy car, a sleek 1942 Packard Clipper, pulled up to the curb, with three other passengers already inside. He squeezed himself in and they headed toward the embassy. Obviously the planned counter attack by the ROK Army had failed. Uijongbu was less than fifteen miles north of the city. How long would it be before they entered Seoul? He didn't want to think about it. By the time he arrived at the embassy, Americans were already congregating in the courtyard, and several busses were parked in the side street just outside the gates. Tom and about a dozen other staff members met in the embassy lobby. After Nick Hogarth briefed them on what they needed to do, they set up tables in the courtyard and the processing started. By eight o'clock more than seven hundred people had been processed and loaded on the busses that would deliver them to Inchon port where an evacuation ship waited.

After the busses carrying the American dependents and other civilians left the compound the ambassador called the entire staff together in the main conference room to update them on the latest events. He told them he still held out hope that the ROK Army would be able to hold off the North Koreans from taking Seoul, but he assured them everything was in place to evacuate the embassy staff on short notice if it became clear that Seoul was lost. After answering several questions from the group, he ended his talk by advising those staff members who lived off the compound to return to their quarters, pack what they needed, and be back at the embassy by noon—just in case. Tom took the advice. As he left the walled-in compound he noted that a small crowd of Koreans had begun to gather near the main gate.

Returning to the embassy shortly before noon, Tom saw that the crowd at the embassy had grown to several hundred people. Some of those in the front were pushing angrily on the bars of the reinforced gate and shouting at the Marine guards standing on the other side. He began to walk around to the side entrance when he heard his name called. He turned to see the young student he talked to just before leaving work on Saturday running towards him.

"Mr. Crandall! Do you remember me? My name is Choe. I talk to you yesterday about my visa."

Tom put down the bag he was carrying and said, "Yes, I remember you Mr. Choe. This entrance is only for embassy personnel. You can't go in this way."

"Yes, I know. But the North Koreans are coming close to Seoul. You said war would not come, but it is here. Can you help me get my visa? Please?"

Tom felt guilt creep through him as he looked at the desperate student facing him. But what could he do now? Then he realized he'd put the student's file in a box to be shipped out and left it sitting beside his desk yesterday. There were a lot of people who wanted to leave, but he'd told this one that he didn't have to worry. He needed to do something.

"I can try," he said. "I have your application in my office. If you wait over there in front of that store, I'll go see if I can find it."

Tom showed his pass to the Marine at the gate and went immediately to his office. He found the file he was looking for, but it still needed to get an approval and stamp from the vice counsel. He walked over to Mr. Stickley's office and interrupted him just as he was putting down the phone. "What is it Crandall? I'm busy?"

"Yes sir, but I really need your signature on this student visa. He's already been accepted at Stanford. The student is here and if we don't do it now, he might not get another shot."

"What good will it do him now. He probably won't be able to get out anyway."

"I know. But if the ROK are able to hold off the Communists and things settle down, then he won't have to start all over. Please."

"Give me the paper."

Stickley scanned the document quickly, scrawled his name on the signature line, and then stamped the paper with an official seal"

"Here. Now get out. I got things to do."

Tom hurried out the embassy side door with the file and saw Choe standing on the other side of the street as he had been told to do. He walked over to him and handed him the file.

"If the North Koreans get to Seoul, you don't want to be caught with these documents," said Tom.

"I know. I won't be caught. Thank you Mr. Crandall. I won't forget you." The two shook hands and the young student disappeared into the mass of people on the street.

By late afternoon it became clear that the situation was untenable. With the North Korean army approaching the city, South Korean President Rhee had left Seoul along with a number of his government officials and fled to Taegu. When the ambassador learned of this, he knew he couldn't put off the decision to leave any longer. He convened the staff, including Korean employees who were present, in the large conference room used for press briefings.

"I've made a decision to evacuate the embassy," he began. "We'll relocate to Pusan and set up shop in the consulate. Because of the imminent threat, we're going to leave tomorrow morning." After waiting a moment for his audience to settle down, he went on. "The evacuation will be by truck convoy, leaving no later than seven tomorrow morning and everyone must be here and ready to go by six."

Someone in the audience raised their hand and asked, "What's going on in Washington? Are there any plans to respond to this attack, or are we going to leave it up to the Koreans?"

The ambassador replied, "President Truman is working with the United Nations to get a ceasefire in place, and the government is evaluating the situation as to further action to take if the ROK Army is unable to stop them before they enter Seoul. However, it would be foolish of me to disregard the threat that exists, and that's why I've ordered this evacuation—not just the American staff, but Korean employees along with their immediate family members, as well. I urge you all to take advantage of this opportunity. If you are interested in leaving tomorrow morning with us, I'd like you to sign up at the table in the back of the room so we know how many busses to line up." After answering additional questions and finishing his remarks, the staff, particularly the Koreans, clapped. Several senior Koreans rushed up to the Ambassador to thank him for including family members.

As the meeting let out, Tom looked around and saw Soon Hi Chung leaving through the rear door. He caught up to her, and said, "Miss Chung, I'm glad to see you stayed in Seoul. If you're coming with us, you better go back in and sign your name on the register. If you need any help in packing or anything, I can help."

Soon Hi looked at him with a pained expression on her face, "I can't go with you. My family— parents and younger brother— are in Suwon, and I need to go there to be with them.

"But if you get caught and the Communists know you worked for Americans, who knows what might happen? Come with us. Your parents can join you later."

"No, my parents won't want to leave their farm if it's not necessary. Suwon's not in danger now. Thank you for offer to help, but I have older brother here in Seoul. He works for *Chosun Ilbo* newspaper. I can go to him if I need help."

Tom nodded, acknowledging that his effort to persuade her was going nowhere. "Okay, but if things go bad, and you have to leave Suwon, then come to Pusan. I'm sure we can use you at the consulate."

"If we must go to the south, then I will remember your kind offer Mr. Crandall. But I think everything is okay." She smiled, made a slight bow, and turned to leave the building. Tom's legs felt wobbly as he watched her go. Was that the effect she had on him? He knew he might never see her again, and it bothered him. He tried to push her out of his mind and went back into the embassy to help clean out files.

. . .

After only a couple hours sleep in his clothes on an office couch, Tom, along with forty-three American embassy personnel and sixty-four Koreans lined up to board four buses for the trip to Pusan. Colonel Wright, the new KMAG commander, provided a twelve-man security detail along with an armored personnel carrier and two deuce-and-a-half trucks to transport what office equipment and supplies could be stuffed inside. The ambassador saw off the staff, but remained behind, saying he would meet them in Pusan later.

As the small American convoy left the embassy compound, the streets of Seoul were beginning to fill with crowds of civilians, watching helplessly as leaderless South Korean troops, with the look of defeat on their faces, started streaming into the city. Once the Americans crossed the Han River, the embassy convoy found the going slow. Throngs of panicky evacuees— white clad men and women, young and old, plodded along, loaded down with their most precious possessions. Carts and wagons, piled high with household goods, rocked laboriously amid a sea of humans. Aged men with wooden A-frames on their backs bent forward under loads fit for mules. Mothers and grandmothers labored on with infants slung on their backs while older children scampered at their heels to keep up. The endless procession moved down the two lane road leading to Pusan like a huge snake, occasionally splitting apart to make way for motor vehicles hurrying south, away from the fighting.

The trip from Seoul to Pusan, about two hundred fifty miles, normally took six to seven hours, but because of the refugee traffic, it took fourteen hours for the convoy to reach its destination. The embassy buses pulled into Hialeah Camp near the Pusan port facility before midnight. Hialeah was a small facility that had been used by the American occupation forces as a staging area for supplies into the peninsula. With the withdrawal of the American occupation forces the previous year, the camp was mostly empty except for two buildings used for American consulate workers and a small contingent of United Nations personnel.

The streets outside the American camp were quiet. The civilian population was aware of the invasion, but initial news reports had indicated that the North Korean attack was being turned back, and residents of Pusan, being so far away from the border, felt little concern about things going on to the north. Although it was near midnight when they arrived, several consulate personnel were on hand to greet the newcomers and to show them to the barracks where they would be temporarily housed. Tom collected his single duffel bag from the bus and followed the others into the barracks. He was glad to see that the staff had put out cots and bedding so they could get some rest. After undressing, he laid down, put his arms behind his neck, and thought about Soon Hi. *Had she made it out of Seoul all right?*

• • •

After leaving the American Embassy around noon, Soon Hi hurried home, to the small rented room where she'd been living for the past year. She laid out some clothing, a few toilet articles, and some photos she didn't want to lose, including one group photo at the embassy, and wrapped it up tight in a large red and blue silk scarf. As she closed the door, she tried to imagine she was just going away for the weekend to see her parents. But she couldn't push away the fear and sadness gnawing at her. Chances were she'd never return to this place. After getting to the street, she found a public telephone and put in a call to her brother, In Yong, to let him know she was on her way to see him.

"The American embassy has been evacuated, but I didn't want to go with them. I need to get home to Suwon. Can you help me?"

"It's a good thing you called. We're shutting down the newspaper right now and getting ready to move the whole operation down to Taegu. You need to get over here quick before we leave."

"How much time do I have?"

"Maybe an hour. They're starting to pack up the trucks now. I think I can get you on one of the trucks with me, but you need to hurry."

Soon Hi put down the phone, and hurried over to a bus stop where two buses were loading passengers. People were scrambling and shoving to get in front of the line. The first bus took off with people hanging out the side doors. Soon Hi hoped to make it on the second bus, but just as she pushed her way unto the top step of the doorway, she felt a rough shove from the side, she lost her balance and fell onto the pavement. She came down awkwardly on her wrist and she felt a sharp pain. Her bundle fell to the side and people were stepping on it. She yelled out and crawled on her hands and knees to recover it. Just as she reached for it, someone stepped on her hand and she screamed. The crowd backed up just enough so that she was able to get to her feet, pick up the bundle, and escape to a less congested area. She dusted herself off, looked down and saw that her knee was bleeding, and she could hardly move her left wrist. It didn't seem broken. Just a sprain, she hoped. It wasn't worth it to try to get on another bus. She made a quick decision to walk the three miles to the Chosun Ilbo building. If she walked fast, she could make it there before her brother left.

After walking for nearly an hour, she finally reached Sejong-no and saw the newspaper building ahead where several trucks with the newspaper logo on the side were parked in front with people hurrying about. When she got there, she saw In Yong loading a box onto the open bed of one of the trucks.

Wiping sweat from his forehead, he said, "Where've you been? You look a mess. I wasn't sure if we'd have to leave without you."

"I got pushed off the bus, and I walked all the way here. I really don't want to walk to Suwon."

"No, you won't have to. You can ride with me."

"Do you really think the North Koreans will come into Seoul?"

He nodded. "They're just north of the city now. They've got tanks, and we don't have anything to stop them. I've heard that the army is regrouping and trying to keep them out of the city, but if they can't…it's going to be bad."

"I need to get to our parent's place," she said. "Whatever happens, I need to be with them."

"Yes, they'll need you," said In Yong. "I wish I could go with you. We're about ready to go. You better get in the rear of this truck now." She climbed in the canvas covered truck bed and saw she wasn't alone. There was a woman with an infant and small toddler already squeezed inside. She found an open space between a file cabinet and a linotype machine, and then heard the tailgate door slam shut. A few seconds later the truck engine roared to life and they began to move.

As the truck jolted over the roadway, her stomach began to turn. The baby began to cry and the woman took the infant and began to breast feed. The older child, a boy of about two, began to climb on his mother and whine for attention. The young mother looked exasperated, and Soon Hi crawled over and took the toddler in her arms. The woman smiled and thanked her as she repositioned the infant more comfortably at her breast. The young boy struggled to get away from Soon Hi, but she found a small peppermint candy in her pocket and gave it to him. That seemed to calm him down. As the truck bumped along, she was able to keep the boy distracted by playing hand games with him, and it helped to pass the time. After about three hours of this, the truck pulled to the side of the road. The tail gate creaked open, and In Yong called to Soon Hi and the other woman to come out and stretch their legs. Soon Hi eased herself down to the ground and looked to see where they were. They were on the outskirts of Suwon, the ancient city gate stood right ahead—she'd been through here many times and knew her way home.

"This is where we part, sister," In Yong said. You can make your way from here on your own. I have to go with the others to Taegu. We've got important work to do in keeping this newspaper going. I know you'll be a help to our parents. Look after that little brother of ours, too, and try to keep him out of trouble."

Soon Hi looked up at her older brother admiringly, then bowed her head and said simply, "*Nay oppa.*"

She turned toward the young woman standing at the rear of the truck, the little boy standing beside her. The woman, whose name she never learned, thanked her for her help and Soon Hi wished her a safe journey. She looked down at the boy who stared back at her with a pouty look on his face. *With war coming, what kind of future can he have?* She leaned over and gave him a hug, then turned away and began walking towards Goto-ri, a village about five miles away where her parents maintained their small farm.

. . .

There was little vehicle traffic on the rural road leading to Goto-ri, but after hiking more than two miles, Soon Hi was able to get a ride on the back of a farmer's truck. When they got to the village, the farmer stopped in front of a dilapidated rice exchange building and let Soon Hi off. She offered to pay him, but he refused, saying, "This is no time to be greedy. We need to help each other." She thanked him and headed to her parent's house, just on the other side of the hill in back of the village. By the time she got to the familiar thatch roofed house with the large persimmon tree in front, darkness had fallen. Light from an oil lamp was visible from the window, and she could see her mother bending over some sewing. When she entered the room, her mother dropped her needle work, rose up with arms outstretched, and shouted, "You're here! I was so worried something might have happened to you. Are you all right?"

"Yes, I'm okay, but the North Korean soldiers are close to Seoul. Many people are trying to leave before they capture the city. Even President Rhee and his government have left."

"What about your brother, In Yong? Have you seen him?

"Yes, he gave me a ride in a truck as far as Suwon. He's fine, but he's going on to Taegu to continue to work for his newspaper."

"Ah, your father will be relieved to hear that."

"Where is father?" asked Soon Hi.

33

"He went into the village to a meeting. He should be back soon." Then looking at her swollen wrist she exclaimed, "What happened? You need to put something on that."

"It's nothing. I had an accident trying to get on a bus."

Her mother scurried into the kitchen and came back with a liquid concoction that she rubbed onto her wrist, then wrapped her arm in a cold towel. After insuring that her daughter was all right, she said, "In Su's in his room studying. Go talk to him while I prepare some supper."

Soon Hi got up and slid open the door to her younger brother's room. In Su had his back to her, his head down in a book. He'd just turned seventeen and was starting his last year of high school. She was glad he was still in school and hopefully would avoid being called up to fight in this war that was on their door step.

"Hi little brother. What are you reading?" She walked over to him and peered over his shoulder—*The Life of Kim Il Sung Our Great Leader*. As In Su turned to look at her, Soon-Hi's mouth fell open in shock, and she stepped back, and said, "Where did you get that?"

In Su, looking innocent, said, "It's just a pamphlet. Some guy was outside the school today and was giving them out to some of us students. It's about Kim Il Sung's life."

"I know what it is. But what are you doing with it. Don't you know you can be arrested for having something like that?"

In Su wagged his head indifferently and said, "I don't think so now. I heard at school today that the North Korean army already defeated part of the South Korean army north of Seoul. Before long they'll take over the whole country. In this booklet, Premier Kim talks about making a new Korea for Koreans, not for foreign imperialists. I don't think that's a bad idea."

"You're being taken in by Communist propaganda," said Soon Hi. "The North Koreans invaded our republic and are killing our people. We must fight them to protect what we have. If we need help, the Americans will help us defeat this invasion."

"You talk like that because you work for the Americans," countered In Su. "Not everyone feels that way. Even father has talked about how bad the policeman have been in arresting people for no reason—just like under the Japanese."

Soon Hi shook her finger at him and said, "Do you think the Communists are better? Why do you think so many thousands of people fled from the north to the south last year? It was because the Communists were arresting and killing people—not just criminals, but small farmers and businessmen like father."

Just then Soon Hi heard her father come in. She abruptly ended her heated discussion with her brother and they both went to greet their father. An Kil Chung looked older than his fifty-two years. A tawny face lined with deep creases, hands brown and calloused, reflected a life spent working in the fields. His family having lived in the village of Koto-ri for generations, he was looked to by many as a leader in the community. Even though he was a farmer by trade, and even though times were difficult, he tried to maintain the air of a gentleman. On this evening he wore clean loose fitting gray cotton slacks and a white cotton shirt under a dark blue jacket. After acknowledging his daughter and inquiring about her injured arm, he sat down on a cushion his wife had set out for him.

"Did you learn anything about the North Korea attack at your meeting?" his wife asked.

Clearing his throat he said, "Mr. Lim brought a shortwave radio to the meeting, and we listened to a speech President Rhee made a couple hours earlier. Rhee said that even though there have been reports of North Korean advances toward Seoul, the South Korean army is still strong and able to defend the city. He said reinforcements are on the way from the south. In the next couple days, he said, he believes the threat to Seoul will be ended."

"Do you think that's true? Maybe we should leave now." said Soon Hi.

"I don't think it's time to panic yet. I want to trust what the president said. We'll stay put for now."

CHAPTER 4

AMERICA INTERVENES

June 27–30, 1950

Marty woke up at six as usual, even though he knew there was nothing to do but wait around for Charlie's call sometime around ten. After taking a shower and dressing he decided to go out for breakfast. He remembered a café a block away from the hotel and started walking. The place, decorated with pictures of sailing craft and local celebrities, was filled with morning commuters. He picked up a newspaper from a rack next to the cash register and took a seat at the counter. A plump, fifty-something waitress wearing a frilly pink apron with a picture of a cup of coffee with the words "Our Coffee Is No. 1 in Hempstead" took his order—ham, eggs over easy, and a No. 1 coffee.

While eating he listened to the conversations around him. No one was talking about Korea. The buzz was about the New York Yankees and their series opener with the Washington Senators later that day. At a table behind him he heard people arguing over a local school bond issue. As far as the people around here were concerned, Korea didn't exist. If he didn't have to go back to the UN, maybe he'd be able to catch the game on the radio.

When he got back to his room, he took out notes from the previous day, and sat down at the desk to compose a memorandum about what he observed at the UN. It was nearly ten o'clock when he finished, and he turned on the radio to listen to the news at the top of the hour. After five minutes of local news, weather report, and a commercial...

In news around the world, the Associated Press reports that North Korea is continuing its incursion into South Korea. The United Nations call for a ceasefire has, up to now, not yielded any results. Because of the continued fighting, the American ambassador has begun an evacuation of American civilians from Seoul, the capital city. President Truman, in response to the North Korean failure to respond positively to the UN demand, issued an announcement this morning that he has ordered the U.S. Navy and Air Force to give full support to the South Korean army south of the 38th parallel. In addition he has directed the Seventh Fleet to move between mainland China and Formosa to prevent an outbreak of hostilities there. In other news...

He turned off the radio and leaned his head back in frustration. *Shit! We're getting suckered into this mess after all. If South Korea was so important, why in hell did we withdraw our troops last year?* He picked up the newspaper and opened it to the crossword puzzle and started working it to get his mind off Korea.

Shortly after ten thirty the phone rang. It was Charlie.

"Hi boss. I heard on the news that the Reds have ignored the UN call for a ceasefire. Any change in that?"

"No. In fact, things have gotten worse. President Rhee has left Seoul and is moving his government down to Taegu. The South Korean army seems on the verge of collapse. That's why the president authorized American air and naval strikes."

"Yeah. I heard that too. Is there anything more planned with the UN?"

"Yes. There's another Security Council session this afternoon at three, and we're going to try to get a tougher resolution passed. I want you there.

"Think the Soviets will attend this time?"

"Your guess is as good as mine. We're not sure what they're planning. If you have a chance before the session starts, see if you can button hole a reporter from TASS or *Izvestia*, and see what you can learn from them."

"I don't speak Russian."

"Doesn't matter. They'll speak English. Just call me when the session ends and let me know what happens."

After Marty hung up, an uneasy feeling crept over him. *What will Truman do if the Soviets openly oppose us? Is this worth it? Why should more American boys die over a place that few in the country had ever heard of?* He had some time before he needed to leave for the UN headquarters. He picked up the phone and dialed Peggy to let her know he wouldn't be home for another night.

. . .

Marty got to the headquarters an hour before the session and stopped in the lobby where people were gathered in small cliques. Most of them, he figured were connected with news media, and as he walked around the room, he noticed a nattily dressed man in a blue blazer and red tie standing by himself next to the coffee machine, and when he drew closer saw that he had a hammer and sickle button on his coat lapel. Marty introduced himself as a reporter for the Chicago Daily News. If the guy was a KGB agent he didn't want to let on he worked at the White House. The man, tall and clean shaven, introduced himself in broken but correct English as Boris Grachkov, a reporter with TASS. After engaging in small talk for a couple of minutes, he asked the Soviet reporter why they continued to boycott the UN Security Council.

"We think it's important to make the point that the current membership is illegitimate without the People's Republic of China represented. Like you, we support our friends."

"Does that mean Ambassador Malik will continue to boycott the meeting today?"

"I don't know. Our government doesn't inform us of those things."

"The Soviet Union is still a member of the Security Council. Since they've called for the North Koreans to stop their aggression and withdraw their forces from South Korea, don't you think the Kremlin should assist in restoring the peace?

"You speak of North Korean aggression. That is your term. Not ours. According to Premier Kim, the South Koreans attacked first, and he was responding to their provocation."

"You can't believe that," said Marty. "Not when the North made coordinated attacks all along the 38th parallel—not just one place—using tanks and massed infantry. It had to have been preplanned."

"You believe what your South Korean friends tell you. We believe what our friends tell us. Excuse me, Mr. Kessinger. I have a colleague I must talk with. Perhaps we'll meet again."

The Soviet reporter— AKA KGB agent— strode off, and Marty stood alone, shaking his head.

A little before two, Marty strolled into the General Assembly auditorium and went up into the press gallery, saw a vacant seat next to Evan Frantz, his friend from the Chicago Tribune, and went to sit beside him.

"Didn't expect to be seeing you again so soon," said Frantz.

"I didn't either. I hoped the ceasefire resolution on Sunday would have brought an end to the fighting, but it apparently hasn't had much effect at all."

"The North Koreans aren't going to stop until somebody makes 'em. The South Koreans sure can't," said Frantz. "The only way to stop them is if the Russians want them to, and right now it seems like they want to let the thing play out."

Marty let his eyes focus on the crowd of people in the chamber below before turning back to Frantz. "If the new American resolution gets passed today," he said, "then that should make the Russians and the North Koreans take notice."

"If is a big word, and it just got bigger," said Frantz. "Malik just walked in with the Yugoslav delegate. There he is on the right with the glasses."

"Oh, fuck!" said Marty. "Excuse the language."

"You took the word right out of my mouth."

Following the formalities of opening the emergency session, the American representative, Warren Austin, introduced a carefully worded proposal, ending in the statement, "…in recognition of the failure of North Korea to comply with Security Resolution 82, this body recommends that members of the United Nations furnish such assistance to the Republic of Korea as deemed necessary to repel the armed attack and to restore international peace and security." After more than two hours of heated back and forth arguments from the

United States and Soviet representatives, a vote was taken. As expected, the Soviets cast their veto and the resolution was dead. The delegates filed out to report the decision to their government, and Marty and Evan hurried to the lobby to call their offices.

. . . .

Dean Acheson was still at work, when Warren Austin called just after six o'clock to tell him the disheartening news that the Soviets had vetoed the proposal encouraging direct military assistance to South Korea. Acheson thanked him for his efforts and immediately dialed the president. When he told him about the veto, Acheson was surprised that the president wasn't more upset.

"It doesn't change anything," said Truman. The Soviets are testing us, and we need to stand up to them. If we back off now and let their North Korean stooge take Korea, they'll keep taking bites out of some other little country. We can't let them do that. I've got Congress behind me on this, and the American people, too. I've given the green light to MacArthur to use the Navy and Air Force south of the parallel. So let's see how those goddamn Reds react to that."

. . . .

Following receipt of the president's directive to provide combat support to the South Koreans, General MacArthur dispatched an advance team led by Major General John Church to Korea to evaluate the situation first hand. Early the next day, MacArthur, in his Tokyo headquarters, carefully read over Church's troubling report. The Communists had taken over most of Seoul, and although ROK General Chae had set up a defensive line on the south bank of the Han River, most of his heavy armament had been abandoned and thousands of his soldiers were left on the north side of the river, captured by the North Koreans.

"Morale is low and the command structure is in disarray," reported Church, "and the South Koreans are not going to be able to hold off the North Koreans for long."

MacArthur slammed his fists on the desk, angry at the evident ineptitude of the South Korean army. "Lieutenant Barker!" he shouted through the open office door.

His young aide rushed into the room.

"Call the airfield and tell them to get the Bataan ready to fly. We're going to take a ride over to Korea. I need to see what's going on over there for myself."

Six hours later MacArthur landed at Suwon Air Base, fifteen miles south of Seoul, where he met with Ambassador Muccio and President Rhee. After receiving a briefing on the situation, he drove up to the battle line and watched with disgust as retreating ROK troops straggled past his unmarked jeep. When he got to the Han River and talked with the overwhelmed ROK commanders, he saw what they were facing. He understood, then, that the South Koreans were outgunned and in such disarray that they were not going to able to stop the North Koreans anywhere unless they got additional help on the ground. American air power wasn't going to be enough.

On his return flight to Tokyo MacArthur drafted a flash message back to the Pentagon. "The South Korean Army," he wrote, "is incapable of counteracting the enemy's attack and the only way I can see to stop them and regain lost ground is by putting U.S. ground combat forces into Korea and using Air Force and Navy assets to attack Communist targets north of the 38th parallel."

When General Lawton Collins, Army chief of staff, contacted him by secure telephone asking for specifics on ground force requirements, he responded, "I want to immediately send in a combat regiment to give the South Koreans a backbone. But I'm going to need two full American divisions to do the job the way it needs to get done. Give me two divisions and I'll turn this thing around."

. . .

It was five thirty in the morning on Thursday, June 29, when Secretary of Defense Johnson was awakened by a call from General Bradley advising him of MacArthur's urgent request for ground troops and authority to strike north of the 38th parallel. After hanging up, Johnson immediately put in a call to the president's hot line which he answered after one ring.

"This is Lou Johnson. I'm sorry to wake you, Mr. President, but we've more bad news from Korea.

"I was already up. What've you got?"

"We have a message from MacArthur that you need to see right away. It looks like Seoul is lost. He says the situation is so critical, if South Korea is to be saved, we need to get American combat forces involved against the North Koreans. He's talking about ground forces in addition to naval and air attacks. I think you should call another meeting of the NSC today."

After letting the information sink in for a few seconds, Truman, said, "I'll have something set up this afternoon.

. . .

Later in the day, a little after five o'clock, the members of the National Security Council again convened at the Blair House to meet with the president. Secretary Johnson laid out the current military situation and conveyed MacArthur's request to conduct air and naval attacks north of the 38th parallel and to deploy American ground troops — two full divisions. The matter was thrown open for discussion. General Bradley and each of the civilian service chiefs gave reasons why they thought MacArthur's request should be approved. There was no dissent.

After listening to the arguments, Truman said, "I can agree with expanding air and naval attacks north of the 38th parallel, but I'm still concerned that the use of American ground troops could draw us into a wider war."

When the president raised the question about the possible intentions of the Soviet Union, Secretary Acheson remarked, "Up to this point, the Soviet reaction has been fairly mild. Although they are verbally supporting the North's position, it doesn't appear that they have any intention of getting their troops involved. They're happy to leave the fighting to the Koreans and perhaps the Chinese."

"I believe we need to take a firm stand here," said Truman. "I want the Soviets to understand that we are going to resist this aggression...but at the same time, I want to avoid a direct confrontation between our troops and the Soviets. I can't be so committed in Korea that we can't meet contingencies that might crop up somewhere else in the world. General Bradley, send a message to General MacArthur giving him authority for air and naval attacks north of the 38th parallel. As for ground force, I need to think on this overnight. I'll make a decision tomorrow morning. We'll meet in the west wing conference room at nine. Until then, goodnight gentlemen."

After mulling over the possible consequences of not acting, he went to the oval office the next morning with his mind made up. His decision was made easier by a late night message from MacArthur in which he predicted total collapse of the South Korean government unless he could introduce some American ground troops to stem the Communist tide. Meeting again with his national security advisers at nine o'clock sharp, he lost no time in telling them, "I've made my decision. We'll give MacArthur what he's asked for—two divisions of ground troops and authority to use the Air Force to attack north of the 38th parallel."

The military officers in the room welcomed the decision with a sigh of relief. Only Secretary of State Acheson appeared to show a slight expression of doubt on his face. Without asking for further discussion, Truman then directed General Bradley to send a message to MacArthur to inform him of his new mission.

MacArthur was pleased when he received the JCS message giving him the authorities he requested, but he couldn't help griping to General Almond, his chief of staff, that they took longer than they needed to respond to his request. After receiving the message, he lost little time before writing out an order for Major General William Dean, 24th Infantry Division commander, directing him to get a reinforced infantry battalion into Korea by the next morning. He ordered him further to prepare the entire 24th Division for embarkation to Korea within the week. Twelve hours later the first American combat troops were on the ground in Korea and heading north to confront the North Koreans.

CHAPTER 5

FLIGHT

June 30–July 4, 1950

The first light of dawn peeked through the bedroom window, a rooster crowed outside, and An Kil Chung rose from his mattress as if it were any other workday morning. His father had worked this land, and his grandfather before that. It was a family treasure that he expected to one day pass on to his eldest son. Leaving the land, even for a temporary period, was something he didn't want to think about. Four days had passed since the Communists had started their attack. From what he heard over the radio, it seemed the South Korean army was still fighting back and holding the Communists at the Han River. But even if they stopped them there, the loss of Seoul would be devastating to the country.

An Kil shuffled out to the living room where his wife was already setting out breakfast for him. Looking as if he hadn't slept well, he eased his tired body down to the floor and slid himself up to the low table. His wife—Nam Hui was her given name—bent down to place an extra bowl of rice for In Su on the table. Nam Hui had never attended public school as a child, but she wanted to be sure all of her children did. Her first two had finished well, and now she just had her youngest to worry about. With this talk of war, he might be called away to fight. She hoped with all her heart the Communists would be turned back, and they could go on with a normal life.

In Su came bounding into the room, pulling up his pants, and then flopped down at the end of the table. "Did you pack my lunch yet? I'm going to be late for school," he said in an off-handed manner.

44

Seventeen years old and in his last year of high school, In Su slurped his soup down and then shoved three or four spoonfuls of rice into his mouth. "I'm finished," he said. Then getting to his feet and picking up his school bag, he was about to go out the door when his mother stopped him.

"Don't forget your lunch," she said. Hurrying to the kitchen, she retrieved the lunch box she'd prepared, tucked it into his pack, and watched with concern as her youngest went out the door.

Since Soon Hi was still asleep, worn out from her long trek, Nam Hui felt free to sit down across from her husband as he finished his meal. The two of them had been through many difficult times, and An Kil had always been able to find a way for them to survive. But this situation was different, and she wasn't sure how they would handle it. She clasped her hands together as if in prayer, holding them tight to her chest. "Do you think we'll be safe here *yobo*? Have you heard any news?"

An Kil raised his eyes to the ceiling for a moment. "I'm not sure. We have to wait to see if the ROK Army can hold the Communists. If the Americans will help, there's a chance. I heard on the radio last night that the American general, MacArthur, came to Korea and met with President Rhee a day or two ago. The announcer said the Americans are going to send help. But I'm not sure it will be in time."

"What are we going to do if the North Koreans come this way?" asked Nam Hui. "What's going to happen to our son?"

"If the Communists get past the Han River, it won't be safe for In Su, or us. We'll have to leave." Letting out a sigh, he said, "Let's not think about that now. It may be for nothing." An Kil got up from the table, put on his rubber work boots at the entry way, and left her sitting at the table alone.

Later that day, about mid-afternoon, An Kil was on his knees repairing a leak in the berm of one of his rice paddies when a neighbor came bicycling up the paddy trail, stopping right in front of him. "An Kil. Have you heard the news? The Communists have crossed the Han River and they're coming this way."

An Kil got to his feet wiping the sweat from his brow and shouted, "What? Where did you hear that? It must be some Communist propaganda."

"No. I heard it from Minister Pak. He has a telephone and talked with one of his church leaders in Seoul. He told him the Communists had taken the city and were killing people there—government workers and any soldiers they find. He said the ROK Army didn't even try to defend Seoul, but they fled and even blew up the bridges, trapping many people who wanted to get away. The North Koreans got across the river, and now there doesn't seem to be anything to stop them from coming here."

His mouth agape, An Kil stood paralyzed by what he'd just heard. "I can't believe it! What about our army? How much time do we have?"

"I'm not sure. Maybe a day or two. Minister Pak said there's a meeting at the village hall at seven tonight, and he asked me to help spread the word."

Scrambling out of the muddy paddy onto the bank An Kil muttered, "I'll try to make it." *I've just got to get back home. Tell Nam Hui.* As the neighbor pedaled off down the trail to tell others, An Kil began racing barefoot back to his house, leaving his boots atop the berm.

"*Ai Goo,*" said Nam Hui, an expression of fear on her face. "Does this mean we have to leave our home?"

"I don't know," said An Kil. There's a meeting tonight in the village. I'll tell you after the meeting tonight."

. . .

It was after ten when An Kil returned home. His wife and children waited anxiously to find out what he'd learned. His face was drawn tight, the corners of his mouth turned down as he entered the room. They could tell the news wasn't good. He sat down slowly and sighed, "It's true. The Communists are running over the ROK Army and there's no stopping them."

Soon Hi said, "What'd they say exactly? Any town officials there?'

"There were a couple town officials, and more than a hundred people in all—mostly farmers like me. Old Mr. Yi was in charge. He said he heard North Korean's making announcements over the radio. They've taken over radio stations in Seoul. They're saying the South

Korean army is defeated, the Rhee government is no more, and everyone should welcome the North Koreans. But Minister Pak said he heard that the North's army has been rounding up and shooting people in Seoul."

"What about our government?" asked Soon Hi. "Is there any word from them?"

"Yes, President Rhee has been broadcasting too. He says South Korea is not giving up, and the government is temporarily moving its operations to Taegu. A lot of the people I talked to said they're going to leave and not wait to see what the Communists do. I think we have to do the same."

Nam Hui put her hands to her mouth in alarm. Soon Hi stared as if not believing what she'd heard. In Su threw his arms up and said, "Why should we leave? They aren't going to hurt us. We don't work for the Rhee government. Why should we be afraid?"

An Kil looked at his son and said, "I'm a land owner. I've talked to too many people who came here from the north. They shoot land owners and then take their land. They'll take you and put you in their army to be killed. No. We can't stay."

Nam Hui, looked frightened. "Where should we go? Where will it be safe?

An Kil turned to his wife. "We'll go to Taegu and find In Yong. It should be safe there. Start gathering things together now, and then we'll try to get a little sleep. We'll have to leave early tomorrow morning before the road gets too clogged. I'd say it's about two hundred kilometers to Taegu. We'll have to walk, but we can fill up the cart and take what we can with us."

Early the next morning, the family loaded up the wooden cart that An Kil used to haul produce to market. In Su lifted the two hitching shafts over his head, took a firm grip on the handle bar, and leaned his weight forward. The cart began to move, and as the family of four started down the rutted country road, leaving their ancestral home behind, An Kil told his son he would spell him when he got tired. They hadn't gone far on the dirt road before several other families joined them, all moving in the same direction. A horn blared from behind as a beat up pick-up truck flew by them, blowing a cloud of dust in their faces. After an hour and a half, they came to Highway 1, the paved road that would take them to Taegu.

When they saw the crowded highway, they all stopped and watched in awe at the unending line, mostly people on foot, including a number of partially uniformed soldiers, but also including animal driven carts, jeeps, jitneys, and trucks of all sizes. It looked like a garish funeral parade. It was the beginning of summer and the women and old men were nearly all dressed in traditional cotton *hanbok*. In Su heaved the cart forward, and they entered the procession, flowing southward like a flood swollen river filled with detritus flowing ever southward. After stopping at the side of the road for lunch, Nam Hui said she needed to relieve herself and asked Soon Hi if she needed to also.

"Yes," she said. "But where?"

They stood at the edge of a large rice field. There were no nearby trees or rocks to hide behind. "Over there." Said her mother, pointing a short distance away towards a rice paddy berm. "No one cares. Everyone has to do it."

She followed her mother, watched her hike up her long skirt, pull down her pantaloons, and emit a long loud fart. People were passing by on the road above them, not more than ten yards away, but no one paid any attention to them. After emptying her bowels, and wiping herself with a handful of grass, Nam Hui looked up at Soon Hi, and said, "It's okay. Go ahead."

Soon Hi, wearing a one piece dress, tried to hunker down behind the berm to lower her panties. She needed to go, but she couldn't make it come. Finally a few drops dribbled out, and she gave up. Pulling up her panties without wiping, she told her mother, "I couldn't."

Nam Hui said, "Sooner or later you'll have to. You just have to get over your nervousness."

By nightfall, they'd traveled nearly thirty kilometers and were on the outskirts of Pyongtaek. It was starting to drizzle when they stopped to spend the night. The *yogwans* (inns) and private dwellings were already filling up with people, but Soon Hi's father found an innkeeper who agreed to take them in in exchange for a fistful of won notes and a bag of precious rice. They put their cart in the center courtyard of the *yogwan* and were directed to one of the rooms. In Su volunteered to sleep outside next to the cart to make sure no one took anything.

Entering the room, only about twelve feet square in size, they discovered they weren't the only occupants. A family of seven, including three children, had already taken up temporary residence, their belongings spread out over the floor. "Make some room for us," said Nam Hui, as she started to make a space. The other family grudgingly moved their things, piling them up against one wall, and watched warily as Soon Hi and her mother laid out their blankets on the floor.

Even though she was protected from the rain, Soon Hi found it impossible to sleep. It was hot and muggy with only one small window. The air was stagnant and the sickening sweet smell of sweating bodies mixed with the thick odors of urine and decaying food, hung like a heavy fog. The sound of snoring and babies crying was almost continuous as Soon Hi tried to force herself to sleep. After lying wide awake for more than an hour, she began to feel an uncomfortable urge in her bowels. She didn't want to get up, but she knew she couldn't hold it forever. Her father was snoring and her mother, she thought, was asleep too, but when she raised up, her mother stuck her head up and said in a whispery voice, "Be careful."

Making her way to the entryway she slipped on a pair of rubber *komushin* (sandals) that looked like hers and went outside. She went around to the alley in the rear where her mother told her she'd find the latrine and saw several women standing in front of a small wooden shack. She got in line and waited. When she got inside, the stench was overpowering. A dimly lit bulb hung from a crossbar above, allowed her to see that there were three spaces, two of them occupied. The floor was slippery as rain leaked through the tar paper roof. She went to an open spot on the end and her eyes fixed on the gaping round hole in the wooden floor. Black slimy sewage bubbled only inches from the top, emitting a sickening stink that made her gag. She took short breaths, removed her panties, and squatted over the hole, praying that no creepy crawly thing would rise up from below and bite her.

Waiting for the urge to return, she listened to the strained grunts of the two women beside her. She closed her eyes and tried to imagine herself alone. Her sphincter muscle finally relaxed, and she felt her bowels emptying. When she finished, she peered around the darkened area to see if anyone had left newspaper or anything that could be used to wipe herself. If there had been, it'd been used already. She felt stickiness between her legs, but nothing she could do. She'd have to wait until daylight to try to clean herself. She stood up, stepped into her panties, and went back out into the alleyway where the air was half-way breathable. She slipped back into the *yogwan*, found her place next to her mother, and laid down to try to get some sleep.

At some point, well after midnight, Soon Hi did fall asleep, but even before the sun had risen she was awake. She noticed her mother wasn't next to her, and she went outside to the courtyard. While standing in line to use the water pump to get a drink and wash her face and hands, she saw her mother on the other side of the courtyard huddled with several other women preparing something in a large pot over a fire. After she finished at the pump, Soon Hi went over to her mother who handed her a cup of watered down kimchee soup, telling her, "Eat this, and then wake your father and brother. We should leave soon."

She sipped the hot liquid. "Tomorrow let's sleep outside," said Soon Hi. "I don't care if it is raining." Her mother nodded in agreement.

Not long after breakfast the family of four was back on the road, hoping to stay ahead of the oncoming Communist army. It was July 4, a date that didn't mean much to her family, but Soon Hi knew it was an important date for Americans. Last year on this date, she was attending a picnic on the embassy grounds to celebrate America's Independence Day. This year there would be no such celebration. Plodding on alongside her mother, she heard the low rumble of vehicles coming from the opposite direction. As they rounded a curve in the road, she saw several military trucks heading towards her, and there were soldiers in the back of the trucks. As the trucks passed, Soon Hi saw they had white stars on the sides, and some of the soldiers waved. She turned to her mother and shouted, "It's the Americans! They came. Now the Communists will be driven back." Others nearby saw the Americans too and began shouting and waving. It didn't take long for the small convoy to pass by, and Soon Hi turned her eyes to the south to see if more were coming, but that was all.

CHAPTER 6

COLLATERAL DAMAGE

July 5–July 10, 1950

Soon Hi and her family had been on the road for four days. They just passed by Taejon, home to a major Korean army base, and she thought it strange—she hadn't seen any South Korean soldiers or trucks on the road today. Although the Americans had entered the fighting, rumors were rife about a battle that had occurred near Osan a day or two before and that the Americans had been driven back. That was worrisome too, but Soon Hi was still confident that once more American fighters came, they would be able to halt the North Korean advance and the tide would turn.

"We're almost to Taegu," said An Kil as he rested with his family along the roadside after finishing the last of the rice they had carried with them. "Another day and I think we'll get there. "We need to leave early tomorrow, because I'm afraid the fighting might get here before long."

The next morning they started out at dawn along with a large number of others seeking refuge farther south. As they moved down the road, they were shunted to the side as military vehicles, both Korean and American moved in the opposite direction toward Taejon. The refugees traveling south were mostly old men, women, and children, many wearing light colored summer *hanbok*. Retreating ROK soldiers were no longer in the group, but Soon Hi noticed a number of youngish men in civilian clothes who looked out of place. The government was drafting young men off the street to add to their military ranks. Could these young men be trying to escape being drafted, she wondered. Or were they perhaps infiltrating soldiers from the North Korean army?

By the time dusk began to fall they had traveled just beyond Kumi when someone suddenly yelled out, "Look. Airplanes!" An Kil looked up and saw two planes swooping toward them at treetop level. He saw a white starred insignia under the wing of one of them, and shouted, "They're Americans." He and others started waving, but then a thin stream of light, firefly-like, emerged from the wings followed by the staccato burp of gun fire. As the refugees realized the planes were shooting at them they scattered and began diving into roadside ditches and rice paddies. Bullets whizzed through the tightly packed crowd of refugees. For a split second Soon Hi stood transfixed. *What's happening?* The scene before her became a slow motion horror show of people falling over like wooden ducks in a shooting gallery. A second plane began to make a pass. Soon Hi, shook herself from her trance, pushed her mother to the ground behind the cart, and fell on top of her.

Soon Hi lay on the ground for a full minute while fearful screams punctuated the air. A few seconds of silence was followed by the sound of gun fire. She raised her head to see two young men in civilian clothes standing just on the other side of the cart firing at the attacking planes as they disappeared in the distance. Who were they? Where did they get the guns?

Once the firing ended, the two young men left without a word. The whole attack had been less than a minute. Soon Hi helped her mother up and tried to gather in what they'd just been through. At least a dozen people, including three or four children were lying about, dead or dying. Cries of pain could be heard from the wounded. Some people walked about like zombies. Others were shouting and rushing about in panic to find their family members.

Soon Hi rushed to the front of the cart and found her father lying flat on his back, blood pouring from his temple, his eyes vacant. Her mother fell on her husband's body with a shriek of agony. Soon Hi turned and saw her brother laying nearby, moaning with his knees buckled up underneath him. She turned him over and saw that he was bleeding from the stomach.

Seeing her mother lying over her husband, crying and shouting for him to respond, Soon Hi pulled her away and yelled out, "We need to get In Su to a doctor. You need to help me."

The two of them managed to get both In Su and her father into the cart and pushed it back onto the roadway. She saw a group of grass roof houses in the distance. "There's a village up ahead. We can get help there."

An old man came up to Soon Hi carrying a young child, the child's clothing soaked in blood. "Help me," he pleaded. "My boy needs help."

She bent down, tore a strip of cloth from the hemline of her dress, and wrapped it tight around the boy's right thigh to try to stem the flow of blood from a deep gash in his leg. Then she helped the man put the boy onto the cart. There were several other dead and injured lying in the road. Most were being tended to by family members. For some, there was no one to tend to them, and bodies were left where they were.

With the old man pushing from behind they got the cart moving, and after a few minutes they left the paved road for a dirt path. When they got to the little mud-walled village, about two kilometers off the main road, people came out to gawk at the arrivals. A village elder came forward and directed the curious villagers to take the injured to a nearby house. One of the older women stepped over to Soon Hi and offered to take In Su and the injured child to her home. The woman said she knew something about medicine and she would try to save him. Soon Hi looked at her and knew that she must be the village *mudang*.[ii] When the old woman unwrapped the cloth from around his torso, In Su let out a scream, then passed out. Seeing that blood was still oozing from the wound in his belly, she cleaned the wound, applied a strong smelling paste, and repeated some strange incantations. Then she wrapped a new cloth bandage around his waist and let him sleep.

The *mudang* said, "He is all right for now, but he must have the bullet removed from his belly. I can't do that. It can cause infection and he will die."

Soon Hi nodded her head in understanding and said, "I'll get a doctor. Can you keep him here?" She reached into the pouch inside her slip and pulled out some money and handed it to the woman, then went out to find her mother.

The village was crowded now with other refugees that had come from the highway. There were more dead and injured lying on the hard packed ground. Soon Hi saw her mother, standing over the body of her husband, talking to a Buddhist monk. "I have to leave," she said. "I'm going to Taegu to find In Yong and bring back a doctor. Can you take care of father?"

"Yes," said her mother. "The monk told me he'll see to a proper burial if we donate some money for his temple. I'll take care of it and wait here. Hurry."

Soon Hi went back to check on In Su. He was awake, but his face was clammy and ashen. She took his hand in hers and said, "Be brave brother. I'll be back as soon as I can." Feeling she might begin to cry, she quickly turned away and hurried toward the highway.

. . .

Soon Hi walked all night long until she came to a river. She could see that there were some refugees camped along the bank, but no one stirred—not at this hour. She strained her eyes looking across the wide expanse of the Naktong, barely detecting the outline of trees and a building or two on the opposite bank, all framed by the gunmetal gray of a starless sky that marked the faint beginning of a new day. She looked along the course of the river, but could see no bridge. The noiseless river, shrouded in a frothy mist, seemed peaceful and inviting, but it was far too wide to attempt to wade or swim across. She scanned the near bank and her eyes caught movement about a hundred yards upstream—perhaps a fisherman tending his boat. She found a path leading down the embankment. As she started down, her feet slipped out from under her, and she slid on her back to the river's edge. As she neared the boat she saw a man leaning over it, unaware of her approach. She called out to him, and he turned with a start. She quickly told him her story and asked him if he would take her to the other side. At first reluctant to waste his time with a stranger, he agreed when she thrust several won notes into his hand.

By the time she reached the outskirts of the city the sun was just coming up. Taegu was an important railroad hub with a normal population of about two hundred thousand people. Refugees streaming in from the north were adding to the population daily. It wasn't going to be easy to find her brother. She was able to catch a bus that took her into the city, and the driver dropped her off near a large market area. From there she walked until she came to a walled compound that appeared to be some type of school. She went through the gate and entered the main building, hoping to find someone to help her. As she walked down the hallway, a bell rang and young girls, all dressed alike in white blouses and blue skirts, began pouring out of rooms along the hallway. Some pointed at her, giggling and shaking their heads. She realized she must look frightening with her blood caked blouse and torn, mud-spattered skirt. She walked up to one of the young girls who didn't shy away. "What is this place?" asked Soon Hi. "I'm looking for my brother who is a newspaper man. Is there anyone here who can help me?"

"This is a Catholic girl's school. I'll take you to the principal's office. She'll help you," said the younger girl. Soon Hi endured more stares while waiting for the dean to see her and was surprised when a short white haired western woman in a black habit came out. "I'm Sister Agnes," she said in faultless Korean. "How can I help you?"

After overcoming her surprise at meeting a westerner who spoke Korean, she explained her situation, telling the nun that she was trying to find her brother who worked for the *Chosun Ilbo*. The nun listened, then told her to wait while she made some inquiries. After fifteen minutes she came back to the waiting room with a faint smile.

"I didn't locate your brother exactly," she said, "but I did find out where the *Chosun Ilbo* people have set up their newspaper." She handed her a slip of paper with the address on it saying, "It's not too far from here."

After effusive thanks, she started to leave, but Sister Agnes stopped her. "Before you go, you should clean yourself up and get a change of clothes. I'll take you downstairs to Sister Rosa and she will see you're taken care of."

A half hour later Soon Hi walked out of the school wearing clean underwear and ill-fitting, but clean, blouse and pants the nuns had provided her. She stood at the edge of the roadway and hailed a passing jitney taxi with two other riders already inside. Pulling the last of the money her mother had given her, she gave it to the driver along with the piece of paper with the newspaper's address on it. "Do you know where this place is? Can you take me there?"

The driver looked down at the hundred won note and grunted before putting the vehicle in gear and stepping on the gas. Fifteen minutes later, after dropping off one of the riders and picking up another, he stopped in front of an old warehouse in an industrial section and hollered back at Soon Hi that the place she was looking for was down the street. She thought the driver must have made a mistake. She didn't see evidence of a newspaper office. Then, at the far end of the building, she saw a small hand painted sign over a door. She ran down the street until she could make out the words: 조선 일보 (Chosun Ilbo). *This is it.*

Soon Hi opened the door and immediately heard a clatter of typewriters and was hit with the strong smell of printer's ink. Two young men, with shirt sleeves rolled up, were bent over a rickety plywood table reviewing a page layout. One of them looked up when she came in, stared for a moment as she entered the room out of breath from running, then pulled up a folding chair for her to sit and offered her a cup of water.

"Where have you come from? Have you been near the fighting? You look terrible."

Soon Hi took a sip of water and gasped, "My brother, In Yong Chung. I need to find my brother. I've been walking all the way from Seoul."

The young newsman looked at his co-worker and asked, "Do you know who she's talking about?"

"One of our reporters. He may be in back. I'll go see if I can find him."

A moment later In Yong came out of the back room, his arms outstretched with a broad smile on his face. "Sister! You made it. Where are the others?"

Choking back a sob, Soon Hi said, "Father's dead. We were attacked by airplanes."

In Yong's jaw went slack. "Dead? Airplanes? I didn't think the North had any planes in this area."

"They weren't North Korean planes," said Soon Hi. "They were American."

Shaking his head in disbelief, In Yong said, "Can't be. How?"

"I don't know," said Soon Hi. But we need to get a doctor for In Su. He's hurt, but still alive."

"What about mother? Where are they?"

"Mother's okay. She's with In Su. In a village along Highway 1 about twenty kilometers from here. We need to hurry."

Quickly gathering his senses, In Yong went to the phone and made a call to a nearby clinic. "We're in luck. My friend is off-duty now and he said he'd help us. We have to go pick him up."

"Is he a doctor? How do you know him?"

"Yes, he's a doctor. We were good friends in high school. He even came to our house one time. You may remember seeing him—Yong Chul Song."

She shook her head.

"We need to hurry. We'll take one of the company jeeps."

He took his sister's hand. Running through the press room, he grabbed a key from a rack, shouted to his boss that he had an emergency, and rushed out the rear door where a jeep was parked. After picking up Dr. Song, he sped out of the city as fast as the traffic would allow. With refugees clogging the highway, what normally would have been a thirty-minute drive took twice as long. When they reached the village, Soon Hi led her brother and the doctor to the hut where she'd left In Su. Her mother was sitting alongside In Su holding his hand and humming softly. When she saw her eldest son, she got to her feet and hugged him, gasping, "In Su's body is very hot. He's been sleeping most of the time, but he says crazy things in his sleep. I'm afraid he'll die like your father."

In Yong sat his mother down. "I brought a doctor. He has medicine. We're going to do what we can."

Song leaned over In Su's semi-conscious body, pulled back the blanket and checked his heartbeat. He had two bullet wounds. The one in his right thigh was superficial and did not pose a problem. Song removed the bandage from the abdomen and saw a reddened patch where the bullet had penetrated. He pressed lightly and In Su's eyes opened and he let out a groan.

"He's going to need surgery," Song said. "First, though, we need to get that bullet out. The wound's been infected." He pulled a syringe from his case and gave In Su a shot of morphine. Thirty minutes later he held up his forceps, displaying a twisted three-inch-long .50 caliber shell. "There it is. I'm surprised it didn't go through his body. It would have been better if it had. The bullet narrowly missed his spine, but it damaged his intestines and pierced his kidney. He has internal bleeding. I think he'll make it, but we need to get him to the hospital in Taegu."

After Song took time to check on the other serious casualties that had been brought to the village, they carried In Su and two others, a woman and a young boy, and put them in the rear of the jeep leaving no room for Soon Hi and her mother. In Yong told his sister he would return as soon as he could.

. . .

Several hours later In Yong returned to pick up his sister and mother. "How's In Su? Where'd you take him?" asked Soon Hi.

"I left him at Kyungbuk Hospital. Dr. Song was able to get him admitted, and he said they'd take him direct to the operating room. We need to get back."

Before leaving, Nam Hui, insisted that they stop by their father's gravesite located on the edge of the village at the foot of a hill. The monk had done a good job of negotiating a favorable spot with the village elders, although it had cost Soon Hi's mother more than they could afford. At the grave, Nam Hui prostrated herself on the grave and began chanting a Buddhist mantra. The sight of her mother in such agony tore at Soon Hi's heart. Finally, In Yong helped his mother up, and said, "We have to go."

Unsteady on her feet, Nam Hui clung to the arm of her son as he led her through the village to the waiting jeep. Soon Hi was relieved that for this final segment of their journey, they would be able to ride and not have to walk.

When they arrived at the hospital later that evening, they were met by Dr. Song. "Mr. Chung, your brother is out of surgery and he came through the operation fine. We had to remove one of his kidneys and also remove some of his lower intestine. He can live with only one kidney, but he's going to need an additional operation in three or four weeks to repair his colon."

When they went into the recovery ward to see In Su they found him unconscious still under sedation, but were comforted to know he was going to make it. The next morning Soon Hi and her mother went to see In Su and found him awake, staring at the ceiling with tubes running into his arm and another running from his side. He turned to his mother when she touched his arm, but he didn't smile."

"Are you in pain?" she said.

"I don't feel much of anything right now. I'm just mad. It was an American plane that shot us, you know? What kind of friend would do that?"

"It was an accident, I'm sure," said Soon Hi.

"Accident hell, they intended to kill Koreans, they didn't care if we were Communists or not. Where's father? Is he here in the hospital too?" In Su's mother turned away, unable to speak, but Soon Hi said in a near whisper, "No, he's not here. He didn't survive. He's gone."

In Su let clenched his fists and a gurgled growl of pain and anger emerged from his throat like hot lava from a volcano. He attempted to rise and pounded his fists on the mattress. "Americans must pay for this," he shouted.

Drawing attention from nurses and other patients, Soon Hi tried to calm him down. "It's a war brother. There were some North Korean soldiers in civilian clothes. I know – I saw them."

"It doesn't matter," said In Su. "This is our country. The Americans can't get away with killing innocent civilians. They killed our father."

CHAPTER 7

REFUGE

July 15–Sep 1, 1950

When Tom and the rest of the embassy staff first arrived in Pusan two weeks before, the post at Hialeah was largely empty, and everyone was getting ready to jump aboard the nearest boat for Japan. Now the place buzzed with activity. American troops were processing through, ammunition, equipment, and supplies were piling up in the warehouses, the port was alive with off-loading ships. From Tom's point of view, it looked like the South Korean army, with American support, might be able to turn the thing around.

Tom was not aware, however, of just how serious the military situation was. The North Korean army was preparing to swallow up their non-Communist brethren and shove the Americans back into the sea. What the Americans and their Korean allies desperately needed was someone to take charge—someone who could create order out of chaos. That finally appeared to be taking place as General MacArthur got President Rhee's agreement to put all ROK and U.S. forces under a single U.S. command and designated Lieutenant General Walton Walker to command the combined allied ground forces.

Shortly after arriving in country General Walker went to the embassy and met with the ambassador and his staff, a meeting Tom was invited to attend. At five-foot-five and a rotund waist, Walker resembled a beardless Santa Claus. Although not physically impressive, the general's confidence, his studied awareness of the situation, and his ready plan for dealing with the multi-pronged North Korean offensive made a strong impression. Walker told the ambassador, "My first priority is to slow down the North Korean advance at Taejon. I'm going to set up a defensive perimeter along the Naktong River. But I need time to get reinforcements here. I've told General Dean he needs to hold them at any cost—that means no retreat beyond the Kum River."

Ambassador Muccio responded, "You're sending those men on a suicide mission."

"In war, there's a human cost," the general said. "Soldiers know not all will survive. They accept that...and I accept it too. It's the price we pay to protect our freedom. If we can hold the Reds off until the end of the month, I'll have the 1st Cavalry Division from Japan and an additional two divisions coming right behind them from the states. With those reinforcements, I believe, we'll be able to hold indefinitely."

The North Koreans were not interested in helping Walker achieve his goal. By the end of the following week, word spread through the embassy that the North Korean third and fourth divisions crossed the Kum River. By July 20 they took Taejon. The rag tag remnants of the U.S. 24th Division, having lost a third of its original 12,000-man force, was in full retreat, and the division commander, Major General William Dean, was missing in action. General Walker ordered his new defense line to dig in at the Naktong River and ordered elements of the 1st Cavalry Division to relieve the disintegrating 24th Infantry Division. Walker knew it was their last chance to stop the Communists. If they broke through this defensive line, it would be impossible to stop them from taking the whole peninsula. Tom, and everyone on the embassy staff, felt the pressure, knowing there was nowhere else to go. They would have to evacuate Korea entirely. Walker made it clear in a message he sent out to his troops, "There will be no retreat from the Naktong."

Fortunately, the U.S. Air Force controlled the skies, and daily attacks by F-51 Mustangs and F-80 Shooting Stars slowed the advance of the North Korean army down highway 1, but only for a short time. By August 1 they were at the Naktong preparing for a major push to take Taegu city. The brief respite had given Walker time to build up his forces and he readied them for a major battle. Recognizing the real possibility that they'd be overrun, he directed the evacuation of civilians from Taegu which had ballooned to more than half a million people. Fearing the worst, President Rhee once again moved his government—this time to Pusan. It was the end of the line. The roads below Taegu were clogged with refugees seeking shelter and safety. The civilians were funneled into dozens of refugee camps, large and small, hastily set up outside Pusan. One of those was at Kimhae where Tom worked as the embassy liaison.

.   .   .

The Kimhae refugee camp, about ten kilometers north of Pusan, was in a barren field surrounded by low hills and rice paddies where the grain was just beginning to ripen. The army had set up hundreds of tents to provide shelter for the massive numbers of refugees pouring in from Taegu and elsewhere. Tom's job was to coordinate the transfer of food and medical supplies from the port to the camp. On his second day in camp, while going over an inventory with a UN medical team member, he heard a commotion outside his tent. He went out and saw a young Korean woman arguing heatedly with another UN worker. He recognized the woman, even with her hair cut short and her face smudged with grime.

"Miss Chung? How did you get here? Is your family okay?

It took a moment for Soon Hi to recognize the American standing in front of her. "Oh, Mr. Crandall? Yes, it's me. I'm so glad to see you. I need help."

"What can I do?"

"It's my brother, he needs medicine. Airplanes attacked us before we get to Taegu. He had operation last month and was supposed to have second one last week, but when everyone ordered to leave Taegu... Now his fever returned and body swelling up. He needs medicine."

"Is he here in camp?"

"Yes."

Tom called to the Filipino nurse he'd been talking to, "Grab your bag and follow me."

They followed Soon Hi through the rabbit warren maze of densely packed tents. Finally she stopped in front of one of the canvas shelters, and the three of them stepped inside. A putrid odor permeated the air. A shirtless man lay on a straw mat on the dirt floor. He thrashed his head from side to side, his body bathed in sweat. An older woman sat beside him attempting to keep a wet cloth on his head. Soon Hi pulled back a tattered blanket covering his lower body. A plastic bag, attached to his side and nearly filled with a black liquid, reeked of excrement. The skin around an incision in his abdomen was bright red and puffed up like a ripe tomato. The nurse took one look and said, "We need to get him out of here and to a hospital. If that wound bursts, he will die."

Tom radioed back to the embassy for medical help. After an hour's wait, an army medic team arrived, and at Tom's insistence, they agreed to take In Su to the American base in Pusan by ambulance. Tom followed in an embassy jeep with Soon Hi and her mother. On the way, he learned that, not only had In Su been shot, but Soon Hi's father had been killed along with several other civilian refugees. Tom knew that infiltration of North Korean soldiers mixing in with civilians was a U.S. Forces concern. He attempted to apologize for what he called a terrible American mistake, but he knew in his heart it had been no mistake, and he feared it would haunt the Americans in times to come.

When they got to the Hialeah compound, he told the ambulance driver to take In Su to the MASH (Mobile Army Surgical Hospital) unit that had been set up to receive and handle American casualties. Tom wheeled In Su into a large tent and a gruff looking sergeant, after eyeing the patient, said, "We can't take a Korean. It's against regulations. We got our hands full with GIs. Take him to a civilian hospital in town."

"I can't do that," said Tom. "He needs surgery now. This is a special case. Where's your commander?"

The sergeant led Tom to another tent where he stood waiting outside for several minutes before the sergeant came out, and told him he could enter. Colonel Sam Shelby was a short bespectacled reserve officer who'd been practicing medicine in Terre Haute, Indiana until called up for service in Korea three weeks earlier. He looked up from his paper work, and said, "I hear you brought in a

Korean civilian. We're not equipped to handle all the Korean population. You'll have to take him to a Korean hospital."

"I understand, sir, but this is a special case. I don't think he can get the treatment he needs in a civilian hospital right now. I found him in the Kimhae refugee camp. I brought him here because my nurse said he'd die, and this was the only place equipped to handle this kind of medical emergency."

"There're hundreds of civilian casualties out there. What's so special about this one?"

"His sister told me that when she and her family were on the road just north of Taegu their group was attacked by American planes. Several people were killed, including her father. Her brother, here, may be another victim if we don't help. I think the American government has a responsibility since we put him in this condition."

"Our pilots don't go killing civilians for no reason. What makes you think what you heard is true?"

"This patient's sister used to work for me at the embassy in Seoul. I know her and I trust what she says. But even more than that, I've talked to some pilots who've told me about North Korean soldiers using the civilians as shields. They've told me they'd been given an unwritten go ahead to decide whether the targets are civilian or military."

"Accidents of war happen, don't they?"

"Yes sir. But accidents can sometimes escalate into big scandals. This guy's older brother is a newspaper reporter, and if this gets into the Korean press it won't look good—could even have repercussions back in the states. We're trying to rally Koreans to resist the Reds. What kind of message does this send? I know the ambassador wouldn't want this to get out now."

"Hmm." The colonel massaged his chin. Then he scribbled something on a notepad, tore the page off, and gave it to Tom. "Take this to the sergeant, and he'll get him admitted."

The next morning, before he had time to finish his first cup of coffee, his office phone rang. It was Colonel Shelby.

"We patched up your Korean friend last night. Drained the infected area and have him stabilized for the time being. But he needs a complicated operation to reconnect his intestines and there's only so much we can do for him here."

"You're not going to throw him out on the street are you?"

"Don't get all worked up," the colonel responded. "He's leaving by hospital ship for Japan this afternoon. They've got surgeons over there that can handle him. Once he has the surgery and gets well enough to travel, maybe in a month, then they'll send him back here."

"Colonel, I don't know how to thank you."

"No need to thank me. I'm doing it to help cover the Army's ass. After he gets back here, he's your problem. Make sure he understands what we did for him."

* * *

Later that day Tom returned to the Kimhae refugee camp, found Soon Hi, and took her to the army port facility to see In Su off. After the ship left the dock, they began walking back toward the parking lot and Tom said, "How'd you like to come back to work for the embassy?"

Soon Hi's eyes widened, "You really think I can?"

"The embassy is looking for interpreters to work with the refugees. You'd be good at it. I'll see if I can set up an interview for you tomorrow."

Soon Hi threw her arms around him and said, "Oh Mr. Crandall you do so much to help my family. I'm so grateful."

Tom felt a warm surge through his body as he felt her arms around his waist and her head against his chest. Suddenly sensing others watching, she released her arms and stepped back. He gently put his hands on her shoulders and said, "No need to be embarrassed. And don't be so formal Soon Hi. Call me Tom. We'll be seeing each other quite a bit before this fighting is over. Let's be friends."

* * *

It was the middle of August and more than 50,000 American soldiers stood alongside roughly 95,000 South Korean soldiers, outnumbering the North Korean forces of 120,000 that were moving in three separate columns, one along the eastern coast, one driving directly south toward Taegu, and the third angling to cut off Taegu from the southwest. American air power was beginning to take a toll on North Korean supply lines, cutting down their flow of arms, ammunition, and food. The Pusan perimeter was holding, but the North Koreans were not through, and success was still not certain.

Up to now, General Walker had deftly shifted his resources to meet each North Korean challenge. By the end of the month, he expected another 40,000 American troops in country. There was a growing sense that the worst was over, and that the Communist effort to drive the Americans from the peninsula would fail. But simply holding off the Communists at the Naktong, was not the endgame anyone would be satisfied with—not the South Korean government officials sitting in Pusan, not the Korean refugees who wanted to return to their homes, not the millions of South Koreans who feared confiscation of their property and worse by the Communists, and certainly not General MacArthur who surveyed the unfolding scenario from his imperious seat in Tokyo with eager anticipation.

MacArthur had been a strong supporter and architect of amphibious landings employed in the Pacific during the Second World War. In early July, immediately after he got approval to inject U.S. ground troops into the Korean peninsula, he ordered his planners to develop a scheme for a delaying action that would slow the Communist advance, followed by an amphibious landing at a point above the invading force.

MacArthur first submitted his invasion plan to the Joint Chiefs of Staff (JCS) on July 10, requesting the call-up of a Marine division to support an amphibious landing. His plan was initially rejected, but the blustery general wouldn't take no for an answer. He resubmitted his request in more detail, identifying Inchon, a port city on the country's western coast less than thirty miles from Seoul, as the point of landing. He put special emphasis on the fact that he needed the Marine division by September 10 for a proposed D-day of September 15. That date was crucial since the widely ranging tide levels would be at their most favorable point on that date. The military leaders in Washington okayed the plan concept and sent it to the president. On August 19, Truman approved the call up of the Marine division while also announcing his intent to expand the size of the military through the draft.

Although these actions allowed MacArthur to proceed with preparations for the landing at Inchon, the decision to launch the counterattack was still in limbo. The JCS as a whole was still leery. General Bradley, the JCS Chairman was a foe of amphibious landings. There were too many things that could go wrong—and usually did. On August 23 Bradley sent two members of the JCS staff, General Lawton Collins, the Army chief of staff, and Admiral Forrest Sherman, the chief of naval operations, to try to dissuade MacArthur from his focus on Inchon. They argued that the tides at Inchon made the window of opportunity for a landing too narrow. There was a risk of ships becoming grounded on mud flats where they could be attacked from the rear, leaving the landing forces vulnerable to enemy artillery. They tried to convince him to choose another spot for the landing farther down the coast. MacArthur, in his characteristic bravado, was undeterred. He argued back that Inchon was precisely the right place, because it would not be expected. It was near the main supply route for the North Koreans and cutting off that route would be instrumental in eliminating the North Korean invading force. He ended the meeting by declaring forcefully, "This is where we will land, and I will succeed."

By September 1 preparations for the landing were nearly complete. An armada of more than a hundred ships and landing craft had been assembled at Sasebo, Japan. Marine and Army units designated for the landing were in place. The troop and ship movements were so large, it was impossible to expect that the enemy wouldn't know that something big was in the offing. Naval batteries pounded the area around Inchon in preparation for the landing, but attacks were also made on enemy posts elsewhere along the coast to create uncertainty as to exactly where the Americans were planning to invade. The plan had a green light, but there was still great concern among members of the administration in Washington. How would the Russians respond? How would the Chinese respond? Even though the preparations were proceeding, no final decision on the launch would be made until the last minute—and that decision would be made by the president.

CHAPTER 8

THE SOVIET CHALLENGE

September 8–14, 1950

Having just wrapped up a meeting with senators from the Armed Services Committee, President Truman was upbeat. He began looking over his calendar when the phone on his desk rang. It was his secretary.

"Give me a moment, Rose, and then you can send in Mr. Eban."

"Yes sir, but I have a call from Mr. Acheson. He says it's urgent. Will you take it?"

"Put him on." After the connection was made, the president said, "Good morning, Dean. I just had a very fruitful meeting with some of our friends in the Senate discussing the situation in Korea. I hope you're not calling with any bad news about that place."

"No sir — it's not about Korea. I just got word from our embassy in Ankara that the Soviets have invaded Turkey."

"What! What's happening?"

"According to the report I received, Soviet tanks crossed into an eastern border region known as Kars Oblast using tanks and infantry early this morning. There's been an ongoing dispute over this area for some time, with the Soviets making claims that it used to belong to Russia and is rightfully theirs."

"What are the Turks doing about it?"

"I understand they're calling for a general mobilization. I have a call in to Warren Austin up at the UN. This is going to get big very fast."

"I was afraid of something like this. I have a meeting now. But you're already on my schedule for noon. I want to see you and the fellas from the Pentagon here in my office then so we can figure out what needs to be done."

Two hours later Dean Acheson, trailed by Louis Johnson, General Bradley, and the four service chiefs, walked stiffly into the oval office and took chairs around the large desk where Harry Truman was hunched over a set of briefing papers.

The president looked up, adjusted the rimless glasses on his nose, and said, "Well, Mr. Acheson, what more do we know about the Turkey situation?"

"The Soviets are claiming that they are reoccupying lands stolen from them that was previously part of historic Armenia. It goes back to the days before World War I when the Turks massacred Armenians and drove them out of Eastern Turkey into Russia. Stalin seems to be settling old scores."

"Yes, I think you're right. Just like he's done in Poland and other Eastern European countries. What's the Turkish reaction so far?"

"According to their UN representative, they're preparing to go to war, unless they withdraw. Mr. Austin has called for a meeting of the Security Council to try to get a call for a ceasefire the Soviets will listen to."

Looking at General Bradley, the president asked, "How does this impact our situation in Korea?"

"It could have a big impact. We're a week away from launching a counteroffensive on the Korean peninsula that will be the biggest thing we've done since landing on Okinawa, and it's unclear what additional forces will be needed once we engage the enemy. We don't know what the Chinese will do. It could draw a lot more of our resources to complete the job there."

"And what about Turkey?" asked the president. "If the Turks ask our help against the Soviets, can we fight there in addition to Korea?"

"It depends on the size of those battles. It would be difficult at best. The problem with that scenario is it would probably not be limited to Turkey. The Soviets would more than likely broaden the conflict and start something in Eastern Europe as well. In the war against Germany and Japan, Britain and the Soviets did much of the fighting. Britain's not in a position to help much now, nor is France. We have only twelve divisions in Western Europe facing maybe eighty Soviet divisions. It could very well come down to a nuclear showdown."

The president pondered what he'd heard, and then said, "That's a very sobering outlook. With the Inchon plan a week away, we've got some time—not much, but a little—to try to find a resolution in Turkey before it gets out of hand." Turning to his secretary of state, he said, "Mr. Acheson, I want a ceasefire proposal put before the UN Security Council by tomorrow morning. Let's put this back in the Soviet's lap. Then I'll consider our options."

. . .

Late the following afternoon the president met in the oval office with his secretary of state. As expected, the Soviets had rejected the American request at the UN for an immediate ceasefire. He was joined by Louis Johnson, General Bradley, and Averill Harriman. Harriman had served as ambassador to the Soviet Union from 1943 to 1946 and had been instrumental in funneling American war materiel to the beleaguered Soviets. He had been with Truman at Potsdam and understood, as well as anyone, the thinking of Stalin.

Truman turned toward Acheson and said, "What do the Russians want? Is this connected to the situation in Korea?"

"Without a doubt, the two are connected. But the Turkey situation is a little different since it plays on a long standing dispute over an area they once controlled. And it involves a humanitarian issue involving the Armenians who were driven out of the area after the First World War ended. There is some legitimacy to their claim, but the Turks aren't going to stand by and let them have it. Just like they've done in Eastern Europe, the Soviets want a government in Turkey that is under their thumb. It will give them access to the entire eastern Mediterranean and the Middle East."

After mulling over Acheson's comments, the president said, "I met with the Turkish ambassador earlier this afternoon. He said Turkey needs our support in terms of arms and possibly soldiers. I told him we would support their position diplomatically, but I made no promises beyond that." Turning towards Harriman he asked, "What do you think is Stalin's objective? Can we deal with him?"

Harriman shifted in his chair. "Mr. President, the Russians are chess players, and Stalin is one of the best. He sees this as a combination chess move. Two of our pieces are threatened. He wants to force us to sacrifice one of our pawns—either Korea or Turkey."

"Well I don't believe in sacrificing anything if I can help it," said Truman. He looked at Harriman. "Averill I want you to go to Moscow. Do you think you can get in to see Stalin?"

"I still have some of my old contacts in the Kremlin. I think he'll see me."

"Good," said Truman. "We need to let him know that we can play chess too, and we have some moves that may make him rethink his strategy. We haven't got much time. After we finish here, you and Mr. Acheson get together to work out the details. You need to be on a plane tomorrow."

• • •

Three days later Harriman was back in the oval office, alone with the president.

"I've read over your memo. Now explain to me what his bottom line is," said Truman.

Harriman cleared his throat. "He wants us out of Korea. If we agree to let the Communists take over the peninsula, then he'll withdraw his forces from Turkey."

"And if we remain in Korea?"

"Then he'll expand his invasion of Turkey and may make a move somewhere else."

The president nodded. "I see. There's some decisions to be made. I have a meeting set up with the NSC tomorrow. I want you to brief them, and then we'll weigh the alternatives."

• • •

The next morning, with all the president's top advisers sitting around the table in the cabinet room, Harriman went over the results of his meeting with Stalin. Truman then asked around the table for comments. Everyone knew that whatever came out this meeting could be the start of World War III.

Admiral Sherman, the CNO, was first to speak. "We're on the verge of turning the tables on the North Koreans. Right now troops are boarding the landing craft in Sasebo. They'll set sail in two days for Inchon. It's too late to turn back. We need to stick to our plan, and damn the Soviets. I think they're overplaying their hand in Turkey. If we can quickly end the fighting in Korea, it will change the calculus in the Soviets thinking."

General Bradley spoke up. "If is a big word. I don't think they're bluffing. They know we're not prepared to fight major wars on two separate fronts. If we land our amphibious force as planned, we'll be committing our forces there for some time. We can't expect to be able to shift them to Europe. It would take six months at the earliest to build up our forces in Europe to anything approaching equivalency. If Russia is successful in Turkey it will threaten the rest of Europe. We can't hope to defend West Germany, and even France would be in play."

General Hoyt Vandenberg, the Air Force chief, interjected. "The Air Force has an answer for that. We have the bomb. If you give the okay, we can send the Soviets back to the Stone Age, and they know it. It was proven effective in bringing the Japanese to their knees, and it'll be just as effective against the Russians. We know they're developing a capability of their own. Now may be our best chance to end that threat forever."

Then it was Dean Acheson's turn to speak. "Once those bombs are released, we don't know where things will end up. Before we start sending anyone back to the Stone Age, we need to look at our long term strategy and how our current situation fits this conundrum. With respect to Western Europe, we've enunciated clear goals through the Truman Doctrine and implemented programs under the Marshall Plan to save Western Europe from economic collapse. If we let Turkey spiral out of control, all of Europe could unravel, our principle post-war policy would be in shambles. On the other hand, we have sought to support South Korea against a forcible takeover from the North. The South Korean government was set up under

United Nations auspices and it is a matter we rightfully referred to the UN, but maintenance of Korea in our sphere of influence has never been considered vital to American interests. Our vital interest in Asia lies in protecting Japan—and we can still do that, even if we have to withdraw from the Korean peninsula. That's the option I would recommend."

After everyone had a chance to speak, Truman tapped his pencil on the table and said, "Thank you gentlemen. I'm going to consider everything that's been said here and think it over tonight. We'll meet here again tomorrow at one p.m., and I'll make my decision."

. . .

It was nearly midnight when the president, sitting in his study, laid down the book he was reading, took one last sip of his drink, got up and walked into the adjoining bedroom where his wife was still sitting up reading her own book. He sat down on the side of the bed. "Bess, I don't know what I'm going to do tomorrow. I feel like a guy standing in an alley with a gun facing down a kidnapper who's holding a woman hostage when I see another guy with a gun coming up behind me. I can fight with the best of 'em...but do I start shooting and maybe end up with a dead hostage and maybe get killed myself, or do I find an exit so I can track down the bad guys later?

"Harry, you don't need me to tell you what to do. You've never been afraid to make tough decisions, and you'll do it again—and it'll be the right decision." Bess put her book down, leaned over and kissed him tenderly. "Turn out the lights Harry, and let's get some sleep."

. . .

The next afternoon, the president's advisers entered the cabinet room as scheduled, most keeping to themselves with little of the normal pre-meeting chit-chat. The president entered and took his seat at the head of the long table. Without wasting time Truman said, "I've made my decision. I've sent a message to Mr. Stalin through the Soviet embassy that we will withdraw from Korea if the Soviets withdraw from Turkey. I've sent a message to MacArthur, also, to put on hold the Inchon landing preparations pending any final agreement with the Soviets. I do not make this decision lightly, but the danger of setting off a new world war is too great to ignore. I was willing to use the atomic bomb in Japan to save millions of lives that would have been lost if we had continued with that war. However, I am not willing to use the atomic bomb to start a new war that has the potential to cause the loss of millions more."

There was a visible sigh of relief from some around the table, while others looked stone faced and disappointed.

"This does not mean we are abandoning Asia. Since the end of the last war, we have been committed to Japan to ensure that they can stand up as a strong democratic state, and we will continue to do that. We will work diligently to finalize a peace treaty with that country and seek to establish a mutual defense agreement. At the same time, I do not intend to abandon those South Koreans who have stood beside us and who are threatened with death once the Communists take over. I am dispatching Mr. Harriman back to Moscow to meet with the Soviets, to determine if their offer to leave Turkey was sincere, and, if it is, to negotiate a means to end the conflicts both in Turkey and Korea with no more bloodshed. Towards that end, I have instructed Mr. Harriman that we must have a ceasefire of sufficient length that will enable us to effect an orderly withdrawal and evacuation of South Koreans who wish to leave. Are there any questions gentlemen?"

CHAPTER 9

DEPARTURE

September 24–30, 1950

From the roof top of the port terminal Tom stared down at the sea of humanity queuing up to board the huge troop ship moored alongside dock number one. Vince Moroni, standing beside him, snapped a wide angle shot of the scene. "I couldn't believe it when the ambassador told me we were getting out of Korea, but when I understood how the situation in Europe could escalate things, it started to make sense."

"Yeah, I was shocked too," said Tom. "I really doubted if it could be worked out peacefully, especially when President Rhee began speaking out publicly against the Americans, saying he wouldn't honor the ceasefire. If he would have stayed on, things could have gotten sticky."

At a rally three days after the ceasefire announcement of the planned U.S. withdrawal, President Rhee was shot and badly wounded at a rally in Pusan. The assassin was a young Cheju-do man who sought to avenge his brother who had been killed the previous year in an anti-Communist sweep by ROK Army units. After the assassination attempt, things began moving fast. The Americans put Rhee, in critical condition, on a plane to Hawaii, along with his European born wife. After Rhee left the country (he would die six months later in a Honolulu hospital), there was little will left within the ROK Army or the South Korean government to further resist the Communist takeover.

What remained of the South Korean government was now operating from the city of Pusan. After Rhee's departure, his vice-president resigned his office, and the prime minister, Yi Pom Sok was sworn in as acting president. Although the forty-five-day ceasefire was holding, the Communist noose was tightening around the small area still controlled by the Americans and their Korean allies. Taegu's population, which had more than tripled in size as evacuees flooded in, had shrunk to less than a hundred thousand. Many who had fled, accepted the inevitable and drifted back to villages to pick up their lives as best they could. Communist organizers in civilian clothes had infiltrated the city and were laying the groundwork for their takeover, and most people having any connection with the local or national government had left the city, seeking to escape through Pusan or other ports where anyone with a boat found they could make a lot of money transporting people to Japan or Taiwan.

"It's a good thing Truman got the North Koreans to agree to the ceasefire," said Vince. "Otherwise, there'd be no way we could do an evacuation on this scale. Just look at the ships out there—like a kid's bathtub filled from one end to the other with rubber ducks and plastic toys."

"Yeah," said Tom. "I heard that when General MacArthur was first notified of the decision to cancel the Inchon landing and withdraw troops from Korea, he had threatened to resign."

"That's true. The ambassador told me he was fit to be tied. The only thing that kept him here, I think, was when Truman sent out General Bradley to sooth his ego and convince him that Japan couldn't survive without him. After that he was all in."

"How many Koreans do you think we'll be able to get out?"

"I think the latest estimate is 300,000. At least that's what they're gearing up for. Japan, I understand, will take up to 50,000 in the home islands. Most will be going to Okinawa, Guam, and the Philippines."

Watching the milling crowd below, Tom said, "So far the ROK Army units have been holding the line pretty well. I'm sure the officers, at least are going to want to get out before the North Korean tanks roll into Pusan. Sure hope we can avoid any panic."

"I'm worried about that, too," said Vince. "Most of the anti-Communist signs and banners have disappeared from the streets, and it's rare to see a South Korean flag now except on government buildings. Most of the people with money and connections have already left, but I'm afraid anybody connected with the Rhee regime is in for it if they don't get out, and I'm sure those people who own property are fearful of losing everything. We're not going to be able to get everyone out who wants to go."

• • •

With a restless throng of evacuees pressing against barrier ropes six feet away, Soon Hi Chung, sat with three other clerks at a table near the gangway leading up to the USNS General Alexander M. Patch. An MSTS troop transport last used during World War II, it had been activated by the Navy just for this purpose. Its normal capacity was around 5,000, including crew, but more than 6,000 refugees would be crammed aboard on this day. Other ships waited in the harbor for berthing assignments to take on more refugees. The number of people seeking a way off the peninsula seemed to be without limit as the camps around Pusan emptied and the people spilled into the city seeking a way out. A crowd of at least 20,000 jostled and pushed for a better position closer to the registration tables where Soon Hi and three other clerks were processing passengers for boarding.

Soon Hi looked up when she heard angry shouts come from the surrounding crowd. Suddenly a squat jowly-faced Korean colonel accompanied by several wild-eyed ROK soldiers emerged from the crowd and stalked toward the gangway. Ignoring calls from Soon Hi and others, the officer pushed aside those trying to stop him. "Out of my way. I have orders," he yelled. When two Marines brandishing M-1 rifles confronted him, the colonel drew a revolver and began waving it. A shot rang out, and another. At the sound of the gunfire, the crowd panicked and, like a human tsunami wave, it began to roll over anyone and anything in its way. Those too infirm or too small to withstand the rolling mass of people were swallowed up and trampled. The swirling mob began to surge towards the gangway. Before she knew what was happening, Soon Hi found herself sprawled on the pavement, the overturned table partially covering her. As she attempted to free herself, other bodies began to fall on top of her. A knee jabbed into her ribs. She couldn't breathe. She felt a hard blow to the head and blacked out.

Sometime later, Soon Hi began to come to. She could hear muffled voices and sensed someone standing over her. She was woozy and her body ached, especially her face. She started to pass out again, but then felt someone touch her on the shoulder and speak to her, "Can you hear me. Open your eyes."

She forced open her eyelids just a crack. At first her vision was a blur. Then, as she opened her eyes wider, a man's face came into focus, a rugged, but not unpleasant, face with deep set dark eyes that seemed to pierce through her. Was she dreaming? A sharp pain when she tried to raise her left arm made it clear she wasn't. She heard a moaning sound to her left and turned her head to see another person laying nearby. People were milling about all around her, but the madness appeared over.

The man kneeling beside her said, "Are you all right?"

"I...I think so. What happened? Who are you?"

"I'm Lieutenant Han. I'm with the security detail. We had a rogue colonel trying to force his way on board the ship with several soldiers, but we've got things under control now. Somehow, in the panic, you got pushed to the ground and roughed up. When I got to the scene, I saw you lying there and figured I better get you out before you got killed. You've taken quite a beating. There's an aide station at the end of the pier. Do you think you can walk?"

Soon Hi tried to get up, but her head began to swim. Her legs gave out, and she collapsed back onto the ground.

"I'll carry you," said the lieutenant as he bent over and picked her up in one swift motion. She put her one good arm around his neck and let her body go limp, putting aside her modesty and felt her body relax as his strong forearms gripped her. When they got to the aide station, he laid her down on a blanket and called a medic over. The lieutenant leaned down and said to Soon Hi, "You'll be all right now. I've got to get back to my men."

She propped herself up on one elbow, touched his arm, and said, "Thank you for saving me. Be careful."

Soon Hi waited patiently on the ground while a single nurse attended to others first. Finally, a young rosy cheeked American with a Red Cross band on his sleeve came to her and asked her to sit up. After taking her pulse and checking her eyes for evidence of concussion, he asked her to raise her arms. "Ow," she cried. "It hurts."

The medic probed her shoulder and clavicle with his fingers. You've got a separated shoulder, and a concussion too, I think." He fixed a sling and adjusted it on her arm. Then, looking at the ID badge on her blouse, he said, "I see you work for us. To be safe, I'm going to send you to the embassy medical unit at Hialeah so they can X-ray your shoulder and check out your head trauma. You should be okay in a day or two."

• • •

The next morning, after spending the night in the infirmary, Soon Hi woke to see Tom Crandall, sitting in a chair beside her bed reading a magazine.

"What are *you* doing here?" she asked.

"I was worried about you. I was at the port facility when the crowd rioted. I saw everything. Didn't know you were down on the dock then, but when I learned you were hurt and brought here, I had to come and see how you're doing."

"How do I look?"

"You look like a tank rolled over you. Your face is blown up like a big pumpkin, but your eyes are a pretty purple, I have to say."

She started to laugh but her jaw hurt too much and she could only let out an exasperated, "Ooww!"

"I wanted to talk to you about getting you and your mother out of here. We've only got a few days before the curtain comes down on our welcome in Korea. I think I can get things arranged for a U.S. visa for you and your mother since you've been working for us. Where do you want to go?"

"I want to go to Japan. We have no one in the U.S. My mother has a sister who lives near Tokyo. Besides, my younger brother must be still there, and we have to find him."

"Okay. There's an MSTS ship scheduled to leave here day after tomorrow for Sasebo. I'll get papers prepared for you and your mother. You'll be going to a refugee processing center, but shouldn't have to stay there too long. Although the Japanese have been trying to put brakes on the number of Koreans to be settled in the home islands, given you've been a U.S. employee, there shouldn't be a problem in your getting permanent resident papers."

Her eyes cast to the side, Soon Hi said, "I know we must go. Maybe someday things will become normal once again. My brother In Yong told me he's staying. He's a newspaperman, you know. Do you think he'll be all right?"

Tom furrowed his brow and shook his head uncertainly. "It's going to be tough for him for a while, but hopefully Kim and his government won't penalize civilians like your brother for being on the opposite side. Whether they'll allow his newspaper to stay in business is a whole other question."

Soon Hi held her chin in her hands, shaking her head slowly back and forth. Raising her eyes to meet his, she said, "I think I can't worry about that. I need to take care of mother, and I need to find my brother In Su. We have no word from him since he went to Japan a month ago. Do you have any idea?"

Tom shook his head, "No, the only thing I know for certain is that the ship he was on was going to Sasebo, and he was to be transferred to some American Army hospital near there. I'll get the exact name and give it to you tomorrow. Since your brother didn't have any papers authorizing him to stay in Japan, he may still be in the hospital. I'll be leaving for the states in a few days, but I'm going to try to get reassigned back to Japan. I don't want this to be our good-bye."

"I know, and I won't forget your help."

. . .

Two days later Soon Hi, standing with her mother amid a crowd of anxious refugees waiting to board the USNS William O. Darby, prepared to say good-bye to her brother In Yong who had come to see them off.

"It's not too late for you to leave Korea. There'll be another ship tomorrow. You'll be safe in Japan," said Soon Hi.

"No," said In Yong, "I have to stay here in Korea. I have work to do here. We need newspapers not connected to Kim Il Sung and his party. We need to hold him accountable to the people. I'm hopeful, once he's taken over all of Korea and no longer feels threatened, that he'll become more moderate. I hope he'll open his arms to all internal groups and will enlist the support of southern leaders—businessmen, scholars, and even politicians—to build one Korea into a real democracy. The Communist newspapers are saying that they will allow freedom of press and they will welcome those who have not actively supported the Rhee regime. They say people below the provincial government level need not worry. We have to hold them to that promise."

"I don't know much about politics, but I think you're taking too big a chance," said Soon Hi. "I want you to write me." She handed him a piece of paper with an address written on it. "Here's the address of Aunt Kim in Kawasaki. Once we get our residency papers in Japan we plan on going there to stay with her for a while. You can reach us through her."

"Okay, I'll write to you and keep you informed on how things are going here. Maybe in a year or so when things settle down, you can return to Korea."

With a troubled look on her face Soon Hi said, "I'm not so optimistic, but I hope you're right."

. . .

Later that day, as the huge troop ship left the harbor and the pilot boat veered away, Soon Hi looked at her mother standing beside her at the railing watching the land they once called home disappear in the distance. Her chin quivered, but no tears emerged from the heavy folds around her mother's eyes. Soon Hi thought about her father, lying in a grave in the small village in Kyongsangbuk-do. Would she ever be able to go back to her father's grave? Would she ever see her brother again? In Yong said he'd write, but would a letter reach her? She knew her mother was thinking the same thing. She put her arm around her shoulder, squeezed her close, and stared at the fading shoreline. As they moved into open water and the boat swayed under their feet, they made their way below deck.

CHAPTER 10

HIRADO

October 1950

After a six-hour trip over rough seas, the ship carrying Soon Hi and her mother sailed into Sasebo harbor on the northern coast of Kyushu. A former Japanese naval base, it had been taken over by the Americans, and now the port was ringed with U.S. Navy vessels of all types. An aircraft carrier was moored along one pier and several smaller warships were tied up near the entrance to the port facility. Cranes were unloading two large supply ships along an adjacent pier. The docks were overflowing with equipment, vehicles, and thousands of containers. Crews of stevedores scurried this way and that, like ants in an upheaved ant hill, busily stacking containers and moving materiel into warehouses lining the docks. When an announcement was made over the ship's loudspeaker for passengers to assemble for debarking, Soon Hi and her mother picked up their meager belongings, a cloth bundle for her mother and a suitcase for Soon Hi, and they joined the mass of passengers on deck, eager to set foot on ground.

Once on land, Soon Hi and her mother were ushered to waiting buses that were to take them to the island of Hirado, about twenty kilometers away, where a half dozen camps had been set up to maintain the Korean refugees until they could be placed in permanent locations. Hirado, an island slightly larger than Nantucket off Cape Cod, was just a stone's throw from the Kyushu coast connected by a single bridge to the larger island. It wasn't by chance that Hirado was selected as a refugee camp. From Japan's earliest recorded history, it had been an entry point for traders from China and Japan. Portuguese and Dutch traders from Portugal in the sixteenth and seventeenth century were allowed to set up trading posts on the island. Now it would be home to the new arrivals from Korea.

After their bus crossed over the bridge onto Hirado, they rode for another three hours before finally arriving at Shimonaka, a refugee camp in the center of the island. Although surrounded by a fence, the camp itself, a former training center for the homeland reserve force, appeared to be well maintained with some trees and green areas and several barracks-like structures that were being used for communal activities. The majority of the area, however, was made up of long rows of tents where refugees were assigned to live. Immediately on arrival, they were ushered to a large assembly area for in-processing. The female interviewer, a Korean member of the anti-Communist community organization called *Mindan*, told Soon Hi that it might be several weeks or even months before they could be placed in Japan, since they needed to find sponsors for each family. When Soon Hi told her they had an aunt living in Kawasaki, the clerk called over an older woman who appeared to be a supervisor.

After looking over her paper work, the woman said, "We may be able to get you out of here in two or three weeks if we can contact your aunt and she is willing to sponsor you."

"That shouldn't be a problem," said Soon Hi.

"Do you have any money? You'll need it on the outside. Our *Mindan* organization has a bank here in the camp. They can exchange your Korean money for Japanese yen."

"We don't have much Korean money, but we have some gold jewelry. Can we exchange that for yen?"

"Oh, of course, they'll pay for gold."

Before leaving the interview, Soon Hi pulled out a piece of paper from her purse, handed it to the woman, and said, "I want to find my brother. The Americans sent him to a hospital here in Japan over a month ago and we haven't heard from him. The name of the place is on that paper. Do you know how I can go there?"

The woman looked at the piece of paper. *118th Station Hospital, Fukuoka.* She gave the paper back to Soon Hi and shook her head, "I can't help. You need to find an American."

The next day Soon Hi took her mother to one of the large Red Cross tents where they were distributing used clothes. The weather was changing, and they had not brought any winter clothing with them. She picked out a wool overcoat for herself and one for her mother. Then she went to a rack of western style dresses, took one down that looked like it would fit her mother and said, "This will be more comfortable for you to wear than your *hanbok*."

Her mother flashed a scowl and said, "No, I'm not wearing that thing. It doesn't look right on me. I'll wash my Korean clothes and wear them until they fall apart."

Soon Hi tried to argue with her mother, to no avail. After her mother stalked away, she picked out two cotton dresses that looked like they'd fit her mother and put them in her bag knowing that someday they would be of use.

While her mother browsed through the clothing tent, Soon Hi began talking with one of the Red Cross workers who introduced herself as Jill Harris. A gray haired woman close to her mother's age, the American expressed surprised at Soon Hi's fluency in English. When Soon Hi told her she had worked for the Americans in Korea, the woman asked if she would like a job helping out as a clothing sorter. Although it didn't offer any pay, maybe this woman or some other American could help her find her brother, and she quickly accepted.

Two weeks later, after receiving their alien registration documents, Soon Hi and her mother packed up their few belongings and prepared to leave. The cash they were able to get for the gold wasn't as much as Soon Hi had hoped, but it would be enough to live on until she could find work. Aunt Kim had written and said they could stay with her in Kawasaki for as long as they needed, so that relieved some pressure. Soon Hi's first task was to find her brother — if he was still alive. Since she had heard nothing, she feared that he may have died from his wounds. She needed to find an answer, and she'd start with the American Army hospital in Fukuoka. Getting around Japan would be no problem for Soon Hi, since she'd had to learn to speak and write in Japanese from her earliest elementary school days. Her mother, having little formal education, spoke Japanese well enough to get around, but she never learned to read or write the language. Getting on an American Army post would pose a separate problem. For that she needed American help, and she turned to Jill who told her she'd been to the 118th Hospital several times and she'd be happy to take her there.

. . .

When they got to the U.S. Army hospital gate, Jill signed Soon Hi in as a visitor, and they left her mother waiting outside. After some searching, they found the hospital records section. Soon Hi stepped up to the counter. "I'm looking for information about my brother. He was a patient here. I have this paperwork." She laid the copy of In Su's travel document that Tom had given her on the counter.

Ignoring the document, the private looked at her and said, "We don't have Jap patients here."

Soon Hi responded, "I'm not Japanese. I'm Korean. My brother sent here by U.S. Army."

The private retorted, "Same goes for Koreans. We ain't got any."

Jill stepped forward and said, "This order says you had at least one Korean. Now check your records."

The private grudgingly went over to a card file, and after fingering through them, said, "Nope. Nobody named Chung in this file. He must have been taken some place else."

Jill said, "This is the reception area for wounded, and he had to have come through here. I want to talk to your sergeant."

The private went to a back room and a ruddy faced staff sergeant came out and Jill thrust the travel document in his hand, saying, "We're trying to find this man, and we're sure he was sent here."

The sergeant looked at the paper, and said, "This was two months ago. Even if he came here, we wouldn't have kept him here. It would take a lot of searching to look through our records, and even if we did find something we wouldn't know where he went. He could have gone back to Korea."

"No," said Soon Hi. "He would write me. If he died here I want to know."

Jill interjected, "If I have to go to Colonel Simpson to have the records checked I will. We need to get an answer.

Frowning at her veiled threat, he said, "That won't be necessary lady. I'll have someone go through the records, but it's gonna take a while, so have a seat."

Forty-five minutes later the sergeant came out of the back room, carrying a book the size of an atlas, and motioned Jill and Soon Hi to the counter.

"I couldn't find any medical records, but I found an entry in this log book for a guy named I Jung for August 17. Do you think that's the guy you're looking for?

"Soon Hi quickly glanced at the entry. "Yes, that's him. What happened to him?"

The sergeant bent over to read the handwritten script. "It says he was shipped up to the 128th Hospital at Camp Zama on August 19. He was alive when he left here, but that's about all I can tell you. Any medical records would have been sent with him."

Soon Hi looked up at Jill for reassurance and said, "Does this mean he's okay. Where is Camp Zama?"

"It means he was alive when he left here. Their job here has been mainly to get patients stabilized and if they need more advanced treatment to send them to places where they can do the necessary surgery. Camp Zama is just a few miles south of Tokyo. That's a long way from here, and I wouldn't be able to go there with you, but I can give you the name of a friend of mine in Tokyo. Her name's Ellie Crawford, and she's head of the Red Cross office near MacArthur's headquarters. You should be able to find it easy. It's right across from the Japanese emperor's palace, and I'm sure she'll help you."

Jill wrote down her friend's name, along with a short note of introduction, and handed it to her. As they walked out the front gate of the hospital compound they saw Soon Hi's mother still sitting patiently on a bench across the street. When Soon Hi told her mother In Su had been there, but was sent up to Tokyo, Nam Hui squeezed her hand, squinted her eyes as if in thankful prayer, and said, "We must hurry to my sister's house, so we can find your brother."

Jill escorted them off the army post, hailed a taxi, and directed the driver to take them to the Fukuoka train station. An hour later Soon Hi and her mother boarded a train for Kitakyushu, the terminus of the Kyushu rail line. From there they had to take a ferry to get to the main island of Honshu.

A twenty-minute ride across the narrow Kanmon Strait brought them to the city of Shimonoseki, the southernmost point on Honshu. As they made their way through the crowded ferry terminal, Soon Hi sensed that people were looking at them in a strange way. When Soon Hi tried to approach a middle aged man to ask directions to the train station, he looked down at them with a disapproving sneer and said he didn't know before hurrying away. When they got to the exit, Soon Hi tried to get a taxi, but was told it was taken, just as a young woman shoved in front of her and jumped into the back seat of the cab. Soon Hi looked around bewildered and saw an elderly porter standing at the curb. She thought his face looked Korean, and she went over to him.

"How can we get a taxi to take us to the train station? People seem to ignore us?"

The porter looked at Soon Hi and then at her mother dressed in her long *chima* skirt, once a pretty pink, but now dingy, streaked with dirt and stains."

"You're probably not going to get a taxi to take you there. They don't like Koreans here. You need to blend in and not be so obvious if you want people to treat you right—just like me. It's only about two kilometers that way," he said, pointing to the north. "You can get there quicker by walking than waiting for a taxi." Then he turned away and quickly wheeled his cart toward a potential customer several feet away.

Soon Hi, carrying her heavy cardboard suitcase wrapped in twine, and her mother carrying large scarf wrapped bundles in both hands, trudged in the direction the porter had shown them. After going more than two kilometers, they finally came to the train station. Soon Hi walked up to the ticket booth, pulled out her purse, and asked the clerk for two second class tickets. The clerk looked at her mother and said, "Those seats are reserved for Japanese. Koreans ride in third class."

Soon Hi started to say something, but then thought better of it. She laid the fare on the counter and took the ticket. She turned to her mother and said, "If you'd worn the western dress instead of the Korean, maybe this wouldn't have happened."

Her mother shook her head and said, "Why should I pretend I'm not Korean. It's who I am."

Soon Hi and her mother stood with about a hundred other homeless vagrants like themselves, all hanging unto a miscellany of baggage and food products that represented their sole possessions. When the call for boarding was made, they were herded toward a rear car with a sign designating it for third class travelers. More than eighty people were packed into the car that was intended to hold half that number. They were able to squeeze unto a rickety wooden bench where they remained except for brief periods when the train halted at station stops and they were able to stand and stretch. After eight hours they finally heard the announcement for Kawasaki station. They grabbed their bags and Soon Hi pushed her mother forward through the packed compartment, reaching the door just before it closed. Exiting the station, they found the taxi line, and this time they found a driver willing to take them. Soon Hi worried how her mother would be able to adjust to her new surroundings.

Kawasaki, an industrial city just a few miles south of Tokyo, was home to a large Korean community. After a few minutes staring out the window of the taxi, Soon Hi noticed that some of the signs in the shops were in Korean and she even saw that a few of the older women on the street wore Korean dress. Mother won't have to feel so much like a foreigner here after all, she thought. She leaned back against the seat cushion and began thinking about her brother. *Where is he?* She pulled out the note Jill had given her and looked at the name. *Tomorrow I need to go into Tokyo and find this woman.*

CHAPTER 11

MINSEN

November-December 1950

Soon Hi's aunt, a widow, lived with her unmarried daughter in a small upstairs apartment above a pharmacy. The accommodations were crowded and they had to share a bath with another family, but Aunt Kim welcomed Soon Hi and her mother to stay as long as they wanted. Soon Hi was grateful for that since she knew it would be a while before she could find work and get an apartment of her own.

Soon Hi's cousin, Yong Ja, four years younger, had left Korea when she was only six. Soon Hi could barely remember her cousin as a shy little girl who she tried to teach to jump rope on the street in front of their house. Then suddenly she never came around anymore, and Soon Hi thought she'd never see her again. Now they were back together, eager to share stories of their experiences.

"Why did your family leave Korea?" asked Soon Hi.

Yong Ja explained, "Father couldn't find any work in Korea, The Japanese government was recruiting Koreans to work in factories here in Japan to replace Japanese men who were being drafted into the army. Father got a job in a chemical factory in Yokohama and after a year he brought us to Japan. He was able to support us okay, and we had a bigger apartment than we do now. Then he was killed in an explosion at his factory. That was eight years ago. Mother found work sewing soldiers uniforms, and Chang Son— you remember my older brother— left home and went to Osaka to work. After the war mother lost her job, and so I quit school and got a job as a bus girl. That's what I do now."

After listening to Yong Ja's story, Soon Hi related her own adventures since leaving Seoul five months before. Yong Ja cried when she heard how Soon Hi's father was killed.

"Do you think you'll ever go back? The Korean language newspapers are saying Kim Il Sung is offering free land to people who return to the fatherland. A lot of people here in Japan have gone back, and the Japanese government has even encouraged it."

"I'd like to someday, but I don't know if it'd be safe to return now. I used to work for the U.S. government in Seoul, and I don't trust the Communist rulers there."

Yong Ja shrugged her shoulders and said, "I understand. Maybe someday."

•　•　•

The next morning, after a short train ride into Tokyo Station, Soon Hi emerged from the bustling terminal and saw the walls of the emperor's palace looming off to her right. Before anything else, she was determined to find out what had happened to her brother. She walked toward the palace and soon came upon the Dai Ichi building, which was the landmark Jill had told her to look for. After passing that block-long building, Soon Hi saw a Red Cross logo on a window. There was no building directory inside, but she found a janitor who directed her to the second floor. Entering the office, she introduced herself to the secretary and gave her the letter of introduction that Jill had written. After waiting several minutes, the secretary told her the director would see her.

Soon Hi walked into the room and saw a plump matronly looking woman, perhaps in her late forties, not more than five feet tall. Ellie Crawford stood up and came around her desk to introduce herself. Soon Hi made a bow and sought to apologize for imposing on her, but the older woman waved her hand and said, "It's no problem. Jill called me and told me all about your situation, and I'm more than glad to try to help, although it may be a tall order to find your brother after all this time."

Over a cup of tea, Soon Hi explained in detail how her brother had been sent to Japan for medical treatment, showed her the copy of the initial travel authorizing document, and told her what she had learned at the army hospital in Fukuoka. Ellie, listened and then said, "I can't take you today, but tomorrow I'll make time, and we'll go out to the hospital at Camp Zama and see what we can find. I'm sure they'll have some record of him still. Can you meet me here at ten?"

. . .

The next morning Soon Hi arrived at the Red Cross office fifteen minutes early, but the secretary told her that Ellie was in a meeting and would be a little late. She worried that perhaps Ellie wouldn't be able to take her to the army base after all. But a few minutes after ten Ellie emerged from her office with her coat on her arm, saw Soon Hi, and said, "Let's go before I get another call."

It was a crisp sunny December day, and as the two of them made their way out the door, Soon Hi noticed a crowd gathering on the sidewalk in front of the Dai Ichi building next door where an older model Cadillac had just pulled up to the curb. It must be someone important, thought Soon Hi. An aging American Army officer, his eyes hidden behind aviator sunglasses, emerged from the car wearing a nondescript olive drab overcoat and a battered tan service cap with faded oak leaves on the bill. He was joined by another American, a bespectacled white haired man in civilian dress, somewhat bent over, wearing a distinctive homburg hat. The two of them strode toward the front of the building with a sharply dressed aide close behind. "Who are those people?" asked Soon Hi.

"The man in the sunglasses, that's General MacArthur," said Ellie. "And the other man I think is John Foster Dulles. I read in *Stars and Stripes* that President Truman was sending him here to meet with General MacArthur concerning the Japanese Peace Treaty. With the Korean peninsula now in Communist hands, the American government is anxious to get that done soon."

"Ah, look," said Soon Hi. "People are bowing. Why are they bowing for a foreigner like that?"

"Oh, it's not just any foreigner. They're bowing for General MacArthur. After the war ended, General MacArthur agreed to allow the emperor to remain in a position of authority in Japan. The people respect him for that so much that they treat him almost like he was the emperor himself. It's as if he were a shogun under the old Japanese empire."

. . .

After a short train ride to Sagamihara station they grabbed a taxi to Camp Zama. Ellie showed her pass to the gate guard and signed in Soon Hi as a guest. Entering the hospital, Ellie went directly to the patient administrator's office where she greeted the female lieutenant behind the desk by her first name.

"We're looking for information about my friend's brother," said Ellie. "He's Korean, but he was treated in the 118th Hospital at Fukuoka, and we believe he was sent up here for surgery in late August or early September. His name is In Su Chung. Can you do a record search to see what you have on him?"

The woman shook her head uncertainly. "We're still trying to get our records organized, and since the patient would have been a foreigner, I'm not sure that we would have kept anything on him. But I'll take you back to the records section and see what they can find."

After waiting nearly an hour in front of the records desk, a sergeant came out of the rear file room with a folder in his hand, a puzzled look on his face. Ellie and Soon Hi went up to the desk and Ellie asked, "Did you find something? Is there a problem?"

The sergeant laid the folder on the counter and said, "I found a file on your Mr. Chung that includes a medical report on surgery that was done on September 3 and a couple follow-up reports when he was in recovery. But that's all there is — nothing to show a release date or final disposition."

Ellie took the folder, scanned the report, and then said, "It says in here that her brother had intestinal reconstruction surgery. That's a difficult operation and he would have had to be in intensive care for at least a few days. I don't know how he could have got off the base on his own, but I don't see any other explanation."

The sergeant shrugged his shoulders. "You may be right. At that time we were in such chaos with all the wounded being brought in from Korea anything could have happened."

Ellie turned to Soon Hi and said, "I'm sorry we couldn't find anything more definite. But we do know he was here and that he survived his surgery. Do you have any idea where he might have gone?"

"The only relative we have here is my aunt, and he didn't contact her. You helped me a lot to find out this much. He's somewhere in Tokyo, I think, and I'll find him somehow."

. . .

That evening, back in her aunt's apartment, Soon Hi sat with her cousin, sharing a supper of spiced noodles and vegetables, and related the day's events.

"I don't know where to start," Soon Hi commiserated.

Yong Ja said, "There are many Korean community organizations where he might have gone for help. I don't know much about them, but I think my high school teacher, Mr. Yon, may have some contacts that can help us."

"You completed high school? What kind of school?"

"Yes, it was a Korean language school run by *Choren* (League of Koreans in Japan). In Japanese it is called *Zainichi Chosenjin Renmei*."

Soon Hi cocked her head to the side and said, "Isn't that supported by Korean Communists?"

"I guess it was, but my mother wanted to send me there because it's hard for a Korean to get into a Japanese school, it's more expensive, and people look down on you. Going to that school I didn't have to be shy about being Korean. A while ago the Japanese closed my school because they blamed Koreans for a lot of anti-Japanese demonstrations. But I think Mr. Yon still gives private lessons, and I see him almost every week on my route."

"I see," said Soon Hi. "I guess it wouldn't hurt to talk to him."

. . .

The following evening, after Yong Ja returned from work, the two girls set out to see Mr. Yon.

They passed a boarded up two story brick building. "That's my old school," Yong Ja said. "The Japanese police closed it down when the war in Korea started. Mr. Yon's house isn't too far from here."

After walking three more blocks, they turned into a narrow side street lined with one and two story wooden buildings huddled close together. Some were dark, perhaps where businesses were closed for the night, but from most of the structures soft light filtered through papered windows and sounds of an occasional baby's cry, a couple arguing, a teenager shouting back at his parents, could be heard from behind the thin walls. Finally they came to a small building set back from the street with a short path leading past a small rock garden near the entrance. Yong Ja knocked on the door, and a skeletal looking old man with a wispy white goatee, wearing pajama bottoms and a t-shirt, peered out at the visitors behind thick rimless glasses. His narrow face lit up upon seeing a familiar face.

"Yong Ja, my favorite student. Come in."

Mr. Yon showed them into a small living room cluttered with books and papers and laid out a pair of cushions on the tatami covered floor and invited them to sit. Yong Ja introduced her cousin and then let Soon Hi explain her situation. After listening to the full story, the old teacher pulled at the whiskers on his chin. "Tokyo is a very big place, but we Koreans have a very close knit community. If he came to the Tokyo area from an American hospital, like you say, someone will know of him, and we will find him."

Soon Hi took a deep breath. "That sounds wonderful. It will make my mother so happy to have him back with us. How long will it take?"

"If he's in this area then it shouldn't take long. But if he went to some other area in Japan, then it could take some time. I will start making inquiries tomorrow, and I will get in touch with Yong Ja when I find out something."

When Soon Hi returned to her aunt's house and told her mother about the progress, she felt the end of their search was near. After a week, though, without hearing anything from Mr. Yon, Soon Hi was beginning to think her brother had gone to another area, and they wouldn't be able to find him at all. Then two days later Yong Ja came home and brought news. "I saw Mr. Yon today. He knows where your brother is."

"Where is he? When can we see him?"

"Mr. Yon said to meet him at a tea room I know just outside Shinjuku Station tomorrow evening at seven. He says your brother is working near there, and he'll take us to him."

The next night Soon Hi and Yong Ja took the train into Shinjuku and, without much difficulty found the *Tomo* Tearoom. Mr. Yon was sitting at a table near the front with a cigarette dangling from his mouth reading a newspaper. He motioned to them to come over, and, no sooner had they sat down, than Soon Hi immediately asked him, "I thought we would hear from you sooner. How did you find my brother?"

Yon drew on his cigarette. "Ah, Miss Chung. Don't be so excited. As I told Yong Ja before, I have many contacts. I went to see a friend in the prefectural office and made an inquiry with the director. It took a little while because your brother apparently changed his name. He didn't want the Americans to know where he was, but we were able to find him. He's actually working under the name Dong Son Chung in one of the pachinko parlors that *Minsen* operates in this area."

"*Minsen*?"

"Yes, it's what we call the Korean Democratic Front. It's a patriotic Korean organization that performs many useful services for Koreans here in Japan. We need to take care of ourselves. We used to have *Chosen Soren,* but the Japanese shut our organization down when the war started in Korea, and we have to be very careful in our activities since the Americans under MacArthur have attacked any groups they believe support the Communist revolution. You should consider coming to a meeting sometime."

"Um, maybe, but what about my brother. Can you take us there now?"

"Yes, of course." He paid the waitress, and they got up from the table and went outside. The street was awash in bright lights, restaurants, bars, a large movie theater, and shops selling everything from clothing to antiques. After walking no more than three blocks, they turned unto a side street with more glaring lights, a row of pachinko parlors on one side and bars on the other. They stopped in front of one of the pachinko parlors where several customers were engaging with the game machines as if they were human. Mr. Yon walked to the rear and began talking with a gray haired man sitting at a cash register. The man went into a back room and before long a young man wearing patched blue jeans and a greasy sleeveless t-shirt, came to the front. He didn't look the same. He was much thinner with long hair down to his shoulders and a scraggly mustache. He looked more like a young mobster than the teenage schoolboy she'd seen last. But he *was* her brother, and she ran up to him and put her arms around him.

"In Su, I was so worried about you. Are you all right?"

In Su, standing stiffly, let his sister hug him but, showing little emotion, stepped back and looked at his sister for a moment before speaking. "Yes, I'm okay, except for missing one of my kidneys and needing special medicine for my bowels thanks to the Americans. How did you find me?"

"Mr. Yon helped us. He said you changed your name. Why did you do that?"

"I was afraid the Japanese police would arrest me. I didn't have any legal papers for staying in Japan. After I escaped from the American Army hospital, I made my way into Tokyo and some Korean friends hid me and got me papers under my new name — people know me as Dong Sun from now on."

"I don't understand how you think. Why did you have to escape from the army hospital?"

"America is the enemy of our fatherland. It's a new age for Korea now," said her brother. "I want to be part of it. I've found people here who support the new Korea and it's given me a purpose. My old life, just like my name, is a thing of the past."

"You can change your name, but you can't change your family. You're my brother, and I'll always call you In Su. Mother is so anxious about you. You must come to see her."

Ignoring her comment about his name, he nodded his head. "Yes, I miss her too. In a day or two I'll come to see her. You can tell her that."

Soon Hi wrote out her aunt's address in Kawasaki, and then after a few parting words left.

Two days later In Su came to the house, shivering in a light jacket, carrying a large bento box filled with a varied selection of *kimbap*, sushi, tempura, and pickled vegetables. Answering the door his mother threw her arms around her son, letting out a cry of happiness, and then, tears streaming down her eyes, she led him into the apartment where Soon Hi and her cousin and aunt were preparing a meal. Most of the evening was spent with the whole family sitting in the living room where a charcoal space heater gave off just enough heat to ward off the cold from outside, reminiscing about what had happened over the previous five or six months. Later that night, after her mother, aunt, and Yong Ja had gone to bed, Soon Hi sat up with In Su and questioned him at length about his worrisome behavior.

"You talk about Korea under Kim Il Sung as if it's a perfect paradise now. Do you really believe that? Are you thinking of returning there?" asked Soon Hi.

"Yes, I think it is much better now that Kim Il Sung has made our homeland one again. Someday I want to return, but not now. There are things to do here in Japan. The socialist revolution in Asia has just begun."

"Where are you getting these ideas? You didn't used to talk like this."

"I've made a lot of friends here. I go to meetings, and I've learned a lot. I understand now that we are just part of a world-wide revolution, and it's starting in Asia now. Under the guidance of Chairman Mao Western imperialism was defeated in China. Now Chairman Kim has evicted the Americans and their toadies from Korea and established a socialist nation. He even changed the name in English to Choson instead of the name Korea that westerners gave us. Now we Koreans must help our Japanese friends to create a socialist Japan as well. Capitalism is dying. It's only a matter of time before it's defeated everywhere."

"You're talking dangerous ideas. You'll be arrested if you get involved in any of these anti-Japanese things. I don't want to see you in prison."

"You can't stop me, sister, and in fact, I hope you will think of joining us. You should give up thinking like an American slave.

Accept what has happened and become a part of the new Choson. If you join with us, I know your past will be forgiven and you can give useful service to the fatherland."

Soon Hi shook her head back and forth, "No, I can't. It's too sudden. I mean I'm glad Korea is unified now, but I don't think a Communist Korea or Communist anything is the answer to everyone's problems. You talk as if America was the only foreign country involved in Korea. What about the Soviet Union, and China? Doesn't Kim Il Sung owe his victory to their support?"

"Certainly they helped, but his victory was inevitable. Korean unification was a victory for international socialism. But now Korea is free and can chart its own path free of foreigners.

"That sounds good for a speech, but what does it mean in reality?" asked Soon Hi. "Your Chairman Kim is still under the thumb of Stalin and, I'm afraid, he'll create a monstrous dictatorship just like Stalin. Why do you think so many people tried to escape to the South when he took control?"

In Su rejoined hotly, "What was the bastard Rhee, but a dictator, backed by all the old Japanese collaborators and comprador capitalists who murdered and exploited the small farmers and working class people so he could stay in power? Chairman Kim loves his people. Give it some thought sister. "

Soon Hi got up and laid out a roll of bedding for her brother in one corner of the room. "I can see we're not going to settle this tonight. It's late. We can talk more tomorrow."

Soon Hi went into the small room where her mother slept, curled up beside her, and quickly fell asleep.

The next morning In Su spoke hardly a word, eating a simple bowl of rice with seaweed soup and kimchi, before leaving. Soon Hi, looked at her mother, as they watched him disappear down the street, and she began questioning her own motives. *Could he be right about Kim Il Sung? Was she wrong to have worked for the Americans? Her brother knew what he wanted, but did she?*

CHAPTER 12

MISSIVE FROM CHOSON

January 1951

It was a bitterly cold January morning, and Soon Hi was alone in the apartment when she heard a knock at the door. She opened it and was met by a short, rather odd looking little man wearing a ratty overcoat and a floppy hat pulled down over his brow so she couldn't see his eyes.

"Who are you? What do you want?" she asked.

"My name is Yang. I'm from *Mindan*," he said in a distinctly North Korean dialect. "Do you know of us?"

"Yes, I've heard of you. But if you're collecting money, I'm afraid I don't have anything to give."

"No, it's not that," said the man. "I have something to deliver to a Miss Soon Hi Chung. Is she at this address?"

Soon Hi took a step back and said weakly, "That's me. What is it you have?"

"I have a letter from Korea, Miss Chung. May I come in?"

Soon Hi stepped back, feeling a bit unsteady. She showed him into the sitting room, laid out a seat cushion, and offered him a cup of tea, which he accepted. After taking a sip of the hot liquid, he pulled out a small envelope from the bag he was carrying and handed it to Soon Hi. It was addressed to her in English in care of the U.S. Army Headquarters in Tokyo. Whoever wrote it knew she could be tracked through the Americans. She opened it gingerly and quickly scanned the letter looking for the signature. She let out a deep sigh when she saw it was from her brother In Yong. She had almost given up hope of

101

hearing from him. She dropped to the floor next to the odd messenger and began to read:

November 10, 1950

Dear sister: I'm sure you have been wondering why you had not heard from me these past weeks since you left our homeland. It isn't because I didn't want to contact you, it was just impossible to send any letter through normal channels to Japan, without it being opened. I was finally able to make contact with an underground organization and I am sending it through their agents.

You probably have been reading quite a bit of praise about what is going on in Korea since the Communist victory. Most of it is false propaganda generated by the tightly controlled political party now running this country. When the Communists took control last month, they announced that people should not fear them. They said they welcomed all classes of people with the exception of those who supported the Rhee regime. They said people in government at the local level should continue to do their jobs as before, that they wouldn't be affected. That lasted about a week before the arrests started en masse. I went into the streets and saw piles of bodies of people stacked up like dead mackerel in a fish market. In the countryside people's committees have begun identifying people for arrest — property owners, business people, and anyone that someone had a grudge against could be identified as a Rhee sympathizer. There is no court system anymore, it is simply mob rule. There is no one to appeal to if you are accused of something. Mass executions are a daily occurrence throughout the country.

Shortly after the arrests started, my editor went to the city hall. He never came back. I'm afraid he may be in one of those stacks of bodies I saw. The next day police came and smashed all our equipment and shut us down. The same has happened to all the other papers except those belonging to the Communist Party. Several of the top people in my paper were arrested. Those who are not executed are sent to "reeducation camps" to learn how to parrot the Communist Party line. This is a sordid dictatorship, one where Chairman Kim is determined to eliminate any opposition. He's creating a cult. It's scary — I can't live under a regime like that. But for the time being there isn't a choice for me. But you do have a choice. I'm glad you got away to Japan. Don't think of returning to Korea? It's not safe for you, no matter what you may hear.

Although a lot of people I worked with were arrested, I managed to escape with the help of friends and am in hiding. Because I have written things critical of the Communists, I'm sure I'm on someone's list. When the witch hunts ends, I hope the new regime will come to realize it doesn't have to fear its people, but will come to understand that divergent views can be empowering. Until then I will try to keep out of sight of the authorities. It won't be possible for you to contact me now, but when I can, I'll contact you again through the underground network. Keep safe, and work toward a better future for our Korea.

Your brother In Yong

Soon Hi put down the letter, her face was white, and she looked at the stranger sitting patiently with his eyes closed as if dozing.

"It's from my brother," she said. It was written two months ago. Why did it take so long? How did you get it?"

Opening his eyes, he said lazily, "It's not easy to receive mail from Korea these days. An American who said he was from MacArthur's headquarters came to my office with your brother's letter and asked that we try to find you. We had to trace you from your stay in the refugee camp."

Soon Hi shook her head slowly. "This letter is disturbing. I'm very worried that I haven't heard from my brother since this one letter. He paints a very different picture of Korea than what we read in the local Korean paper. I'm afraid that something has happened to him. He cautions me about not trusting Communists. But most of the people I meet here seem to support Kim, and I'd be afraid to say anything against him. Who can I trust?"

"You must have faith, Miss Chung. There are many people working to free Korea from the Communist web. If you are interested, there is going to be a talk in Okubo this coming Friday evening. Maybe you'd like to attend." He wrote down an address on a piece of paper, and added, "You may make some contacts that can help you find out more about your brother."

She took the paper as the stranger got up and began walking to the door. "By the way," said Soon Hi, "You said someone in the American military headquarters recognized my name and sent the letter to you. Do you know who the American was?"

The stranger paused and thought a moment. "I believe his name was Ku-landal, or something like that," he said with a toothy smile.

"You mean Crandall?" she asked excitedly as he exited the door.

The strange little man was gone, and Soon Hi was left wondering whether it was actually Tom Crandall who had been responsible for her receiving the letter. If he was working in MacArthur's headquarters building, then she knew where to go to start looking.

. . .

The next morning Soon Hi took a train into Chiyoda and easily found the Dai Ichi Building, now better known as the Allied Powers command center. At the front door she was met by a military security guard who asked her for her identification. She showed him her alien registration card, and he shook his head.

"This isn't any good here."

"But I'm looking for a Mr. Crandall who works here. I need to see him."

The guard ogled her for a moment and said sarcastically, "Yeah, there's a lot of you girls trying to hook up with Americans. You need to take care of your business outside in the street, not here."

Soon Hi turned around and began walking away, angry and embarrassed at what she suspected the soldier was implying. She was about to give up and return home when an obvious solution came into her head. *Ellie can get me in. Her office is just down the street.* She hurried out the door and walked briskly the two blocks to the Red Cross building. When she got to the office, the secretary told her that Ellie would be out of the office until one. It was only nine thirty, but Soon Hi waited, and finally Ellie came through the door. When she saw Soon Hi she immediately went up to her. "What brings you here? Were you able to find your brother?"

"Yes, I found my younger brother and he's okay, but now I have another problem, and I need your help," she said meekly.

"Anything. What is it?"

"I need to find an American man I knew in Korea when I worked at the embassy. I think he is working at MacArthur's headquarters, but when I try to go there and find out, the guard won't let me in because I don't have American ID."

"Sure. I can help you. What's his name?"

"Tom Crandall."

"Is he military?"

"No he's civilian. He was an embassy officer. I don't know what he does now."

"Okay, we'll walk over there and see if we can find your Mr. Crandall."

When Soon Hi reentered the American headquarters this time, the guard looked at her suspiciously, but didn't say a thing as Ellie signed her in as a guest. They walked to the end of a long hall and stopped at a desk where a second security guard waited. Ellie told the guard they were looking for a Mr. Crandall and asked to see an office directory. The guard handed her a mimeographed booklet and she quickly traced her finger through the names.

"I don't see your Mr. Crandall on this list—but I do see a State Department Liaison Office headed by Minister Sebald. Maybe his office will have some information."

Ellie, using the guard's in-house telephone, called the number in the directory, and after three or four minutes of conversation and waiting, she hung up, and turned to Soon Hi. "We found Mr. Crandall. He's on his way down here now."

A moment later Tom Crandall appeared at the foot of the stairs and with a broad smile came up to Soon Hi and gave her a big hug. Suddenly realizing that Ellie was standing there, he quickly introduced himself and thanked her for helping Soon Hi. Ellie, seeing that she was no longer needed, said she had to get back to work and left.

Soon Hi, looking as if she would hyperventilate, said, "I received the letter from my brother in Korea. Was it you who helped get letter to me?"

Tom smiled. "Yes, it was me. I've been working in the State Department liaison office here in SCAP[iii] since January. Your brother's letter ended up in our office, and one of our translators brought it to my attention. I had been kind of hoping that I'd be able to find you here in Japan, but didn't know where to look. When I saw what I thought was your name on that letter, I took it as my responsibility to try to get it to you. I'm really glad our contacts were able to locate you, and now you found me."

Later, at lunch in the cafeteria, Tom explained how, after returning to the United States for just three months, he'd been selected as part of a combined military-civilian task force to work on finalizing a security agreement that could be tied to the soon to be ratified Japanese Peace Treaty. He told her, "Once the peace treaty gets signed, then we'll set up an embassy here, and I hope I can get permanently assigned to Japan."

Soon Hi recounted to Tom what she'd gone through over the past six months since leaving Korea— her time in the refugee camp, her move to Kawasaki living with her aunt and cousin, and her concern over her younger brother's pro-Communist attitude. She said, "I don't know what I can do to change him, and I'm not really comfortable living with my aunt and cousin. They treat mother and me okay, but they make it clear they don't like that I used to work for Americans. We don't talk politics, but I think they support the People's Republic."

"Why don't you move out?"

"I wish I could, but I don't have a job. We had a little money when we left Korea, but now almost gone. I've tried to find job, but because I'm not permanent resident yet, it's hard."

Tom scratched his head. "Being a non-resident is a problem. SCAP has a policy that we have to hire Japanese citizens for any of our local jobs, and I don't see a way around that."

Soon Hi's chin dropped, hating the thought that she and her mother would have to continue to depend on her aunt for help. But then Tom added, "There may be another solution. Do you know about *Mindan*?"

"Yes, they were involved in the refugee camp. And the man who delivered the letter from In Yong was also from *Mindan*."

"That's right. The American government has been working closely with them ever since the Reds pushed us off the peninsula. One of the things we've done is provide them funds for social programs to help win more support for their cause among the Koreans here. In fact, we're backing a medical clinic that's supposed to start up soon over in

Okubo. There's a Dr. Yi, who I met last week, who is going to be in charge of it."

"But I'm not a nurse. What could I do there?"

"I know," said Tom, "but he'll need administrative help, and you do know something about that. Let's go back to my office, and I'll look up his address. You need to go and talk to him."

"I'll do as you say, but I don't think he will want hire someone like me."

"Nonsense. You're exactly what he needs. I'll write you a note of introduction."

"I really do need job, and I hope you're right. These days I'm very confused. My two brothers pull me in different directions. The one tries to make me feel ashamed I worked for Americans, and wants me think about returning to Korea. The other tells me how dangerous it is in the new Choson People's Republic. Some people I talk to say forget about Korea. Now that you live in Japan, learn to be Japanese. I love my Korea, but is there any hope for a Korea that I love? Or must I resign myself to live as a Japanese?"

Tom listened to her sympathetically. "You don't need to give up hope for Korea, and you don't need to be ashamed of having worked for Americans. There are a lot of Koreans who support democracy and oppose the Communists, and America is going to continue to support them. Did you know that a group of people, former ROK government officials, have set up a government in exile on Okinawa?"

"No, I didn't know about that," she said.

"Well, it's true, and, although we haven't actually recognized the exile government yet, we're supporting them, and so are the British. There's a man by the name of Yi— Yi Pom Sok— took over as president. He used to be the prime minister under Rhee."

"But the Choson People's Republic controls Korea, and they have the support of the Soviet Union, and even China. What hope is there?"

"There is always hope. The international situation can change. But nations, just like people need to prepare for change and be able to react to it when it happens. That's why the security treaty my office is working on is such an important thing. Don't give up on Korea and don't give up on America."

Soon Hi smiled weakly and nodded.

Tom took Soon Hi back to his office and asked her to wait while he located the file on the medical clinic. He wrote out a short note in longhand, put it in an envelope and after penning the address in English and Japanese, handed it to Soon Hi.

Surprised, Soon Hi said, "You write Japanese. I didn't know."

Tom chuckled. "I didn't have any need for it in Korea, but before going to Korea I went through an intensive course in Japanese with the Foreign Service Institute. That's one reason I got assigned to this task force. Now take this letter and go see Dr. Yi."

He walked her out of the building and to a taxi stand nearby. Tom gave her money for the fare and said, "I know you don't want me to come by your aunt's apartment, but I want to know how things turn out for you. You have my office telephone number. Call me from a public phone after you see Dr. Yi and let me know how it goes."

"I will," she said as she lowered herself into the taxi. He stood and watched as the taxi drove off.

CHAPTER 13

A NEW NORMAL

February 1951

It was past five when Tom got back to his office after an all-day session with Josh Bolton and Ray Crossman, two officers from the SCAP plans section. Although they were working on the stationing plan for U.S. forces once the occupation ended, he was having a difficult time concentrating. He was thinking about Soon Hi. It had been a full week since he'd talked to her— time enough for her to have gone and talked to Dr. Yi about that job. Perhaps things didn't pan out for her. He stopped at his desk and saw a note his secretary had left. He picked it up and read it: *A Miss Chung called. She thanked you for helping her get a job, but didn't leave any phone number.*

It had been only six months since the American withdrawal from Korea, but it seemed like ages ago. After Soon Hi left Korea he figured it was the last he would ever see her. Tom had tried to convince himself it was for the best, and that their relationship never had a future. But when he returned to the states, he couldn't forget her. When he returned to Japan and the letter from her brother fell into his hands, the improbable likelihood of that happening had revived his hopes that fate was looking out for him. But did she have any real feelings for him? He still didn't know.

Tom stared at the note a moment, then went to his file drawer and pulled a folder where he remembered he had kept the papers on Korean outreach projects. He quickly found the paper with Dr. Yi's contact information, wrote down his address, and stuffed the note in his pocket. He glanced down at his watch. *Too late to go today.*

Early the next morning Tom left his apartment, grabbed a taxi, and directed the driver to the address in Okubo that he'd written down. The driver at first balked at going into the old Korea town area, but when Tom laid three thousand-yen notes in his palm, he changed his mind.

There were no numbers on the storefronts, and they all seemed to look alike, Tom told the driver to slow down as they approached the block where he thought the clinic should be. He stared out at the storefront signs with their mix of kanji and Japanese characters, looking for a hospital or clinic symbol. "Keep going," he told the driver. Finally, he spotted a sign with a red cross and the kanji characters 診療所 (*Shinryousho*) painted on it. "That's it. Stop!" Tom hollered.

He jerked forward in the seat as the driver slammed on the brakes, paid the cabbie his fare, and got out. Entering the small street-side clinic, he saw three women, one with a baby, sitting on a bench along the wall. He approached a young girl at the counter and asked in English, "Is Dr. Yi here. I'm a friend."

The girl replied, "He busy. Please sit. Wait."

Tom had met the doctor one time three months ago when he came to a meeting in the Dai Ichi building to discuss funding for a clinic to serve Korean immigrants. Yi had been a surgeon at the Taegu General Hospital before the war and came to Japan with others who were evacuated. Tom was impressed by the man and his commitment to providing medical and social services for his community. He was confident the SCAP funds were being put to good use, and when Soon Hi said she was looking for work, he knew it would be a perfect place for her.

After waiting fifteen minutes, the doctor came out of the back room, stopped at the front desk, and began talking to one of the clerks. Tom jumped up, went to the counter and said, "Excuse me, Dr. Yi. I'm Tom Crandall. Can I have a word with you?"

Turning his head toward Tom, he said, "You are American? Do I know you?"

"We met a few months ago at the Dai Ichi building. I work for SCAP and helped get you the funding for the clinic."

"Ah, Mr. Crandall, of course. Good you have come. What can I do for you?"

"Last week I referred Soon Hi Chung to you for a job interview. She sent me a note to say she was hired here, but I don't see her."

"Yes, Miss Chung works for us now. But she is next door in other building. She is working there. You can go see. Now I'm busy, but later we can talk if you have time."

Tom shook Dr. Yi's hand and thanked him before hurrying out to the adjoining structure, windowless, except for one opening covered over by opaque plastic. Entering he found himself in a dimly lit open spaced area that looked like a large storage room with boxes stacked up along the walls. Towards the rear two people seemed to be unpacking boxes.

"Hello." said Tom, attempting to draw their attention. The two looked up and walked to the front where Tom recognized Soon Hi, despite the masculine sweater she was wearing and the kerchief wrapped around her neck.

"Soon Hi! I got your note that you got the job, and I had to see you."

The other woman looked at Soon Hi as if to ask "Who is this foreigner?"

Soon Hi, surprised at first, thanked Tom for coming and introduced her companion.

"This is Myong Sin Pak. She hired me for this job. She's my new friend."

"What job is this? I thought you were going to work for the medical clinic?"

"This *is* part of medical clinic. Dr. Yi told me he wanted to start a food bank for Koreans, because many people can't afford to eat. When I told him I like to work there, he sent me to Miss Pak for interview, and she hired me."

"That's wonderful. We need to celebrate. After you finish I'll take both of you to a nice restaurant for lunch."

Soon Hi explained to Myong Sin what Tom had said about going out to a restaurant, but the other girl shook her head. "No, I need to stay here and work, but you go with your friend and have a good meal."

Reluctant to leave her friend behind, but wanting to let Tom know that she appreciated his help, she said, "Okay, I go with you to lunch after I finish unpacking those boxes over there. Myong Sin will stay here."

Thirty minutes later Soon Hi returned to the counter. "I finished. We go now."

Since Tom wasn't familiar with the area, he let Soon Hi lead him. She took him to a small Japanese noodle house, tucked away in an alley. The place was nearly full with customers, but they were able to find a table when another couple got up to leave, and Tom ordered for the two of them. After an uncomfortable few moments of silence, Tom asked "What are your plans now that you have a job? Are you going to move out from your aunt's apartment?"

"Yes, as soon as I can find apartment I can afford. Mother is anxious to move, too."

"What about your brother, the one you found working at the pachinko parlor? Will he help you?"

"No, I haven't seen him for weeks. I'm worried about him. I think he's becoming some kind of radical—maybe mixed up with Communists. He talked as if he believes Japan will become Communist just like Korea and China. I'm afraid he's going to get in bad trouble."

"He could very well find himself in real trouble if he gets involved with them. My government has been very concerned about Communist subversion here in Japan. That's why SCAP outlawed the JCP (Japanese Communist Party) last year. Even though the American occupation will probably end next year, the Japanese government is going to be just as tough on them—won't put up with a lot of anti-government shenanigans. And the Americans aren't leaving either."

"So you don't think there's danger of Communists taking over Japan?"

"I didn't say there wasn't a danger. But we're prepared for it now. We're not going to let Japan go the way of China and Korea, you can be sure of that."

The waitress brought a tray of food to the table, a dish of *yakisoba* for Tom and a steaming bowl of *udon* noodles for Soon Hi. She picked

112

up a slice of *kamaboku* with her chop sticks, popped it into her mouth, and slowly chewed, while looking off into space.

"What are you thinking about now?" asked Tom.

"I'm thinking of my older brother in Korea. Here I am safe in Japan, but In Yong is in hiding, somewhere in Korea, for fear of being arrested. There's nothing I can do for him. I feel helpless. Do you think things will change there?"

"Eventually, maybe. But your brother is in a very difficult situation. I know there are a lot of Koreans here in Japan who are not content with the way things have gone in Korea, and they hope the old republic will be reestablished just as before. Right now, it doesn't seem likely, but who knows?"

They finished their lunch and as they left the small restaurant, Tom said, "I would really like to see you again, and I meant what I said about helping you move. Give me a call at my office when you're ready."

"I will," she said as they parted in separate directions.

. . .

A week later Soon Hi called Tom and told him she had found an apartment in Okubo and would be ready to move on Saturday. Although he didn't have a car of his own, he did have a friend in the motor pool at Camp Zama. He called Sergeant Glick who he'd become friends with back in Pusan, and persuaded him to sign out a sedan to him for Saturday with the understanding that it was for "official business."

"If the MPs catch you doing personal stuff, you're on your own brother," said Glick.

"Understood," said Tom. "I'll have the vehicle back Saturday evening."

Finding her address in the maze of streets wasn't easy, but he finally located the Kurasaki drugstore that she had directed him to. Her apartment was the one above that store. He got out of the car and hurried up the steps to the apartment and knocked on the door. Soon Hi was waiting for him and pushed two suitcases outside, telling him, "Take these down. I'll be down with mother in minute."

Tom lugged the suitcases downstairs and Soon Hi and her mother soon followed, both carrying bulging bags under each arm. Tom stuffed the suitcases and bags into the trunk and then helped her mother into the back seat. He glanced up to see people looking down at them from apartments on either side of the road.

Soon Hi got into the passenger side, and he shut the door. "Please, let's go," she said. "People think it strange to see American car here. Many people don't like."

Tom didn't ask why. He started the car and drove off. He knew the way to Okubo, but Soon Hi had to direct him to her new address. Finally telling him to stop in front of a two story building housing a furniture store on the ground level, Soon Hi, pointed up to the second level. "Here. This is where my apartment is."

Tom stopped the car. "This doesn't look like any improvement over where you've been living."

"No," she said. "But it is ours."

Tom carried the suitcases to the upstairs landing while Soon Hi went to the furniture store to get the key from the owner. The apartment was small, with just three rooms, but it did have electricity and running water, including an indoor toilet. For bathing they would need to use the public bath down the street, but Soon Hi told him they were used to that.

Soon Hi looked at her mother. "What do you think? Do you like it?"

"It's not like my old home," she said. "I want to go back to Korea. I want to be able to visit your father's grave."

"I know mother. I want to return to Korea too. But we can't now — not until things change. Maybe someday."

Sensing that Soon Hi and her mother would want to be left alone, Tom excused himself and started to leave. Soon Hi followed him to the door, and as he stepped outside he turned to her. "I'd like to see you again, Soon Hi. Maybe go out to supper together?"

Up until then, Soon Hi had seen their relationship as one of pure friendship, and she very much appreciated all that Tom had been doing for her. But she wondered if he saw their relationship as something more. She wasn't sure about her own feelings, but she knew she couldn't say no.

"Yes, I will go."

· · ·

It was six the next evening when Tom arrived at Soon Hi's apartment. While she was putting on her jacket, Tom asked, "Would your mother like to come with us?"

Soon Hi translated the offer for her mother who made a slight bow towards Tom and then shook her head emphatically from side to side, pushing her daughter toward Tom and telling her to go and enjoy herself.

The area around the Okubo station was well lighted and crowded with people—many travelers coming and going, shoppers peering in windows, and couples, like them, on a date. They strolled down a low-lit side street and looked in the windows of restaurants where artful replicas of the chef's most popular dishes were on display. They stopped in front of one where they found dishes they both liked, went inside, and found a table. A young waitress came by and took their orders, Tom ordering a sukiyaki dish that he saw in the window, Soon Hi ordering a fried egg plant dish and miso soup. Even though he wanted to ask her about her brother's activities, he decided he'd better stay away from that. For a few minutes they sat silently without saying anything while trying to ignore curious eyes from other tables. Finally, Soon Hi broke the silence. "Tell me about your family and where you grew up."

"There's not too much to tell. I grew up in a small town in the state of Illinois. You know where that is?"
She shook her head no.

"How about Chicago? You know where Chicago is?"

"Oh yes," she said. "I heard Chicago. I read poem about it in English class. Very dangerous rough place."

Tom smiled, "That must have been Carl Sandburg's poem titled *Chicago*. It was written many years ago, but Chicago can still be a dangerous and rough place. I grew up in a small town about fifty miles from there—very peaceful. My father still runs a grocery store there and my mother is a school teacher. I have one younger sister who is in nursing school. As for me, I went to the University of Illinois and studied history and got a law degree. After I finished school, I was hired by the State Department. That's about it."

"Your family isn't Japanese. Why do you speak Japanese?

"Well, that's kind of a long story. When I was in college the war with Japan was going on, I got interested in learning about the country we were fighting. The college offered courses in Japanese, and I studied it for two years. After I got hired by the State Department, since I already had some knowledge of Japanese, they sent me to a full year of intensive training. After I finished that I thought, for sure, they'd send me to Japan. But I guess when the job in Korea came open, they didn't have anyone with Korean language skill to send, and since a lot of Koreans speak Japanese, I was a good second choice. At least that's how I think it happened."

He poured a half cup of sake for Soon Hi and poured a full cup for himself, took a gulp, and let the warm liquid trickle down his throat. "Now tell me how you wound up working for the Americans in Korea."

Soon Hi thought a moment on where to begin. "I was staying at home when your war with Japan ended. I never finish high school because during last year of war, they closed my school. After that war, my family heard American missionary lady opened school near our village. I want to learn more, especially English, and so my older brother took me there and enrolled me in her school. The lady's name was Miss Andrew and I think she liked me, because she spent time after school with me to practice. After one year, I left and went to a women's college in Seoul to study English and secretary skill. When I graduated, I found job with American Embassy in Seoul. Miss Andrew wrote me a letter of recommendation to help me get job. I miss her."

"What happened? Did she go back to the states when the war broke out in Korea?"

"Soon Hi's eyes clouded, "No. She stayed in Korea after Communists came down. Don't know what happened to her."

"Ahh, that's bad. I know there were a number of missionaries who stayed on thinking the Communists would leave them alone and permit them to continue to work. I don't think it's worked out that way. I'm sorry about your Miss Andrew."

Their meals came and they finished eating without saying much more. Upon leaving they asked the cashier about any movie theaters in the area and she directed them to the next street over. The first theatre they came to had a sidewalk display of samurai warriors in full battle dress. Tom looked at Soon Hi, "Here?"

Soon Hi shook her head, "No, let's see happy movie."

They walked on until they came to another theater, this one with a picture display of a family in an old jalopy bouncing down a road—a comedy.

"How about this? It's even in color."

"Yes," said Soon Hi, her face brightening, "I like. Never saw color movie. First time."

When they left the theater Tom was relieved that Soon Hi's mood had been lifted by the movie. She'd laughed a lot. When he suggested that they stop at a tea room, she agreed and they sat listening to record music for a half hour before she said she needed to go home. On the taxi ride back to her apartment, he stretched out his hand to take hers, and she didn't pull back. He held it fast until they arrived and then helped her out of the cab and walked her up the flight of stairs to her apartment. Standing there he took both her hands in his, and said, "I like you a lot Soon Hi. Maybe next weekend we can do something else together?"

Her eyes cast towards the floor, she whispered, "Yes, I like you too. Maybe I…"

He lightly raised her chin with his right hand, and with his left hand drew her near and slowly pressed his lips to hers. She didn't resist, but felt a warm comfortable sensation. She didn't know what to do with her hands. They remained frozen against her sides. It was the first time a man had kissed her and she felt a little embarrassed as he released her. Fumbling for her key, her mother suddenly opened the door and the spell was broken. She shooed her mother back inside, then hastily said good night and went inside herself, leaving him standing alone on the landing. He stood there for a full minute before bouncing down the stairs and out to the street to look for a taxi.

CHAPTER 14

A RALLY FOR THE ROK

May 1951

Soon Hi sat in the clinic reception area waiting to see Dr. Yi who was in with a patient when she noticed someone in a military type uniform walk in. Was it a Japanese uniform? What business would he have here? She picked up a newspaper and sat back down to read it when the uniformed man took an empty seat next to hers. She glanced over at him out of the corner of her eye. A broad face, heavy eyebrows, and deep set eyes, there was something familiar about him. She shifted in her seat, trying to build up the courage to say something.

"Are you here to see Dr. Yi?' she asked in Japanese.

The man turned and said in Korean, "Why are you speaking Japanese? I'm Korean like you. Can't you tell?"

Soon Hi, was taken aback, "The uniform — it's not American. I thought..."

The man laughed. "No, it's not American, and I'm not in the Japanese Army. I belong to the New Republic of Korea Army. I guess you haven't heard of us."

He put out his hand to introduce himself, "I'm Lieutenant Han — Chae Hoon Han."

Soon Hi swallowed hard. Now she remembered the face, and the name.

"Were — were you in the South Korean army in Pusan during the evacuation?"

"Yes, I was with a security detachment there. My unit was one of the last to leave the port with the Americans."

He noticed her nervousness. "What's wrong?"

"You...you rescued me from being trampled to death in the riot on the dock. Don't you remember?"

He craned his neck to look closer at her. "My god, it is you! I would never...you were all beaten up then. But I never got your name."

"My name is Soon Hi Chung, and I'm so happy to meet you again Lieutenant Han. I didn't expect... Oh, I don't know what to say. What made you come here?"

"As I said before, I'm with the New ROK Army. It's the military arm of the Korean exile government in Okinawa. You've heard of that haven't you—Yi Pom Sok is our president."

She nodded. "Yes, I've heard of it, but I didn't know they had an army?"

"Right now it's just being created. When the Communists took over our homeland, thousands of ROK soldiers like me escaped but ended up in many different places. Most of us believed, like President Rhee, if the Americans had not abandoned us, we could have turned back the Communists and defeated them then. But now we are regrouping, and soon—very soon—we plan to return. Now we are setting up a unit here in Honshu. We want to recruit *Zainichi*[iv] Koreans who love Korea and want to help restore democracy there. I came here to meet with Dr. Yi to get his help in advertising a rally that is going to be held this next Saturday in the Kankoren Theater to raise funds for our army. "

He pulled out a flyer from his briefcase and showed it to her.

FREE KOREA RALLY
ALL WHO LOVE KOREA WELCOME
MAIN SPEAKER: COL PARK CHUNG HEE
NEW REPUBLIC OF KOREA ARMY
May 21, 1951, 7 PM
Kankoren Saijijou, 5–1 Shibuya-ku, Sendagaya-machi, Tokyo

Soon Hi stared at the paper and then looked at Chae Hoon, "Who is this Colonel Park?"

"He is chief of staff to General Chong Il Kwon. Colonel Park will be talking about our plans for reestablishing a free and democratic Korea and how Koreans in Japan can help. I think you'd be interested in hearing what he has to say."

"Do you know him personally?"

"Yes. For the past three months I've been working with him as his aide."

"Oh, I see. But what makes you think Koreans in Japan will want to listen to him? From what I've seen, many of them, maybe most, favor Kim Il Sung and what he's done in Korea."

"That may be true. But it's a false image they have. We have to change that perception and convince people we have a better vision for the future of Korea—a future not of a totalitarian police state, but a true democracy. People are starting to hear a lot more about the bad things that are going on in Korea since the Communists took over. Syngman Rhee isn't the leader of the opposition any more, and I think people will be more open minded towards us."

"Perhaps you're right. I heard from my brother who is a journalist in Korea that things are very bad there. He said he had to go into hiding to keep from being arrested."

"Yes, Colonel Park is very familiar with how the Communists operate and he'll address that in his speech."

"I think I do want to hear what he has to say. I'll try to make it next week."

Just then a receptionist at the desk called out, "Mr. Han. Dr. Yi can see you now."

Chae Hoon rose and before leaving said, "Nice talking with you, Miss Chung. I'll look for you at the rally."

Soon Hi sat for a moment, her mind in a blissful daze after meeting the man who had rescued her from possibly being killed. He certainly spoke with the confidence of a man who was sure of himself and his cause. She liked that. And he was handsome, in a rough masculine sort of way, slender with an athletic build, and quite tall for a Korean—almost as tall as Tom...She sighed and then suddenly remembered, Tom had invited her out to supper that evening. She looked at the clock on the wall. Almost noon time. Her meeting with Dr. Yi could wait. She got up and returned next door to the food bank.

.   .   .

Soon Hi finished her work an hour early so she could stop by a used clothing store down the street from the clinic. It was her first real date, and she was nervous — she couldn't afford to buy new clothes, but she wanted to wear something dressier than what she had. She picked out a mid-calf length skirt and a flowered blouse with a floppy bow at the neckline. Both looked as if they'd never been worn, and the price was right. She knew she shouldn't feel ashamed of wearing used clothes. After all, a lot of people were in the same situation as she was, and she hoped Tom would understand.

When Tom arrived at her apartment to pick her up, he immediately remarked how nice she looked, and she let out a sigh of relief.

"I'd like to take you some place different than what you're used to. Would you like to go to an American restaurant?"

"Oh yes, I would like very much," she said.

"Good I made a reservation at the Army-Navy Touchdown Club. It's right in the center of the city, near the Ginza. If there's time we can walk through the shopping area. They have a movie theater too. They're playing a new film tonight. Would you like to see that? It's a musical called *An American in Paris*. Ever hear of it?"

"No, but I'm sure if it has music, I will like."

They arrived at the club and Tom escorted Soon Hi through security and signed her in as a guest. Soon Hi could see that it wasn't just a restaurant but it was like a big hotel with a game room and slot machines in a room off the main lobby — in fact it had once been a hotel, but after the war, the American Army had converted it into an R&R haven where GI's on leave could relax and enjoy themselves in a manner that, for most of them would be beyond their means if they were civilians back in the states. After taking an elevator to the sixth floor, she found herself in an elegant restaurant with white table cloths with candles bouncing reflections of light off fine glassware.

122

Tom gave his name to the host manning the reservation desk, and they were quickly guided to a table by a Japanese waiter in white shirt and bow tie.

Soon Hi felt uncomfortable as she sat down, seeing other women dressed in stylish dresses that made her look like a country girl. Some wore dresses with low-cut necklines that drew looks from some of the male diners, others with more conservative fare displayed expensive jewelry. Soon Hi touched the cotton bow at her neck.

"Something's bothering you. What is it?" asked Tom.

"I...I don't belong. Everyone is dressed so nice. I'm not..."

Tom glanced around and said, "Don't worry about anyone else. You're prettier than any of them." He pointed to the menu, "What would you'd like to eat. I'm having a steak. Why don't you try the filet mignon?"

Later, between bites of her filet, Soon Hi asked, "Did you ever hear about New Republic of Korea Army?"

Tom sat back with a puzzled look on his face and said, "Yes, but how did *you* hear about it?"

"A man came to our clinic today to talk to Dr. Yi about distributing posters for a meeting and rally to support an anti-Communist Korean government in Okinawa. I talked to the man, a Lieutenant Han. He said they were trying to recruit Koreans to join an army that they were forming, and he invited me to attend the meeting. A Colonel Park is going to speak. I'm interested to go. Do you think it safe? Do you think I should go?"

Tom knew a lot about the exiled South Korean government, as well as its efforts to maintain and grow a military capability, but he didn't want to reveal what he knew to Soon Hi. It was no secret that the U.S. government had provided a haven for thousands of Korean refugees in the Philippines and Guam and had transported the surviving South Korean government leaders, including Yi Pom Sok, to Okinawa. Although there had been no formal recognition of this government, there had been speeches in Congress in support of the exile government, and Secretary of State Acheson had openly espoused the hope that the Korean peninsula was not yet a lost cause. Less publicized, however, was the fact that the U.S. government had transported more than 30,000 ROK Army soldiers to Okinawa in the last days before the Communist takeover of Korea, and, with the tacit support of USCAR[v], the exiled South Korean government was now busily reconstituting its army.

"Yes, I think you'd be safe," said Tom. "It's a legitimate organization, and I'd be interested in hearing what you find out if you decide to go."

"Okay, I'll go. I'm not exactly sure why. I don't want to see war return to my home, but after reading that letter from my brother in Korea, I'm sure that communism will be bad for Korean people. I need to know more about what's going on there, and then maybe I can convince my younger brother."

"I hope you can. The Japanese government is not going to take lightly these Communist demonstrations."

"But it's the Americans who control things. Why do you say Japanese?"

"The American occupation isn't going to be lasting much longer," he said. "The peace treaty with Japan is probably going to be completed before the end of this year. When that's done, my job on this task force is finished. Not sure what will happen after that."

"You'll be leaving Japan then?"

"Yes, I'll be leaving, but..." He struggled to come up with words to express his feelings, and said, "I really care about you Soon Hi, and I want to keep seeing you as long as I'm here."

Soon Hi blushed, and lowered her head. "Yes, I like you too. I'm sad you'll be leaving."

She did like Tom, felt at ease with him, but she didn't want to lead him on to think of her as more than a good friend—especially since he would be leaving soon and they would probably never see one another again. For now she just wanted to enjoy the friendship they had, and by the time the night ended, she felt happier than she had since coming to Japan. On the ride back to her apartment, she let him put his arm around her, and as they got to her apartment door she wasn't surprised at all when he leaned down, took her face in his hands, and pressed his lips to hers. She responded this time by wrapping her arms around his waist and holding him tight. Finally, fearing her mother would come to the door, she released him and stepped back.

"I'll stop by your work next week and see you," said Tom, as she stood and watched him go down the stairs, unsure where her feelings were leading her.

. . .

Soon Hi arrived at the theater just as the doors were opening. There was a long line of people waiting to get in, which surprised her — mostly young men, but also a number of older men, and even a few women her own age. The area in front of the theater was festooned with balloons and large posters advertising the evening's event and a barker screamed unintelligible words from a megaphone. When she got inside she found herself jostled by the compacted bodies of people, all trying to make their way to the seating area. It was a large open auditorium with rows of folding chairs set up in front of a stage at the far end of the room. She heard her name called and turned to see Chae Hoon making his way over to her.

"Glad you were able to make it," he said, pulling her away from the crowd. "Come with me. There's someone I'd like you to meet."

He took her hand and she felt her heart skip a beat at his touch. Embarrassed at her own reaction, she reflexively withdrew her hand from his as he led her toward the side of the stage where four men, all in uniform except for one, were talking.

Walking up to the group, he addressed the man in civilian clothes, "Colonel Park. I'd like to introduce my friend, Miss Chung."

The colonel, dressed in a dark blue business suit turned around, removed the lit cigarette from his lips, and nodded politely to Soon Hi.

Although the colonel was no taller than her, and a full six inches shorter than Chae Hyon, she could tell from the way the others acted around him that his short stature didn't detract from a commanding presence. His piercing brown eyes, dark complexion, prominent straight nose, and square jaw gave him the look of a bull terrier, a fighter not to be taken lightly.

"I'm very happy to meet you, Miss Chung. Lieutenant Han has told me about you, and how you almost were killed in a brawl during

125

the evacuation from Pusan. I hope you're doing well now. Did your family get away safely?"

Soon Hi let her eyes fall to the floor, "Not all. My father was killed on the way to Taegu. My older brother is still there. He is a newspaperman, and I'm worried about him."

"I'm sorry to hear about your father. We have a speaker tonight who recently escaped from a labor camp in Korea. You may be interested in what he has to say."

"Yes," said Soon Hi. "I'm very interested."

The colonel wished her well and turned back to the other men in his group to continue his conversation. Chae Hoon led her to a reserved seating area near the front. "You sit here," he said. "I have to stay with the colonel. I'll see you after the speakers finish."

Two hours later, when the speeches had ended, Soon Hi remained seated as the audience began to file out of the auditorium. After waiting ten minutes, she started to get up to leave when she saw Chae Hoon emerge from a side door, hurrying towards her.

"I thought you might have left. Sorry to keep you waiting..."

"I know you're busy. I shouldn't have stayed."

"No, I wanted to talk to you some more. I'm glad you waited." Sitting down next to her, he asked, "What did you think of the presentation?"

"Colonel Park spoke with a lot of passion about recovering a free Korea. I don't think most of the people knew what to expect when they came, but after his speech, it was clear he'd won this crowd over. As for me, I was interested in the talk by the man who escaped from Korea. What he said about what's going on in Korea confirmed what my brother wrote me. The labor camps—it makes me shudder. I wonder if my brother is in one of them. I wish I could find out what has happened to him."

"Maybe there is some way to find out about your brother," he said. "We've got a number of agents in Kyongsang-do and Cholla-do. If he was working as a journalist, there's a chance he may have had some contacts with people in our underground network. If so, someone is likely to know where he is. I'll make some inquiries and see what can be done."

"Oh, thank you lieutenant. I wish there was something I could do to help."

"There's nothing really you can do right now. But you can stop calling me lieutenant. It's okay just to call me Chae."

Soon Hi lowered her eyes with a slight smile.

Not realizing that the place had emptied out, they continued talking. She learned, to her surprise, that before the North Korean invasion, he was living in Seoul, not far from where she was staying. They reminisced about places familiar to both of them. Finally, after sitting there more than a half hour, they both heard the clatter of chairs being folded up and realized that it was time to go. Chae Hoon escorted her outside and waited with her for a taxi. Opening the taxi door for her, he leaned down and said, "I have to go to Osaka tomorrow, and then I have to go back to Okinawa, but I'll come back and see you. It may be a two or three months. Hopefully by then I'll have some information for you about your brother."

Soon Hi replied softly through the window, "Nay, nay." (Yes, yes).

Chae Hoon stepped away from the taxi, made a short bow, and watched as the vehicle sped off.

CHAPTER 15

A CALL FOR REVOLUTION

June-September 1951

In Su sat in the large auditorium spellbound as he listened to the renowned Kim Chon Hae describe the growth of the socialist movement in Asia since the end of World War II. Kim had lived in Japan for many years and had served as an officer in the JCP Central Committee before returning to Choson last year following the Communist victory. Now he had come back to Japan, an emissary sent by the "Great Leader" Kim Il Sung himself, to urge young Koreans and Japanese to be a part of the new socialist revolution that was coming to Japan.

Ever since his father had been killed, In Su had felt a rage building in him like a festering sore. After coming to Japan and joining up with *Minsen* (Korean United Democratic Front) he'd found comfort in being surrounded by people who had a similar view toward the American occupation. He'd attended meetings and paid his monthly dues to the organization, but until now he had shied away from participation in any of the violent demonstrations. But under prodding from his friend Min Yong, a second generation *Zainichi* whose father had immigrated to Japan more than twenty years before, he agreed to go hear speaker Kim. His sister's words of warning about the Communist Party propagandists stuck in his mind. He remembered what she'd told him about his older brother hiding from the Communists in Korea, fearful for his life. But the excitement of being part of this revolutionary class struggle sweeping through Asia was just too strong to resist.

128

Sitting next to his friend in the packed arena, In Su listened to Kim as he described in glowing terms the workers' paradise that was now being established in the new Choson. In Su stood with the rest of the audience to applaud when the speaker recounted Kim Il Sung's victory over the Americans. It made In Su proud, for once, of being Korean and having a Korean hero to look up to. With his arms upraised, his voice echoing off the walls, Kim declared, "Imperialism has been defeated in China; it has been defeated in Choson. Now it is Japan's turn to join in the world-wide class struggle against imperialism. The people are ready, but they need the help of activists like you to show the way for the Japanese working class to throw off their chains. Take to the streets and show them you are with them, and the people will rise up with you."

Speaker Kim left the stage, leaving rally organizers to take over. Like leaders at a pep rally, they began directing the revved up crowd, made up almost entirely of young men in their late teens and twenties, to the street outside the auditorium where they passed out banners and colorful *hajimaki* embossed with inspiriting *kanji*. In Su picked up a headband, "Victorious Rebel", and wrapped it around his forehead. Min Yong was given a banner reading, "Down with American Puppet Yoshida."

Numbering nearly a thousand, the youthful crowd filled the plaza outside the hall. At a signal from the rally leaders, with banners raised high, they began to move at an orchestrated trot down a thoroughfare lined by shops and apartments, swaying like a drunk python and chanting slogans to a rhythmic[vi] *taiko* beat. It was late afternoon, and as they entered a major intersection, traffic was stopped and people came out of shops along the street to watch. After proceeding another quarter mile they came to a technical school where the marchers stopped and called out to the students to join them. More than a hundred did. After going another mile the pulsing mass of bodies entered Shibuya, a more commercialized area that included some government offices. At the first major intersection, the marchers were met by a line of police, blocking any further advance. When the police, with protective shields in front of them, began pressing forward, some demonstrators picked up bricks and began throwing them into the police lines. The riot police responded with tear gas resulting in more brick and bottle throwing. A second line of police moved up from the rear preventing the demonstrators to flee the way they had come. Demonstrators began to panic, and began to push and shove in all directions. Some fell and then were trampled by others. The police began grabbing anyone they could lay their hands on and beat them with sticks before taking them to waiting busses to be hauled off to the district jail. In Su and Min Yong, near the center of the procession ran up an alley along with several others. A half dozen police were in hot pursuit. As they turned a corner, Min Yong spotted a fish monger's shop, its door open, and he pulled In Su inside where they hid behind a counter. The shop owner, wearing an apron with fish blood smeared on the front, looked down at them, "What are you doing here?"

Fearing they would be turned in, In Su pleaded, "We're students. Just marching peacefully, and the police are trying to arrest us. Please don't turn us over to them."

The shop owner smiled. "Don't worry. I've had run-ins with police myself. You're safe here."

Thirty minutes later, after all seemed quiet in the street outside, In Su and Min Yong left the shop, taking the back alleys on their way back to their Okubo neighborhood. Once they were out of Shibuya, Min Yong slapped In Su on the back, "That was fun, wasn't it?"

"Yes," said In Su, nodding his head in agreement. "It's exciting to be part of something so big and important. I feel like I'm making a difference in the world. I'll see you at the next *Minsen* meeting for sure." In Su was hooked, and through the summer he participated in several more demonstrations, each one exhilarating in its own right as he became adept at escaping from the police.

. . .

On September 8, 1951, the long awaited peace treaty between the United States and Japan was announced with fanfare. In Su, who had become leader of his own *Minsen* circle, had looked forward to the treaty signing since it would mean the end of the American occupation and the departure of the Americans GIs from Japan. However, he and his left wing friends were hugely disappointed when they learned that, along with the signing of the peace treaty, the United States and Japan also inked a military security agreement that bound the U.S. to defend Japan in the event of attack. Worst of all, as far as he was concerned, it provided for the indefinite continuation of U.S. military bases in Japan. The Japanese Communist Party issued a call to arms aimed at all left wing organizations to take action to oppose this embarrassing treaty that left Japan as a vassal of America. *Minsen* leaders in Okubo passed the word down to their members.

Five days after the signing of the peace treaty, Sanjiro Mori, a conservative member of the National Diet, was giving a fiery anti-Communist speech in Tokyo's Uenu Park, calling for an amendment to the constitution to allow for the re-creation of the Japanese army, when shots rang out. Mori, hit by multiple shots to his head and chest, died on the podium. The shooter, a Korean, was quickly apprehended. Right wing politicians screamed for revenge against the Korean menace in their midst, and a Tokyo police dragnet sought out others involved in what they labeled as the foreign menace, focusing on the Korean community of Okubo.

Talk of the police crackdown on Koreans suspected of being involved in anti-government demonstrations worried Soon Hi. In Su normally stopped by the apartment at least once a week to get a home cooked meal, but he hadn't come by this week. She wondered if he'd been involved in some of those demonstrations and got picked up by the police. She decided to go to the pachinko parlor where he worked. When she got there, she asked a young boy working the game room if he knew anything about In Su. He said that he'd just started working and didn't know anything about him. She went to the rear and knocked on the manager's door.

"What ya want?" a voice came from inside.

"I'm Dong Son Chung's sister," she shouted, using his alias. "Have you seen him?"

The door opened, and an old man, unshaven, wearing a dirty sleeveless t-shirt poked his head out the doorway. "After the shooting last week, police were all over this area looking for people they could blame. Came in here and took him away."

As she approached the open door, she nearly gagged as she caught a whiff of his liquor laced breath. "Do you know where they took him?"

"Don't know. Don't care. I got a place to run."

Soon Hi had what information she needed, and thanked him for his time and left. Grabbing a taxi she told the driver, "Take me to the Shinjuku police station."

Arriving at the station, she walked hesitantly inside and went to the counter where a tough looking officer stood. "I'm trying to find my brother. I was told he was arrested in Okubo a few days ago after the big demonstrations, but I haven't heard anything from him."

"We don't keep any of them here," he said. "Most of those picked up from the riots were taken over to the Katsushika Detention Center. You need to go over there and check with them."

She turned away and returned quickly to the street. It was nearly noon and she stopped for a quick lunch from a sidewalk vendor before catching a bus. Katshushika was on the city's outskirts, too far to pay for a taxi.

An hour and a half and two transfers later, she got off the bus at the detention center stop. An imposing walled in facility, it stretched as far as she could see. Passing through the main gate, the guard directed her to the administration building. Once inside she found herself in a line waiting to see a clerk. Finally after a thirty minute wait she got to the counter and told the clerk she was trying to find her brother. He gave her a form and told her to fill it out. Completing the form and handing it back, she waited for her name to be called. Finally, after more than an hour, she heard her name.

She hurried back to the counter. "My name is Soon Hi Chung. Can I see my brother now?"

Looking up from the paper in front of him, the clerk said indifferently, "Visitation time is past. You can come back tomorrow at ten."

Exhausted, she wanted to yell at the clerk, but she held her tongue. She walked out, her head hanging down, angry at the bureaucracy, but glad, at least, she knew where In Su was. When she got home well after dark, she found her mother distraught, worrying over what had happened to her son. The next morning, the two of them set out for the detention facility. This time, after signing in at the reception desk, they were given a number and instructed to go to another room where In Su would be brought to them. Separated by a glass partition, In Su, his head shaved clean and wearing washed out blue pajamas, was brought into the reception area and set down in front of them.

Soon Hi's mother put her hand on the glass and began to cry. Soon Hi, retaining her composure, asked her brother, "What happened? Were you involved in those demonstrations?"

In Su leaned forward with a slight smirk on his face. "Yeah, I was demonstrating, along with a lot of other people, and proud of it. The police picked me up two days ago. Accused me and others of destroying public property and attacking police."

"Did you? Did you attack the police?"

"I'd say the police attacked us. But it doesn't matter. I'm stuck here until they decide to let me go. Supposed to see a judge in a couple days. This fascist government's afraid of us. They signed some agreement with big bad America to defend them. America may be materially wealthy, and that may attract greedy Japanese fat cats by promising to make them richer, but they are not interested in helping the Japanese common man. The Communist Party is educating the Japanese people about these truths, and eventually a majority of Japanese will realize they are being used by the westerners and the people will overthrow Yoshida and his government. Once that happens, then international socialism will become victorious in Japan— just like Choson. I'm not afraid to stay in here for months, even a year. I'll be with friends, and when we get out, we'll be even stronger."

"You've been brainwashed brother. America is not weak, and neither is Japan. You need to get away from those people who've been filling your head with such one sided ideas. You're not thinking straight, and I'm not going to let you stay here. I'll find a lawyer."

In Su shrugged. "You can try. But it won't matter. I know what I know."

Perturbed by his attitude, Soon Hi shook her head and slid her chair back and let her mother talk to In Su. After a few minutes a guard came up behind In Su and told him his time was up and led him out of the interview room. Soon Hi left with her mother, unsure of where to find legal help.

On the bus ride home, Soon Hi's mother said, "Why don't you ask your cousin Yong Ja. She must know people who can help."

Of course, thought Soon Hi, I'll go see *Yong Ja. She knows people in Minsen. They would have lawyers. I don't like relying on them, but it may be necessary.*

After dropping her mother off at her apartment, Soon Hi took a bus to Kawasaki. Yong Ja didn't get home until nearly dark, but after she arrived they talked, and Yong Ja suggested that they go see her former teacher, Mr. Yon. Soon Hi had met him before when she was trying to find In Su. Surely he would be willing to help her now.

•   •   •

After knocking several times, Mr. Yon came to the door, greeted them warmly, and invited them in. But when Soon Hi asked him if he could help her get a lawyer for her brother, he hesitated and then shook his head slowly side to side. "There are no lawyers available. Too much is going on. Besides you don't belong to *Minsen* and..." Then rubbing his whiskery chin, he said, "As I recall you used to work for Americans. You know them. Now if you would be willing to help us in some way, then I might be able to introduce you to..."

Soon Hi looked at her cousin to gauge her reaction. Yong Ja gave an encouraging nod. Soon Hi rose abruptly from her chair, her eyes narrowed. "No. I'm not getting involved with that kind of thing. Let's go."

As she headed for the door, Yong Ja made a quick bow, apologizing for her cousin's rudeness, and quickly followed Soon Hi into the street.

Walking toward the bus station, Soon Hi could see that Yong Ja was clearly upset with her, but she refused to express any regret for her behavior. She told Yong Ja she wasn't going to be trapped into becoming a spy of *Minsen*. Yong Ja angrily accused her of forgetting she was Korean. They parted at the bus stop without further words.

Later that night, lying on her mattress, Soon Hi tried to think what she would do the next day. She couldn't leave her brother. If he didn't have a lawyer, he'd get some kind of jail sentence. Where could she turn? She didn't want to get Dr. Yi involved. *Tom — Tom would know what to do. I'll call him tomorrow morning.*

The next morning, after arriving at work, Soon Hi called Tom at his office.

"Crandall speaking."

"Tom, it's me, Soon Hi."

"It's pretty early to be calling, what's the matter?"

"I need help. My brother In Su is in jail. He was arrested after riots. I'm afraid for him. I…"

"Hold on. Tell me where he is and exactly what he's accused of."

After she detailed his situation and gave him his prisoner identification, he told her he would talk with his friend in the SCAP legal office and would get back to her by the next day. The following afternoon he called her back at work.

"I talked to Fred Kirchoff in legal about your brother. Normally, there wouldn't be much we could do, but in this case, since he walked away from our custody when he was in the hospital last year, he's actually still our responsibility. Your brother has a hearing day after tomorrow, and Fred thinks he can get him released to our custody. We'll have to turn him over to the American MP's, but it should only be a matter of completing some paper work to set him free."

"Oh Tom. If you can free him…I don't know how to thank you."

• • •

A week later Tom stood with Soon Hi in the waiting room of the MP station at Camp Zama. In Su emerged from a door at the rear with a smile on his face. Soon Hi ran up to him and put her arms around him. Then she guided him over to where Tom was standing.

In Su knew only a smattering of English and Soon Hi spoke in Korean. "This is my friend Mr. Crandall. He works at the American Embassy and he is the one who helped get you released from the Japanese jail. You should be very appreciative."

In Su looked first to the side and then at Tom before making a half bow and saying, "*Komapsumnida* Mistuh Kandoll."

Tom offered his hand and In Su shook it without any noticeable facial expression. Tom said to Soon Hi, "Tell him that I was glad that I could help him, but now he has to stay out of trouble. If he gets arrested again I may not be able to help. If he will let me, I'll try to find him another job so he can start over."

Soon Hi translated. In Su nodded in apparent understanding and told his sister he did appreciate Tom's help and he would think about getting another job. The three of them went together back to Soon Hi's apartment where Soon Hi's mother had a meal prepared for her returned son. When Tom left later that evening, he felt confident he'd made a good impression on In Su.

CHAPTER 16

JUST BETWEEN FRIENDS

December 1951

Snowflakes were starting to fall when Tom knocked at the door of Soon Hi's apartment. Tom had just gotten word he was being reassigned back to Washington. Since his work with the Japanese security agreement was finished, he knew it was just a matter of time before they moved him somewhere. But he was reluctant to leave Japan—especially what with his budding relationship with Soon Hi. How would she react? He was falling in love with her. Did she feel the same?

As they left the house together, snow was starting to come down heavier, the sidewalk becoming slippery. Tom took Soon Hi's arm as they made their way carefully to the main street where they could catch a taxi.

"Where we go tonight, Tom?" she asked as they waited in the taxi line.

"I want to take you to a nice sushi house that I've been to a few times. It's not too far from my apartment in Shinjuku. Afterwards I thought maybe we could go there and listen to some music. I have a record collection I know you'll like."

"Oh…okay," she said. He hadn't asked her to his apartment before, and at first, she hesitated. She wondered if her mother would frown at her going to his apartment, but then pushed that thought aside. *We've been dating for several weeks now, and I am twenty three. There's no reason we shouldn't be alone.*

The place was small and it looked like they may have to wait for a table. Even the seats at the sushi bar were filled. Then Tom spotted an empty table in the rear, took Soon Hi's hand, and hurried to take it. Candles flickered on the tables, adding a touch of romance. A waiter came by and left a menu with glasses of water. Soon Hi opened her menu, and Tom noticed her unconsciously lick her lips. It had been nearly a year since she tasted fresh sushi, and her eyes feasted over the pictures of the varied creations. When the waiter returned Tom ordered a bottle of warm sake to go along with a combination dish of sushi and sashimi that they could share. As they waited for their meal, they talked about In Su.

"I want him to get a different job," said Soon Hi. "He needs to be away from those *Minsen* people. They'll get him into trouble again."

"I agree. He really needs to stay out of trouble," said Tom. "I was able to help him this time because the U.S. still has influence over the Japanese. But when the occupation finally ends—probably in the spring—things will be different. I'll try to find some places where they might hire him, and you can try to get him to go."

Once the meal arrived, they forgot about talking and simply savored the epicurean delight the waiter set before them. Soon Hi felt almost guilty as she popped the last morsel of eel into her mouth and took a final sip of the sake that Tom had poured for her.

When they left the restaurant the snow had stopped, but the temperature had fallen, and the wind had picked up. Even though they both wore winter overcoats, it was shivering cold and Tom put his arm around Soon Hi as they stepped outside.

"The apartment is only about two blocks from here. Do you mind walking?"

"It's Okay," she said as she drew closer to him.

Arriving at the apartment, they stamped the snow off their shoes at the entry and Tom helped Soon Hi off with her coat.

"How about some coffee? I can heat some up in a jiff, said Tom."

"It's good. I like coffee," said Soon Hi, rubbing her arms as if still feeling the outdoor chill.

While Tom busied himself in the kitchen, Soon Hi noticed a copy of the English language *Japan Times* on the coffee table, sat down, and began scanning the front page.

Tom came out a few moments later carrying a tray with two steaming cups of coffee and a plate of cookies. He set it down, went over to a rack of records, flipped through disc covers, and picked up two albums. Holding them up for her to see he asked, "Which one would you like?"

"I don't know. You choose," she said.

"I think you'll like Artie Shaw," he said as he put the record on the turntable and switched on the player.

Tom sat down on the sofa, close so their shoulders touched. Soon Hi pointed to the headline in the paper. "Do you know about this? You think it's good idea?"

Japan's Diet Considers Constitutional Amendment
Rearmament Proposed in face of Korean Threats

"Ah, that. Yes, I know about it—and, if it passes, I think it will be good for both Japan and the U.S."

Soon Hi cocked her head to one side and said, "Why? I thought Americans wanted to punish Japan."

"Well, we did. When the Second World War ended we were concerned about making sure Japan never was a threat to us or any other countries again, and we made sure that their new constitution banned the creation of an army or any kind of offensive military capability. But since then, we've come to realize that the real threat to U.S. security is not a resurgence of the Japanese military, but the threat from the Communists taking over. The American government has made an about face in its approach to remilitarization, not just in Japan, but also in Europe, where the threat is just as great. When the Communists took over the Chinese mainland in 1949, we saw then that we needed a Japan that was strong militarily once again. If there's going to be a fight with the Communists in Asia, we don't want it to be just Americans and other westerners."

"But I think Japanese people don't like war any more, and they won't support having new army."

"That's been true until recently. But the sinking of a Japanese coast guard boat a couple months ago by Choson gunboats raised a red flag for a lot of Japanese."

"Oh yes," said Soon Hi, "I read about that. They were fighting over who owns those little islands in the East Sea. They should be able to find peaceful way to decide."

"That's just it. The Communists don't want peace. Just look at the reaction to the assassination of that Japanese Diet member last month. The public mood's changed. People are scared. The new law may not pass this time around. But it shows that there's support for rearming. In any case I think the Japanese government is going to reevaluate its options. The American government is putting a lot of pressure on Yoshida."

Soon Hi leaned back and sighed. "I hate war, but I think I understand what you say. But Kim Il Sung has all Korea now. Why isn't that enough for him?"

After the last Artie Shaw tune played, Tom got up to put on another record—this time a Woody Herman album. He stood with his arms outstretched and said, "May I have a dance, madam?"

Soon Hi rose with an amused smile and let him wrap his arms around her waist as the soft lilting melody of *Sentimental Journey* began to fill the air around her. She leaned her head on Tom's shoulder swaying gently back and forth with the music. At the song's end they returned to the sofa, and holding her hand, he said, "There's something I have to tell you, and maybe it won't matter to you, but it matters to me."

"What's that?" she said puzzled.

"I'm getting reassigned back to the states. I'll be leaving next month."

"Oh Tom. I'm sorry. I don't want you to go now."

"I'm sorry too. Sorry, because…because I don't want to leave you. I think I've fallen in love with you."

Startled at the hearing the word love, she leaned back against the sofa, speechless. She wasn't' sure how to react. She liked Tom a lot. But she couldn't say she loved him— not like *he* meant it. After a moment she bent forward, put her arms around his neck, and hugged him tightly."

As she began to draw back, he pulled her towards him, pressing his lips hard against hers. With his chest against hers she laid back on the sofa. She felt his hand on her breast and then his fingers fumbling at the buttons of her blouse as their lips remained locked together. She began breathing heavily and felt a strange wave of excitement enveloping her as he opened her blouse and began kissing her breast. She felt his hand on her back, working to unhook her bra.

One part of her brain urged her to let him continue. Another part said no—not until you're truly in love. As the bra hook popped open she suddenly sat up straight, holding the loose bra by one hand and pushing Tom back with the other. "I'm sorry, Tom. I'm Sorry. I can't do this. It's not right. Please understand."

Standing up with a pained expression on his face, Tom said, "Don't be sorry, Soon Hi. I should apologize. I do understand. I wouldn't do anything to hurt you."

Soon Hi looked up at him while refastening her bra. "It's okay, Tom. But maybe you take me home now."

When they arrived at the apartment, Tom helped her out of the taxi. "I don't want this to be the last we see of each other. Even though I'll be leaving soon, I want to keep in touch with you. I intend to come back to Japan sometime in the future. Will you write to me?"

She looked up at him with an expression he couldn't quite decipher. "Yes, Tom, I know you care much for me. I will write."

Relieved at her response, Tom said, "I'll stop by your work before I leave and give you my new address."

She hoped her mother would still be asleep, but when she opened the door to the apartment, she saw her mother's face peering from her bedroom. "I couldn't sleep. Where were you?"

"I was with Tom Crandall, the American.

"Why are you so late?"

"After supper we went to his apartment and got to talking. Lost track of time. Nothing else happened, mother."

"Good!" Her mother turned, went back into her bedroom, and closed the sliding door.

CHAPTER 17

THE SECURITY AGREEMENT

March 1952

Two months had passed since Tom left Japan. He had been writing weekly to Soon Hi, and last month he put down in writing what he'd been feeling for a long time—he asked her to marry. When he received her reply, it hurt—really hurt. He read and reread the last paragraph of her short letter. "...*You have been very good to me and my family and I care for you a lot, but I think that's not enough. Anyway, I cannot consider thinking about marriage now. Too much is unsettled with my brothers, and I cannot leave my family. I don't want to make you feel bad, but it is for the best if you go on with your life and don't think about me. Soon Hi.*"

Putting the letter back in its envelope one last time, he tried to convince himself that she was leaving the door open. *She's not in love with me. Maybe she'll change her mind. Should I write again? Should I just try to forget her? I'll talk to Phil. See what he thinks.*

Assigned as a country analyst in the Northeast Asia Bureau, Tom was glad when he learned that he'd be working with Phil Crosswaite, who he already knew from Korea. Since his return to Washington, the two of them had been meeting for lunch once or twice a week, and Tom looked to the senior analyst as a sort of mentor. The next morning, after collecting his regular cup of coffee with one sugar, he sat down at his desk to a stack of Tokyo newspapers. One of his primary tasks was to review the Japanese papers and prepare daily summaries of important articles for Mr. Allison, the bureau chief. John Allison had just been assigned to his job last month, but he was

142

no novice on Asian affairs, and Tom felt lucky to be able to work under him. Before coming to State he had served as deputy to John Foster Dulles and was a regular participant in the Japan Peace Treaty negotiations. Now that the peace treaty had been signed, it was a hot topic in the papers and Tom was having to prepare position papers on that subject almost daily. Today he wanted to find something different to write about.

Tom began paging through the *Mainichi Shimbun* to see what stories might be of interest. Disputes between Choson and Japan over fishing rights in the Sea of Japan continued to be regular issues. On the inside second page he noticed an article in which Choson was claiming ownership over Tsushima Island. That large island, halfway between the southern tip of Korea and the island of Kyushu, had been part of Japan for centuries. *What are those Koreans thinking? Nobody's going to recognize their claim now. That's already been decided.* He pulled out a scissors and cut out the article to show to Phil. *They're probably just blowing hot air, but Phil should see this.*

After writing out translations in longhand on two articles, one on the Tsushima Island matter, and a second on the upcoming elections for the National Diet, he looked up at the wall clock. It was almost noon. Glancing over at the elevator he saw that Phil was already heading downstairs to the cafeteria. Handing his notes to Miss Morikami, the office secretary, he said, "I'm off to lunch. I'd like to get these into Mr. Allison this afternoon."

At lunch Tom was unusually taciturn, trying to decide how he could bring up the subject of his Dear John letter without looking like a schmuck. Between bites of his tuna sandwich, Phil asked him, "Why the long face? You look like a puppy who's just had his rump rapped for piddling on the floor."

Tom gave a wan smile and asked, "Do you remember the clerk in our office in Korea, Soon Hi Chung?"

Phil thought a moment and said, "Yeah, I think I do. Really cute girl."

"Well...before leaving Korea we were dating, pretty seriously—at least I thought it was serious even though we never actually talked about marriage—just that we'd write. After coming here I realized I really was in love with her and I wrote her and told her I wanted to marry her..."

"And..."

"And yesterday I got a letter from her. She said she wasn't ready for marriage. She didn't say absolutely no, but she didn't say yes either. She said she didn't want to leave her family back there. I'd like to keep writing to her. Maybe she'll change her mind. What do you think?"

Phil, four or five years older and married with two kids at home, said, "I think she was trying to let you down gently. I wouldn't count on her changing her mind. I know you want to think there's a chance, but you need to give up the thought of marrying her. She's on the other side of the world now, and you're here. You're only making yourself miserable. You need to chock this one up as an experience and start looking elsewhere for your feminine company. There's plenty of fish on this side of the pond you know. In our own department, I'll bet there are four or five single girls who'd jump at the chance to go out with you."

Tom bit his lower lip in resignation. "Yeah, you're probably right. She told me no, and I need to face up to it. The last thing I want to do is make her feel bad by pressing her too hard. She may already have someone else she's in love with. Maybe if I do start dating it'll help me get over her."

"That's the spirit," said Phil as he drained his coffee.

That evening, back in his apartment, Tom considered what Phil had told him. He sat down and began writing.

Dearest Soon Hi,

I'm writing to you to let you know I received your letter in which you said you could not marry me. After first reading your letter, I was despondent over the thought that you did not love me as I have come to love you. After giving it some time to sink in, however, I know I have to respect your feelings. Love isn't something that can be manufactured out of thin air — it's something that is in the heart. I wish only the best for you and won't push you on the subject of marriage any more. I hope you find the one you are truly looking for to make your life complete.

Although I'm sad tonight, it won't last. Tomorrow I'll be fine. I'm ready to move on. But I won't forget you. Too much has gone on between us. In the past you came to me for help, and I was happy to do what I could. Although now I'm in the states, I expect to return to Japan within a couple years, and if an occasion comes where you again need American help, I want you to know that you can call on me anytime. I hope you will write to me once in a while to let me know how you are doing and will not throw away our friendship.

I remain yours, Tom

It was a dreary drizzly morning as Tom left his apartment for work, a typical April day in the district. He hardly noticed the weather. He felt a weight had been lifted from his shoulders as he dropped his letter to Soon Hi in the mailbox. Having put the thought of marriage aside, now he felt he could concentrate on work. He might even look for a date for this weekend. When he got to Foggy Bottom he went straight to the cafeteria for some breakfast. He saw Herb Chao from the China desk sitting alone reading a paper, and after going through the cafeteria line, went over and sat down opposite him.

"What's new?" said Tom.

Looking up from the paper, Herb said, "You haven't heard? Truman announced last night he's not running for another term in office. There's a front page article right here."

"Hot damn! I thought for sure he'd run. Maybe he'd lose anyway, but now the Republicans are going to run away with it. If Taft gets in, it's going to throw our whole foreign policy upside down."

. . .

The day after Truman's decision was announced, Tom sat down to lunch with Phil, and their conversation quickly turned to the hot topic of presidential politics.

"Now that Truman has said he won't run," said Tom, "who do you think the Dems will try to run in November?"

"It's hard to say. Right now it kind of looks like Stevenson has the inside track. Rumor has it that Truman asked Ike to run as a Democrat and he turned him down."

"I worry about who the Republicans are going to nominate. If it's Taft, it'll really shake up the State Department. You think there's anyone else?"

"I've heard that MacArthur's considering putting his hat in the ring now that he's retired. He came out looking pretty good after the Korean debacle, and got most of the credit for the way things in Japan have turned out. He certainly has name recognition. He's a possibility."

"I'm not sure we'd be any better off with him than Taft. He'd probably have us at war with somebody a month after he took office. What about Eisenhower. Think there's any chance?"

"I don't know," said Phil. He's over in Europe setting up that new NATO command now. He'd have to resign his commission. I think he could win no matter which party he belonged to, but I doubt he'll do it."

. . .

The signing of the peace treaty paved the way for the reestablishment of the American Embassy in Japan and also signaled the formal ending of the American military occupation of Japan. On April 16 the president announced the nomination of Robert Murphy as his choice as the new ambassador. Two days later he came to the State Department for a briefing to prepare him for his Senate confirmation hearing. Although Tom didn't have to present anything, since he had prepared two position papers for the meeting, Phil asked him to attend as a subject matter expert in case questions came up.

The briefing room, one of the larger conference rooms on the third floor, was nearly full when Tom arrived and took a seat along the wall in the rear. John Allison stood at the far end of the table and began his introduction. The tall graying ambassador-designate sitting in the first chair on the left side of the long conference table, was a popular choice among the staff. Even though most of his experience had been with Europe — he was leaving a position as ambassador to

Belgium—Robert Murphy's name was legend within the diplomatic corps as a man well versed in international gamesmanship. Tom had read over his bio and was in awe of his accomplishments. As President Roosevelt's personal representative, he'd played a key role in gaining French cooperation for the allied invasion of North Africa in 1942 and was a man who General Eisenhower had relied on heavily in his North African campaign. In Europe he had played a role in bringing former enemy West Germany into NATO and strengthening security in that region. Now, Tom thought, his diplomatic skills were going to be needed for the U.S. to help transition Japan from a once discredited adversary to a reliant partner with the U.S. in pursuit of its foreign policy aims in Asia.

After several briefers spoke, Phil Crosswaite rose to present information on the current political situation with respect to relations between Japan and Choson, the new official name for Korea, and Murphy raised a question about the status of Korean exiles in Japan.

Phil said, "We still have a relatively small number of refugees in Kyushu that have not yet been placed—about 5,000. Our biggest concentration of Korean exiles is on Okinawa where we have about 40,000, mostly ex-soldiers, living in large camps separated from the local population. The Koreans have established a government in exile there with an office in Naha. It's headed by Yi Pom Sok, who was Rhee's prime minister, but we have yet to formally recognize them."

Murphy looked concerned. "What do the Okinawans say about that? I imagine they're not very happy about having so many Koreans in their midst."

"No, they're not happy about it, but under the Mutual Security Agreement that we just signed with Japan, Okinawa will remain under a U.S. trusteeship arrangement indefinitely."

"It's been more than a year since we evacuated Korea. Shouldn't we be whittling that number down? I want to know what's going on. Who's paying the bill?" Murphy asked testily.

A bearded man in a tweed coat sitting near the rear of the table raised his hand. Murphy squinted his eyes and after a moment said, "Don't I know you? Where have we met?"

"Ted Graziola, CIA. Formerly OSS—French Morocco 1942."

"Ah, of course, Ted. I hardly recognized you. Ten years makes a difference," he said leaning back in his chair. "Do tell me how this little program is being financed."

Sitting up straighter in his chair and clearing his throat Graziola replied, "The great majority of the Koreans on Okinawa are former ROK soldiers, including a lot of their family members, taken there as part of the evacuation. General Chong Il Kwon, the former ROK Army chief of staff, has attempted to maintain them as cohesive units with an objective of returning to Korea eventually. We've provided them with land and housing, but right now they're relying on funds their leaders squirreled away in foreign banks and some donations from Korean ex-patriot groups for their operating expenses."

"What's the CIA's involvement?"

"We have a number of advisers working with them. We've infiltrated a number of teams into the Korean peninsula to set up underground cells in the event their needed in the future."

"It doesn't seem that justifies keeping such a large force intact. I can see why the Koreans don't want to give up, but I'm not so sure it's in our best interest to allow them to remain. Shouldn't we be relocating these people?"

"We think the political situation is still fluid as to what might happen with regard to Korea. We believe we need to continue to back them because they provide a contingency force in the event a new war breaks out."

"And are we expecting a new war to break out soon?"

"The way Mao is pushing revolution and the way Kim Il Sung is behaving toward Japan, it's a real possibility, and I think we need to be prepared."

Murphy tapped his pencil on the table looking somber, "If war doesn't break out—which I hope it doesn't—having such a large concentration of Korean soldiers in Okinawa is going to create a political tinderbox. Even though we may have authority over that group of islands now, the Okinawan natives aren't going to be happy, and it's going to be fodder for the Japanese opposition parties to cause trouble."

"True. I guess that's something that you'll have to deal with as ambassador."

"I guess I will," said Murphy as he turned toward Phil at the opposite end of the table. "Continue with your briefing."

After Phil finished speaking, Murphy asked a final question. "What do you see as my most important task when I take over as ambassador?"

Phil responded, "Sir, I think the most important thing for you to do, and probably the biggest challenge, will be to convince the Japanese government, and the people, that they must build up their national defenses — to be able to defend themselves. At the same time, we'll need your help to convince Congress to provide funds for military aid that they will absolutely need."

Murphy nodded his head. "I have no more questions. Thank you." After a short summation by Allison the briefing was over.

. . .

Later that morning, just as Tom was getting up from his desk, the phone rang. It was Phil. He wanted to see him right way. Gulping down a mouthful of coffee that he didn't want to waste, he hurried over to his office. The office door was open, and Phil was sitting at his desk with his back to the door, looking intently at a wall map of East Asia. Tom knocked on the doorpost. Phil swiveled around in his chair and invited him to take a seat. His mind still on another track, Phil picked up a pipe from his desk, lit it, and took two or three puffs before asking, "How do you think the briefing went this morning?"

"I think it went fine," said Tom. I was struck by how concerned ambassador Murphy seemed to be over the Korean fighters in Okinawa."

"Good observation. He did make quite a point of that. And I think he's right in being concerned. If that Korean army stays there too long, the shits going to hit the fan."

"What did you think of what the CIA guy said about the likelihood of a new war?"

"I can't argue with his thinking," said Phil. "I really believe something's going to break within the next year or so. The Reds aren't stopping with winning Korea. Look at the map behind me,"

Phil drew on his pipe and exhaled a smoky halo before continuing. "Mao is pushing every Asian button he can. Pressuring the French in Indochina, putting the squeeze on the British in Malaya. Indonesia still is a question mark; and the Philippine government is just barely holding its own against the Huks. Just by the law of averages, at least one of these countries is likely to go Communist."

"I think you're right," said Tom.

"The Japanese, up to now have seemed pretty content to let us be a shield for them," said Phil, "but the pressure's mounting there too, and they're going to have to take more responsibility for their defense. They seem to be at least moving in that direction now to expand their police reserve and coastal navy. Now we've got to get Congress to make sure we give them the tools to build up those defenses. The secretary is scheduled to go up on the hill next week. I want you to prepare a position paper for him on foreign aid—we need to furnish him with some specifics on what's required along with ball park dollar figures."

"Isn't it too late for this session?"

"I'm sure it is. But the president can still request a supplemental appropriation bill. Get with your contacts over at the Pentagon and come up with something quick."

"I'll get with Frank Gibson over at Plans and Ops today and have something on your desk by Friday."

CHAPTER 18

THE LIEUTENANT RETURNS

March-April 1952

It was nearly closing time. Soon Hi, standing on a small ladder, was stocking shelves in the back storeroom of the food bank when she heard someone come into the room. Assuming it was the young girl who was working the counter, she said without looking, "Would you hand me that carton of dried milk Kun Ja?"

Turning around to take the box, she was startled to see, not Kun Ja, but Chae Hoon. Her balance shifted and the ladder began to tip."

"Look out!" he yelled, holding out his arms.

She fell unto him like a crippled bird with its wings flailing, nearly knocking him over, but he steadied himself and eased her to the floor. With his arms around her waist, her eyes locked on his, they remained motionless, seemingly mesmerized for several seconds before she managed to squeak, "I...I wasn't expecting to see you."

"I'm sorry if I scared you. I should've called out to you when I came in the door."

Pulling away from him she said in a somewhat scolding tone, "I thought you'd forgotten about me. It's been what—nearly a year since the time I attended that meeting to hear your friend the army officer—I forget his name—give a speech."

"Yes. Colonel Park is his name. I still work for him. I've been tied down in Okinawa all this time and couldn't get back here until now. I didn't forget you, Soon Hi. I didn't have your address to write...but I did find some information about your brother in Korea."

Her face brightened. "Really? Tell me."

"We know that he's alive. But he's in a labor camp.

"What? How do you know that?"

"We have agents in Korea. There are still many people who are struggling to fight against the Communist's control. They can no longer be open, but there are groups that are active and our exile government is in contact with them."

"What do you know about In Yong? Do they know where he is exactly?"

"He's being held in what they call a "reeducation" camp outside Chonju. According to the information we received he was arrested about three months ago. For a short time after the North Korean army took over the country, they allowed newspapers, like the one your brother worked for, to continue publishing. But then they cracked down on them and forced them to close. The *Nodong Sinmun* became the only public voice permitted. Some journalists, like your brother, went underground and continued to try to publish a paper that could tell the truth. Naturally, they had to be careful because they knew they would be arrested if the police could find them. Your brother, along with several others, were discovered hiding out in the mountains, not too far from Taegu. They were arrested, put on trial, and convicted. Your brother was sentenced to ten years."

Soon Hi stared blankly, remaining silent for several seconds before asking, "Is there anything we can do to get them to release him? What am I to tell mother?"

"Nothing can be done right now. If he's as smart as I think he is, he'll be able to survive. Maybe the regime will at some point reduce the sentence, but I don't see any way for him to escape."

Soon Hi covered her eyes with her hands. "I feel so alone," she sobbed. "My father's dead. My brother In Yong is lost to me. My younger brother, I can't talk to, and he'll probably end up in jail, or worse. I'm a stranger in this country. I wish I could go home to Korea. But I can't."

Chae Hoon put his hand on her shoulder. "Be strong, Soon Hi. Things can turn around. You're not alone. You still have your mother, and…you have me. I'm going to be staying here for a while.

"You are?" she said, raising her head and wiping away tears from her cheeks.

"Yes. I've been reassigned to Honshu indefinitely, so you may be seeing more of me."

Surprised, she asked, "Where are you going to be working?"

"I'll be working out of an army base about a hundred kilometers from here in Shizuoka Prefecture. We think that war with Choson is likely in the near future, and General Chong wants to add to the force we already have in Okinawa by creating a separate unit here in Honshu. Up until last month we didn't have any place to house or train Korean soldiers on this island. But with the American occupation about to end here in Japan, the Americans agreed to provide us space on a former Japanese Army base located near Mount Fuji. I've been assigned here primarily as a recruiter for the new unit."

The idea of a new war scared her, but if his assignment meant that she really would be seeing more of him…

"I'm really glad you'll be here," she said.

"I am too. Colonel Park was even able to persuade Prince Yi Un to come out of retirement and serve as the formal commander of the *Zainichi* Brigade. With his name we'll be able to attract a lot more recruits."

"Yi Un, a crown prince? I didn't know any of the royal family were still alive. How can he help you?"

"Yes, some family members are still alive. He was one of the sons of King Kojong. If the old dynasty had continued, he was next in line after Sunjong. Instead he was sent to Japan as a boy and became an officer in the Japanese Imperial Army. He was promoted all the way up to lieutenant general, but when the war ended, he was forced out of the army. When Colonel Park found him he was running a grocery store in Osaka, and no one paid any attention to him. Now he can receive some of the respect his name deserves."[vii]

"No Korean in his right mind wants to return to the Yi Dynasty. Is that what Yi Un wants?"

Chae Hoon laughed, "No, not at all. He simply loves Korea and wants to see a free Republic of Korea restored. His name recognition will be a real help in recruiting young men who never thought of putting on a military uniform—especially a Korean uniform. But enough talk about my work. I know you probably have other plans for tonight, but I'd like to see you again. How about getting together for supper tomorrow evening? Are you free?

Hesitating for just a moment, she felt her heart begin to beat faster. *Is he really asking me?*

"Yes, yes I'd like that."

. . .

The *Silla Wangjo* restaurant was crowded and, as they entered, the tantalizing fragrance of steaming beef broth and piquant spices made her mouth water. Myong Sin had told her about this place, but she'd never had the chance to go. So when Chae Hoon asked, it was her first choice. After sitting down, she looked over the menu and pointed to the *solleongtang*. He ordered the same, along with a large bottle of Kirin beer.

While waiting for the waitress to return, Soon Hi said, "You know about my family's story. I've told you everything. But you haven't told me about your family and why you became a soldier."

"You're right," he said, "and I owe you that." When the waitress returned with the beer and several plates of *banchan*, he filled her glass, then his own. "I grew up in the north – in Wonsan. My family left there in 1946 and we resettled in Seoul."

"I was pretty sure you were from the north from your accent. I know many people came south after the Communists took over. Since I never actually had to live under them, I'm curious as to why it was so bad. Tell me about your family."

"I have two sisters, one older and one younger. My mother and sisters were able to evacuate from Korea and are living in Osaka now. My father – I'm not sure about him since he stayed in Seoul when the North Korean army invaded. I haven't heard from him since."

"Oh, I'm sorry," said Soon Hi, her hands clasping her chest. "We've both lost our fathers. What happened to make your father decide to come south?"

"My father lost his job and had no way to support us. He didn't like what he saw as the new political system and felt we had to leave."

"Why did he lose his job? Did they consider him pro-Japanese?"

"No, it wasn't that at all. I'll start from the beginning. My family was Christian and the Communists didn't much like Christians. We weren't wealthy—my father was a school teacher—but we had a decent house and enough money to live on. In his youth he attended a Christian missionary school and that's where he got his early education. As a teacher, my father was well respected in our community. After the announcement that the Japanese had surrendered, Koreans began organizing and established a People's Committee in Pyongyang—a first step to establish a government. My father was appointed as a representative for our area. Some of the people in his committee were Communists, but not all."

Chae Hoon paused as a waitress came and set two large steaming bowls of thickened beef broth with strips of beef and scallions floating on top. He waited until Soon Hi first took a taste, before trying it himself. Smacking his lips with satisfaction, he reached across the table with his chopsticks to snatch a piece of kimchee from a plate, popped it in his mouth, and washed it down with a long swallow of beer.

"When the Soviet army came in, they brought with them many Russian speaking Koreans from Manchuria and the Soviet Union. The Communists took control of all the government committees. Father was willing to work within that kind of system as long as they didn't bother him. But in the first weeks after the Soviet army entered Korea, father told me he saw Russian military trucks day after day removing equipment from factories and from the shipyard around Wonsan harbor. When they finished, hardly anything was left. He heard of Russian soldiers taking goods and raping women. He saw friends arrested and disappear for no reason. He saw mobs beating up people and taking over property of people he knew had worked hard to acquire and maintain it. He knew they weren't collaborators."

When Chae Hoon paused and lifted his beer glass to take another swig, Soon Hi said, "Your father had a good position. Did he try to do anything about what he saw?"

"Yes. At one political meeting father spoke up against the criminal acts against loyal Koreans, but he was shouted down. Afterward, two policemen came to our door and they arrested him. When asked why, they said that someone had accused him of being a pro-capitalist traitor. He spent a week in jail and after that he was paraded through the streets with a large number of others. They had embarrassing signs around their necks that said things like "fascist pig" and worse. My mother and I had to go watch. After he was released from jail, he was fired from his teaching job, and there was no hope of getting another one. Except for members of our Christian community, people began treating us like lepers."

Soon Hi, shook her head in disbelief. "I understand now why your father felt he had to leave the North."

"Yes, it wasn't what he wanted. Now my hope is that someday I can return and find my father again. I keep hoping he may be still alive."

"Soon Hi thought about her own father. "I wish I could see my father again too, but for me, it's not possible. It's my dream, though, and the dream of my mother, to return to our homeland, to visit father's grave, and to see my older brother In Yong again."

"It may seem impossible right now," said Chae Hoon, "but someday I believe it will happen. There are still many in Korea who strongly oppose the Communists, but they are powerless to fight against them. They need help. We're becoming stronger, but we can't really fight them alone. We're going to need allies, like the United States, and also Japan."

"What makes you think the Japanese will work with you? From what I know, most Japanese don't like us. They would be just as happy if there weren't any Koreans in Japan."

Chae Hoon agreed. "Exactly. Koreans get all lumped together and most Japanese would like us to disappear. But we have friends in the government who realize not all Koreans are the same, and they understand our goals are not contradictory. They see Choson as a threat to them. We want to defeat Choson. So our aims are complimentary. If our exile group is successful and can create a friendly government on the Korean peninsula, it would solve two problems for the Japanese. It would relieve them of having a large Korean minority here, and it would eliminate the immediate threat of an enemy state on their doorstep."

"I see what you mean. But the Japanese have their own economic problems and they didn't do anything after the Choson gunboats sank their ship in the East Sea last year. I still don't see why you think they will help you."

"What you say is true. The Japanese are limited in what they can do militarily right now. But the U.S. is urging them to change and, over time, they will rebuild. The big concern now of the Japanese politicians is the internal threat of Communists. The Japanese Communist Party has spoken openly of a revolution to overthrow the government. They want to see Communist states in all of Asia. There have already been incidents of sabotage and the Communists are riling up the big labor unions against the government. That has the Japanese power brokers, the politicians and members of the *zaibatsu*[viii] frightened. Its common knowledge that a large percentage of those Communist activists are Koreans and they are looking to us to help identify and stop them. In short, they look to us for help in their counter-espionage efforts. While we're on that subject, you told me before that your younger brother had been involved with the *Minsen*. Is he still involved with them?"

"I hope not. A few months ago he was arrested after participating in a demonstration. A friend of mine who worked for the American government helped him get out of jail. After that In Su promised to change his ways. He got a new job as a warehouseman in Yokohama."

"Do you see him often?"

"He usually comes here on the weekend to eat with us. He should be here Saturday evening. Why are you asking these questions about him?"

"I'd like to meet with him. That's all."

"No, there's something more you're not telling me."

"All right. I don't want to lie to you. Earlier I told you I came here to work as a recruiter, and that's true. But I'm also working with Japanese counter-intelligence to help them identify Korean Communist cells. Next weekend is May Day weekend, and the Japanese are expecting mass demonstrations that could get ugly. They're worried about assassination attempts and sabotage. Since your brother was involved with *Minsen* in the past, maybe he has useful information he'd be willing to share. That's all. Would you ask him if he'd meet with me?"

Soon Hi knit her eyebrows in concern. "Did you plan this from before? Is that why you asked me out? To get to my brother through me?"

"No, no! I asked you out because I wanted to get to know you more. It's *you* I'm interested in. Really. If you don't want me to talk to your brother that's okay."

Soon Hi pursed her lips together, feeling tugged in two directions— not wanting to turn Chae Hoon away from her and at the same time wanting to protect her brother. Gripping the table she leaned forward. "All right, I'll talk to him and if he agrees, then I'll arrange for us all to meet. But don't pressure him."

Chae Hoon reached over and put his hand on hers. "Thank you Soon Hi. I won't push him into anything he doesn't want to do. If he doesn't think he can help us, then that'll be the end of it." He handed her a piece of paper. "Here's the name of the inn where I'm staying and a telephone number where I can be reached. Call me Monday and let me know either way."

CHAPTER 19

MAY DAY

April 24–May 2, 1952

Although he seldom called in advance, In Su almost always came by the apartment on Sunday evening for a home cooked meal. Soon Hi waited anxiously for him all day, eager to talk with him about her conversation with Chae Hoon. Her mother had prepared one of In Su's favorite meals, seafood *jiggae*. That should put him in a good mood, she thought. But when darkness came and he still hadn't shown, Soon Hi began to worry. By eight o'clock the stew had grown cold, and they knew he wasn't coming. Soon Hi warmed up the soup and ate a small bowl, but her mother said she wasn't hungry, cleaned up some dishes, and went to bed.

Later, lying awake in bed, Soon Hi couldn't help but wonder why her brother hadn't shown up. She had no way to contact him by phone. But she had an idea where to go look for him. She remembered he had told her he was working as a dock worker on Mizuho Pier. He'd also mentioned the company name, but she couldn't quite recall what it was. She'd just have to go to the pier and look around. But she couldn't go tomorrow. It was the first day of the workweek, and Myong Sin needed her to take a complete inventory of what they had on the shelves. Another day shouldn't matter.

. . .

Soon Hi started out early for the pier on Tuesday, catching the commuter train at the Shinjuku station. A half hour later, getting off

159

at Motomachi, she looked around and spotted a baggage handler loading boxes onto a wagon.

"Can you tell me how to get to Mizuho Pier?" she asked.

He looked up, grunted, and pointed across the street, "Two blocks over that way. Go to your right and keep walking. Can't miss it."

She thanked him and headed in the direction he'd pointed. After two blocks she came to the waterfront with clusters of small fishing boats and dories anchored this way and that like leaves scattered aimlessly atop a waving field of grain. She looked down to her right and saw far down the line, piers jutting out from the landing and was sure that one of them must be Mizuho. As she started down the long quay, she saw busy construction gangs putting up new buildings, one after another, including one large concrete warehouse-like building. Anti-American graffiti and garish posters advertising May Day events in big red and yellow characters seemed to jump out at her from the wooden fencing separating the construction sites from the walkway. She could tell that the area had been devastated by bombing during the last war. Signs of that destruction were still evident in some vacant spaces, but the remnants of the old waterfront were fast disappearing, being replaced like so much else in the new Japan.

The first pier Soon Hi came to extended about a hundred meters into the harbor and had several fishing boats moored at it. But there was no sign that said Mizuho. She kept walking, and after passing two more piers she was beginning to think that the bag handler didn't know what he was talking about. Walking a little farther she saw a fenced in area ahead extending out into the harbor. At first she thought it was simply the end of the wharf, but then she saw smokestacks and antennae looming up over buildings on the far side. She realized those weren't buildings, but large seagoing ships. *That must be it.* She walked another fifty yards before reaching a gate with a sign in English that read: Mizuho Pier.

At the gate was a guard house. As she started to pass through, the guard stopped her and said, "Where you going?"

Flustered because she couldn't remember the name of the place where In Su worked she pointed and said haltingly, "My...uh...brother works over there. I need to take him his lunch."

The guard pushed a log book towards her. "Sign in and write down where you're going."

Soon Hi scanned the register hastily seeking a name she could put down. The name "Mitsui" caught her eye. Now she remembered. That was the name of the company In Su had mentioned. She smiled at the guard and calmly filled out the register. Leaving the guard house, she saw that the pier stretched on for three or four hundred yards. It was like an island with rows of concrete warehouses lining the waterfront where large freighters were moored. Workers were busily unloading crates. Huge cranes loomed over the ships like vultures preparing to pick up their prey. She checked the signs on the buildings. Halfway up the pier she was surprised to see a large gray gunship flying a United States flag. Fascinated by the sight of the American ship, she almost missed noticing the sign posted on the side of a large brick building on her left, the words written both in English and Chinese characters — MITSUI TRANSPORT CO LTD.

Looking for an entry, she came to a door marked "Office" and went in. She caught the attention of a female clerk typing behind a counter. "Can you help me? I'm looking for my brother. He works here as a warehouse worker."

The girl got up from her desk and came over to Soon Hi. "If you give me his name, I can look him up in our employee register. But unless you have a company business pass, you can't go in the work area."

"I really need to talk to him," she said. "Can you just tell me if he's here? His name is…she hesitated, trying to recall the false name he'd started using. Dong Son, Dong Son Chung." She took a pencil and wrote the name down.

The clerk looked at the paper, told her to wait, and went to the back of the room. Five minutes later she came back. "Yes, we have employee with that name, but you can't go back there."

"Can I send a note to him to let him know I'm here?"

The clerk said, "I guess you can do that. But even if he's there, he can't leave until his shift is over. That'll be three o'clock. They have to come by this way on their way out."

Soon Hi wrote out a short note, folded it up, and gave it to the clerk. "I'll wait," she said.

The clerk took the note, tossed it in a mail bin for a messenger to pick up on his next run through the building, and went back to her desk.

Soon Hi sat and waited for two and a half hours, getting up and walking outside periodically to pass the time. She worried her brother might not be at work today. She didn't know where he was living. If he didn't show up, what could she do then? Finally she heard a whistle blow, and then men started coming out from various exits along the building. She stood and watched as they passed, hearing occasional crude comments that made her cringe. At quarter after three, she began to think that her effort had been for naught. Then she saw him ambling slowly down a ramp and coming towards her. She stepped away from the side of the building and waved, and he stopped for a moment before coming up to her.

"What are you doing here?"

"I was worried about you. You didn't come for dinner this weekend, or the last."

Shifting his feet, and looking down at the cement pavement, he said, "I went out with friends. Since you don't have a phone, I couldn't call you. You don't need to worry about me."

"Okay. But with all the talk about demonstrations coming this week, I wasn't sure if maybe you'd got into some kind of jam. You're not involved with those troublemakers in *Minsen* are you?"

"No, quit bothering me about that. I haven't changed my mind about the Americans, but I'm not going to any of the big rallies tomorrow. I'm staying away from that. I learned my lesson. I know what I'm doing."

"I hope so."

Leaving the pier, Soon Hi asked him if he wanted to stop and get something to eat. "No, I don't have time," he said. "I have to meet some friends."

"Well, then walk me to the station so we can talk some more." At the station, just before boarding, Soon Hi said, "Will you come to the apartment this weekend for sure? I need to tell mother."

"Yeah, for sure. I'll come over Saturday after work."

"Good, we'll be expecting you."

As April 1952 drew to a close, officials in Tokyo and other major Japanese cities began readying their police forces to deal with an expected outbreak of anti-government demonstrations on May 1. The first of May had been celebrated in Europe as a joyous springtime festival day for centuries. But following the Bolshevik Revolution in Russia in 1917, the Communists took it over as their day to celebrate the triumphant march of socialism as a new world order. As communism spread throughout the third world, revolutionary groups, Communist sympathizers, and newly established socialist regimes followed in the Soviet Union's path and recognized May Day as a day to demonstrate their commitment to the international socialist movement. Now, as *this* May Day approached, Japanese left wing radicals prepared to make it one that would ignite a new revolution—one that would lead to a socialist Japan free of foreign occupiers. Although the American occupation had formally ended on April 8, following the signing of the Japanese Peace Treaty, a security agreement between the U.S. and Japan had guaranteed the continued presence of American bases in Japan. That agreement enraged every leftist element in the country— from the moderate socialists to the most radical student groups. It energized the Japanese Communist Party (JCP) to unite the disparate groups, promising the biggest demonstrations Japan had ever seen.

. . .

Soon Hi opened her eyes and stretched her arms. She hadn't slept very well. It was the first day of May. She wasn't looking forward to today. She dressed, had a quick breakfast, and started out for work as usual at seven. More than likely there'd be demonstrations around the emperor's palace, and she'd heard that there was a big rally scheduled for Meiji Shrine Park around noon, but those places were far enough away that they shouldn't affect the clinic. Looking out from her bus window on the way to work, she noticed two buses loaded with blue uniformed riot police going in the opposite direction.

As throngs of Japanese began to converge on Tokyo's Meiji Park to hear rabble rousing anti-American, anti-government speeches, Josef

Stalin was presiding over the massive military parade held annually on this date in Moscow's Red Square; Mao Tse Tung was preparing to make his appearance in Beijing's Tienanmen Square to celebrate the Red victory over the Nationalists three years before; and workers in Seoul were arranging chairs on the reviewing stand in front of City Hall where Kim Il Sung would soon appear to applaud the nation's military for unifying the country under communism less than two years before.

By the time the first speaker took the dais at one o'clock in Meiji Park, the crowd of people had mushroomed to more than four hundred thousand, stretching as far as the eye could see. Banners and signs were sprinkled through the crowd. Some posters showed demeaning images of Americans—one displayed a beggarly Prime Minister Yoshida bowing submissively with his hand out to a Fagan-like Uncle Sam. The first speaker, Eiichi Iwata, a fiery Communist member of the Tokyo Municipal Assembly, told the assembled people that he hoped the large May Day turnout would show the emperor in no uncertain terms that the Japanese people want the Americans gone, and they want the Yoshida government gone. He shouted out, "Japan is a proud nation, put to shame by a government that bows down to foreigners like a slave. Our socialist brothers in China have eliminated western imperialists from their land; so have our socialist brothers in Choson. We must do the same. We must demand that the emperor abrogate the treaty with the American imperialists and throw the Americans out of the country."

Although the speeches in Meiji Park continued on through the afternoon, following Iwata's speech several large groups of demonstrators broke away from the main crowd and headed out of the park, snaking through the city streets like great boa constrictors lofting signs with pictures of Mao, Lenin, and Japanese Communist heroes, chanting anti-government slogans, daring the police to stop them. One particularly large group, perhaps five thousand in all, made up of trained Communist toughs, hot-headed students, young hoodlums looking for excitement, and angry Korean dissidents, many carrying stones and sharpened bamboo spears, headed towards the Imperial Palace about two miles away. They were met by a line of police who confronted them in front of the palace moat, and a back and forth shoving match ensued.

The pent up demonstrators outnumbered the police and many broke through the cordon and attempted to force their way into the palace grounds. Hand to hand fighting broke out, the stones and sharpened sticks of the rioters against the batons and shields of the police. Backed up to the foot of the palace wall, several hundred police put on tear gas masks and counterattacked the mob, some firing tear gas canisters while others fired warning gun shots over the heads of the rioters. The mob scattered, running every which way, creating havoc and destruction outside the palace walls. More than a thousand angry protestors escaped across the street, besieging the Daiichi building where until a week ago, General MacArthur had held court, and where U.S. military offices continued to operate. The rioters were unable to get into the building, defended by Marines inside, but they broke most of the windows on the lower floors and overturned American cars outside, setting them on fire. Several unlucky off-duty GIs, standing outside the American compound, were spotted by the rioters, caught, and severely beaten.[ix]

The clinic where Soon Hi was working was three or four miles away from the rioting, but she still feared that it would spread to them. She and Myong Sin spent much of the afternoon with their ears tuned to the radio, listening to what was happening. Although the demonstrations didn't hit their area, towards the end of the afternoon, a number of people, mostly young men, began to show up at the clinic for treatment of injuries. Because of the numbers, Dr. Yi called them over to the clinic to help screen the patients coming in. Soon Hi and Myong Shin locked up the food bank and rushed over. With a clip board in hand, Soon Hi began interviewing, taking down information from the young men waiting in line outside the clinic. Some had been beaten quite severely and some had bullet wounds. They had to be seen first. Others were less critical. Most of them, she suspected, gave aliases to avoid police dragnets that were bound to follow. She worried that she would see her brother come through the door, but when she finally left for home near midnight, In Su had not appeared, and she was relieved.

The next morning, on her way to work, she heard people talking about some bombing over in Yokohama. When she got to work she found a newspaper and saw big black headlines that screamed

SHIP EXPLODES IN TOKYO BAY
Five Americans Killed

Beneath the headline was a picture of a large gunship alongside a dock with a big hole in its side. She skimmed over the first paragraph of the article:

The U.S.S. Atherton, a U. S. Navy destroyer escort, berthed in Yokohama Harbor with 252 men on board, was sabotaged by an explosive device. The explosion tore open the ship's hull at midsection at about ten o'clock yesterday evening (May 1) killing five American seamen and injuring more than forty.

Atherton? Could that be the same American ship she saw on Mizuho Pier yesterday? She believed it was. *This is terrible. Where can In Su be? Surely he hadn't been involved with whatever mad men had done this.* Even if he wasn't involved in the sabotage, just the fact that he was working near there would put him under suspicion. He'd be scared. She wanted to help him, but even if he showed up at the apartment, what could she do. She dug into her purse for the phone number Chae Hoon had given her, went to a phone, and put a call into him. He answered on the third ring.

"Chae Hoon. I'm so glad I was able to reach you," Soon Hi said breathlessly.

"I've been concerned about you with all the rioting going on," said Chae Hoon. "Is everything all right?"

"I'm all right. But I'm worried about In Su. I saw him yesterday. He's working on the pier where that American ship was bombed."

"Do you think he was involved?"

"He said he wasn't involved with *Minsen* anymore and that he wouldn't do anything foolish on May Day, but I'm not sure... I wonder if he's been arrested, or if anything's happened to him. He told me he would come by our place tomorrow night for supper, but if something's happened to him, I want to know."

"It's early and police are still probably compiling their arrest records. I can try to check to see if there's any record of his being arrested. If he was injured there's no telling where he might have been taken. I'll come by your apartment Saturday evening. If he's there, it'll be a good chance for us to talk. If he's in trouble and is willing to work with us, I can help him."

Chae Hoon's reassurance had a calming effect on Soon Hi and she worked through the rest of the day feeling confident that tomorrow would turn out okay. Arriving home after work she told her mother about her conversation with Chae Hoon and she agreed that they should trust In Su's word and expect him for supper Saturday evening. After supper, they cleaned up dishes together, and then Soon Hi began reading a book while her mother busied herself with some needlework. At ten o'clock her mother put down her material, took out bedding, and laid it out on the tatami floor of the small bedroom she and her daughter shared. Soon Hi came into the room a few minutes later and laid down next to her mother. Still lying awake, her mother lamented in the darkness, "I'm getting old. My children should be married, having children of their own, and I should be a grandmother. These times are so hard. Will life ever be as it should be?"

Soon Hi turned towards her and said, "Times will never be the same. But you will be a grandmother someday. I promise."

CHAPTER 20

THE ARREST

May 3–May 15, 1952

Soon Hi was awakened by a hard pounding on the front door. She groped for the lamp and turned on the light. *How long have I been sleeping*? She looked at the clock on her dresser—it was one o'clock. She'd only been sleeping for a couple hours. *Who could be knocking?* She got up, wrapped a cover around her, and tip-toed warily to the door.

"Who is it?" she called uncertainly from behind the door.

"It's me. In Su. Open up."

She quickly unlocked the door and let in her brother. Looking wild eyed like a frightened animal, he slammed the door shut and locked it.

"They're looking for me."

"Who? Who's looking for you?"

"The police. They think I was involved with blowing up that American ship. I need your help."

His mother, looking on drowsily from the bedroom doorway, said, "*Musun Irini*? (What's happening?).

"In Su came. Go back to bed mother."

Her mother closed her door, and Soon Hi took out a pair of cushions from a closet and put them on the floor. "Sit down In Su. Tell me what happened. Were you involved? Are you still seeing those *Minsen* crazies?"

In Su sat down cross-legged on the floor and Soon Hi sat facing him.

168

"Yes, I *am* a member of *Minsen*," he said. "I believe in their cause. But I didn't take any part in that."

"What is their cause? What could be the purpose of blowing up an American ship?"

"They oppose American bases in Japan. They believe that Japan, like Korea, should be free of foreigners. You saw how many people turned out for May Day demonstrations all over the country. They thought it could inspire a national uprising against the Americans and the Yoshida government."

"How stupid! Blowing up an American ship is only going to make the Americans more determined to remain here. And it will give ammunition for the Japanese militarists to have their way in shutting you down."

"I know. I tried to convince them of that."

"Tried to convince them? Just how deep into this were you?"

"I was in a meeting last week where it was planned out. There were eight people there. I tried to tell them it was a bad move. It wouldn't achieve what they wanted. Me and one other guy spoke up against it, but we were outvoted. The two of us walked out before the meeting ended. I promise you I wasn't involved in the actual bombing."

She slapped the floor angrily. "Oh In Su! Even though you didn't do the actual bombing, just your association with those who did means big trouble. I wish you had listened to me."

In Su agreed. "I know. But it's too late to worry about that now. If any of those guys get captured my name will come up. I need a place to stay tonight and then find somewhere to hide out. Will you help me?"

"Of course you can stay here tonight, but as for going into hiding...the police will eventually find you." She leaned back against the wall and thought for a moment, then bent forward wagging a finger at him. "I think it would be better for you to turn yourself into the police and give them information that they want to know about those who planned the bombing. Otherwise, if they hunt you down, you'll surely be lumped in with those criminals, maybe killed."

"If I do that, then *Minsen* will have a contract out on me. Either way I'm dead."

"No, I don't think so. I have a friend who can help you. He's coming here tomorrow night. I told him about you, and he wants to talk to you."

"One of your American friends?"

"No, he's Korean. He's an officer with the New Republic of Korea Army. Have you heard of it? He has contacts in the Japanese government. He can work out a deal for you."

"I've heard about it. I can't go to them. They don't speak for me. If I give information about my comrades, they'll be killed. I'm not a traitor."

"Your comrades are not interested in you. I am. You don't have to give up your allegiance to Choson. But Japan is not going to go Communist. I think you know that. By staying loyal to these radical revolutionaries you're eventually going to be caught and put in prison, or worse. If you cooperate with the Japanese police, you can separate yourself from *Minsen* and the Communists and start a new life here. Just talk with my friend and see what he has to say."

In Su nodded, indicating he would think about it. Soon Hi picked herself up off the floor. "I have to go to work tomorrow morning. I need to get some sleep. Stay here tomorrow. You'll be safe. I'll call my friend and he'll come over tomorrow evening and we can all talk this through. I'm sure he'll have a good solution."

When Soon Hi left for work the next day, In Su was still sleeping in the front room. She told her mother who was standing over the stove preparing breakfast, "Don't let In Su go anywhere. If he says he's going to leave call me from the phone downstairs. I'll be home by six and Chae Hoon will be here for supper."

• • •

While unloading boxes of CARE packages received from the United States, Soon Hi was interrupted by Myong Sin who said she had a telephone call at the clinic. She hurried next door and took the phone.

"*Yobosaiyo?*"

"He's gone."

Hearing her mother's words brought home her worst fear. "What do you mean he's gone?"

170

"In Su left with two men about two hours ago. He hasn't come back."

"I'll be home as soon as I can."

. . .

An hour and a half later, Soon Hi rushed into her apartment where her mother waited.

"You said that In Su left with two men. Were they policemen?"

"No. I heard them speaking Korean. In Su said he had to go out, but that he would return in an hour. That's why I didn't call you right away. I'm sorry."

"Don't feel bad. It wouldn't have mattered if you'd called me an hour earlier." She put her arm around her mother's shoulders. "Chae Hoon will be here soon. Maybe he can help find him before the police do."

When Chae Hoon arrived he questioned Nam Hui for several minutes as to exactly what she heard and saw. She told him she saw them get into a small black car and drive away.

Chae Hoon said, "It sounds like they were definitely *Minsen* people. I can have some feelers put out as to who might have him, but I don't think it'll do any good. They'll probably try to smuggle him out of the country—to Korea. For your sake, I hope they do. If the police catch him he'll be tortured for information and go to prison for sure."

. . .

A week had passed and Soon Hi had heard nothing about her brother. Then one day two men, both in dark brown business suits, came into the food bank and waited by the door while she tended to a customer. She looked up and said she'd be with them in a moment. After packing up her customer's order, one of the men, stocky with close cropped hair and a pencil thin mustache, came up to the counter. She smiled. "How can I help you."

The man, without returning the smile, slowly reached into his jacket pocket, pulled out an official looking badge, and laid it on the counter. "I'm Sergeant Miyomoto with the Metropolitan Police. This is detective Oshiro. We've come to talk to Miss Soon Hi Chung."

She wrinkled her brow. "I'm Soon Hi Chung."

Putting the badge back in his pocket, he said, "We have some questions to ask you about your brother. You have a brother named In Su Chung, also known as Dong Son?"

"Yes, I do. Why? Is anything wrong?

"We believe he was involved in the bombing of the American ship in Tokyo Bay a week ago. We were hoping you could tell us where he might be. We want you to come down to the police station with us so we can discuss this matter."

"I don't think I have anything to say. I don't know anything. I don't want to go with you."

"Miss Chung. We have reason to believe your brother came to your apartment after the bombing. Aiding a felon is a serious business. If you don't come voluntarily, then we'll get a warrant and be back to arrest you."

Myong Shin had come out of the back room and approached the counter looking puzzled. She could tell something was wrong by the look on Soon Hi's face. "What's happening here?"

"These men are police officer's," said Soon Hi. "They want me to go with them to the police station. They're looking for In Su."

Myong Shin quickly became angry. "What do you want with her? She doesn't know anything,"

"It's procedure in matters like this," said the officer who identified himself as Miyomoto. "It shouldn't take more than a couple hours." Raising his arm and pointing in the direction of the doorway, he said, "Shall we go Miss Chung?"

Soon Hi knew she didn't have a choice. She picked up her purse from under the counter, rummaged through it for a piece of paper, and handed it to Myong Sin. "I'm not sure what's going to happen. Go to my apartment and tell my mother to call Chae Hoon. His phone number is on this paper."

After getting permission to close the store early, Myong Shin took a bus to Soon Hi's apartment and told her mother what had happened. Nam Hui insisted that Myong Shin stay until Soon Hi returned. When it started getting dark and she still hadn't shown, they both went downstairs and asked the store owner to use the phone. Myong Shin made the call to Chae Hoon, and he picked up on the second ring. When she told him what had happened, he said he'd go to the police headquarters building right away to try to locate her.

When Chae Hoon arrived at the downtown police headquarters, it was past eight o'clock. A brusque desk sergeant told him that she was being held for interrogation regarding her relationship with a suspect involved in the American ship bombing. Since it was after eight o'clock, he wasn't permitted to see her but was told to come back another day.

. . .

The next morning, Chae Hoon returned to the police headquarters and filled out a request to meet with Soon Hi. He was directed to a separate wing of the building that housed the jail, and after walking through a long dimly lit corridor, reached a room with a sign over the door saying "Visitors Area". The room was fairly small, with one outside window opened half-way to let in air. There were about a dozen straight-back chairs for visitors lining the walls. All but one was occupied. At the rear of the room was a three foot high counter where three or four people sat talking with prisoners through a glass partition. He took the empty seat next to a heavy-set man whose overpowering body odor reeked of rotten eggs, and he waited. After enduring as much stink as he could, he was about to get up when a guard called his name. He looked up and saw Soon Hi, wearing a baggy gray jail uniform, take a seat behind the glass paneled partition. He hurried over and sat down in a chair opposite her. There were dark rings under her eyes. She looked tired but unharmed as she attempted a weak smile.

"Thank you for coming," she said. "I was afraid mother wouldn't be able to reach you."

"I came as soon as I could. Have they told you why they're keeping you here?"

"They think I knew about the bombing and that I helped my brother escape. They tried to get me to admit to that, but I told them I didn't know anything about it, and I *didn't* help him escape."

"I believe you. But did you see In Su after the bombing?"

"Yes, he came to the apartment, and then left the next morning when I was at work. Mother said two Korean men came and got him."

"Did you tell the police investigator that?

"Yes. Was I wrong? Can they keep me here? Am I going to prison?

"No, you did right. If you lied about his coming to your apartment the police would find out, and they would use that against you. They're fishing for information. They can't keep you here indefinitely, and they can't charge you with something without proof. I have a lawyer friend that I think can help. I'll go see him after I leave here."

A short while later a buzzer went off indicating that the visitation time was up. Chae Hoon put his hands on the window and she placed her hands against his. "They may keep you one more night, but I'll be back tomorrow and we'll get you out."

• • •

The next morning Chae Hoon was back at the Metropolitan Police Station accompanied by Kanoru Sato, a young attorney and aide to influential Diet member Nobosuke Kishi. Chae Hoon had been working closely with Mr. Sato in connection with several counter-intelligence projects, providing him with useful data on Koreans associated with *Yakuza*ˣ syndicates. When he explained Soon Hi's situation, he readily agreed to help.

• • •

Two hours after the attorney's arrival, the three of them walked out of the police station. At the foot of the stairs Soon Hi bowed and then shook Mr. Sato's hand for helping her. He downplayed his contribution, saying that he owed Chae Hoon a favor, and besides, she wasn't guilty of anything. As Sato left to catch a cab, Soon Hi looked at Chae Hoon. "I don't understand why they came to arrest me. If they haven't arrested In Su, how did they know about me?"

"That puzzled me too," he said. "But I found out that there was an article in *Nodong Sinmun* a few days ago celebrating the return to Choson of three "heroes of the revolution" who participated in the bombing of an American ship. In Su Chung was one of the "heroes". The article was reprinted in the *Akahata Shimbun*. Once the Japanese police had the name they started tracking down relatives. That's how they traced you to him."

"Ahh, so he made it out of the country. I guess I'm glad of that. But it almost cost me *my* freedom?"

"Yes, but that's behind us now. I'll bet you're hungry. Let's go find a place to eat before I take you home."

It was still light out when they finished eating. The restaurant was only about a mile from her apartment, and they decided to walk. They stopped along the way at a bakery and he bought a small cake to share. When they got to her apartment he went upstairs with her. She stood for a moment at the door looking up at him with liquid eyes, wanting to reach out to him, but afraid. "I don't know what I would do without you," she said.

Touching her cheek softly with his right hand, he said I feel the same Soon Hi. He lowered his face to hers and she lifted her chin. Their lips touched and they kissed gently. He wrapped his one arm around her and the other he placed on her breast. They kissed again — more passionately. Then she pulled away, seemingly embarrassed. "No, no. I'm sorry. I shouldn't."

Smiling, but feeling like a deflated balloon that had just been pricked with a needle, Chae Hoon said, "Don't be sorry. It's all right. But I do want to see more of you — much more. Will you go out with me this coming Saturday?"

Soon Hi unlocked the door and turned her head toward Chae Hoon, her heart beating so fast she could hardly breathe. "Yes, of course I will."

CHAPTER 21

A FRIEND IN NEED

August 13–15, 1952

Tom sat at his desk daydreaming, staring out the fourth floor window of his office watching a group of children, probably on a school outing, romp around the San Martin statue in Triangle Park. He was thinking about his time in Japan and Korea. It had been eight months since he'd transferred back to D.C., and he still thought about Soon Hi. She had written to him shortly after the May 1 riots in Tokyo. She told him about her brother's disappearance and that she had started dating a Korean, an ex-soldier. He was glad for her, and told her so in another letter. He knew he'd never be able to totally forget her, but he was finally able to admit to himself that his dream of marriage was over. He'd even taken Phil's advice and started dating again. That had done wonders to relieve the mental pain that had been keeping him awake nights.

Today he had an appointment at one o'clock— someone by the name of John Choe who said he was representing the ROK exile government. In setting up the appointment he told the secretary that he'd met Tom in Korea before the war started. Tom couldn't recall meeting anyone by that name during the time leading up to the war. He wasn't sure why the man wanted to see *him*, since he wasn't a money guy. He'd probably just have to refer him to some other department. At one o'clock on the nose, the secretary in the lobby downstairs called to let him know there was a visitor to see him.

Standing in front of his cubicle, Tom saw a tall well-dressed Asian man—appeared to be in his mid to late-twenties—emerge from the

176

elevator at the end of the hallway. The young man had a flattop haircut and wore black horn rim glasses. He looked somewhat familiar, but Tom couldn't place him. Had he been an employee in the embassy in Seoul? He began walking towards him, and as they drew closer, the stranger held out his hand in greeting. He shook Tom's hand firmly and said, "Hello Mr. Crandall. I'm John Choe. My Korean name is Chong Kyu Choe. You look like you don't remember me."

Suddenly it all came back. Breaking out in a broad grin, Tom said, "*You're* the young student whose visa I approved just before the North Korean attack. I often wondered if you'd made it out all right. Come on over to my desk and we'll talk."

Sitting down behind his desk, Tom said, "Can't believe it's been two whole years since that time in Korea. Tell me what you've been doing and why you're here."

"As you may remember," said Choe, "I came to the U.S. to attend Stanford. In June I receive my doctorate in economics. Ever since coming to the U.S. I've been active in groups trying to raise funds for the new Republic of Korea government—the one headed by Yi Pom Sok in Okinawa. Recently Mr. Yi personally contacted me and asked me to work for them directly to try to get financial support from the U.S. government."

"I see. But I'm not involved with any programs concerning foreign aid or military assistance. Why did you come to *me*?"

"Because we met before. I think you understand our need. And I think I understand the kind of person you are. I thought I could count on you to help me. I've contacted some Congressmen in California. They just tell me they're sympathetic to our situation, but they can't do anything."

"What's your aim—what does your organization hope to accomplish?"

"After the Communists took over the Korean peninsula, it seems that people wrote off Korea as an American ally. But there are tens of thousands of Koreans who evacuated Korea and millions in Korea who still believe in a free democratic Korea. If given the right kind of help, they'll be willing to fight to overthrow the vicious dictatorship that has taken control of our country. As an economist, I'm convinced that the communist system being installed by Kim Il Sung and his

Soviet advisers will only bring misery to the Korean people. In my doctoral thesis I created a model for a market oriented land reform program. I hope someday I can put my ideas into practice in a free Korea."

"I understand your feelings, and I'd like nothing better than to see a democratic government, friendly to the U.S., restored in Korea. But right now Kim Il Sung looks to be pretty entrenched, and providing help to an unrecognized Korean exile movement is going to be a hard sell. There are too many people who would see it as throwing money down a sewer drain."

Choe was disconsolate. "So you won't help me?"

"I didn't say that," said Tom. "Just what is it you're asking for?"

"General Chong, who heads up our military arm, needs tactical vehicles, communication equipment, and guns. We've got more than 30,000 soldiers on Okinawa, but nothing really to fight with. As for funding, we're looking at five million U.S. dollars for now."

"The United States government isn't going to simply bankroll an uncontrolled paramilitary force belonging to a self-proclaimed exile government unless its own national interest is at stake."

"I understand that. But Choson is already creating problems for U.S. interests in Japan. Look at what happened this past May Day with the bombing of the American ship. It's only a matter of time before they take the next step that will force the Americans, and Japan, to take some kind of retaliatory action."

Tom sat back in his chair and thought about what Choe said. He looked him straight in the eye. He didn't blink.

"Okay, you have a good point. There are people I know who may be willing to help. I can try. Give me a couple days to make some calls. Where are you staying?"

"I'm staying at the Madison Hotel. It's on K Street." He pulled out a hotel business card from his pocket, wrote down his room number on the back and handed it to Tom.

"I can't guarantee anything, but I'll call you by Friday."

Choe nodded, thanked Tom for seeing him, then got up and walked briskly back towards the elevator.

That afternoon Tom made a call to Stan Webster with the Technical Assistance Group (TAG) in the State Department. The office had just recently been set up under the president's Point Four Program to provide a vehicle for economic assistance to emerging nations.

"I can't help you," said Webster. "We can only provide technical assistance for economic development, not for military assistance. Besides the South Korean exiles don't control their own territory. The situation just doesn't fit our criteria. Sorry."

Next he put in a call to Jeff Kimble who headed up the Military Assistance Program at the Pentagon to see if there was surplus equipment that could be transferred to the Koreans.

"That doesn't fall under any category we can cover," said Kimble. "Every bit of surplus we've got in the Pacific is being transferred over to the Japanese. I think the best thing for the Koreans to do is to join up with the Japanese. I can't do anything for them apart from that."

As his day came to an end Tom felt discouraged. He didn't want to let Choe down, but he didn't know where else to turn. He thought of Fran. This was Wednesday, and she didn't like to go out on week nights. Whenever he asked, she always begged off saying she had too much reading to do. But he needed her advice. She would know people that he didn't. It was nearly five o'clock when he made the call. She picked up and, after an initial refusal, agreed to get together at six after she wrapped up some things.

Tom had met Fran at a Republican political rally in April some four months before. At the time he was still trying to get over his feelings for Soon Hi. He was lonely. He hadn't dated any girls since returning to the states and needed somebody to lean on. When he first saw Fran Burstein standing by herself with a glass of wine in her hand, she was wearing a fitted jacket and calf length pencil skirt with low heel shoes. She was nearly as tall as he; a little skinny he thought, but with a nice figure that her tight wardrobe accentuated. He approached her and, after introducing himself, learned that she worked at the State Department too, in the Bureau of International Organization Affairs. With drinks in hand they found two vacant chairs in a corner of the large auditorium where they could still barely hear one another amidst the clamor of voices around them.

Tom and Fran grew up under different circumstances. She'd grown up in a Jersey suburb of New York City, the only daughter of a wealthy surgeon. He had a younger sister and grew up in a small town in Illinois where his father operated a neighborhood grocery. Her family was Jewish. His was Presbyterian. Despite these differences, as the evening wore on, they soon discovered they both hated the Taft isolationist wing of the party and considered themselves progressive internationalists. Ike was the man both of them wanted to see as the next president and they couldn't stop talking about the upcoming convention.

Fran wasn't pretty. Her nose was a bit big for her face, her mouth a little wide, and the bangs on her forehead didn't do anything for her. But it wasn't her looks that had attracted him. It was a common interest in history and politics and a shared idealism that the work they were doing would help make the world a better place. When the evening was finished, he wanted to see more of her. The following Monday he'd asked her for a date. She said yes, and they'd been an item ever since.

Shortly before six Tom went over to the other side of the building where Fran worked and waited outside her office. It was six thirty by the time she came out. They drove to Georgetown and he took her to a below-street level bar and grill called Rick's Cellar. He'd been there two or three times before with friends from work. They took a seat in a booth along one wall. He ordered a mug of beer to go with his burger and fries; she a Caesar Salad and glass of merlot.

While waiting for their meal they talked about the upcoming presidential elections in November and how glad they were that Eisenhower had been nominated as the Republican candidate. Although Ike was a popular figure, when the convention began, there was considerable doubt as to who the nominee would be. Robert Taft started out with a small lead in convention delegates, and he had an equally popular military man in his corner—General MacArthur—who agreed to give the nominating speech for Taft. There was no mistaking the fact that the retired general, who had been the virtual emperor of Japan, resented the praise being heaped on Eisenhower, and hoped to cut down his former aide de camp to size. But when it got down to voting, the aging MacArthur had little impact over the crucial undecided delegates. Ike gradually pulled ahead and won the nomination comfortably. As for the Democrats, both Tom and Fran liked the Illinois governor. He was from Tom's home state, a good administrator, intelligent, witty, and not a hint of scandal.

"You must feel a little split over who to vote for." she said.

"Not really," said Tom. "Stevenson has the smarts, a good sense of humor, and a great job resume, but I don't think he's tough enough. He's not a man to lead the country. We need a world leader. I do worry some that Ike's lack of political experience may hurt him, but he's the one I want to see elected."

"I don't think we need to worry," said Fran. "The country's tired of the Democrats. They've been in way too long. In the last year Truman couldn't do anything right. I remember this past spring how the court overruled him on his seizure of the steel mills; then there was that corruption scandal in Internal Revenue; and he's been pilloried over being soft on Communists. People haven't forgotten that he gave up on Korea. No, I can't believe the country will elect another Democrat."

"I think you're right. If there's anyone that can give the country a lift, it's Eisenhower. The Reds will think twice before trying anything else. I heard a news report the other day that he pledged to go to Japan to reinforce our commitment and to urge them to take more responsibility for their own defense. I really like that. From all the opinion polls I've seen, he should win easily. But then Dewey was expected to defeat Truman easily too, and it didn't happen."

As they finished eating, a pianist sat down at the piano bar on the other side of the room and began playing a Cole Porter tune. The waitress came over and Tom ordered a second round of drinks. As the plaintive melody *Love for Sale* floated through the room, Fran drew a cigarette from her purse and put it to her lips. Tom leaned over, lighted it, and then took out one of his own.

"There's something that came up at work that I need your advice on."

"What's that?"

"This young Korean guy who I helped get out of Korea just before the North Korean attack came to see me. He's representing the Korean exile government now and wants my help to get our government to provide arms and equipment for a military force they're maintaining over in Okinawa. I'd like to help him, but I'm not sure there's any way. I talked to Jeff Kimble over at DOD, but he said they're concerned with getting aid to the Japanese. They see the Koreans as Japan's problem."

"I thought we were supposed to be looking at relocating those people from Okinawa."

"State's been working on that, but up until the treaty signing, Koreans living in Japan were considered Japanese. Now with the occupation ended and with this new immigration law Congress just passed they can be classified as refugees and we can start trying to move them out. We've got to find states that will agree to take them, though, and that'll take time."

He stubbed out his cigarette in an ashtray and lowered his eyes. "I'm really not in favor of relocating those Korean ex-soldiers right now even if we could. My friend gave me a pretty convincing argument that Choson is probably going to try something against the Japanese soon, and I think it'd be in our interest to build up an anti-Communist Korean force before that happens. I just don't know if I can convince anyone else of that. I've contacted people I thought might be able to help but no one wants to touch them. Can you think of any program that would fit? The Mutual Assistance Program? That comes under your department doesn't it?"

Fran shook her head. "No, there's no help for them there. Have you thought about TAG, the new foreign aid group that Sam Hayes is running?"

"Yeah. I talked to them already. It's a no go."

Fran took a sip from her wineglass, leaned her head back and took a long draw on her cigarette. "What about the CIA. They get involved with all kinds of under the table stuff. Do you know anybody over there?"

Tom's eyes lit up. "Of course, the CIA may be willing to get their hands dirty on this. And I know just the man who may be able to get my Mr. Choe a hearing."

Fran looked at her watch. "We'd better go," she said. "It's getting late."

Tom waved over the waitress for the bill.

When they arrived at her apartment door, Tom put his hands on Fran's shoulders and lowered his head as if to give her a good night kiss. "Aren't you going to invite me in?"

"I told you I have work to do. If I let you in, don't plan on staying long."

She unlocked the door and he followed her inside. While she went to the bedroom to get out of her work clothes, he went to the kitchen, poured a glass of wine for her, and opened a bottle of beer for himself. Returning to the living room he set the drinks on the coffee table, tossed his jacket and tie on a chair, slid his loafers off, turned on the TV, and plopped down on the sofa. After a few minutes Fran came out of the bedroom wearing a pair of pajamas and slippers, plumped up the sofa pillows, and sat down beside him.

"What are you watching?"

"It's an old Charlie Chan movie. Is that okay?"

"Sure. I like Charlie Chan movies," she said, settling back against the pillows and then taking a sip from her wineglass. "But I really don't know why they have to put a Caucasian in the role of a Chinese detective. It seems like they should be able to find Chinese actors."

"I agree," said Tom. "It's like Americans think they can represent an Asian better than an Asian actor. It's the kind of thinking that's gotten us into a lot of trouble politically the way we always know best how Asian countries should be run. We've got some hard lessons ahead if…"

She put her hand to his mouth. "Let's not talk politics now. Let's just watch the movie."

She leaned against him as he put his arm around her shoulder and his feet on the coffee table. Later, as the final scene of the movie came to the end, Tom let his hand drift to Fran's neck, undid the top buttons of her pajama top, and moved his hand to her breast. She moved closer to him and they kissed pressing their bodies tight against one another. He heard the sounds of the national anthem signaling that the TV station was going off the air for the night and started to get up. She freed the remaining buttons of her top, took off her pajama bottoms and laid on the sofa with her arms outstretched.

"I thought you wanted me to leave early," he said.

"Did I say that? I don't remember."

He removed his shirt and slacks, kicked them to the side of the room, and edged himself back onto the sofa, half covering her. He laid his head between her inviting breasts. They were like small luscious melons, and he had to have them. She held his head and pulled him tight against her. His hand went between her legs and she moaned. Slowly, very slowly, he slid down her perspiring body, his tongue tracing the centerline of her torso. He came to her naval and licked the salty sweat from her rounded belly. He lifted his face, and she breathed huskily, "Don't stop now."

"I won't," he said, and dipped his head to continue where he left off.

CHAPTER 22

THE ARRANGEMENT

August 18–26, 1952

It was nearly eight o'clock when Tom got to work — later than usual. Jumping off the elevator he stopped at the admin office and picked up a telephone directory for the CIA. Sitting down at his desk he paged through the booklet and found the name he was looking for. He looked up at the clock. *He's had time to get his coffee. Should be able to reach him now.* He dialed the number.

After going through a secretary, a gravel laced voice came over the line.

"Graziola here."

"Mr. Graziola. Good morning. This is Tom Crandall. I'm with the State Department in the East Asian Affairs Bureau."

"Morning. What can I do for you?"

"You may not remember me," said Tom, "but we met a few months ago at the briefing for Ambassador Murphy here in the State building. After the meeting we talked about the Korean military refugees on Okinawa."

After a moment of silence he replied, "Yeah, sure I remember."

"Well, the reason I'm calling is I had a young Korean man come by to see me a couple days ago. His name is John Choe. He said he was representing the Korean exile government that's been operating on Okinawa for the past year. I know the young man from when I worked in the embassy in Korea, and I trust him. I don't want to go into what he wants over the phone, but I told him the State Department isn't the right agency for what he's looking for. I didn't say anything to him about the CIA, but it's something I think you might be interested in. That's why I'm calling. Would you be willing to talk to him?"

"I *am* familiar with the situation in Okinawa. And you're right. We've been keeping an eye on the Korea situation — but we haven't been real active in that theater recently. Old Harry Truman hasn't been our biggest supporter... Of course, he *is* on his way out. So, yeah. Maybe it's something we would be interested in pursuing. I have an hour free at three o'clock. If you can have your man here, I'll listen to what he has to say."

. . .

Immediately after hanging up the phone, Tom called the number Choe had given him. Although another person answered the phone, Choe called him back in a matter of minutes and immediately agreed to meet Tom that afternoon in a parking lot across from the CIA entrance gate. The meeting with Graziola went well — so well that Graziola agreed to set up an appointment for them to meet with the deputy director the following Tuesday.

. . .

Ten o'clock on Tuesday morning Tom sat outside the CIA deputy director's office, a bit nervous since he was about to meet a man he'd been in awe of ever since he started working for the department, a man whose career had become part of agency lore. Allen Dulles, the younger brother of John Foster Dulles, had begun working as a diplomat with the State Department before the start of World War I. During the 1920's he worked for a prominent New York law firm and became an adviser to delegations working with the League of Nations on arms limitations. He gained his spy credentials with the OSS during World War II, serving as a station chief in Europe. In 1950 he'd become head of the CIA's Covert Operations Division, and later that same year he was promoted to his current position as deputy director of the agency.

Tom felt a bead of sweat drip from his armpit. He was nervous. Choe, sitting on the chair right beside him, his head buried in some notes, seemed perfectly at ease.

When finally admitted to the inner office, Tom noticed Ted Graziola sitting on one side of the room. Graziola rose, as did Dulles, and made introductions. After a brief exchange of small talk, Choe began explaining in detail what the Korean exile government was seeking— a long list including funds for training, communication equipment, small arms, anti-tank weapons, howitzers—enough to field at least three full infantry divisions.

"Even if we could provide you with all that stuff, why should we?" queried Dulles puffing on his pipe. "Our government isn't going to just arm you and let you barge back into Korea and start a war."

"We don't intend to start a war, Mr. Dulles," said Choe. "But a war is coming, we're quite certain of it."

"What do you mean? I know Koreans have been making trouble in Japan with assassinations and bombings. But they can deal with that. You're in the same boat as the Chinese Nationalists on Taiwan. They want to return to the mainland and are hoping for a war to start. But your people are on Okinawa. That's part of Japan, and the Japanese people aren't going to want to have a standing army on their territory for an indefinite period. We're already making plans to relocate your people to other areas. Isn't that right, Mr. Crandall?"

"Yes sir. That's right," said Tom.

"We don't plan to have an army in Okinawa for a long time. We realize we can't stay there forever," said Choe. "But war will come within the next year. That's what we believe,"

"How? What gives you that idea?"

"It will start over *Daemado*. Kim Il Sung wants it, and we have information that he will soon invade that island to take it back."

"*Daemado*? What's that?"

"You may know the name better as Tsushima Island in the Sea of Japan."

"Tsushima? That's an issue that we decided several years ago when Rhee was in charge in the South. I remember the South Koreans made a claim over that island, MacArthur's staff considered it, and decided it's rightfully Japan's territory—has been for more than a thousand years—and Rhee accepted it."

"What President Rhee agreed to means nothing to the people running Choson today."

"Why would they start a war over an island that the Japanese have occupied for centuries?"

"During Rhee's campaign to put down Communist resistance on Cheju-do and Cholla-do many people feared they would be killed for siding with the Communists and fled to Tsushima where some Koreans already had roots. Now they are claiming that they are being oppressed by the Japanese. It's a perfect excuse. Remember Hitler's takeover of the Sudetenland?"

"Of course. But this isn't the same. The Japanese have occupied that island for centuries. Korea knows they're not going to just give it up. And we just signed a security agreement with Japan."

"Yes, but the United States left Korea without fighting for it. And Japan has no army and has a constitution that outlaws war. Kim Il Sung sees this as a perfect opportunity. He doesn't believe that the United States or Japan will fight. I believe you will. And if war comes, you will be glad to have our help."

"Hmm—you make a good case Mr. Choe." Tapping ashes from his pipe into a silver tray, Dulles said, "I can't make any promises...but if we were able to come up with some type of aid package, it wouldn't be directly in military hardware; it would be dollars. You would have to purchase your own equipment on the open market—I'm sure your people are aware of the non-government sources for such things."

"Yes, of course. If we receive the money, that's all we'll need."

Dulles looked over at Graziola, "Ted, I want you to get a team together, go out to Okinawa, meet with their leadership, and see if a plan can be worked out. We'll need to have our people get with Ambassador Murphy to get his read on this too."

As they left the office, Tom noticed a sense of satisfaction on his friend's face. *Nothing's set in stone, but there's a good chance he's going to get what he came for. If war comes, it'll be a bargain to arm the Koreans. If it doesn't, no one except a few people in government will ever know where the money went.*

CHAPTER 23

LOVE AND SEPARATION

November 1952

Sitting alone in the tearoom, Soon Hi stirred another teaspoon of sugar into her second cup of black tea. Taking a cautious sip, she looked out the rain-streaked window and watched the people going by, all hunched over under a cold November drizzle. A ragged vendor on the corner appeared to be selling out his stock of flimsy plastic umbrellas that would almost certainly disintegrate before the buyers got home.

Chae Hoon had said he'd meet her at five o'clock and it was already five thirty. She was starting to worry, and then she saw him come in the doorway, shaking water from his clothes. She waved at him and he came over, took off his jacket, and sat down with a broad grin on his face. She said stiffly, "You're late, and *I'm* not smiling."

"Sorry honey. I can't help it. Got some great news today."

"What news?"

"I just came from a meeting and learned that the U.S. is giving us five million dollars for our army. When we started this business right after the evacuation, there was an expectation that we would go back to Korea within a few months to continue the fight. Morale was high. But after two years the Okinawans want us gone, and we'd just about given up hope. We know the Americans have been talking to President Yi about disbanding his army and relocating the soldiers to other places. But now, with this new American support, we won't have to. We're going to reclaim Korea."

Soon Hi had a frown on her face. "It may make you happy. But not me. I don't want to see another war. My brothers are over there."

"This wouldn't be a new war. It'd be a continuation of the war we didn't finish. Kim isn't going to stop his efforts to turn Japan Communist. There's going to be war. And when it comes, we're going to finish what they started. When it's all over, I'll come for you and take you back to Korea."

Soon Hi stared down at the table, saying nothing.

"What's the matter? Don't you know I love you? Don't you want to go back to Korea?"

Soon Hi looked up at him, tears welling up in her eyes. "Of course I want to go back—more than anything, but...isn't there some other way?"

"No, either we fight our way back, or we give up on returning to Korea. Kim Il Sung isn't going to change his attitude toward people like us. You used to work for the Americans. They're not going to ignore that. This will be our one chance to take back our homeland and help to make it free. I need to be part of that. Don't you see?"

"I do, but...you said you love me, and I love you too. I'm afraid you'll be killed. Then what's this worth to our future?"

"I don't intend to die. I intend for us to spend a long life together. But I have to do this."

He took her hand, "Please don't worry. Nothing's going to happen to me."

She wiped tears from her eyes. "I understand why you feel the way you do. I just wish it didn't have to be this way."

After a moment of silence Chae Hoon tried to break the tension. "Let's get out of here. I'll take you to a good restaurant tonight. We should be celebrating, not crying."

Knowing how much Soon Hi loved seafood, he took her to a small restaurant off a main thoroughfare in Shibuya where he'd been a couple times before. Although most of the tables were occupied, he found a table near the rear of the restaurant. Japanese flute music and low lighting lent a dream-like air to their corner of the room. Surrounded by beautiful floral plantings and decorative bamboo panels, she felt as if they were completely alone in a secluded garden. For an hour and a half Soon Hi was able to put aside her fears of the future and enjoyed being with the man she felt closer to than anyone. And when the meal was finished, she didn't want the night to end.

On the taxi ride back to her apartment Chae Hoon suggested that, since it was only eight thirty, they go to his apartment to spend some time together before he had to take her home. Soon Hi thought about how to respond, and then, giving in to her emotions, said, "My mother is away this weekend visiting her sister in Kawasaki. We can go to my apartment if you like. I can fix some tea."

Chae Hoon waited a moment before replying, not wanting to appear over-eager. Finally he said, "Sounds good to me," and then directed the driver to her address.

It was chilly in the apartment when they entered. Normally Soon Hi's mother would have had the heat on, but since she was gone, there was nothing but the residual floor heat from the shop below. After taking off their coats, Soon Hi pointed out where the spare kerosene was for the space heater. While Chae Hoon tended to the heater, Soon Hi went to the kitchen, turned on the small electric stove—nothing more than a two burner hotplate, and began boiling a pot of tea. After a few minutes she came back into the living room with a platter of sliced apples and pears along with a pot of steaming tea, setting it down in front of Chae Hoon who sat cross- legged on the floor close to the heater. She kneeled down, poured his tea, and then offered him a slice of pear before sitting down herself and filling her tea cup.

For a while, they talked nostalgically about Korea as it was, about what had happened to them since leaving Korea. Chae Hoon told her, "I've dated several girls before, but you're the first girl I've ever been in love with."

She blushed when he told her. Did he mean what he said? She told him about Tom, how he'd helped her and how he'd helped get In Su out of jail, but she didn't tell him everything. She rose to her feet and picked up the cups to take them to the kitchen.

"It's getting late," she said. "You probably should go."

Chae Hoon followed her to the kitchen and put his arms around her from behind. "I don't want to leave tonight," he said, turning her around to face him.

She touched his face with her hands. "I want you to stay too. But I think we should wait. We need to be sure of our feelings."

"I am sure of my feelings," he said. "That won't change. And what about you?"

"I—I do love you—with all my heart," she said. This time she had no doubts about her feelings. The only doubt she had was whether she should commit herself wholly to him tonight.

He lowered his face to hers and they kissed. She pulled away and began walking into the living room. "You said you love me, but what do you mean by that? Is it only because you're lonely now? What of the future?"

Quickly moving in front of her he grabbed her by the shoulders. "I want you forever, Soon Hi. I want you for my wife. But the future is uncertain, and I think marriage has to wait for a while until things are more settled—maybe six months, a year at the most. Can you wait that long?"

Hearing those words reassured her. "Yes, I can wait. I just needed to know you'll come back for me."

"I will. I promise." He picked her up, twirled her around, and kissed her. Tripping over a cushion, he lost his balance and fell awkwardly to the floor, cushioning Soon Hi's fall with his body. They laughed and rolled over, he ending up on top of her. Stifling his laugh, he looked down at her. "I want you more than anything Soon Hi. I'm not sure what the future holds. I just know I don't want to wait to make love to you. But if that's what you want…"

Gazing up at him she hesitated. "I won't make you wait. I know you love me."

He pushed himself off her, stood up, and helped her to her feet. She touched his arm and said, "Wait here while I get undressed." She went to her mother's room and closed the door.

Chae Hoon sat back down on one of the cushions and waited. When she called him, he went to the door and slid it open slowly. She was lying motionless like a porcelain doll covered by a thin blanket up to her chin. Her eyes followed him as he took off his clothes. When he removed his underpants and stood over her, she gasped and playfully pulled the blanket up over her eyes. He knelt next to the futon and slowly removed the blanket to reveal Soon Hi in her full nakedness. He laid down beside her, caressing her small rounded breasts. Her nipples grew erect, and his lips softly settled over one and then the other, while the tips of his fingers gently explored the nether parts of her slender body. After a period of foreplay, as tenderly as he could, he pushed himself inside her. She let out a short cry and then began to move rhythmically with him. After several minutes, breathing heavily, her body slick with perspiration, an intense surge of electricity coursed through her entire body. She let out a low moan, and almost simultaneously Chae Hoon did the same. They kissed and fell apart, staring at the ceiling, their hands touching, taking in what had just happened.

.   .   .

When Soon Hi opened her eyes, the first hint of dawn was visible through the bedroom window. She looked at Chae Hoon who was still sleeping. She knew her mother would be aghast. But she loved him, and she feared for what the future might hold. She wasn't going to worry about old mores. She leaned over to kiss him, and he opened his eyes, put his arms around her, and pulled her on top of him. After the previous night's experience, she wanted more and so did he. She slowly lowered herself onto him, and they began to make love with even more fervor than before. After finishing, they fell back to sleep until awakened by the clatter of traffic and voices in the street outside their window. Soon Hi got up, and after taking a bath, started preparing breakfast. Chae Hoon got up only when called by the irresistible smell of the spicy pot of *jjigei* coming to a boil in the kitchen. After he left, Soon Hi spent the rest of the morning cleaning up the apartment, hoping her mother wouldn't suspect that she'd had a visitor.

.   .   .

One morning, just after finishing breakfast, Soon Hi felt sick to her stomach and went to the toilet and threw up what she'd eaten. Since she felt better after getting rid of what was in her stomach, she didn't think any more of it, and went on to work. However, the next morning it happened again. Her mother noticed and urged her to go to the pharmacy on the corner and get some pills for her stomach. She told her mother she would, but she didn't. When she got to work she talked to Myong Shin, who was fully aware of her relationship with Chae Hoon.

"How long has it been since you last saw Chae Hoon?"

"About a month, I think."

"And you haven't had your regular period?"

"No."

"You need to go see Dr. Yi and have a test done. You might be pregnant."

"But it was only that one time?"

"It doesn't matter. It just takes once."

The next day after getting the test results back, Dr. Yi called her over into his office. She sat down and waited for him to pull out her file.

"Congratulations, Miss Chung. You're going to have a baby."

Soon Hi tried to smile, pretending it was good news, but she started to cry. *How will Chae Hoon react? Will he keep his promise? Will he use this an excuse to run away?*

She received her answer the next weekend when he came to her apartment to pick her up for supper. They walked to a familiar neighborhood restaurant near her apartment. Neither said much on the way. She noticed that he seemed even less talkative than usual.

"What's bothering you? You don't seem yourself," she said.

"I got a call today from Colonel Park. I'm being ordered to Camp Fuji in two weeks."

Soon Hi dropped her head. "Oh, I hoped you wouldn't have to go at all. I...."

"I know there's something else on your mind. What is it?"

"I...I'm pregnant, Chae Hoon."

He stopped in mid-stride, grabbing her by the hand. "What? What did you say?"

"I said I'm pregnant. I guess I'm unlucky, she said with downcast eyes."

"Unlucky? I think it's wonderful," he said laughingly while picking her up off her feet, drawing stares from passers-by.

When her feet hit the ground she started laughing too. When they got to the restaurant Chae Hoon asked her if she was sure, and she told him about her meeting with the doctor.

"This changes everything," he said. "We'll have to get married before I leave. Do I need to get down on my knees? Will you?"

"Will I? Yes, yes, of course."

After hastily finishing their meal, they returned to the apartment and confronted Soon Hi's mother together. Chae Hoon explained that they planned to be married right away because of his new assignment. Soon Hi had the embarrassing task of telling her mother she was pregnant, a revelation that she took surprisingly well, cushioned by the fact her daughter was marrying the father.

A week after the wedding Soon Hi stood on the platform of the Shinjuku train station and waved as he set off on his military assignment, not knowing when, or if, she would see him again.

CHAPTER 24

TSUSHIMA

February 1953

On March 1, 1953 artillery guns of the Chinese People's Army began bombarding the small off-shore island of Quemoy, still garrisoned by Chinese Nationalist forces. Was it a signal the Communists were about to attack Chiang Kai Shek's bastion on Formosa? A month earlier, President Eisenhower had ordered the withdrawal of the Seventh Fleet from the Taiwan Strait under pressure from the Republican Party's right wing. After a hastily called meeting of the National Security Council, the fleet was ordered to return to the strait to prevent any invasion of the Nationalist held island.

Eight hundred miles to the north, while American eyes were focused on Taiwan, four figures clad in black wetsuits slipped into the sea from the side of a silent midget submarine less than a mile off the northern tip of the Japanese island of Tsushima. On most regional maps Tsushima appears as a single cigar shaped island. But it's actually a compact island group composed of two major islands, Kamino-shima and Shimono-shima which are separated by a jagged, sometimes narrow, waterway with many small islets dotting its winding course.

It was a dark moonless winter night, the temperature just above freezing, as the four intruders waded unseen onto the shore of Sasuna Bay. One separated from the others and headed for a lighthouse sitting on a nearby promontory. A night watchman dozed in his quarters at the base of the lighthouse tower, unaware when a shadow passed behind him with a wire garrote and tightened it around his neck. He struggled briefly and then collapsed dead.

While the lone frogman took care of the lighthouse watchman, the three others proceeded another three miles down the shoreline towards the village of Sasuna where fishing boats bobbed peacefully in the harbor. Two policemen, sharing the night shift, sat playing cards in the dimly lit station. A rap on a window brought one of them to his feet, pistol in hand, to check out the noise. Behind him the door flew open and two figures with blackened faces rushed in. Surprised, he turned toward the door and began to raise his gun, but before he could get a shot off, a burst of bullets from a Soviet AK-47 nearly cut him in half. The second policeman ran to the wall where a telephone hung, but as he put his hand on the receiver, a nine inch bayonet blade chopped through his wrist like a guillotine. He looked at the stump at the end of his arm and opened his mouth to scream, but nothing came out as the knife blade sliced through his windpipe. He fell to the floor, blood gushing from his throat.

As the rest of the island slept, a signal lamp flashed from the light house, and as dawn neared, four landing craft and a cargo vessel appeared out of the mist like huge whales. Sliding quietly into the bay, the landing craft settled unto a beach a few hundred yards above the village. A full battalion of camouflage clad soldiers flying the red, white, and blue banner of Choson spilled out and began securing the area. The cargo ship continued into the harbor and found a mooring site at the edge of the village. As local villagers came out to begin their day, they were awestruck to see foreign soldiers patrolling their streets and a huge cargo ship tied up at their docks unloading vehicles and crates of supplies. Seeing what they were up against, without any way to defend themselves, the residents offered no resistance.

Sasuna had been selected as an entry point by the invaders because, not only did it have a good harbor, but it also was the starting point for the only major road that ran the length of Tsushima Island. The island's interior was of little concern to the Koreans since it was heavily forested, mountainous, and sparsely populated. There was little police presence on the island other than a constable or two in the larger towns along the highway. By mid-morning the Koreans began moving south along the highway leaving a token military presence in each town they passed through. By nightfall the Koreans had established control of all the population centers along Route 382 without losing a single soldier to hostile fire.

Tsushima's local government was quartered in Izuhara, located on the southeast corner of Shimono-shima, about a hundred thirty miles from the Japanese island of Kyushu. It was early evening when Mayor Suzuki finally got word of the invasion by a frantic call from a townsman on the upper island, Kamino-shima. The size and intent of the invading force was unclear. Suzuki immediately contacted his chief of police, Kato Hamaguchi, directed him to go to Kamino-shima and to report back what he found. Hamaguchi set out that night with six officers. When he reached the channel separating the two islands he saw through his binoculars Korean soldiers encamped on an island in the channel and others on the opposite shore. He estimated their numbers to be in the hundreds. Early the next morning, after hearing Hamaguchi's report, Mayor Suzuki sent a radiogram to the prefectural governor in Nagasaki, advising him that Koreans had invaded his island, and asking for immediate military assistance. This set off a flurry of bureaucratic activity both at the prefectural level and the national level.

During the early stages of the American occupation the Japanese were barred from establishing anything resembling an army. To maintain internal order municipalities were allowed to set up local police forces, but creation of a new national military force was prohibited. However, in June 1950, following the North Korean attack on South Korea and the sending of U.S. occupation forces to Korea, the Japanese government, with the approval of General MacArthur, established a 75,000 man National Police Reserve (NPR) plus a coastal safety force to provide some degree of defense against outside aggression as well as to assist in natural disasters at home. Following the peace treaty with the United States in 1951, the Japanese government increased the NPR force level to 110,000. However, until now, the government had not called on it to confront a foreign attack.

Upon notification of the Choson invasion, Kyushu governor Masatake immediately sent out a call to activate members of the NPR within his prefecture. At the same time he put in a call to the prime minister. Prime Minister Yoshida agreed they should send a contingent of soldiers to the island to protect the residents, but they should not engage the Koreans unless fired upon. Yoshida told the governor he wanted to negotiate their withdrawal and do everything he could to end things peacefully.

After hanging up the phone with the Nagasaki government, Yoshida put in a call to the American Embassy and reached Ambassador Murphy at his residence. Murphy agreed to meet the prime minister later that evening.

. . .

Meeting together at the prime minister's residence, Yoshida told the ambassador, "Our Tsushima has been invaded by the Koreans. This action seems to fall under our mutual security agreement. What action is the United States prepared to take in this situation?"

Murphy, through an interpreter, said, "I understand a territorial dispute is involved here. Because of that, I can't recommend any unilateral military action. I think it's something we need to go to the UN about and get a resolution for the Koreans to withdraw."

"There's no territorial dispute," said Yoshida. "You Americans decided several years ago that Tsushima belongs to us."

"Yes, we did. But the international community needs to make that decision now."

"But America has pledged to defend us. We have no army. We need you to honor that pledge."

"And we will," said Murphy. "But my government is not going to act alone. Japan needs to play a role in its own self-defense."

"That's not what our agreement was. Our constitution forbids creation of an army."

"Circumstances have changed Mr. Prime Minister. This is not just a fight between Japan and Korea. China is involved, and we know the Soviets had a role to play in this. Be assured. We won't abandon you, but we want to avoid World War III if possible. This is a matter for the entire free world to deal with."

Yoshida glanced at his foreign minister, Katsuo Okazaki, who was sitting off to the side, and nodded his head solemnly.

"I'll notify the secretary of state tonight, and we'll get this matter before the Security Council within a day," said Murphy.

After Murphy left, Yoshida turned to Okazaki. "What's the best way to reach out to Premier Kim? Who do we have here in Tokyo that can make that connection?"

"There are a number of Koreans here in Tokyo, but I think we should talk to a man named Kim Chon Hae. He used to head up the old Korean *Choren* Party. He now has a key position in *Kyosanto* (Japanese Communist Party). He likes to brag that Kim Il Sung and he are like brothers."

"Let's see how much of a brother he is. Let's talk to him. See if he wants to help."

. . .

Two days later, after efforts to negotiate directly with Kim Il Sung had failed, the ocean going ferry *Gosei Maru*, under cover of darkness, departed Fukuoka harbor with five hundred police reserves on board en route to Tsushima Island. The night was clear, the sea was calm, and the temperature hovered just above freezing. The one hundred and thirty mile crossing of the Tsushima Strait appeared to be an uneventful one for which Captain Takeo Yamada was grateful. His ship had only one fifty caliber machine gun to defend itself against enemy gunboats. After passing Iki Island, he ordered extra watches on deck to be on the lookout for enemy craft, but none were seen. As dawn approached and the hazy outline of the Tsushima coastline appeared on the horizon, he felt he could relax. Soon he would unload his cargo of men and vehicles and return to Fukuoka safely. Suddenly there was a huge boom, the ship rocked and the captain clung to the bulkhead. He hurried to the phone and called to the engine room.

"What was that? What happened?

Chief engineer Kimura responded, "It looks like we hit a contact mine. It blew a two foot hole in the cargo area and we've got two badly injured men. We're taking on water, but we're working to contain it. We should be able to make it to port without any problem. No damage to the engines."

"Good said Yamada. The harbor is only five miles away. We'll need to get some repairs before heading back."

Yamada put down the phone, and instructed his helmsman to veer thirty degrees to starboard before heading for port. A minute later a huge blast shook the ship as if it were a toy, throwing the Captain to the floor. As he struggled to get up, he felt the ship rolling violently from a shock wave. He reached for the phone. This time there was no answer from the engine room. A second mine had blown a large hole below the water line, completely destroying the engine room. Vehicles thrown loose from their moorings in the hold rolled to one side, causing the ship to list at a forty five degree angle. Sensing the ship was going down, the captain ordered all aboard to abandon ship. Because of the list, life boats could not be released and many of the soldiers were simply thrown into the cold murky sea.

. . .

Within thirty minutes the ship was gone. Fishing vessels from Tsushima were on the scene quickly, picking up survivors. Some were able to make it to drifting lifeboats, but most waited in the frigid water to be rescued. With the water temperature just above zero, many didn't make it. Of the 520 men on board, 190, including the ship's captain, lost their lives.

Although the bulk of the Choson invading force had not yet reached Izuhara, an advance element, learning of the sinking of the troop ship, was quickly sent ahead, took up positions at the port, and captured survivors as they came ashore. Eighty-five reservists were put under guard before fishermen were able to alert those coming in as to what was happening. Immediately the Japanese boats began steering clear of the harbor and dropped the survivors off in remote coves elsewhere along the coast.

The surviving police reservists who escaped capture were without any arms, the battalion commander was apparently lost at sea, and many survivors required medical attention. Those who were able discarded their uniforms and melted into the local population as best they could. Major Taro Kawabata, the second in command, began rounding up as many as he could and set off with a hundred thirty men into the rugged mountains. By the next morning the Koreans had taken complete control of the coastal areas of Shimono-shima and the Tsushima mayor formally surrendered to the Korean commander.

When word of the disaster off Tsushima reached the main islands of Japan, there was a universal outcry from public figures of every stripe for mobilization of an army to strike back. Prime Minister Yoshida, meeting before a joint session of the Diet rejected the call, saying he had no authority under the constitution to create an army or to make war against Choson. He told the members of the Japanese parliament, if the United States would not take action on their own, they must rely on the United Nations to take the necessary action to demand Choson's withdrawal. This met with angry retorts from Diet members, calling for his resignation.

Ichiro Hatoyama, a leading right wing member of the House of Representatives rose to speak before the assembly. Barred from participating in politics since 1945 because of his past relationship with militarists, the bar was lifted when the American occupation ended, and he'd run successfully for office in 1952. Until the invasion of Tsushima his views on rearmament had been in the minority, but his words were not in the minority on this day as he spoke forcefully before the parliamentary assembly.

"Since the end of the war we have endured the unendurable and survived," said Hatoyama. "Defeated in war we have had to accept the loss of lands that have long been a part of Japan. Sakhalin and the Kurile Islands have been lost to the Soviets. Okinawa is under American administration. When the war ended we were in no position to stop those great powers from taking control. Now the Koreans have invaded and taken over Tsushima. Soviet ships guard our northern borders. This is intolerable! Will Hokkaido be next? Where will this end? We must take action to defend our land."

Pointing to the prime minister who was sitting to the side, he shouted, "Prime Minister Yoshida refuses to act in the defense of our country claiming our constitution forbids it. He is wrong, and if he continues in this way, he will lead our nation to utter destruction. Even as it is written, that is not what the constitution intends. Japan has a moral right to defend itself like any other nation in the world. Because Mr. Yoshida has failed to stand up to these Korean invaders, he no longer deserves to lead this government. He must resign and allow those who will defend the nation to lead. We need a government that will rebuild our nation's strength—not to prey on other people—but to defend our lands and protect our own people."

When the speech was finished, the house members stood up as one and applauded for five minutes. The following morning Yoshida announced his resignation as prime minister and called on his colleagues to name a new leader. The next day, a joint session of the Diet overwhelmingly elected Ichiro Hatoyama as the new prime minister.

In the days following Hatoyama's election, left wing activists in the country stepped up their efforts to disrupt the government and demand removal of American bases from Japan. Sabotage incidents occurred almost every day. Two days before, a bomb had exploded at the entry to an American military base, killing four civilian passers-by. The next day there was a suspicious train derailment resulting in thirteen deaths on the Osaka-Tokyo line. Students were demonstrating at universities in Tokyo, Osaka, and Kobe, forcing the call-out of the police reserve. Hatoyama had long wanted to strengthen the nation's security forces, but up to now he'd been in no position to do anything about it. Under Yoshida's leadership, the party had taken the stand that any kind of military establishment would be a violation of the constitution.

In the face of the Korean occupation of Tsushima Island, public opinion polls reflected a change in the people's attitude about rearmament. Hatoyama's political supporters urged him to take political action to do something about the Tsushima matter. Even some of the moderate socialists came to change their view about limited rearmament for purposes of self-defense. Believing the time was now right, Hatoyama submitted a bill to the Diet proposing a law that would authorize the creation of a Japanese Self Defense Force—a real army that would replace the toothless police reserve. After three days of haggling within the House of Representatives, the Self-Defense Force Act was approved with near unanimity. On the following day, Hatoyama spoke before the House of Representatives with tears in his eyes and said, ""Once again Japan can hold its head high among nations."

CHAPTER 25

A TITAN

March 6–8, 1953

As he left his hotel room and headed for the elevator, Tom ran through his mind all that had happened in the three weeks since he'd returned to Japan. The invasion of Tsushima was a surprise; the Chinese action against Taiwan not so much. What worried him more was what the Soviet intentions were. They'd been no help at the UN—blocked the resolution calling for Choson's withdrawal from Tsushima. He'd seen reports that Soviet subs had been identified entering the Sea of Japan to bolster their Pacific Fleet. Then last week the announcement of Yoshida's resignation created more uncertainty. Tom was concerned about the new prime minister. Yoshida had been a steadying influence in Japanese politics and had been a good partner for the Americans to deal with during the transition. *The right wing military is going to be strengthened for sure. Is this the start of the next war?*

When he got down to the hotel lobby he noticed a stack of newspapers on the counter and picked up a copy. It happened to be the *Yomiuri Shimbun*. A picture of Josef Stalin on the front page caught his eye, and he stared at the headline, SOVIET PREMIER STALIN DEAD. *Wow. This could change everything.* He hurried outside with the paper in hand and caught a taxi to the embassy. It was seven thirty when he arrived. He went to the second floor cafeteria for some breakfast before going to the office. Slowly making his way through the line, he picked up a box of corn flakes, a carton of milk, a glass of juice, and looked for a table. He saw Ed Harper, the new deputy public affairs officer, sitting at a table with his nose in a newspaper. Tom picked up his tray and walked over.

"Mind if I have a seat Ed?"

Harper looked up. "Oh, hi Tom. No have a seat. I was just engrossed with this story."

Setting his tray down and pulling out a chair he said, "Yeah, that's something with Stalin dying. Looks like you're going to have a busy day ahead."

"Many busy days. But it's what I thrive on. I love the excitement of breaking news events like this. The ambassador has a meeting at nine with General Clark. He's the new Far East Commander who took over after MacArthur's retirement. There's a press conference at eleven. I'm sure that'll be a hot one. This afternoon he's got an appointment to meet Hatoyama."

"Do we have any idea who's in charge over there now with Stalin gone?"

"At this point, I doubt whether the Soviet Politburo knows who's in charge. TASS is saying Malenkov is the new premier, but that could change overnight. They might end up with some kind of collegial ruling group rather than one strongman."

"What's your gut feeling as to how this will impact our situation here?"

"It's hard to say. I know the Japanese are scared shitless the Russkies are going to use this situation with Tsushima to try to make a move on Hokkaido. They know if the war hadn't ended when it did, the Russians would have taken that island and more back in '45 and split the difference with the Americans, just like they did with Korea. We'll just have to see if that will change under new leadership. In any case, the change should give us some breathing room while they figure out who's in charge."

"This could really affect how we're going to deal with the Tsushima issue, don't you think?"

"It could," said Harper, as he looked at the clock on the wall, took a swig from his coffee cup, and jumped up from his chair. "I have an early staff meeting. Gotta go. Catch you later."

Tom finished his cereal and went downstairs to his first floor office. The consular section, easily accessible to the public, had a large window looking out onto the street. Passing by the front lobby he saw a line of people already queuing up. It was going to be another long day.

. . .

The death of Stalin had come as a surprise to leaders throughout the world, including those in the United States. When President Eisenhower convened his National Security Council for his regular Wednesday morning meeting, topic number one was the death of the long-time Soviet dictator. As the president entered the cabinet room, everyone around the table stood up. Taking his seat between Secretary of State Dulles and Defense Secretary Charles Wilson, he nodded for everyone to sit down before making a few opening remarks regarding the significance of Stalin's death. Then he turned to Allen Dulles, sitting at the end of the table. "Allen, go ahead and give us the CIA assessment as to what Stalin's death means for us internationally."

Dulles opened his briefing book, cleared his throat, and said, "Thank you Mr. President. My agency has been working with the Intelligence Advisory Committee over the past several days to develop a sound estimate. Based on our analysis we expect this transfer of power is going to be a difficult one for the Soviets. There could be some internal upheavals that could affect their posture towards the United States. Stalin has been in power for almost thirty years—ever since the death of Lenin. There is no precedent for the peaceful transfer of power within the Soviet Union. However, it appears the Soviets have taken an important first step by transferring governmental authority to Georgy Malenkov. Because of the speed with which this transfer has been accomplished, we believe the leaders around Stalin had some idea this could occur—may have anticipated if not abetted his death— and had prepared well in advance for the change."

Pausing for a moment to see if the president had any questions, Eisenhower simply nodded for him to continue.

"Malenkov has held key positions in the Communist Party for many years," said Dulles. "He's played a prominent role within the party since 1948. Given the praises laid on him at Stalin's funeral, he appears to have the backing of the party leadership, and we don't see any immediate challenges. Of course, he's always operated in the past with Stalin's backing, and just how that will play out in the future we can't predict. A struggle within the Communist hierarchy could develop at any time, but we don't think it's likely to threaten the hold the Communist Party has over the country."

Eisenhower raised his hand to interrupt. "Do you see any change in their approach to the U.S.?"

"Malenkov has indicated in statements made through TASS that he wants to reduce tensions with the West and avoid war. In the long run, though, we think the Soviets will continue their efforts to expand their influence in the world through whatever means necessary. The most dangerous area for us now is the Asian Far East where the Soviets backed the North Korean takeover of the Korean peninsula, and they continue to support them in their invasion of the Japanese island of Tsushima. Within Japan itself they're giving financial support to the Japanese Communist Party. We believe the Far East is where we need to focus our attention."

"Thank you Mr. Dulles." Eisenhower then turned to his Secretary of Defense. "Charlie, what's our situation in Japan now that Hatoyama has taken over as prime minister? What are we doing to get ready if the situation with Tsushima blows up? And what about the Chinese?"

Wilson glanced down at a point paper before addressing the group. "Currently the Seventh Fleet has taken up a position in the Taiwan Strait to curtail any effort by either side to start something. As for Japan, Prime Minister Hatoyama, in contrast to Mr. Yoshida, is much more willing for Japan to take on a bigger role in their defense. Last week the Japanese Diet passed new legislation called the Self Defense Force Law that authorized the creation of a legitimate military force capable of putting up a fight, although, right now, it wouldn't stand a chance against a major power like the Soviets or even the Chinese Reds. When the Koreans sank their ship last month in the Sea of Japan, the resistance to Japanese rearmament kind of crumbled. I'm going to let General Collins talk in more depth about our own military preparedness."

"Thank you Mr. Secretary," said Lawton Collins, the Army chief of staff. "It's been the Army's position ever since the Chinese takeover on the mainland that the Japanese need to be able to defend themselves. With this new law and the willingness of Hatoyama to work with us, we can expect a significant upgrade in Japan's defense capability over the next year. American strength currently within the Far East Command is just over 110,000. The army has the 24th Infantry and elements of the 7th Infantry Division in Japan. The 1st Marine Division is in Okinawa, and the Fifth Air Force has both a fighter wing in Japan and a bomber wing in Okinawa. The Seventh Fleet of course has a task force still occupying the Taiwan Strait. We're prepared to deal with any immediate threat, but if general war breaks out, we need Japan to step up and defend itself. We think they're ready to do that now."

Pushing his glasses to the top of his head, Eisenhower asked, "What do you think the effect of this new law will have on their force structure?"

Referring to his notes Lawton said, "Last year, after the May Day riots and the bombing of the American ship in Tokyo Bay, the Japanese government agreed to expand the NPR to 110,000 and create a National Safety Agency (NSA). They aren't quite there yet, but with this new law, they're planning to grow their military force to 300,000 within two years. At present they have little in the way of heavy weaponry. But last December we implemented an intergovernmental agreement with Japan and began transferring some of our excess from the last war—howitzers, some medium and light tanks, mortars, as well as lighter arms suitable for infantry. We've also transferred a dozen ships to the Maritime Safety Force— that includes six of our older destroyers.

"What are we doing about training and joint operations?" the president queried.

"Last December we set up a combined command with their National Safety Agency. We've sent over fifty military advisers to train them on the new equipment, and we've brought at least ten of their senior and mid-level officers to the War College and C&GS School for training here in the U.S. We've been war gaming several scenarios with them and have a joint exercise planned with them for later this month. I also should note that the Korean exile army—a 30,000 man force made up of former ROK soldiers—has been participating in training exercises with the Marines on Okinawa. If we do go to war, those ROKs will play into our OPLAN."

"Hmm. It sounds like we've got our ducks in order. What do you think the likelihood is that this thing in Tsushima will widen into a larger war?" And if it does, what are the Russians going to do?"

"We have a security agreement with Japan to help defend them in the event of an invasion, and in reality, that's already happened, although Japan has not invoked the treaty. Currently the situation on Tsushima seems to be at a standstill. The Koreans have taken effective control of the populated areas of the island, but there are some guerilla units in the interior that we've been supplying with air drops. The situation over Formosa also appears to be at a standoff right now. Last week we saw a squadron of Soviet submarines move into the Sea of Japan which could have meant they were preparing to challenge us over control of that body of water. But after Stalin's death, it appears the new leadership wants to avoid any confrontation. The submarines have apparently returned to their home base on the Kamchatka Peninsula. With respect to the whole Asia-Pacific Theater, we're in a wait and see mode right now."

"Thank you," said Eisenhower before turning to his right, "Mr. Dulles, I'd like to hear the State Department's views on what's just been said."

Adjusting his glasses on his nose the senior Dulles stood up. "As we've heard from my brother, there are momentous changes going on within the leadership of the Soviet Union—and that's all true. However, the nature of communism and the goals of communism have not changed, and they will not change by themselves. The Soviet Union has vetoed our efforts through the United Nations to demand the withdrawal of the Koreans from Tsushima. They are intent on expanding their ideology throughout Asia and the world. President Truman had the idea we could limit their expansion through what he called a policy of containment. Where has that led us? The Communists have succeeded in extending their odious system to Eastern Europe, to China, to Korea and now seek to add Japan. Containment hasn't worked." Crimson faced and leaning forward with his fists on the table, Dulles said loudly, "The Reds have pushed us around since the end of the war. If we don't demonstrate our will to fight, Japan could be lost. The Philippines could be lost. We need to PUSH BACK."

He then said more calmly, "The death of Stalin has created an opportunity for us to reexamine our approach, and to take a more aggressive stance against the Communist aggressors and to free those people who have been swallowed up by the Red giant. The Soviets, for a short period at least, will not want to enter into any conflict with us. Now is the time for us to use this to our advantage. I hope you will take this into consideration Mr. President."

Eisenhower lowered his head, taking in what Dulles had said. "Thank you for your observations and recommendations Mr. Dulles. I do recognize the threat the Communists pose to the world, but I don't intend to be the first to break a peace. If directly challenged and called upon, however, I am prepared to fight for what we believe in and to defend our allies with all that we have."

CHAPTER 26

THE ULTIMATUM

April 1953

In the wee hours of April 15, the Japanese destroyer escort Asahi passed Shita Point on the northeast coast of Tsushima. This was Captain Ariaki's second night on a mission to watch for and intercept any boats coming from Choson that might be trying to smuggle in supplies to their forces on Tsushima. Sighting a suspicious vessel two miles in the distance, the captain ordered the helmsman to steer toward it at top speed, unaware that nearby a steel gray predator, a Soviet Shchuka Class submarine manned by a Korean crew, lurked silently below the ocean's surface waiting to pounce. Suddenly a watchman on the Asahi called to the bridge, "Torpedo to port side at ten o'clock!" Ariaki, still asleep in his quarters, was awakened by an explosion that rolled him out of his bunk. He rushed to the bridge to learn the ship had been struck amidships, creating a hole the size of a small car. The surging seawater caused the boilers to explode, killing the crewmen in the compartment. A fire control team quickly sealed off the area, and the chief reported to the bridge that the area was secured.

The ship's engines were undamaged and Ariaki ordered the helmsman to swerve to take evasive action to try to avoid any further hit. Too late—BA-ROOM. A second torpedo slammed into the aft section hitting the ships magazine compartment. The resulting blast tore through the main deck creating a fiery inferno topside that soon engulfed half the ship. After frantic minutes trying to put out the fire, the captain ordered the ship evacuated. A Mayday call was sent out

211

by radio, but Ariaki knew there was no help nearby. Although life boats were lowered, only about half the crew made it into them before the ship went down amidst flaming oil slicks. Only 130 of the 245 man crew made it safely to shore. Those who did make it were quickly rounded up by enemy patrols and taken to a dismal concentration camp on Kamino-shima to join others who had been captured earlier.

When word of the sinking of the Japanese ship and loss of life was received in Tokyo the following day, a cry of outrage was heard throughout the country. This time the Japanese Diet took decisive action. After receiving assurance from the American government that they would back them, Japan issued an ultimatum to the Choson government through the Indian Embassy: *Begin the withdrawal of your forces from Tsushima within seven days, or Japan will initiate action to remove you by force of arms.*

• • •

Tom hadn't had a chance to look at the morning paper before he walked into the employee lounge to get his first cup of coffee. Several people were chattering excitedly.

"What's the big news today? Did the Russians announce they're giving up communism?"

"Haven't you heard" said one. "The Japanese have given the Koreans an ultimatum. Get out of Tsushima or get kicked out. It looks like the Japanese are ready to fight."

"No kidding?" He saw a copy of the *Stars and Stripes* laying on a chair, picked it up, and scanned the headline and first paragraph of the article. "It's true. They gave the Koreans seven days. They're not going to give it up voluntarily."

Tom filled his coffee cup and went to his office without saying anything more. He sat down at his desk to consider what this all could mean for his personal plans. He'd been in country just a month and a half and one of the things he intended to do was to try to look up Soon Hi, but he'd been avoiding it. Maybe she didn't want to see him again. But there was something still tugging at him to see her again. Was she still working at the clinic? He needed to find out, and now was the time to do it. He put down his cup and went across the hall and knocked on Kate Keeler's office door. Kate, who had been his co-worker in Korea, now was the vice counsel and his direct supervisor.

"Good morning Kate. Sorry to interrupt but I wanted to ask if I can take off from work a couple hours early this afternoon on some personal business."

She glanced up from the paper she was reading. "You know your schedule better than I do. Go ahead if you don't have anything pressing."

Tom left the office at three. He still remembered the location of the clinic food bank where she last worked. Arriving by taxi, he found the building unchanged from before. Entering the front door he saw a woman at the counter waiting on a customer. He waited to ask her if Soon Hi still worked there when he heard a familiar voice coming from the back room. Looking pretty as ever, but a little heavier than when he'd last seen her, she came up to the counter and began to say something. Then she recognized him. She gave out a cry of surprise and came out from behind the counter with a big smile on her face. As she came up to him, he saw why she looked heavier—she was several months pregnant.

Uncertain at first how to react, he gave her a gentle hug, then looked down at her belly and stammered, "You, you look great. When's the baby due?"

She laughed. "In three months. I'm sorry I didn't write and tell you I married."

"Well congratulations, I'm happy for you."

"You're not angry at me?

"Oh no. I felt bad at first when you told me you couldn't marry me, but I got over it. I've dated other girls."

"You didn't married?"

"No, the girl I was seeing in the states wasn't the marrying type, but when my time comes, I'll find a girl whose right for me, just like you found the right guy. Is your husband here in Tokyo?"

She shook her head back and forth. "No. He's at some army camp near Mount Fuji. He's an officer with New Republic of Korea Army. I think you know about it."

"Oh. Yes. I remember you told me before. Do you expect him to be able to come here for the birth of the baby?"

"I hope so, but I'm worried because of what's happening with Tsushima. Do you think there'll be a war?"

"I don't know. I *do* know the Americans are trying to work through the United Nations to get Choson to withdraw. We need to wait to see what happens there. You have a right to be concerned, but hopefully it will all blow over. Whatever happens, I want you to know you have a friend at the American Embassy, and if you need anything, call on me. For tonight, I'd like to take you to supper and help feed that little tyke growing inside you."

She smiled and said, "Yes, I can go. I'd like that."

. . . .

Three days after the sinking of the Japanese destroyer, the United Nations General Assembly issued a condemnation of the Choson regime for its continued occupation of Tsushima. It had no effect. With Japanese patrols in the Korea Strait suspended, Kim Il Sung's response was to shuttle an additional four battalions of ground troops across the narrow strait. That brought the total number of Choson military on the little island to more than eight thousand. An editorial in the *Nodong Sinmun* (Worker's Daily), addressed to the Japanese people, scoffed at the Japanese claims to the island. It called instead for the Japanese people to embrace the socialist revolution and to throw out all those who side with the American imperialists."

. . . .

Japanese Prime Minister Hatoyama, fully aware that his newly created self-defense force did not have the capability to dislodge the Choson military from Tsushima, decided the time had come to call on the United States to honor its security commitment. After meeting with key cabinet and Diet members, he made a formal request to the United States for military assistance under provisions of the Japan-U.S. Security Treaty.

Before replying to the Japanese request, President Eisenhower sent a message to the new Soviet Premier Malenkov in a last ditch effort to try to get the Korean Communists to the negotiating table. Two days later Soviet Ambassador Zarubin delivered Malenkov's response, telling the American president, in effect, that the Soviet Government had wiped its hands clean of Choson and didn't want to get involved. He said it was a matter to be resolved between the Koreans and the Japanese. Like a hot potato, the problem was thrown back into Eisenhower's lap.

Later that evening Eisenhower met with his National Security Council in the White House cabinet room. There was little disagreement over what needed to be done. Addressing General Bradley, he said, "Where do we stand on implementing the OPLAN?"

"Phase one is set to go. Phase two is in its final stages of preparation and will depend on Choson's response."

"What about China. How do we expect them to react if the fighting starts?"

"We've still got an aircraft carrier and a destroyer squadron patrolling the Taiwan Strait and we don't see any evidence that they've built up their forces in the past couple weeks. I don't think they're ready to start anything with us."

"All right. I'm going to sign off on this agreement understanding that the initial phase will be limited to Tsushima with Japanese ground troops. If the Koreans attack our ships, then I'll consider implementing the second phase."

The next day Eisenhower met with key members of Congress and informed them of his decision to provide air and naval support to Japan in its effort to oust Choson forces from Tsushima. He also advised them that he was implementing a naval blockade in the Korea Strait to prevent Choson from reinforcing their troops by sea. There was no dissent.

CHAPTER 27

PUSH BACK

May 1953

The skies were clear over Tsushima on the early morning of May 15 as barelegged farmers standing in rice paddies and fishermen setting out to the open sea on their fishing boats, lifted their eyes to the thrumming sound of aircraft high overhead. As antiaircraft fire opened up from shoreline batteries, offshore destroyers manned by newly trained Japanese sailors began firing salvos at targeted Communist positions. In the distance parachutes could be seen coming down like raindrops as a dozen C-119 Flying Boxcars began dropping crates of supplies, ammunition, and weapons into the mountainous interior where they would be picked up by guerilla fighters still holding out against the Choson invaders.

When he made the decision to invade Tsushima, Kim Il Sung was counting on the Soviet Union to back him up. He had signed a security agreement with them. However, with Stalin's death, he could no longer count on their help. The new Soviet leadership had recalled its advisors and told Kim he was on his own. Despite this setback, Kim was still confident that Japan, with its public committed to pacifism and their government facing protests in the streets, would not put up a fight over Tsushima. Now it appeared he had miscalculated.

Later that night four frigates, former U.S. Navy ships recently transferred to the new Japanese Maritime Self-Defense Force, entered the narrow channel dividing the two major islands of Tsushima. Moving undetected amidst the channels many islets, four battalions of

Japanese soldiers, more than 3,000 men, were lowered into boats and put ashore on the southern island of Shimono-shima where they quickly sought out and overpowered unsuspecting enemy outposts. In the morning, aided by guerillas who had already scouted the area thoroughly, they split up into two separate forces, one attacking and overpowering a battalion sized post at Mitsushima and the second group surrounding the Garrison headquarters at the port city of Izuhara. With the U.S. Navy patrolling the sea around Tsushima, Colonel Bang Yu Gu, commander of all KPA (Korean People's Army) forces on the southern island, realized he was trapped, and on May 18, he agreed to surrender to the Japanese.

The KPA still held the northern Tsushima island of Kamino-shima. Only thirty miles of ocean separated it from the southeastern coast of the Korean peninsula, and the stranded Choson commander maintained hope that reinforcements from the mainland would soon arrive. On the night of May 20, under a moonless cloudy sky, two destroyers and three patrol frigates of the U.S. Navy maintained their regular picket line midway between Pusan and the northern tip of Tsushima to block any attempts by Choson to funnel in reinforcements. On the patrol frigate USS Tacoma, radar man Paul Pollard stared at his screen. Two blinking blips, then four, then eight. As the blips grew larger signaling they were drawing closer he called out, "Chief! Come look at this I'm not sure what we've got."

Chief Petty Officer Rollins came over, peered over Pollard's shoulder, and said, "It looks like high speed torpedo boats, and their heading right for us." He called to the bridge to alert the captain, and a general alarm was given. Gunners sprang to their stations and ammo was readied for a potential attack. As the attacking torpedo boats neared, they fanned out and began circling the American ships like a pack of wolves surrounding their quarry. Because of the darkness, visual identification was difficult. Suddenly a torpedo, unseen by the lookouts, ripped into the hull of the USS Gallop, exploding with a roar. Seconds later a second torpedo struck the engine room of the three hundred foot long frigate, and it began to sink. Soon crews on two other ships were also fighting fires, but damage was not so severe as to threaten the ships themselves.

The two destroyers, Kidd and Bradford, responded to the torpedo attack by opening up with their deck guns into the darkness. One of the torpedo boats, made visible by bursting flares, was hit, and sunk. Two others were hit, but managed to limp away. As fast as the attack had begun, it was over, and the torpedo boats sped off to the northwest. Captain Richard Wells was about to order the entire squadron to pursue the escaping boats when he saw on radar a new set of blips, indicating larger ships heading their way from the northeast. It was clear to him then the torpedo attack was meant to lure them away so that the enemy supply convoy could pass by them and get to Tsushima.

Captain Wells ordered the destroyer USS Barton to pursue the torpedo boats, but the other frigates would remain on station to intercept the approaching convoy. As the lead ships of the convoy came into view, Wells sent out flare signals to order them to stop and identify themselves. When the convoy appeared to be changing course to avoid the picket, the USS Fairchild sent a shot from one of its five inch guns across the bow of the lead vessel. With this unmistakable signal of "We're not kidding," the convoy stopped, turned around, and headed back to the northeast.

The captain of the USS Barton reported later that night that he had sunk two of the escaping torpedo boats, and had taken some captives, but terminated the pursuit when he neared Chinhae Bay because of potential mine fields. On the American side, ten sailors were lost as a result of the sinking of the USS Gallop. It was the first loss of life for Americans in this new encounter with Communist Korea. It was, also, the trip wire for America to implement a new tougher policy in dealing with Communist aggressors in Asia.

. . .

Back in the West Wing of the White House, following notification of the attack on the American destroyers, the president huddled with his military chiefs and other key security advisers, including the two Dulles brothers.

Ike looked at his secretary of state. "Is Hatoyama on board with us?"

Dulles replied, "He's agreed to use Japanese flagged ships with civilian crews to transport the Koreans we've been training, but he won't commit Japanese troops to Korea. Even though he's been adamant about that in the Japanese press, the Reds aren't so sure, and we want to keep them guessing."

"Good. I think that's a smart move," said the president.

After querying each of the service chiefs in turn and receiving assurances that China and the Soviet Union were not going to intercede, Eisenhower slapped the table with the palms of his hands, and said emphatically, "Okay men. Operation Pushback is a go."

. . .

When the Joint Chiefs of Staff began making plans for returning to the Korean peninsula, General Bradley decided to dust off the plan developed in 1950 by General MacArthur in which he proposed to backdoor the Koreans with an amphibious landing at Inchon. It was still a good plan, General Bradley thought, but for its success, they needed to draw off KPA forces from the Seoul-Inchon area. When the plans were laid out, he was pretty confident they would accomplish just that, but now that the president had given the go ahead, he was beginning to have second thoughts. Would Kim Il Sung take the bait?

On May 28, just a week after the president made the decision to send U.S. forces back to the Asian mainland, Naval Task Force Nine led by the battleship Iowa and the aircraft carrier Kearsarge left Yokosuka Naval Base for the western coast of Korea. As the armada of ships rounded the southwest corner of the Korean peninsula they were joined by a second battle group out of Okinawa transporting a combined force of upwards of 35,000 including the 1st Marine Division and more than 20,000 South Korean soldiers. As the huge carrier group passed the island of Wido, the cruiser USS Toledo and several destroyers broke off from the main task force. They headed for Kunsan at the mouth of the Kum River where they intended to land a diversionary force of 5,000 Marines, hoping to draw KPA forces away from the main objective of Inchon further north. After battering the area around Kunsan harbor for two days, Brigadier General Lewis Puller led the Marine assault on Kunsan. . By June 2 they had captured the town and had established a thin line of defense three miles inland along the Kum River bank.

General Puller hoped to break through the enemy's coastal defenses before Communist reinforcements could arrive, but KPA General Mu Chong had fought the Americans successfully in the previous campaign in 1950. He wasn't about to give them an opening. Surveying his defensive positions five miles inland, he was confident he could keep the Americans boxed in along the shore. Turning to his aide, rubbing his thumb and forefinger together, he said, "Once the new divisions arrive from the north, I will squeeze the miserable Americans like a ripe pimple until the Kum River runs red with their blood."

American air and naval bombardment on enemy positions seemed to have had little impact on the Communists, as KPA artillery, well entrenched in the surrounding hills, maintained an almost continuous shelling of the tenuous American position. Despite the mounting death toll among his Marines, General Puller knew withdrawal was out of the question. If the Inchon landing were to succeed, his men had to hold out and draw more KPA forces south.

Within hours of the Marines landing at Kunsan, American ships began bombarding targets at Wonsan, Samchok, Pohang, and Ulsan on the eastern coast of the Korean peninsula. With KPA commanders trying to predict the Americans next move, the Americans, on June 3, finally struck where they were least expected, at Ulsan, forty miles north of Pusan. General Maxwell Taylor, recently installed as commander of the U.S. Eighth Army, watched from the bridge of his flagship, the USS St Paul, as a multitude of LSTs shuttled troops of the revamped 24th Infantry Division into Ulsan Bay where, after wading ashore, they were met by stiff resistance from Communist batteries defending the high ground on both sides of the narrow inlet. Twenty four hours after the initial landing by the Americans, the 5,000 man Korean *Zainichi* Brigade landed ashore where the fighting was still heavy.

Chae Hoon, leading a forty man infantry platoon, flopped down on the beach, and as bullets whizzed close by, he yelled for the men behind him to keep moving forward to reach the headland where several large boulders would provide some cover. Every so often someone would yell out that they'd been hit. He hoped it wasn't one of his men. He and several others hunkered down in a shell hole waiting for the firing to subside before moving further up the beach. As minutes turned to hours, the continuous cacophony of gunfire and explosions began to get to him, his head began to reverberate as if someone was using it as a drum. As he laid in a ditch with bullets and shrapnel flying around him, Chae Hoon felt disconnected from reality. He thought back to when he'd left Korea on an evacuation ship, how he feared he would never see his homeland again. He'd been dreaming for so long of returning, and now he was back. He clenched his teeth. *Is this how it ends? Will Soon Hi ever know?*

CHAPTER 28

INCHON

June 4–June 25, 1953

Meeting with his chief of staff, General Nam Il, at his headquarters in Seoul Kim Il Sung went into a rage when Nam informed him of the American landings at Kunsan and Ulsan.

"If Stalin were still alive," he shrieked, "the Americans would not dare to attack us like this. They think because we are small, we are weak. We will show them who is weak. We *must* stop them before they're able to establish any permanent foothold. We need to send everything we've got to the south now and destroy them to the last man. We can't allow the imperialists to foul our beautiful country again."

General Nam said, "We need to be cautious about vacating defensive positions here in the north. I have reports that American ships are bombarding the area around Inchon. I'm afraid they're landings to the south may be a trick. I think they may be planning to attack us here through Inchon. Shouldn't we wait to see what their true intentions are?

"Hah. If they try that, they are truly fools. Their boats will be stranded on Inchon's muddy flats. Their army will be wiped out. Tens of thousands of sea birds will fill their bellies with the rotting entrails of their soldiers."

Not wanting to contradict his leader directly, Nam responded, "You are right sir. That would be a stupid move on their part."

"The Americans are like lumbering oxen," said Kim. "They are big and strong, but dumb. We are like the stalking tiger, and we will outsmart them. We need to concentrate on dealing with the immediate threats in the south. I want you to send the two divisions here in Kyongi-do south to Kunsan immediately. As for the landing at Ulsan, I want you to have Kim Chaek move two of his mechanized infantry divisions to deal with the landing at Ulsan. We need to destroy them."

"Yes sir. I'll order those movements immediately. But I'm still worried about protecting Seoul? I'm afraid we might be taking too much away from Seoul's defense."

"I've thought of that," said Kim. "I've already contacted General Pak up north and told him I want him to transfer three divisions of his III Corps down here to Seoul to replace those divisions that are being sent south. They should be here in a few days."

"Ah, your foresight is truly worthy of a great leader," said Nam.

．　．　．

Two days after the joint American and Korean landing at Ulsan, the incoming fire from the KPA forces surrounding the small fishing port abated. Continuous aerial bombing had been effective in forcing most of the defenders to retreat further inland. Chae Hoon felt almost giddy that he was still alive after what he'd just been through. Although he wasn't given to showing much outward emotion, he couldn't help but cheer when he saw units of the 1st Cavalry Division come ashore with their tanks and mechanized artillery. With little time to rest, General Taylor ordered General John Holcomb, the 24th Division commander, to drive diagonally across the peninsula to cut off the southern port city of Pusan. Anxious to escape from their exposed position on the beach, General Holcomb ordered the division westward toward the small town of Miryang. Chae Hoon gathered his platoon together—he'd lost three of his men in the landing, but it could have been worse— and began the march to Miryang where two KPA divisions, augmented with an armored tank battalion, were approaching to do battle.

．　．　．

While KPA reinforcements rushed south to turn back American forces there, the main body of the U.S. task force began to anchor off Inchon. On June 5, as the American Marines waited aboard ships to begin their assault, the sixteen inch guns of the USS Iowa began pounding critical positions inland. On June 6 two battalions of Marines forced their way onto Wolmi Island, a rocky bit of land that sat in the center of Inchon Harbor. After a six hour fire fight, they raised an American flag over the island. The big guns of the battleship Iowa and the cruiser Juneau hit targets inland as far as Kimpo Airfield, silencing enemy air defenses. Some Yak fighters escaped the shelling and attacked the fleet like a swarm of bees protecting their hive from an intruding bear. F-9 Panthers manned by Marine pilots off the aircraft carrier Kearsarge shot down several of the Soviet made Yaks and the remaining enemy aircraft flew north leaving one destroyer and a cargo ship aflame but the remainder of the task force was intact. The shelling continued for another two days in an effort to eliminate as much of the enemy defensive network as possible.

American military planners had studied the tidal tables carefully and knew they had a narrow window in which to schedule a landing when tides would be highest. In the early morning light of June 8, 1953, General Mark Clark watched through binoculars from the USS Iowa as thousands of Marines poured out of landing craft just a few hundred feet from dry land. He'd witnessed such a landing before when he commanded landings in Italy and he knew today would be the last day for many of these brave men. He kept his eyes peeled to the scene as shoreline batteries blasted Marines slogging through the shallow surf. The American bodies floating in the water were too numerous for him to count. Nevertheless, the LSTs continued to unload their human cargo and by mid-day more than 4,000 Marines had reached the muddy beach and were digging foxholes.

Facing an imposing eight foot seawall, the Marines were stuck on the beach throughout the day and into the night, held in check by machine gun and mortar fire. Then suddenly, as the rays of sun appeared on the eastern horizon, Douglas Skyraiders from the USS Essex appeared overhead and blasted enemy positions on the other side of the sea wall. With the incoming fire suppressed, at least for a short time, the Marines scrambled over the barriers, using extension ladders, and before next sunset American and Republic of Korea flags were waving on a hilltop just inside the city.

Two days after the Inchon landing, reinforcements that Kim Il Sung had counted on had still not reached Seoul. B-29's out of Yokota had performed continuous bombing runs slowing down their advance and forcing the columns to travel only at night. With little resistance, the American Marines captured Kimpo Airfield on June 10 and Navy Seabees were close behind, quickly repairing the runways. Within days, F-86 Saber Jets were flying out of Kimpo. Kim Il Sung, Choson's great leader, realized then that General Nam Il had been right—the Kunsan landing was a trick—but it was too late for him to do anything about it. He gathered his relatives and key party leaders together and told them, "This is a temporary setback. We will relocate our capital to Pyongyang for now, but this is only the beginning of our fight."

.　.　.

More than a week had passed since the Americans had landed at Inchon. Seoul was now in the hands of the American 1st Marine Division. Following the landing, The New ROK 1st and 2nd Infantry Divisions, backed up by a Marine artillery regiment, began moving south down the Seoul-Pusan highway to relieve the U.S. Marines at Kunsan, The KPA commander Mu Chong, who had been bolstered by the addition of the two additional divisions was preparing for an all-out assault on the Marines strung out in bunkers within two miles of the shoreline. For seven days the Marines had withstood constant shelling. The day before, they had fended off a probing attack by a battalion size force, but General Puller knew the next attack, could be different. With the number of able-bodied men whittled down to a third of what he'd started with, there was no way they could hold them much longer. Nevertheless, he told his Marines to stand fast, help was on the way. He had to give them some straw to hang onto.

Overnight the sound of artillery could be heard in the far distance, and Puller hoped it was a good sign. As the sun rose in the sky, there was only silence. There was no artillery shelling or bugle calls signaling an enemy assault. The KPA were pulling back. During the night the KPA forces had been caught unaware when the ROK divisions attacked them in their rear, hitting them hard with their artillery. With the ensuing panic in his ranks, Mu Chong had been forced to order an ignominious withdrawal, leaving behind one division as a rear guard. That opened the way for General Puller to begin his breakout. With the support of Marine artillery and fighter aircraft called in from nearby carriers, the rear guard KPA troops were soon driven off, their dead strewing the roads and hillsides. By June 20, the main body of forces under Mu Chung, pursued by the revitalized ROK Army, had retreated to the central Sobaek Mountain range moving north where they hoped to be able to regroup beyond the reach of the Americans and their ROK allies.

. . .

While the ROK Army was battling with the KPA II Corps along the western coast of the peninsula, in the southeast the KPA 2nd and 12th Divisions, supported by at least fifty Soviet-made medium and light tanks that had proven such an important element of their success in their earlier war of liberation, came into contact with elements of the American Eighth Army just outside Miryang, This time, the Communist gunners were not dealing with a lightly armed and undertrained army as in 1950. Armed with the newer 3.5 inch M-20 super bazookas and employing more than sixty M-46 Patton tanks, the 24th Infantry Division quickly eliminated the more lightly armed KPA tanks and steadily drove the Communist forces back, taking hundreds of prisoners in the process. Some of the KPA units, made up of recently recruited southerners simply disappeared as soldiers threw off their uniforms and vanished into the countryside. In other cases whole units surrendered without firing shots. By June 23, the two KPA divisions had been reduced to half, and the remnants straggled helplessly north in small units.

. . .

The victory at Miryang was important, but it was only a means to help General Taylor achieve his primary objective which was the port of Pusan. While the fighting was still going on at Miryang, he sent the newly arrived 25th Infantry Division along with the Korean *Zainichi* brigade led by Brigadier General Yi Un directly south. The American and Korean forces encircled the city by land. With the greater Pusan harbor walled off by American ships, the KPA Garrison with more than 4,000 soldiers, was trapped. Would they fight to the last man, or would they surrender? Over the next two days, more than 100,000 civilians left the city and were guided to hastily erected refugee camps. Once the bulk of civilians had been evacuated, American tanks entered the city, with the *Zainichi* Brigade following close behind. They encountered stiff resistance at first, with several tanks disabled by suicide bombers. However, after holding out for three days in his embattled garrison compound, KPA Colonel Yu Sang Kon, surrendered his forces, and the city of Pusan, including its invaluable port and airfield which were largely undamaged, belonged to the Americans. Two days later, Yi Pom Sok, the exiled president of the Republic of Korea, appeared at a celebratory rally in the heart of the city and declared to the cheers of thousands of anxious residents that the Communist regime of Kim Il Sung was finished. "New national elections will be held soon," he promised.

CHAPTER 29

A CHANGE OF HEART

July 1953

The People's Army was on the defensive throughout the southern half of the Korean peninsula, reeling from the combined American and ROK Army attacks. Only in the southeastern provinces of Cholla-do, were they still able to maintain some semblance of territorial control. Everywhere else south of the old 38th parallel, the local populace welcomed the return of the ROK Army, having had their fill of the promised communist "paradise."

Even though Communist forces were retreating north, for prisoners in Chonju Labor Camp #2, nothing had changed. Located in the foothills of Moak Mountain, the camp was no more than twenty five miles from Kunsan. There had been rumors of an invasion by Americans for days, but then the camp commander had taken three of the prisoners, accused them of spreading American propaganda, and executed them publicly for all the other prisoners to witness. After that, the rumors stopped.

Soon Hi's brother In Yong, who she'd given up for dead, was at Labor Camp #2, working in a small ammunition plant. Every day the routine was the same. But one morning In Yong thought he could hear artillery in the distance. He was afraid to say anything, and no one said anything to him. The next morning, he stood at the window of his cell watching guards and workmen running helter-skelter. Something was happening. Judging from the position of the sun, he thought it must be about seven o'clock. Normally a guard would have come by a half hour before to unlock his door so he could report for

228

his work detail. *What's happening?* From his lone window he saw trucks lined up in the dirt lot across the way. They were being loaded with equipment and boxes. *Are they moving the camp?* Now there was no mistake. He heard sporadic rifle shots in the distance. Someone began shouting nearby and he strained his neck to look. What he saw chilled him to the bone. A group of about fifteen men in baggy work clothes, the same clothes he wore, were being directed with hands tied behind their backs into a truck at gun point.

A year and a half—that's how long In Yong had been living at the camp, for the past six months in an eight by eight foot cell. The last contact he had with his sister was in early 1951. He was still a free man then. After the Communist takeover in September of that year, he continued to work out in the open for the *Chosun Ilbo*. But when the Communists shut the paper down and arrested the editor and top managers, he went into hiding, along with two friends from the paper, including one who was a typesetter and the other a newsman like himself. They found refuge at Haein Temple where the monks took them in, letting them stay in one of the remote hermitages on Mount Kaya. Using the temple as a cover they dressed in monk garb and, with the approval of the head monk, began publishing a newsletter they called *The Public Voice*, speaking out against excesses of the Communist regime. They continued publishing the newsletter until December of that year when a nosy Communist patrol discovered some of their printing plates hidden among the historic *Tripitaka* tablets. Their identities were soon uncovered and they were arrested, convicted, and sentenced to ten years of hard labor.

After arriving at the Chonju camp he was assigned to a barracks with forty other men. Six days a week they went out to work in the ammunition plant. On the seventh day they attended reeducation classes where they were required to study Kim Il Sung's writings and to spout back communist liturgy. Poor performance would mean loss of meal rations and in some cases a physical beating. The days were broken up by a noontime meal in the mess hall. In the evening, just before lights out, workers had a chance to gather and talk to one another in the barracks, but loose talk was dangerous. Anyone could be a spy for the camp commander. Six months earlier he'd been turned in by one of those spies for trying to plot an escape with two other workers. After that he was moved to this small cell isolated from the others, except when taken out to work. The only good thing about that was he didn't have to attend the damned classes anymore.

In Yong turned away from the window and sat down on his mat on the floor. Sweat began to run down his sides. *Is it over? Are they going to kill me?*

The door creaked open and he looked up to see two guards standing in front of him dressed in khaki, red stars on their billed caps. One had a length of cord in his hands, the other a gun drawn. He got up off the floor, about to berate them for their cowardly behavior, taking innocent people to their death, but when he raised his head and looked the men in the eyes, he was shocked to see that the one with the gun in his hand was his brother.

"In Su! Is it you? What are you doing here?"

With a malicious grin he responded, "Yes elder brother. It is me. We've come to take you away on a little trip for your own safety."

"I saw the soldiers taking people away with their hands tied behind their backs. I heard the gunshots. They're killing us. How can you be a part of this?"

Tightening his jaw, In Su said, "Unfortunately you're right. But it's necessary to protect the fatherland. We have been invaded once again by foreign imperialists and their Korean puppets. The current situation requires that we move our forces to a better defensive position to defeat this scum that is infecting our land. Unfortunately we can't take the likes of you with us. I feel badly that you chose the wrong side brother, but that was your choice"

In Su looked at the other guard and signaled him to tie up In Yong. When the guard moved behind In Yong and began wrapping the cord around his wrist, In Su moved behind him and with a violent swing brought the butt of his pistol down on the head of the guard who crumpled to the floor unconscious.

In Yong looked at his brother. "Wha — what are you doing?"

"I'm getting you out of here."

"I thought you wanted to kill me. What are you doing in that uniform?"

"I'm a KPA soldier, but I'm not a killer of innocent people. A year ago I might have been willing to kill you for the party, but no longer. I escaped from Japan last year following the May Day riots. The Communist underground smuggled me into Choson, and after I arrived I was conscripted into the KPA. Maybe it's because I was educated in a bourgeois school where people think for themselves. I'm not sure, but I finally realized that their whole system is built on a bunch of lies. Anyone who criticizes party dogma is arrested and usually shot as an example. They're trying to make a god out of Kim Il Sung—something I just can't accept."

"How did you find me?"

"A lot of luck. I'm attached to the 27th Security Battalion and we were assigned the job of closing out this camp before the Corps moves north. I saw your name on a list of prisoners, and that's when I decided to do something about it. Now, no more talking. Let's get this guard's clothes off him and on to you before we're discovered."

In Yong removed his clothes, took off the guards clothes and put them on. The uniform was too large, but it would do. The two of them then struggled to put In Yong's clothes on the guard before he woke up. Leaving the cell, In Su spotted a small pick-up truck parked aside a nearby building. The two of them sauntered over to the vehicle slowly so as not to draw attention. In Su looked in the window and saw that the keys were in the ignition. He looked around and saw a shovel against a barracks wall. He picked it up and threw it in the back.

"Get in," he said. "We'll use this to get out of here."

In Yong got into the passenger side and In Su started toward a gate about a hundred yards away. At the gate a guard held up his hand for them to stop, checked the back truck bed, and then walked to the driver's window.

"Where you going with an empty truck?" said the guard.

"They need more people for a burial detail out beyond the fields. Uh, we're supposed to collect shoes and things that can be reused."

"Show me your identification."

In Su pulled his ID from his pocket and gave it to him. The guard looked at it briefly and then handed it back.

"You too," said the guard pointing at In Yong.

In Yong hadn't thought to check for the guards ID card. He stuck his hand in the pant pocket and breathed a sigh of relief when he felt the hard plastic. He pulled it out and handed it over to him. The guard glanced down at the card and his face twitched slightly. He looked up and gave In Yong a long stare and then pulled a gun from his holster.

"Get out of the truck. Both of you," he ordered.

"What's wrong?" asked In Su, trying to act innocent.

"This picture isn't the same person. Now get out."

As they got out of the vehicle In Yong tried to come up with some explanation to explain away the image. "It's an old picture," he said. "I've lost weight."

"What's your name?" said the guard, the gun pointing at his midsection.

In Yong tried to stall for time. "You have it right in front of you," he said.

He remembered seeing the name "Lee" on the ID, but what was the first name? "Lee," he blurted.

"You don't know your first name? The guard poked the gun in his ribs.

"Min Ho" In Yong mumbled, hoping the guard couldn't actually read.

The guard grinned malevolently. "Wrong answer."

Turning and pointing the gun at In Su he told him to remove his pistol and drop it on the ground. The guard picked it up and shoved it into his waistband. "Now move," he ordered, pushing them toward the small guard shack ten feet away. The guard went to a phone and as he started to dial, In Su made a lunge for the guard's gun. They wrestled on the floor rolling over, first with In Su on top, then the guard. A shot rang out and In Su cried out in pain. As they began to untangle In Yong spotted the second gun on the floor, having fallen out from the guard's waistband while he was wrestling with In Su. He picked it up and aimed it at the guards head. Suddenly seeing that In Yong had a gun, the guard turned to fire. But In Yong's shot first, and the guard fell back dead, the bullet striking him in the temple.

In Yong went to his knees and lifted his brother's head. He was still alive, but barely. He leaned over him, blood soaking through the front of In Su's shirt. In Su's eyes fluttered open. He tried to speak, but could only whisper. "I can't—I can't help...You must tell people the truth." Then his eyes went blank.

In Yong laid his brother's head back on the floor gently and looked outside. It seemed that no one had noticed the shots since there were other gunshots going off every few minutes from different points around the camp, but it wouldn't be long before a vehicle would pull up soon. He needed to figure another way out. He peeked outside the gate house and saw there was an outer fence he'd have to go through. He'd never make it walking. He turned and looked back towards the barracks area. Trucks were still parked there loading up people. In his KPA uniform no one would notice him. His best chance to get outside the fence was to get on one of those trucks. He was able to make his way over to the barracks parking lot without anyone noticing and joined a group of soldiers clustered at the end of one of the trucks. After two or three minutes a sergeant came up behind them.

"Take a rifle and get on board. Hurry up!" the sergeant yelled. There was a rack of carbines along the barrack building. In Yong grabbed one and climbed into the rear of the truck with the others.

After everyone was aboard, the truck jerked forward, behind two other trucks filled with camp workers—workers like him. He knew that if In Su had not come for him when he did, he would be one of those in the front trucks. Instead, he was going to be one of their executioners. He glanced quickly at those around him. No one was talking, just staring straight ahead. After leaving the camp they drove an additional mile before stopping in a dirt field. In Yong got out of the truck with the others and an officer lined them up twenty feet in front of a long trench. In Yong could see bodies already in the trench. A group of workers were led to the edge of the trench. Some were shouting, one appeared to be weeping with his head down, but most were stoic, standing straight, and waiting to die.

The officer ordered the rifle team to prepare to fire. In Yong had not shot a rifle before. He wasn't sure if his gun was loaded, but he tried to follow the man next to him and brought the rifle to his shoulder when ordered. He knew he had to pull the trigger, but he didn't want to kill anyone. He looked through the sight and raised the barrel just enough he hoped that any bullet would fly above the man he was supposed to be aiming at. On the order to fire, he closed his eyes and pulled the trigger. The rifle stock bucked back into his shoulder and he staggered a little. He looked up and saw that almost half of the workers were still upright, some standing and some kneeling. The lieutenant ordered the soldiers to continue firing. He saw others pulling back on the rifle bolt to reload and he did the same and put the rifle back on his shoulder and fired again above the targets. This time when the firing stopped no one was standing. Agonizing groans could be heard from the trenches. The lieutenant directed four or five of the soldiers to go over and finish the job on those still alive.

While the attention of the officers and NCO's was directed at the pile of the dead and dying, In Yong, as inconspicuously as possible, snuck behind the vehicles which were parked near a copse of trees. From there he managed to make his escape into a nearby wooded area. Where would he be safe? Which direction should he go? There were mountains he could see above the tree tops to his left. He decided that would be the safest place for now. After walking for three hours through brush and up dry rocky stream beds, he came upon a narrow trail leading further upward. Near dusk, after two more hours of climbing he came to a small Buddhist temple. A young priest, seeing that In Yong was near exhaustion came up to him and offered him water. After drinking his fill from a spring fed pipe, he explained his situation, trusting that the monk was not connected with the Communists, and asked if he could stay there for a while. The young monk told him he needed to ask the senior monk. He went to the building next door and brought the elder monk back with him.

The elder, with a grave look on his face, eyed In Yong in his beat up KPA uniform, "You are one of Kim Il Sung's soldiers?"

"Oh no," said In Yong. "I was a prisoner of the Communists. Please believe me. I stole one of their uniforms and escaped. I'm not a Communist. My brother lost his life in our escape attempt. I hope you'll help me *sunnim*."

The old monk didn't display any emotion but gazed, almost hypnotically into In Yong's eyes. Finally a smile emerged and he said, "Yes, I believe what you say. You do not lie I'm sure. The Communists are not our friends, and you will be welcome to remain with us. However, we have no weapons, and if they come for you, we cannot help you."

In Yong bowed several times and thanked the monk for his generosity. He told him, "If I know the Communists are coming, I will leave this place and will try not to put you in danger."

. . .

After sitting with the monks for a meal of porridge and mountain vegetables, In Yong helped them clean and put away the utensils. The monks excused themselves, saying they must perform their evening chants. While they attended to their ritual, In Yong wandered around the small temple area. There were just three buildings. The walls were made of clay, but supported by wooden beams with tile roofs, the red and blue paint decorating the timbers, once bright, was now worn and peeling. The largest building, which housed three statues of Buddha in different poses, was clearly used for ceremonial purposes. Another building was used for sleeping. The third building was a kind of kitchen and storehouse. A chicken coop where several hens pecked the dirt completed the physical structures. There was a large garden where cabbage, turnips, beans, and several things he couldn't identify were growing. As darkness fell, he went to the building he figured was the living quarters and sat down on the stoop to wait for the monks.

In Yong didn't have any way to tell the time, but thought it must be about nine o'clock by the position of the moon. When the monks finally finished with their evening ritual, the elder invited him into their quarters, and the younger monk got out a straw mat and a coarse pillow from a storage chest and handed it to In Yong. He told him, "We rise at sunrise and will fix breakfast before morning prayers. You will join us?"

"Yes, of course," said In Yong, not sure if he would need someone to shake him awake after the difficult day he'd had.

The two monks put out their mats and laid down to sleep. In Yong did the same. Laying there in the dark he thought about his brother and began to cry softly. He didn't want any harm to come to the kind monks, and if he stayed with them there was a real danger the KPA would find him, just as they did before, and they would destroy this temple and probably kill the monks. He couldn't let that happen. The young monk said he knew of a guerilla unit operating in the area. Perhaps he would be able to direct him to where they were. He remembered what his brother had said as he was dying: Tell people the truth. He couldn't wait to start writing again and telling the truth as he knew it. But he couldn't do anything in this isolated mountain. *I'll leave tomorrow. Once the Communists are driven out, a free press will have a big part to play to in determining what kind of government takes its place. I need to stay alive.*

CHAPTER 30

BITTER TRIUMPH

July 1953

The joy and relief Chae Hoon felt after the victory at Pusan was short lived. Less than a week later he learned that his unit was being sent on a new combat mission—nobody told him what it was. Although the Americans and their Korean allies had delivered knockdown blows to the Communists at Inchon, at Ulsan, and at Kunsan, the Reds weren't ready to quit. There were still over 60,000 Communist troops actively operating south of the 38th parallel, with the largest concentration maintaining a strong position in the southeast province of Chollanam-do. General Taylor, the operational commander for ground forces in the peninsula, had in excess of 90,000 men on the peninsula, including the ROK forces brought in from Japan, but they were spread out across the southern portion of the country. With only a single understrength American combat unit remaining in the southeast sector, the vital Pusan port was a tempting target for the nearby Communist forces camped in mountains just twenty miles to the west.

On the evening of July 3, Tae Yong Kim, Chae Hoon's company commander entered the barracks where he and his men were billeted and told them to prepare to move out in the morning. Asked what the assignment was, he answered, "I haven't received the specific orders yet, but from what I hear, the KPA is building up their strength around Masan. General Taylor thinks they're going to try to take back Pusan. I think he's sending us there.

The next morning Chae Hoon, along with the rest of Bravo Company, boarded trucks that took them to a cantonment area near Kimhae, just a few miles outside Pusan. Chae Hoon recognized it as a former refugee camp used during the June 25 War (the first Korean War). Later it had become a "reeducation" camp for the Communists. Over the next few days he'd kept his men busy checking and rechecking their equipment, he sent them out on clean up details around the camp, joined with them in athletic contests with other companies, and in the evenings reviewed small unit tactics with them.

Finally, after five days in the camp, they were moving out. That evening Chae Hoon sat anxiously in the Headquarters Company Quonset hut, along with the other platoon leaders, waiting for Captain Kim to return from his meeting with the regimental brass. They were anxious to know what tomorrow would bring. The makeshift windows were propped open, but it was close to ninety degrees in the tin hut. Wearing wool uniforms furnished courtesy of the U.S. Army, they were all sweating like pigs on a spit. The captain had told them to wait for him inside, and that's what they did. The last few days in camp had been nerve racking. They all knew, for some of them, this would be their last day on earth. Everyone in the room just wanted to get on with it. Waiting was hard. The captain had been gone for more than an hour when the door to the Quonset opened

Kim entered the metal hut accompanied by a tall American soldier dressed in olive drab khakis, his lower pant legs bloused into his scuffed up boots. He wore no rank insignia, but there was a unit patch on one shoulder. A holstered .45 pistol hung from his web belt and a trench knife was strapped to his lower right leg. He stood more than half a foot taller than Captain Kim, who was not short by Korean standards, but his height, along with his broad shoulders, penetrating blue eyes, and dark beard growth gave him a fearsome appearance. Chae Hoon was glad he wouldn't have to face him in hand to hand combat.

When the platoon leaders started to rise, the captain motioned them to stay seated. "This is Sergeant Sam Hatcher," he said. "The Americans have assigned him to Bravo Company to help us coordinate with the American units. He'll meet with each of you individually so you understand his role within this company. He doesn't speak Korean, so I'll assign *you* Lieutenant Han and *you* Lieutenant So to act as interpreters for the others since you know some English. I want you to pay attention to what he says, because we need effective coordination with the Americans if we are to be successful in defeating the Red dog turds."

Then Kim gave them the news they'd been waiting for. "We'll be moving out of here tomorrow morning at 0600."

"Where are we going?" asked one of the lieutenants."

"Not far," said Kim. "We'll take up positions on Chongbyongsan, about twenty kilometers west of here. The American artillery has been pounding the area for the past two days and we don't think there are any KPA left there—at least not in any strength. Now, before I go over tomorrow mornings movement orders, Sergeant Hatcher wants to say a few words."

The big American stepped forward and, with Captain Kim translating, said, "I'm not much for words, but I think it's important for you to know who I am since we're going to be buddying up pretty close for a while. I'm not just an American GI. I'm a U.S. Army Ranger," he said, patting the patch on his shoulder. I'm part of a special ranger company assigned to Eighth Army to work with our Korean allies. I wasn't here when the North Koreans came down in '50, but I know some of you were part of the ROK Army then, and you got your asses kicked. We're not gonna let that happen again. I know you all joined up with this outfit to help reclaim your country. You all know it ain't going to be easy. As an American, I'm here to tell you we aim to help you get your country back. But you gotta do your part too."

There was a nodding of heads and murmuring among the platoon leaders as the sergeant continued. "Now I haven't fought against these Choson Reds before. But I fought plenty of Japs on Kwajalein and Okinawa, and these guys have nothing on them. We can take em, but we need to be a team. My job with you is to be your liaison with the 1st Cav and with the flyboys that'll be keeping watch overhead. I'll be meeting with each of you lieutenants before we head out tomorrow just so we get to know each other better before the shit starts hitting the fan. Are you with me?"

A shout of HUAH went up from the young officers.

Later that afternoon Sergeant Hatcher found Chae Hoon outside his tent with his first sergeant looking over a map. A couple open cans of C-rations sitting on a rock to the side.

Chae Hoon stood up when he saw the American coming toward him and the sergeant excused himself. Hatcher craned his neck to read the name stenciled over Chae Hoon's chest pocket, then held out his hand and said, *"Annyong haseiyo Jungui Han."* While shaking his hand, he added, "I'm sorry but that's about all the Korean I know. Captain Kim told me you speak English and could introduce me around to the other platoon leaders."

"Ah, yes. I—know English a little. I am expecting you." When the captain told him he was going to have to interpret for the American he was a little unsure if he could do it. At his father's urging, he'd spent four years in the American Missionary School in Wonsan. Pastor Thompson told him he was one of his best English pupils. But that all ended when the June 25 War started. Although he'd been reading manuals in English, he hadn't spoken English in a long time, and he was nervous about it. He wasn't sure if the sergeant would understand what he said, or if he would be able to understand everything the sergeant said to him.

Hatcher looked down at the open ration cans on the rock. "I see you've been sampling some of army's gourmet cooking. You like it?"

Chae Hoon wrinkled his nose. "Not much. It doesn't fit stomach."

"So you're not eating it?"

"No," he said, pointing two tents down where some of his men were squatting around an open fire, where a large pot was warming. "We make our own food. You want to try?"

"Maybe later, after your men finish. Captain Kim has briefed me on the company's operational capabilities and weaknesses. Before you take me around to meet the other platoon leaders and some of your men, I want to know your thoughts about any weak spots I should be aware of and what you want from me."

Chae Hoon suggested that they go into his tent where each took a seat on a cot opposite one another. They spent a half hour discussing the lack of real combat experience for most of the soldiers. A few, like him, had been in the old ROK Army, but most had spent their lives in

Japan and had never seen actual combat. The recent walkover in Pusan had been nothing. This next battle would be the real thing. After going over the tactical scenarios, the two of them got up and started to leave. Hatcher noticed a picture of a young woman, obviously pregnant.

"This your wife? She's very pretty."

"Yes, and she speak English better than me. She worked for American Embassy in Seoul." Caressing the picture with two fingers, he said, "I can wait see her again."

"You mean you *CANNOT* wait to see her?" he said with an amused smile.

"Yes, yes, I *CAN-NOT* wait"

"When's the baby due?"

"Expect baby very soon. When we finish defeating Reds, then I will bring them here to live. I hope soon."

Patting him on the shoulder, Hatcher said, "Don't worry. It won't be long. We'll have these bastards on the run and you'll be able to bring your wife over here before you know it. Now let's go and meet some of your compadres."

. . .

Chae Hoon and his men began boarding trucks at five o'clock the next morning. The Americans had moved out two hours before. The American 1st Cavalry Division consisted of two brigades and was to occupy the center of a nearly fifteen mile line of defense where the brunt of any attack was expected to come. They would be backed up by two field artillery battalions and a 2,000 man Korean infantry regiment that was to provide support by occupying the flanks. Chae Hoon's Bravo Company was assigned a position on the right flank, atop a promontory called Hill 509, the name simply referring to the hill's metric height.

After a bumpy hour-long drive, Chae Hoon's convoy halted at the foot of Chongbyongsan. It wasn't really a mountain as its name implied. It was more a range of high hills and bluffs with rocky escarpments. Although they weren't as high as the interior ranges, these hills provided a far better defensive position against an impending attack. The soldiers got out of the vehicles, and after collecting their gear, started the rest of the way up the mountainside on foot. After an hour's hike they arrived at just below the crest where Captain Kim, the company commander, set up a base camp. They'd encountered occasional sniper fire, but hadn't lost any men on the march up. The American artillery had apparently done its job in eliminating any Communist defenses on the mountain, but Chae Hoon and the other platoon leaders knew the easy going wouldn't last for long. They just hoped that they would have a day or two to prepare.

. . .

Once they'd gotten close to the summit, Captain Kim ordered the men to fall out, and he met briefly with his four platoon leaders, assigning them positions along the rock strewn crest line. Chae Hoon was in the center. The third platoon led by Lieutenant Cha was on his left and the 1st platoon headed by Lieutenant So was on his right. The fourth platoon was kept back in reserve. Chae Hoon knew he could depend on Cha, but wasn't so sure about So. He seemed more interested in himself than his men. Captain Kim had set up his command post about half way down the slope. Chae Hoon felt good about the men in his forty man platoon. They wouldn't panic. But it was good to know there was some back up, just in case."

As soon as he reached the rounded summit Chae Hoon immediately set his men to work collecting rocks, filling sandbags with dirt, and digging trenches across the half mile stretch of land he was assigned to protect. A whir of helicopter blades blew up dust before dropping heavy crates of ammo, rolls of concertina wire, and other supplies in an open area. Private Im, the radio operator picked up coils of cable and started laying out communication lines. Chae Hoon assigned one of his machine gun teams to set up a barbed wire perimeter about forty yards down the forward slope. Others he assigned to start constructing bunkers at fifty yard intervals. Chae Hoon, and First Sergeant Bae pitched in building a bunker for themselves, set back a few feet from the others. Two weapon teams, each manning .50 caliber machine guns, he placed in bunkers at the ends. A third team, manning a 75mm recoilless and carrying a 3.5 inch bazooka just in case any tanks showed up, he assigned to a bunker closer to the center.

The first night on Hill 509 was quiet, quieter maybe than Chae Hoon would have liked. He woke up in the middle of the night, went up to the ridgeline to take a piss and looked out over the valley below. There were few lights in the city of Masan, and the quarter moon in the sky cast a dim glow over the landscape. He couldn't see any sign of the enemy, but he knew they were down there and in the dark hills beyond. He wondered what their commander was thinking. Would he retreat into the mountains and wait for the Americans to come? Or would he attack first, before the Americans built up their strength? He was betting that they would attack first. He went back to his bunker and tried to sleep, but it didn't come easy.

On the second day, Chae Hoon kept his men busy strengthening the bunkers. After dark, he sent out a patrol to check for any attempts at infiltration. The patrol came back around midnight reporting everything quiet, and Chae Hoon decided that it was okay to try to get some sleep. An hour later he was awakened by the rat-a-tat of machine gun fire. He jumped up and ran up to where the firing was coming from. It was the left machine gun bunker.

"What happened?" said Chae Hoon as he squeezed into the bunker.

Corporal Paek, manning the .50 caliber gun, said, "We heard movement out there at the wire. I'm sure we got whoever was out there. Any we didn't get, are running like scared jack rabbits back to where they came from."

"Good work. As soon as dawn breaks I'll send out another team to see what we caught in our net."

He went back to his bunker and called up Captain Kim to let him know about the incident. Kim told him they had another action on the southern flank. "They're just probing us. I don't think anything more will happen tonight."

The next morning Chae Hoon went out with a patrol to check the wire perimeter. They found four enemy bodies hung up, all dead. He ordered his men to pull them out and bury them. That evening the Communists began shelling the entire line with heavy artillery fire.

Chae Hoon and his men huddled in their bunkers as whistling Katushya Rockets bombarded their camp. The firing continued for most of the evening, with shells hitting feet from the bunker, bits of shrapnel even finding its way into the bunker. As he lay on the dirt floor with Sergeant Bae, he could hear cries from outside and knew that some men were dying, but there was nothing he could do until the shelling stopped. It was near morning when the rocket barrage finally stopped, and at first light he, Sergeant Bae, and the medic, Private Yu, went outside to survey the damage. There were some shell holes and lots of scattered debris. At first sighting it looked like the camp was still pretty much intact. Looking off to his left, he saw a bunker, though, with its roof caved in and a smoky vapor rising from it. He rushed over to find four men—or pieces of them—scattered inside. He bent over and vomited.

Turning to Sergeant Bae, he said, "Nothing we can do. Get a detail together to take care of the bodies." Then he continued checking on the other bunkers to see how the other men were doing. In all, they lost five men during the night and had two more wounded who would have to be evacuated, but Chae Hoon felt lucky that it hadn't been worse. He knew, though, that the worst wasn't over.

During all that day, Chae Hoon had all his men work on reinforcing their bunkers, laying up a good supply of ammunition, and making sure their weapons were in the best operating order. The night started off quiet, like the previous two nights had, but as a timorous moon peeked from behind an invisible cloud, Chae Hoon heard bugle calls in the distance followed by the susurrate sound of a huge wave coming ashore. The sound soon became audible as half-human shouts meant to frighten defenders. He still couldn't see them, but he could hear them coming—screaming now like banshees from hell. Illumination flares suddenly lit up the night revealing the initial line of the oncoming horde. He passed the word to all the bunkers, "Don't shoot until Sergeant Bae fires first. We wait until they get to the wire,"

"Now! Now!" yelled Chae Hoon as the first line of the enemy broached the wire perimeter. The machine guns on both sides began spitting fire. The whole line began firing non-stop, but the enemy soldiers kept coming, even though bodies were beginning to fill up the concertina wire. The line was holding when Private Im said he'd heard over the phone that So's platoon was pulling back. The two squad's on his right reported they were taking fire from the side. If the enemy was able to bypass them they could get in behind the 1st Cav positions... He couldn't let that happen. He shifted an extra squad over to the right flank and ran up to the machine gun bunker where Corporal Son was putting down steady fire. Just as he got there, Son said, "Look, a T-34!"

Chae Hoon looked out the bunker opening and saw a big T-34 tank busting through the wire. "How'd he get up here?" he said without expecting an answer. Son began firing at the T-34, but the bullets just bounced off. Since the tank was on the upslope, its cannon couldn't hurt them, but if it was able to get past them and over the top, it could devastate the company base camp below. Before Chae Hoon could think of anything to stop it, an enemy sapper who had gotten through the fire tossed a grenade that reached the bunker and exploded. Chae Hoon was thrown back and stunned momentarily. He struggled to get up and saw both Son and his ammo carrier lying on the bunker floor with gaping wounds, probably fatal. He found his phone and got Sergeant Bae. "I need the anti-tank gun. Get the bazooka up here quick."

As the T-34 slowly ground forward, crushing bodies in its path, Private Oh ran up to the bunker where Chae Hoon was holding out. "I'm here Lieutenant. What's the target?"

Chae Hoon pointed straight ahead. "That tank. Stop it."

The private shoved a charge into the barrel of the 3.5 inch tank killer, kneeled, took aim, and fired. The shell hit home, penetrating the rear of the hull and tearing through the engine. The tank stopped in its tracks. As Chae Hoon started to congratulate Private Oh for good shooting, the tank hatch opened. The tank commander or one of the crew popped up and began firing a machine gun. Chae Hoon flung himself down on the ground, but he heard Oh yell out as he let the bazooka fall to the ground. Seeing his gunner laying there badly wounded, he picked up the bazooka and reloaded it. He'd practiced on this kind of rocket launcher only a couple of times. He reloaded the weapon, knelt down, and fired true, blowing the entire turret off the tank.

After the tank was destroyed, the attackers retreated for the time being. With a temporary lull, Captain Kim sent up another platoon to take over the right flank. After an hour, a new wave of attacks started up all along the north side of the hill where Bravo Company was dug in. In seemingly endless waves, the enemy started breaking past the wire and hand to hand combat at the trenches ensued. He was losing too many men. Chae Hoon feared that this time they might get overrun. He called down to the forward observer post. "Hatcher. Hatcher. Are you there? I need air support. There's too many of them."

He called twice but no response. Then the reply came. "This is Hatcher. We got you covered buddy. Flyboys on the way."

Chae Hoon put down the phone and went up to the front bunkers to see if he could help. He picked up a BAR and began firing as the enemy kept coming. He bent down to reload and a Red soldier leaped wild eyed over the trench berm, pointing his carbine at him. A shot rang out. Chae Hoon looked up to see Hatcher on the other side of the trench with an M-1 aimed in his direction, and the enemy soldier at his feet, dead.

"I thought you might need some help," said Hatcher.

Chae Hoon nodded and said "Thanks for coming."

No more than two minutes later a squadron of F-84 Thunderjets out of Yokota Airbase in Japan came swooping down over Chae Hoon's platoon, unleashing bombs of napalm jelly onto the forward slope of Hill 509 that exploded into fireballs, engulfing the oncoming enemy. Those who weren't killed or maimed, turned and ran. Although sporadic firing could be heard. The Communist had attacked all along the line that night, and Bravo Company had played its part. By morning, the battle was over, and the line had held. The enemy was retreating to the mountains west of Masan.

With the coming of dawn, Chae Hoon wiped his brow, bowed his head, and said a small prayer of thanks. Hatcher was still with him, and Chae Hoon suggested that they go out to the forward slope to look around. Dead bodies were strewn everywhere, many piled on top of one another. As they walked close to the wire perimeter, he heard someone moan and walked over toward the sound. As he bent down to check out the badly wounded KPA soldier, he noticed movement out of the corner of his eye. Another soldier lying on the ground to his left rolled over and pointed a burp gun directly at him. Chae Hoon sought to pull out his sidearm, but not fast enough. Three quick bursts slammed into him and spun him around. Hatcher, who saw what was happening, fired three rapid shots into the assailant with his M-1 and then ran over to Chae Hoon, lying on his back, gasping for breath. Hatcher kneeled down next to him and saw that he was hurt badly, blood oozing through the front of his jacket.

Hatcher put him on his shoulder and carried him fireman style back to the main bunker, calling out, "Medic! Medic!"

Private Yu met him at the bunker, ripped open Chae Hoon's shirt and began applying compresses to stop the bleeding. The medic was able to stanch the external bleeding, but Hatcher knew from previous experience in the Pacific that it was the internal bleeding that could kill a soldier, and this didn't look good. *The wound in the arm won't kill him, but the hole in his torso sure can.* "You're going to be all right pal. We'll get you down to base camp and they'll medevac you and get you fixed up in no time. Hang on."

Chae Hoon looked up at Hatcher with blurry eyes, "If — if I don't live, please Sergeant, please tell my wife what happened. Tell her I love her. I love my baby."

Leaning close to his ear, Hatcher said, "Your wife. What's her name? How can I find her?"

There was a pause before Chae Hoon was able to respond weakly, "My — my wife Soon Hi. In Japan. Please."

Wiping a strand of mucous from his nose with a dirt smudged paw, Hatcher said, "I'll find her. You're gonna be okay though. You're not going anywhere except to a hospital ward somewhere safe."

Two soldiers helped lift Chae Hoon onto a litter and Hatcher accompanied them as they carried him down to the base camp. There a senior medic took over, placing him on a cot in the medical tent to wait for the next chopper to come in.

Sergeant Hatcher sat with Chae Hoon who passed in and out of consciousness while waiting for the chopper to arrive. Captain Kim came through to look in on Chae Hoon and just shook his head.

"That's three lieutenants we lost last night. Where am I going to find new ones?"

When the chopper finally came in after more than two hours of waiting, Hatcher watched as they loaded an unconscious Chae Hoon aboard. After seeing his friend being flown out of the battle zone, he trudged back up the hill and went into Chae Hoon's bunker to see what he'd left behind. Seeing the snapshot of Chae Hoon's wife taped to a stanchion in the rear, he took it and stuck it in his pocket.

CHAPTER 31

A PROMISE TO KEEP

August 1953

One week after forcing the retreat of the battered KPA 6th Division back into the mountains of Chollanam-do, American tanks entered the city of Masan, opening up the entire Chinhae Bay for American ship traffic. Despite their battlefield success, Sam Hatcher hardly felt like celebrating. The night before Captain Kim had called him into his tent and showed him a unit casualty report issued by the American Army hospital in Pusan. He'd underlined one name: Lieutenant Chae Hoon Han, died from combat wounds, July 29, 1953.

"I'm sorry sergeant. I know you were friend with Han. So I think you like to know what happen."

Hatcher hung his head, and then tried to shake off the hurt. "Shit happens, captain, and we move on. Thanks for letting me know. You know where the body is, where he'll be buried?"

"I think Americans will take care that. You need to talk with somebody at hospital in Pusan. Can't let you go now, though."

Hatcher nodded. "Thanks, may do that," he said. Then he turned and walked away abruptly as tears clouded his eyes.

After Chae Hoon's death and the victory at Masan, Sam Hatcher's job with the *Zainichi* Brigade was over, but he still had unfinished business to take care of—he meant to keep his promise to Chae Hoon and find his wife. Before reporting to his home unit with the 4th Ranger Battalion, he got approval for a week's leave, but where to start? The only things he knew about her was that she was somewhere in Japan, and he knew her first name—Soon Hi. She had written her name on the back of the picture in hangul, but her family name was a mystery. The best place to start he decided was at the 121 Evacuation Hospital.

After saying his good-bye's to everyone around the camp, Hatcher hitched a ride with a convoy into Pusan and went directly to the army hospital. Hatcher knew a lot of people from his various tours over the years, and he knew someone in virtually every unit in Korea, including the 121 Hospital. The NCO in charge of patient administration, SFC Benny Calvert, had once been attached as a medic to Hatcher's unit in the Philippines, and he was more than happy to help an old friend.

Calvert walked Hatcher over to the records section, and after a twenty minute search a private brought out a slim medical file and handed it to him. The file record confirmed what he expected. According to the record, Chae Hoon had died following surgery caused by internal bleeding and complications from a ruptured spleen and liver. Hatcher peeled through the pages looking for some next of kin. There was nothing. He looked at Calvert and asked him if he had any idea of where he could find out anything about the next of kin.

"I think your best bet is with the ROK Army. They have their command post here in Pusan now. It's located on the other side of town in the Dong-ku section. If you want to go there, I'll have one of my Koreans write up directions for you."

"That'd be a big help."

As Hatcher exited the hospital, carrying a slip of paper with an inscription he couldn't read, he caught sight of three young waifs sitting on a rock wall at the edge of the parking lot. He walked towards them and hollered, "Any of you speak English?"

The shortest of the three hopped off the wall, stood up straight, and gave a stiff salute. "I talk English," he said.

Hatcher eyed him carefully. He seemed to be nine or ten years old judging from his small stature, but he was probably a little older. Each of them had their head shaved and wore cut-off cotton pants and dirty sleeveless under-shirts. All of them looked like they hadn't taken a bath in a month, which they probably hadn't. Their legs and faces were coated with grime. Their bare feet were squeezed into rubber *komushin* (sandals) that looked two sizes too small. He motioned to the boy who saluted to come forward.

"What's your name?"

"My name Chong-hi."

He handed him the piece of paper with the directions in Korean and said, "I need to get to the Korean Army headquarters in Dong-ku. Do you know where this is?"

The boy took a long look as if studying it for grammatical errors. "Yes, I know," he said.

"Can you really read Korean? Don't put me on," warned Hatcher. "I'll have your ass kicked off this post."

"I no shit you GI. I read. I take you there for five hundred won."

Hatcher didn't believe one bit that the kid could read, but he probably did know his way around the city, and he didn't have any other good option. "Okay shorty," he said, "let's go." As they walked away, the other two boys shuffled back to the sidewalk and retook their seat on the wall.

. . .

Standing in front of a fenced in Korean military compound after a two and a half hour ride on three different buses, Hatcher looked down at the bronze-skinned elf, waiting expectantly for his money. "It took a while, but you got me here— just like you said." Hatcher took his wallet out of his pocket and handed the boy a thousand won note.

The boy's face lit up with an impish grin. Holding the bill in his two hands, he just stared at it and said, "Thanks GI."

"You earned it kid. Share some of that with your mother." Hatcher turned and started toward the front gate. *Fuckin A. I shouldn't have mentioned his mother. The boy probably doesn't have any, at least none he knows of.* As he approached the gate, he looked back, but the boy had vanished.

At first the Korean guard didn't want to let him enter. With his little interpreter no longer available, he was getting frustrated with the run-around. But after throwing out some Korean names that he figured the sentry would recognize, the guard made a call inside. Soon an officer who spoke English came to the gatehouse. After

Hatcher explained what he needed and showed the officer the hospital record that included Chae Hoon's name and unit designation, he escorted him inside and led him to the adjutant's office.

The officer told him, "Here we keep all personnel records." He handed the document to an enlisted man behind the records counter and rattled something off in Korean before turning back to Hatcher. "Private Kim will help you. Please have seat and wait."

Hatcher sat down on a hard back chair to wait while the clerk exited into a back room. With nothing to read, thoughts of those events leading to Chae Hoon's death kept running through his mind. *If only I'd spotted the shooter a few seconds earlier. Why him and not me? Just dumb luck of war.* After a half hour, the private returned with a folder under his arm. He laid it in front of Hatcher and opened it up. Hatcher, paged through the file, but it was in Korean. He searched his mind for a familiar Korean word, and then said, "Anything about his *jip-saram*, his wife?"

The young Korean, who spoke some English, said, "I look." He began paging through the file, and then stopped. "Here," he pointed with a long finger. "*Jip-saram* is Chung Soon Hi."

"I'll be damned! Does it give an address?"

"No address. Just name."

Hatcher took a deep breath. Shoving a piece of paper he drew from his pocket, he said, "Write down her name in Korean."

While the sergeant jotted down the name, Hatcher considered his next move. *I go to Japan and check with Japanese immigration and Korean social organizations to try to locate somebody by the name of Chung Soon Hi. Who am I kidding? That's a pretty common name – like looking for Mary Smith in the New York telephone directory. I'll never find her. If there was someone who knew her in Korea...*Then, a revelation. He recalled something Chae Hoon had told him when they first met – she knew English and used to work at the embassy in Seoul. *That's it! I'll go to the embassy in Tokyo. There must be someone there who was in Seoul at the time of the invasion who'll remember her.*

Hatcher, all of a sudden, realized the Korean clerk was standing there, the piece of paper still in hand. He took it with an apologetic smile and pumped the man's arm as if to break it. "*Kamsa Hamnida.*

Kamsa Hamnida my friend," said Hatcher. The sergeant nodded his head, unsure of why the American was so excited.

Early next morning, after spending the night in the MATS terminal at Kimhae Airbase, Hatcher caught a hop on a C-119 flight to Tachikawa Air Base, just outside Tokyo. It was Thursday, and the embassy would be open. Wasting no time after getting off the plane, he took a military shuttle bus that dropped him off in Akasaka in front of the Daiichi building where MacArthur had held sway during the occupation. Then following a tourist map, he walked another mile before finally coming upon the huge three story American embassy. Entering the crowded lobby, he worked his way to the receptionist's desk and told the clerk he needed to see the army attaché.

"Do you have appointment?" asked the pert twenty something Japanese girl behind the counter.

"No. I don't. I just got in from Korea. It's important."

"You'll need to make appointment sir."

"Tell him Sergeant Sam Hatcher, a family friend, is here. It's kind of a surprise. Just do it."

Appearing a little peeved, the girl dialed a number and after talking to someone on the other end of the line, said, "Someone will be out and get you in few minutes. Please wait."

After ten minutes he was escorted up to the second floor to the attaché's office. Wearing the rumpled khaki service uniform he'd slept in the night before, he knocked on the door and heard a sharp "enter" response. The thin hawk-nosed light colonel sitting behind a large mahogany desk didn't even look up from papers he was examining as he came into the room. Finally raising his eyes to meet Hatcher's the colonel said, "Have we served together before sergeant? I don't recognize you."

"I don't think so sir."

"Then what's this about being a family friend?"

"I am a friend of a family…but it's not anyone you know sir. It was the only thing I could think of to get in to see you without an appointment.

The veins on the colonel's stork-like neck began to pulse and the creases on his face deepened. "I'm not amused by your little subterfuge sergeant. I suggest you state your business quick — and it better be good."

Still standing at attention, Hatcher said, "I've just come from Korea. I'm assigned to the 4th Ranger Battalion and was attached to a Korean company as an adviser. One of their platoon leaders was killed outside Masan a month ago, but before he died I promised him I'd try to contact his wife. She's somewhere here in Japan. That's the family I was talking about."

The lines of the colonel's face began to soften, but he let Hatcher remain at attention for a few seconds before he spoke. "Okay sergeant. You can relax. You've said all you need to. I'm with you. I lost several friends during the last war and family members need to hear bad news from someone who cares. But she's Korean, isn't she? Why have you come here to the embassy?"

"Sir, before Lieutenant Han died, he told me that his wife worked in the American Embassy in Seoul — that was before the North Korean invasion. I thought that there must be some embassy people here in Japan who were in Korea then. They might know her name — know where she is. I even have a picture of her." He pulled out the picture and showed it to the colonel.

"Nice looking girl," he said. "I wasn't in Korea then... but I do know at least one person here in this building who was. She's the vice consul. I'll give her a call and see if she's in."

.   .   .

Kate Keeler was a busy woman with her appointment book full, but she agreed to meet the sergeant in the cafeteria during the lunch period. Sitting down over cups of coffee, Hatcher, with a tired hang-dog look on his face, laid the picture on the table. "Her name's Chung — Soon Hi Chung. Do you know her?"

She examined the picture. "Yes — yes, the face is familiar. She was a clerk in our department. Why are you looking for her?"

"I served with her husband in Korea. He was killed and I promised him before he died I'd let his wife know. You know where she is?

Her mouth dropped open. "I'm so sorry to hear that. No, I don't know where she is. But I think I know someone who might—Tom Crandall. He works for me."

Hatcher gulped down his coffee. "I'd like to talk to him."

. . .

Thirty minutes later, sitting across from Tom in Kate's office, Hatcher went over every detail of what happened to Chae Hoon and how he'd promised to tell his wife. Tom was shaken. A month ago, shortly after the baby was born, she'd gotten a letter from her older brother in Korea telling her that her younger brother had been killed helping him escape from a prison camp. *Now this? It's too much for anyone to shoulder.*

"Do you know where I can find her?" said Hatcher.

"Yes," said Tom. "She lives with her mother in Okubo. I visited her not too long ago after she had her baby. She may be at work now, but if you want to go, I'll take you there. She knows me, and it'll be easier."

"Okay. You don't think she already knows do you?"

"I'm almost positive she doesn't. Because of the unsettled situation and incomplete records, the Korean army isn't able to do much of anything in regard to notifying next of kin when someone dies. Korean family members have to initiate an inquiry to the Army to find out what happened."

. . .

It was after five in the afternoon when they got to Soon Hi's apartment. The two of them climbed the steps and Tom knocked on the door. He heard a pitter patter of feet coming toward the door and a soft voice behind it ask, "*Nuguseiyo?*" (Who's there?).

"It's Tom Crandall, American Embassy."

The door opened slowly and a slight elderly Asian woman stood holding a small baby in her arms. She recognized Tom and welcomed the two of them inside, putting the infant into a wooden cradle on one side of the room. She made it clear to them that Soon Hi would return from work soon, and she set out pillows and directed them to sit while she made tea.

A half hour later the front door opened and Soon Hi came in carrying a bagful of groceries. When she saw the two men in the room she almost dropped the bag.

"Oh, Tom! I'm so surprised to see you. Who is this soldier?"

"This is Sergeant Hatcher. He just got in from Korea."

Hatcher nodded his head in greeting, trying to ignore the sick feeling in the pit of his stomach. "Pleased to meet you Miss Chung."

She put the bag down on the floor and held out her hand, her face breaking out in a smile. "You're from Korea? You must know my husband. How is he? I haven't heard from him for more than month ago."

Hatcher cleared his throat. "Yes, I knew your husband, ma'am. We were in the same platoon. I...uh....I'm afraid I have some bad news."

Her face turned from a look of elation to one of sheer anguish, her lower lip quivering. "What are you saying? Is he hurt?"

"Ma'am, he was killed in action. Outside Masan. It happened a month ago. He wanted me to find you and tell you. I couldn't leave Korea until now. I..."

"*O-moh-moh! Chongmallo? Ohtohkkeh?* (Oh, no! Is it real? How?)" She turned to Tom with pleading eyes, "It's not true Tom. Tell me."

Tom put his arms around her as she began to sob. "It is true Soon Hi. He showed me your picture that Chae Hoon carried with him. I'm so sorry— so sorry." He felt her legs collapsing and he eased her gently down to the floor where she began weeping uncontrollably, her head in her lap. Her mother sensing what was happening went to console her. After two or three minutes the baby began to cry and Soon Hi slowly raised her head. She stood up, wiping the tears from her eyes, and went over and picked up the baby, cooing to him softly. Holding the baby to her chest, she turned toward Hatcher, her face a frozen mask of determination. "Do you know where my husband buried?"

"They told me at the hospital that he was buried in a military cemetery in Pusan."

"I must go there. I must go see my husband's grave."

Tom spoke up, "It's too dangerous. It's not possible for you to go while they're still fighting. Think of the baby."

"Mother will take care of the baby. I need to go there, Tom. Korea is my home. I'm not afraid of any danger. But I must go."

"Okay. Okay. Don't try anything on your own. You'll get yourself in trouble. I'll see what I can do. But you need to give me a little time."

"All right," she said. "But hurry."

CHAPTER 32

RETURNING HOME

September-October 1953

By mid-September American troops had captured Seoul. To General Taylor and his Eighth Army staff it seemed like only a matter of weeks before they would destroy the entire KPA army and end Kim Il Sung's dictatorial regime once and for all. Almost lost in the newspaper headlines regarding Korea, was the surrender in August of the last remnants of the KPA army on the island of Tsushima. With most of the southern portion of the peninsula liberated from Communist control, Yi Pom Sok moved his government operations to Taegu and announced plans for national elections by the end of the year.

In the three months since initially landing at Inchon, the ROK Army had doubled in size, with new recruits and deserters from the KPA swelling its ranks to more than a 120,000. With the combined U.S. and ROK Army troop strength now exceeding 200,000, they not only outgunned the Korean Communists but outmanned them. After capturing the old capital city of Seoul and having purged the southern half of Communist combatants, General Clark, Commander of Combined Far East Forces, sent a top secret message to Washington requesting authority to continue the pursuit north to finish the job of defeating Kim Il Sung's army and unify the peninsula. With little debate, the Joint Chiefs of Staff responded with a quick approval, the lone proviso being that American troops were not to approach the border with China.

On October 1, 1953, while Air Force B-29 bombers pummeled targets north of the 38th parallel and Navy cruisers blasted shore facilities with their eight inch guns, Eighth Army began a two pronged ground attack. The U.S. 7th and 2nd Infantry Divisions supported by an armored brigade began moving up the western corridor with its objective to take Pyongyang. On the other side of the peninsula, the Marine Corps' 1st Division, backed up by a newly reorganized Korean division under General Paek Sun Yop began driving north to capture the important port city of Wonsan. Sensing his own defeat was near at hand, Kim Il Sung fled from Pyongyang and escaped to the northwest corner of the country, to the city of Sinuiju on the Manchurian border.

. . .

While the fighting dragged on in Korea, Soon Hi was becoming more and more anxious about finding a way to get back to her home and to her husband's grave. She had written to her brother In Yong, but he'd been unable to help. Tom hadn't been able to make any headway with the new South Korean government either—too dangerous, people said. The new government was just getting organized and it was difficult to get any answers. Tom was finally able to make contact with an old acquaintance who he knew to be working in the Yi administration, now operating in Taegu. Chong Kyu Choe, the man who had come to him when he was in Washington asking for help for the exile government, was now a special assistant to the new president. After returning to Korea, Choe discarded the Americanized first name. He was sympathetic and promised to help Tom but confessed that immigration was not at the top of the list of priorities and it could take some time. Day after day, he waited.

. . .

The phone on his desk rang, and he picked it up. "This is Tom Crandall."

It was Soon Hi, her voice tense. "Tom, I've found someone who takes people by boat to Korea. It's a big price, but I won't have to get

259

anyone's approval. They charge a lot but, I can't wait any longer. My older brother is in Taegu. He'll help me when I get there."

"Soon Hi. Don't do anything foolish! If you go there on some smuggler's boat you'll be picked up and thrown in some refugee camp—or worse, you could be accused of being a spy and sent to a prison camp. Your other brother was a Communist. The authorities there will know about him, and you'll be arrested. Give me a chance. You know how government offices work. I can get your authorization in a day or two, I'm sure."

"You are very good person Tom. I know you try. Maybe I try to wait a little more. But I can't wait long."

"Thank you Soon Hi. I worry about you and don't want anything to happen to you. I'll contact you as soon as I get word back."

He hung up the phone, and immediately placed a priority call to Korea—to the one person he hoped would come through for him with an entry authorization. Finally he reached a secretary who spoke English. "Mr. Choe is out of the office this afternoon," she said.

Tom left a message with the secretary asking him to return his call regarding Soon Hi's entry visa. The next afternoon Choe called him back.

"Mr. Crandall, I'm sorry I wasn't able to get you an answer on Miss Chung before now. Things have been like—how do you say—everyone runs around like chicken."

"I understand Mr. Choe, but have you been able to come up with anything?"

"Yes. I was able to get the special entry authorization signed just a short time ago. I'll send a telegram to confirm it later today, and I'll send the signed document in a diplomatic pouch. It should get to you by late tomorrow or next day."

"I don't know how to thank you."

"She won't have any trouble entering Korea with this document. I can't help everyone like this, but for you—I owe you much. I'm glad I can do for you."

After getting off the phone Tom tried to concentrate on his work, but he couldn't. The normal delivery of routine messages wouldn't be until the next morning. He wanted to get that authorization and go to Soon Hi before she did something stupid. Finally, he got up and went to the communication center to check to see if the message from Choe had been received. The desk clerk grudgingly brought him a six inch high stack of routine incoming messages. Towards the bottom of the pile he found what he was looking for— the immigrant entry authorization. He pulled the message out, signed for it, and rushed back to his office.

Tom called Soon Hi's work number but was told that she had left work at noon and hadn't returned but they would leave a message for her to call. When she hadn't returned his call by the end of the work day, he decided he'd better go to her place to check on her. When he got to her apartment, her mother answered the door and invited him in. Not seeing Soon Hi, he asked her, using Japanese as the common language between them, "*Soon Hi wa doko desu ka*? (Where's Soon Hi?)"

Her mother, wringing her hands together, said "*Ichijikan maeni Shinjuku eki e itta*. (She went to Shinjuku train station an hour ago)."

His shoulders slumped as if a hundred pound bar bell had been laid across them. "*Doko ni ikimasuka*? (Where is she going?)"

"*Osaka e*," she said.

"*Akachan*? (The baby?)"

The old woman pointed to the crib on the other side of the room. *Good. At least the boy's safe. Maybe I can get to her before she boards.* He thanked the old woman and hurried out the door and into the street. Luck was with him as an empty cab came by right away. The terminal concourse was teeming with people. He checked the departure boards and saw two trains leaving for Osaka. An express train was leaving from track #1 at 6:15, in ten minutes. Another train, a local, was scheduled to leave in thirty-five minutes. There was a line at the ticket counter but he knew he couldn't get through the gate without a ticket. He stood in line, checking his watch every few seconds. By the time he got his ticket, his watch showed 6:11. He ran toward the gate, thrust his ticket into the gate keeper's hand, and went down the stairs two at time to the platform. The big steam driven engine was belching smoke, preparing to leave as he got to the platform. He ran alongside the passenger cars, looking into each window trying to spot Soon Hi inside. He didn't see her. Was she on the other side of the car? The train started to move and, for a moment, he thought of jumping aboard. He stopped himself. What if she's taking the other train? He stood there, frozen, as the cars rolled past him. When the last car passed, he looked across the empty tracks. There on the other platform he saw Soon Hi waiting in line to board another train. He yelled out, "Soon Hi!"

She looked his way, and then turn her head away. With a surge of energy he ran up the stairs to the main floor, crossing over to the next platform. By the time he got to the train, she had already boarded, but he wasn't sure which car she might be in. He climbed aboard the front passenger car and began walking through car by car. In the third car he saw her seated with an elderly woman.

Soon Hi looked up at him as he stood over her. "Don't try to stop me. I know you try, but you can't help me. I have to help myself."

"I *can* help you." He pulled out the message from his coat pocket. "Here is the authorization for you to go to Korea legally. You don't need to rely on any smuggler. I'll buy you a plane ticket and you won't have to fear being arrested. C'mon, let's go home."

At first she frowned as if not believing what he said. She took the paper from him and looked at it for several seconds. Then, with a wan smile on her face, she nodded her head, picked up her small suitcase from underneath the seat, and said, "Okay. We go back home now."

• • •

Four days later Soon Hi stood on the tarmac at Haneda Airport, waiting to board a plane to Korea. Tom stood beside her, along with her mother who was holding her grandson. Soon Hi tried to remain strong, but when she touched her son's head, she could no longer hold back the tears. She picked him up and held him tight to her breast. Sobbing, she told him, "I'm sorry my son. I'm sorry. I have to go to your father's grave." She choked on her words as she handed the child back to her mother. "I'll send for you soon. Be a good little boy for grandma." She brushed the tears aside and turned to Tom. "Thank you for everything."

"You know I would do anything to help you Soon Hi. Write to me when you get settled. I'll check in periodically on your mother and baby."

She reached out, put her arms around Tom, and began to cry again before pushing herself away. Her eyes met her mother's. She bowed, bending her head forward with eyes closed out of respect. Then, after several seconds, she stood erect and, without further words, strode briskly towards the airplane that would take her home—home to Korea. Tom, still in love with her, stood transfixed, wondering if they would ever meet again.

. . .

Forty-five minutes after leaving Haneda the plane landed at Pusan's Kimhae Airport on the Korean peninsula. As she stepped onto the tarmac she saw someone waving from behind a fence at the edge of the landing strip. Was he waving at her? After she passed through the security gate, and what passed for customs, she saw him up close— she could hardly believe it. It was her brother In Yong. "*Oppa*," she screamed as she ran into his arms, heedless of other people around her. After recovering her composure, she stood back to gather in the brother who she hadn't seen in more than three years. He was much thinner, his face drawn, the high cheekbones standing out like rocky crags on a barren cliff. The rumpled gray suit he wore looked a bit oversized on him and made him look older than he was. His time in a labor camp had taken its toll, but to her, he looked wonderful.

"How did you know I was coming?"

In Yong motioned to the man standing beside him. "This is Mr. Choe. He works for President Yi. He's the one who's responsible for getting your visa approved."

She bowed her head and said, "Thank you, Mr. Choe. How did you know to find my brother?"

"Ah, it wasn't so hard Miss Chung. Your friend, Mr. Crandall, is my friend also. He told me about your brother and that you would want to find him when you arrived. I wanted to save you the trouble. Your brother is a much respected journalist in Taegu, and I had little trouble tracking him down."

She thanked the government official again, and then said to her brother, "I'm so happy to be home in Korea, but my husband Chae

Hoon is the reason I had to come now. Do you know where my husband is buried?"

"Yes," said In Yong. "He's in a military cemetery in Pusan—not too far from here. I'll take you there, but not this afternoon. We'll go back to Taegu, to my apartment, where you can get some rest. Then tomorrow, we'll come back and go to the cemetery."

At first she wanted to argue, but then she realized he was right. Taegu was only an hour's train ride away. Tomorrow would be soon enough.

• • •

The next morning Soon Hi woke earlier than normal, but her brother was already up and had breakfast heating on a small gas range in the next room. She noticed he'd left a half-filled bucket of water and a small hand mirror on the floor next to her bedding. She dressed quickly, splashed water on her face and arms and fixed her hair as best she could using the mirror her brother provided, and she even added a little makeup from a small supply she'd brought with her.

Over breakfast they discussed what they would do about bringing their mother and the baby to Korea. In Yong assured his sister that he would bring them to Korea as soon as the military situation settled down. She hated being apart even for a day, but knew she had to wait. He didn't want to talk about their brother In Su, but she insisted she needed to know everything. As he went over the scene of how In Su had helped him escape but was killed, tears streamed down her face. When he'd finished, she sniffled softly and wiped away the tears from her eyes. "When I saw him last," she said, "I thought the vengeance he had in his heart had driven him from our family forever. But knowing what he did to save you, even though he died, makes me so proud and happy that his love for family was more important than anything."

In Yong touched her gently on the arm, his own eyes turning glossy, and got up from the table. "We'd better be going to catch our train for Pusan."

• • •

When they arrived at the cemetery on the western outskirts of the city, they stopped at the custodian's shack to ask for directions to Chae Hoon's grave site. The custodian pulled out a large sheet of paper with grids marked out by hand. In Yong looked at the map and saw that the grids were arranged by date groupings, a separate grid for each month. The names of people buried within the grids were not shown. In Yong asked Soon Hi, "When did Chae Hoon die?"

She thought for a moment. "I think it was near the end of July, July 29, is what Sergeant Hatcher told me."

"Okay, he must be in this grid here," he said pointing. He thanked the custodian and they started out toward the far end of the cemetery. There were hundreds of grave sites, and he was glad that they had at least a rough map to go by. When they got to the section marked "July" they began checking the stone markers for names. Most of the markers had names written in Hangul, but some simply said "unknown soldier." Chae Hoon had died in an American hospital and they were certain his name would be inscribed on a marker, but when they reached the last one in that section without finding his name, they were mystified. They went through all the markers again, but still nothing. Soon Hi stomped her feet and shouted, "What have they done with my husband? He's not here!"

In Yong stood staring at the ground, searching his brain for an answer. *He has to be here.* Then it struck him. *Maybe the grid date doesn't indicate date of death. Maybe it means date of burial.* "Let's check the next grid over," he said.

After a five minute search they found a marker with the inscription:

Han Chae Hoon
1st Lieutenant, ROKA
Died July 29, 1953
Kyongsangnam-do

The two of them stood for a moment without saying anything. Soon Hi, holding a bouquet of flowers, bent over and laid it on the grass in front of the stone. Then she took a small bottle of cider from her purse, opened the top, and poured it over the grave, whispering silently words her brother could not hear. Then the two of them knelt before the gravestone, bowing with arms outstretched for more than a minute. Soon Hi didn't cry. She had found her husband, had honored his memory, and now it was time to move on.

As the two rode back on the train to Taegu later that afternoon, Soon Hi stared out the window at the barren hillsides that had been laid waste by the fighting that had gone on over the past year. In Yong asked, "What plans do you have now for your future?"

"I was hoping I could stay with you for a while until I can find work."

"You're welcome to stay with me, but I'm not sure how long I'll be here in Taegu. Since Seoul is now freed from the Communists, it looks like my newspaper will be moving its main offices back there in a month or so. So...that means I won't be here very long. But maybe I can help you find something. What kind of work are you looking for?"

"I can do a lot of things. I can do office work. For the last year in Japan I was managing a food bank and clothing outlet on my own. But if I have to do factory work, or work on a farm, I'll do that."

In Yong thought for a moment. "I just finished doing a story on orphanages in the Taegu area. There are so many kids without parents, and they're being overwhelmed. One, in particular, I remember. An American missionary over on the west side. Mill something...I don't remember the name right now, but I can look it up. Spoke fairly good Korean. He told me they needed a Korean office manager who also knows English to handle their business accounts and to work with adoption agencies. Do you think you might be interested?"

Soon Hi smiled, "I think that would be perfect."

CHAPTER 33

CHINA COMES IN

October 1953–November 1954

By late September U.S. and ROK forces had crossed the 38th parallel and were approaching the Taedong River, just south of Pyongyang. Air Force bombing raids were devastating what was left of any industrial capacity in the northern half of the peninsula. Kim Il Sung's vaunted fighting force was no more. At least half of the original force had been killed or captured, and the rest was in disarray. But even with Soviet Foreign Minister Molotov urging him to leave Korea and regroup, he was not ready to give up his fight.

After evacuating Pyongyang, Kim set up his new government in the far northwest city of Sinuiju on the border with Manchuria and boasted that he would defeat the American imperialists and their Korean lackeys by pursuing a guerilla war. Despite these public pronouncements, he knew he could not hold off the Americans alone. In desperate effort to save his dying regime, he appealed to the Chinese for help.

Ever since the Chinese Communist victory over the Nationalists in 1949, Mao Tse Tung had been threatening to invade the island of Formosa where Chiang Kai Shek had set up his exiled Republic of China government. Only the United States had stood between his goal of wiping Chiang and his despised minions from the face of the earth. Mao had no navy to challenge the American Seventh Fleet that protected the island nation where Chiang held sway. He didn't have the ships or weaponry to fight the Americans on the sea. What he did have was foot soldiers — lots of them.

When the call for help came from Choson, there were already 300,000 Chinese troops ensconced in the hills of southern Manchuria, opposite the Yalu River. Mao had made no secret of his determination to respond militarily to any encroachment of the Manchurian border by American forces or their proxies. He had made his position clear through direct statement in the Communist press as well as through diplomatic channels friendly to the Chinese People's Republic. By mid-November, U.S. forces had taken Pyongyang in the west and Wonsan harbor in the east. Intelligence reports indicated that Chinese forces were now in Korea. Although exact numbers were in dispute, intelligence estimates provided to General Taylor put the figure at no more than four divisions, or perhaps 50,000. In actuality there were a lot more.

In an effort to identify the real Chinese threat, General Taylor ordered the 2nd Division's 23rd Regiment north into Pyongan Province to search out enemy forces, and they found them. On November 3, near the village of Kaechon, fifty miles north of Pyongyang, they ran into a full division of the Chinese Fourth Field Army. They fell upon the Americans from the surrounding mountains like a rolling wave. During the first few minutes of the fighting Brigadier General Brent Rogers the regimental commander was killed. Outnumbered by nearly ten to one, facing possible annihilation, the acting commander, Colonel Michael Madison fell back with his entire regiment into the protective cover of some low hills where he was able to use his howitzers to hold the enemy at bay for a full twelve hours until Air Force Thunderjets arrived. By nightfall the fighting had fallen off enough to allow Madison to gather his survivors and begin a full retreat back to Pyongyang.

The attack at Kaechon marked the beginning of a broad Communist counter-offensive to defeat the Americans and their ROK allies. By early December, the Communists had forced the Americans to evacuate Pyongyang and retreat farther south. By rushing two new army divisions north of the 38th parallel, General Taylor was able to halt the Chinese offensive and a tenuous line of defense was established by Eighth Army across the waist of the peninsula running from Wonsan on the eastern coast to Haeju on the western side.

Early winter storms seemed to ensure that there would be at least three or four months before the enemy would start serious offensive operations, but General Clark, the allied theater commander, knew for certain that when spring came, the Chinese would have more men on the line and would start pushing again. He didn't want to wait until spring to do something about it. Even though he might be able to inflict punishing casualties on the enemy with the men he had, the Chinese had virtually an unlimited supply of soldiers that could be sent in to Korea. Unless their supply of men and material could be cut off, the American Army couldn't force the Chinese off the field of battle. He knew it would require a 500,000 man force, plus whatever the ROKs could provide to defeat the Chinese. The Congress wasn't going to go for that. No, he needed a bigger punch—a nuclear punch. Only the president could authorize that, however, and in mid-December he sent a proposal to the Joint Chiefs of Staff, outlining his plan for a winter offensive and requesting that he be allowed use of tactical nuclear bombs to destroy the Chinese supply bases in southern Manchuria and to make the Korean-Chinese border so radioactive it would be impassable to human traffic.

. . .

It was just a few days before Christmas. Snowflakes filled the late December sky, as Admiral Radford approached the entrance to the West Wing of the White House. After showing his badge to the security guard, he made his way through the hallway to the cabinet room where the NSC meeting was scheduled to start in ten minutes. He was the first one there, other than James Lay, the executive secretary. He opened his briefcase and took out a file folder containing his briefing material. He'd attended these meetings almost every week for the past three months, ever since he took over as chairman of the JCS, but he hadn't had to make a proposal like the one he was about to make—a proposal to use tactical nukes in Korea. While he read over his papers, Robert Cutler, the president's special assistant came in and began putting copies of the agenda on the table.

Charlie Wilson, the Secretary of Defense entered the room, but said nothing, seeing that Radford had his head down in his notes. He took a seat next to Radford and was soon joined by Nathan Twining, the Air Force chief, and Matthew Ridgway, the Army chief, who he'd asked to attend in case questions arose over the disposition of air or ground forces. CIA Director Allen Dulles came in the room talking with two CIA aides who took seats along the wall. Dulles sat down at the far end of the table. George Humphrey, the Secretary of Treasury walked in with a cadre of aides and took a seat beside the CIA chief. Secretary of State Foster Dulles, Allen's older brother, lumbered in like an aged bear, and sat down next to the empty seat at the head of the table. He was followed in by Walter Robertson, his chief adviser on East Asia and Henry Cabot Lodge, ambassador to the UN. Finally, Vice President Nixon came in, looked around to see that everyone who was supposed to be there was, and instructed Cutler to tell the president they were ready to start.

President Eisenhower entered the room and, after acknowledging greetings, looked briefly at the agenda, and then asked Allen Dulles to open the meeting. After the customary intelligence briefing on current world hot spots, the secretary of state gave a quick rundown on the current food crisis in East Germany, and then George Humphrey spent ten minutes detailing his concerns about the inflationary impact of the war in Korea. With those preliminary discussions out of the way, the president turned to Admiral Radford.

The admiral stood up, confident in knowing the Policy Planning Board had already given a thumbs up on the proposal, and began his presentation. Eisenhower listened carefully as he outlined the planned offensive. He ended his fifteen minute briefing telling the president, "The use of tactical atomic bombs is the *only* way to end the war honorably on our terms, just as we ended the war with Japan." Eisenhower winced when he added, "What I learned from General MacArthur is that the only thing the Chinese understand is overwhelming force. And so, as chairman of the JCS, I'm recommending that we employ tactical nuclear bombs immediately."

The president asked for comments from others around the table. There was no disagreement from any of the members. Foster Dulles, said, "We've been telling the Chinese we will use atomic weapons if they attempt to invade Taiwan. This is no different. We should tell them to withdraw their forces from Korea or we will use the atomic bomb. If they don't leave, then we should use it. If we don't, they won't believe any threat we make."

Eisenhower listened to the others, all concurring in Radford's position. Then he slowly took off his glasses, laid them on the table in front of him, a weary look on his face. "Let me tell you something gentlemen. Several years ago, during the Potsdam Conference in Germany, President Truman asked my advice about dropping the A-bomb on Japan. I told him I was against it. I thought we could get the Japs out of the war without that—maybe we wouldn't even have to invade Japan to get them to surrender. He didn't take my advice. That deeds been done, and it can't be undone." He paused before continuing, "I've never said I wouldn't use the atom bomb under any circumstance. But I want to be damn sure that if we ever use it again, it's necessary to our vital national defense. Working with Secretary Dulles, I've developed a nuclear defense policy based on a concept of massive retaliation. It's aimed at preventing enemies from attacking our homeland. That policy is intended to prevent wars—not create bigger wars—and up to now it's been successful."

There was a nodding of heads, and then the president addressed Radford directly, "Let me ask you, admiral. If we were to bomb targets in southern Manchuria with tactical nukes, and then China decided to launch an attack on Taiwan, wouldn't we be expected to respond with other tactical nukes on mainland China, since we told them we would?

"Yes sir. I believe that would be our response."

"And would the Soviet Union sit idly by? Certainly China would demand the Soviets aid them in accordance with their mutual security pact. Would they respond with their own tactical nukes?"

"It's very likely they would sir."

Eisenhower continued, "And where would that lead? What if the Soviets decided to use their tactical nukes in support of the Chinese? Or what if the Soviets took this opportunity to make a play for Berlin again, this time shooting down any of our attempts to supply the city by air. Would this be the start of a new shooting war in Europe?"

After several seconds of mute response, the president answered his own question. "Gentlemen, I respect your desire to end this war in Korea honorably and to slam the door on Communist aggression. But the risks, I believe, are too high for the gain we would possibly achieve by going all out in Korea. I will not approve the request for use of atomic weapons. It's been just over ten years since the end of World War II. I don't want this to be the start of World War III."

After a momentary pause to assess their mute reaction, he continued, "I think the Chinese and North Koreans are exhausted and they have to know they can't win through the use of force. I have no problem with letting the Chinese think we *might* use nuclear bombs, but I think it's time to see if they're ready to negotiate an end to the killing. We've pushed the Communists back to where they were before this Korean mess began and given new life to the Republic of Korea. If we can get the Communists to the table now, I'll consider our efforts a success. If it doesn't work, then we'll have to relook the options. But let's give negotiations a chance."

When the president completed his remarks, Vice-president Nixon spoke up. "I think everyone here fully understands the position you've taken, and we will fully support it without reservation. If we can bring the Communists to the table, you'll be applauded by the nation for ending Truman's war."

After the meeting concluded, as everyone was leaving the conference room, Secretary Dulles grabbed hold of Ambassador Lodge's shoulder and said, "Henry, I know the Soviets have been making noises at the UN about a ceasefire. I want you to talk to Vishinsky and let him know we might be interested. I'll send a message to Bohlen in Moscow to have him get with Molotov."

CHAPTER 34

A TENUOUS PEACE

January – September 1954

Despite freezing cold, with snow and wind sweeping the northern half of the Korean peninsula, sporadic fighting continued unabated through the early months of 1954 — some involving division size clashes. As rumors of a possible ceasefire surfaced in the media, the battle line separating north from south shifted as both sides, like two bulldogs tugging for possession of an old sock, jockeyed for an advantage. In January an air wing of new B-47 bombers was relocated to Kadena Air Base in Okinawa, reinforcing the impression on China and the Soviet Union that the U.S. was serious about its threats to use the atom bomb.

Although China's Mao Tse Tung boasted openly that he had no fear of America's threat to use atomic weapons, the Soviet politburo seemed to take a more cautious view and, in secret communiques, urged the Chinese to begin talks by threatening to withdraw economic aid as well as military equipment and supplies. While publicly maintaining a tough stance, out of the spotlight serious talks were taking place in Beijing. A small coterie of men who had been together since the Long March now had to decide whether Korea was important enough to risk an atomic attack on China or whether it was time for negotiations. Mao Tse Tung was the party chairman and the undisputed leader, but he relied on the advice of his trusted lieutenants that included Chou En Lai, Chu Teh, Chen Yi, and Liu Shaoqui. On a frigid winter night in a modest cement building off Tienanmen Square, the five men met. After going over and over their options for more than four hours, they finally reached agreement that by pushing the United States and their ROK allies back to the 38th parallel they had achieved their aim of maintaining a sufficient buffer to protect Manchuria. They had lost nearly a quarter of a million men in the fighting just completed, and further fighting would endanger plans for developing the Chinese industrial base which the Soviet Union had promised to support. Chu Teh, the oldest of the group at sixty-seven years old, summed up the consensus, saying, "Now is not the time to confront the United States. We need time to build up our strength." Mao nodded his head and said, "You're right comrade Chu. We'll report our recommendation to the full politburo at next Tuesday's meeting. In the meantime, you will advise General Peng in Korea of our intention, and he, then, can inform Comrade Kim.

. . .

When Kim Il Sung was told by General Peng of the Chinese decision to seek a negotiated settlement of the war, he broke into a tirade. "No! No! Mao can't make this decision on his own. I fought too hard to unify this country. Now the Americans have taken back what I fought for. I am a loyal Communist. Mao must support me and continue to fight against the imperialist capitalists."

"Calm down,' comrade Kim. Chairman Mao doesn't march to your orders," cautioned Peng. "You are not even in charge here in Korea. Let me remind you that it is the Chinese People's Army that saved you from extermination. You should be happy with that."

"I *am* grateful General Peng, but you have not finished the job you came for."

"I follow the orders of my chairman—not you. I have simply passed on information that has been given to me."

"Then I want to see Chairman Mao. If China won't help me, then you can take your soldiers and leave, and I will fight the Americans on my own."

"You're in no position to make demands on us. Don't make threats you can't back up Comrade Kim."

With that, Kim turned around and stormed out of the room. If Mao wouldn't support him, he would use his leverage to obtain the support of his other Communist patron. Playing one country off against another had worked in the past, and he was sure it would again. The following evening he boarded a Soviet military transport for Moscow, an arrangement he negotiated with Colonel Ivor Pugachev, chief of the Soviet advisory team attached to the KPA. To his relief, the Chinese didn't try to stop him.

Kim spoke passable Russian, learned during his years of forced exile as a guerilla fighter in the Soviet Far East when the Japanese controlled Korea. The colonel had told him he couldn't guarantee that he'd be able to see Khrushchev, but someone from the politburo would meet with him.

When he arrived at Kubinka Air Base outside Moscow, he was met by a KGB officer who introduced himself as Colonel Kerchenko and took him to a hotel not far from the Kremlin. Kim hoped he would be able to meet with Khrushchev himself, but the officer told him that would be up to the politburo and he would let him know as soon as he was given directions. Kim waited, confined to his dreary hotel room, paint peeling on the cracked plaster wall and a lonely picture of Lenin the sole decoration. Restricted from going outside, he was served his meals in the room. For lunch he had cabbage soup and bread. For supper he had a boiled soup with a fatty pork hock along with more bread. No rice, and no kimchi. For Kim it was a kind of torture.

Finally, on the fourth day, the KGB officer returned and told Kim he had an appointment at one o'clock with Chairman Khrushchev in the Kremlin and that they should proceed there now. Kim put on his overcoat and picked up his briefcase. As he walked the several blocks toward the Kremlin, he practiced in his head what he would say to the Soviet party leader. He'd been here once before. He'd come in 1950 and met with Premier Stalin to get his approval to invade South Korea. Now he was back to ask again, but Stalin was no more. How would Khrushchev respond? He wasn't sure.

When he and Colonel Kerchenko entered the immense marble floored office of the first secretary, his eyes focused on the pudgy bald-headed man dwarfed behind a huge desk. Vyacheslav Molotov, the foreign minister was to his right sitting on a sofa. Molotov was first to get up from his seat and came up to shake Kim's hand.

Khrushchev, more deliberate, came around his desk with a broad smile on his face as if he were about to greet an old friend, and gave Kim a big bear hug. "You have had a long trip, comrade. Would you like a glass of good Russian vodka?"

"Thank you, no, Mr. Secretary. I want to make my presentation to you with a clear head."

Khrushchev went back around his desk and sat back down and Molotov took his seat back on the sofa. "All right Comrade Kim, tell us why you have come."

"Yes, yes," he said, shuffling his feet nervously. "Five days ago I was informed by General Peng that the Chinese People's government intends to negotiate with the Americans to end the fight for Choson." He paused and glanced first at Molotov and then to Khrushchev, trying to get a clue as to their attitude. Their faces remained fixed like stone. He cleared his throat and went on, "This is intolerable to me. I fought my whole life to remove foreigners from Choson. I even defeated the Americans. Drove them and their South Korean lap dogs off the peninsula. Now they have snuck back in and taken away what I fought for. I can't defeat them alone. I need the help of the great Soviet Union. Four years ago, I came here and asked Premier Stalin for help. Now I come here to ask you for help. I have here some messages from Premier Stalin saying how the Soviet Union would provide assistance..."

He bent down to pick a document out of his briefcase, and Khrushchev raised his hand to interrupt. "No need to show me those documents comrade. I'm sure I'm familiar with them already. We appreciate the difficult situation you're in. But Premier Stalin is no more. Our interests have changed since then, and you...I'm afraid you have no real authority any more to represent your people."

"What? What are you talking about?"

With a Cheshire cat-like smile on his face, Khrushchev said, "Last night we received intelligence that a coup has occurred within your party headquarters in Sinuiju. According to information I've been given, General Peng arrested several members of your standing committee for anti-party conspiracy activities. A meeting of the party central committee was then held and they voted to remove you from office and elected Pak Il U as the new chairman of the Korean Workers Party."

Kim's face went white. "Pak Il U-*sippalnom baibanja!*"

"What's that you say comrade?"

"I said he's a fucking traitor. That's what he is. The Chinese brought him in just for this. You have to help. I have to return."

Khrushchev's belly began to vibrate as he chuckled to himself. "No, no, comrade," he said. "You can't return now. They'll arrest you as soon as you enter and put you before a firing squad—but don't worry. Of course, we will help you. I am aware of your many years of loyalty to the Soviet Union and to the Communist cause. I can assure you we will approve your request for asylum here in the Soviet Union. Colonel Kerchenko will assist you with the paperwork. I should tell you we are opening up new lands for agriculture in Kazakhstan and we are looking for good people to manage our collective farms."

Khrushchev got up from behind his desk again, patted Kim on the back and said, "Now, comrade. Would you like to have that glass of vodka before you leave?"

"*Dah,*" said Kim, his head hanging down in resignation.

. . .

Following the coup in Choson, Pak Il U, the new party leader, quickly endorsed Red China's position on negotiations. A few days later the Chinese Communist Party newspaper, *Jen Min Jih Pao*, printed a short article in the corner of the front page announcing that China and Choson had agreed to negotiate an end to the Korean conflict.

. . .

As the mountain streams of central Korea swelled with the spring runoff of melting snow from mountains denuded of forests by years of artillery shelling and aerial bombardment, an end to the fighting seemed finally to be near. On April 2, 1954, in a small brick building in the village of Kaesong, military representatives of the United States, the Republic of Korea, and Japan sat down with representatives of the People's Republic of China, and the Democratic People's Republic of Choson to begin negotiations for an end to hostilities.

The Chinese and their Choson allies didn't give ground easily, but after more than three months of hard bargaining, and occasional firefights along the border, the two sides came to an agreement. The territorial dispute with Japan over Tsushima was settled quickly. The Japanese had regained complete control of Tsushima the previous year, and once the issue of POWs was settled, the Choson negotiators agreed to give up any future rights to that island. However, issues related to prisoners of war on the Korean peninsula and the exact boundary line that was to separate the two Koreas took longer. Finally, on July 8, they signed an armistice document that provided for an exchange of POWs and established a line of demarcation to separate Choson in the north from the Republic of Korea in the south until such time as peaceful unification could be worked out. A final article inserted at the end of the armistice agreement recommended that the governments of both sides meet within ninety days, at a place to be decided, to discuss the withdrawal of foreign forces from Korea and the peaceful unification of the Korean peninsula.

.　.　.

In October, after several weeks of diplomatic back and forth, each of the nations that participated in the Korean armistice talks sent diplomatic representatives to Geneva for an international conference on Korean unification. Initially intended to be limited to issues related only on the Korean peninsula, it was expanded, at the request of France and the Soviet Union, to also cover unresolved issues in Southeast Asia related to Vietnam which had boiled over following the French defeat at Dien Bien Phu.

Talks over Korean unification of the Korean peninsula did not go well from the start. South Korea, backed by the United States, refused to back down from having UN-supervised elections throughout the country and wanted to maintain U.S. troop presence in the country as long as the threat of renewed fighting continued. China and Choson insisted that all foreign troops be withdrawn from Korea immediately and that an all-Korea commission, divided equally between Republic of Korea and Choson representatives, be set up to supervise elections and plan for unification. Although a tentative agreement was reached between North and South Korean representatives to meet in the future to discuss unification, everyone left the conference with serious doubts as to whether unification would ever be possible.

CHAPTER 35

REUNION

April 1957

Tom Crandall peered out the plane's window as it bumped to a landing and taxied toward the Kimpo Airport terminal. So much had happened in the six years since he'd left on an evacuation flight back in 1950. After spending the last two years in the states, he found he really missed Asia, and he had to admit to himself, he wanted to see Soon Hi again more than anything. He'd kept in touch with occasional letters, but he couldn't be sure if there was any feeling other than friendship for him. He needed to stop in Seoul to process through personnel before reporting to the consulate in Pusan. That would give him the weekend to stop in Taegu to look her up.

Although more than two years had passed since the fighting had ended, signs of an active military presence were very much in evidence as Tom stepped off the plane. Several Air Force fighter jets were parked on the far side of the field near camouflaged hangers, and a C-47 military cargo plane was just touching down on an adjacent runway. He looked around and saw the terminal, a low rectangular building with corrugated metal walls and a tin roof, all painted a dull green—not very impressive. It seemed pretty clear the place was still on a war footing.

After picking up his luggage, one suitcase and a duffel bag, Tom went outside the terminal and caught sight of a gaunt fiftyish looking Korean man wearing an untucked white shirt and tan pants holding a sign that read, "Welcome Mr. Crandall." Walking up to the man, he soon understood he was a driver sent from the embassy. After introductions, he followed the driver over to a black Willey's jeep with embassy tags, his limousine for the ride into Seoul.

Bouncing painfully with every rut and hole in the partially paved road that ran alongside the Han River, he gazed out at the squatter huts dotting the river's flood plain where farmers in traditional white garb busily tended their muddy fields. *When the rains come in June, they'll all be flooded out.* As he got closer to the city, he could see a lot of evidence of damage done during the war. Whole blocks were wiped out in some places, but in other areas, damage was slight. The worst thing was that many people had lost their homes, and the hillsides were packed with hastily built shelters of stone, brick, and, mud where people had carved out niches clear to the hill tops. A bad rainstorm would create landslides that would kill a lot of those people. Crews of workers alongside the road worked mostly by hand repairing the road bed. He could see also that there was a lot of construction going on, as every block had new buildings framed with wooden scaffolding to which workers clung like insects caught in silken spider webs.

As he neared the center of town, he mused about the future of South Korea. He wasn't surprised that the two-Korea talks that followed the Geneva Conference had failed after a mere three months. Now they were back to throwing threats and accusations against each other. But he was optimistic about the south's chances for success. Under continued American prodding, new elections under UN supervision were actually held in 1955. Most people in the State Department that he'd talked to before leaving, viewed the elections as a positive sign for democracy in South Korea, particularly since the leader of the opposition party, Chang Myon, the former ambassador to the United States, had been elected president over the old Rhee protégé Yi Pom Sok. Now he was talking about reopening talks with Choson. *He has a big challenge to get South Korea on its feet, but he'll succeed, as long as there isn't another war.*

.   .   .

After completing his in-processing through the embassy the next day, Tom packed up his suitcase once again. Early on Saturday morning he caught a taxi for the Seoul train station, one of the few western style buildings that survived the war nearly intact, and purchased a ticket for Taegu where he hoped to find Soon Hi. Taking a seat next to an elderly Korean man in a weathered gray suit and a battered felt fedora, he introduced himself and tried to start a conversation. While in the states, Tom had attended six months intensive Korean language training and he was itching to use his new skill. After a few halting exchanges the old man became bored with having to repeat himself and, while Tom was thinking of what else to say, he pulled the brim of his hat over his eyes, and leaned his head against the window, pretending to take a nap.

Tom, shrugged his shoulders, leaned back in his seat and pulled a letter he was carrying from his jacket pocket. It was the last letter he'd received from Soon Hi—that was two months ago. He began reading it over again:

Dear Tom:

I receive your letter one week ago. I am very busy these days with office work at Mu Kung Hwa. Every week we receive new orphans, but it's difficult to find new parents. We have more than seventy children staying here. Many have disable condition. Some have foreign fathers. Mothers give away and no one wants to adopt. They are taken care now, but I worry for them when they become adult. They have no place to go.

Pastor Millbrook and his wife Sarah are very kind to me, and I like them both. I work as secretary for pastor. He has given me a room here at the orphanage, and I am able to save some money for Tae Woo's future. Miss Sarah is school teacher and she wants me to study Bible, but I'm not a very good student. Although my husband Chae Hoon grew up as Christian we didn't talk about it. I still believe my mother's Buddhism, but Miss Sarah says I can't have both. I must choose one or other. It confuses me. But I don't want her be angry with me, so I try to be good student.

Living here in orphanage is good for Tae Woo and me. Tae Woo is even learning some English words. He has many play friends every day. He's three years old now (western calendar) and becoming big boy looking like father. If you return to Korea, please stop here, and I will show you my orphanage.

Always your friend,
Soon Hi

Tom laid the letter in his lap and leaned his head against the seat back. *I wrote to her after that, but she never wrote back. Why? Maybe she has a boyfriend or fiancé. Wouldn't she have said something? No matter. Tomorrow I'll go to the orphanage.*

. . .

Soon Hi stood in the playground with a soccer ball over her head ready to bounce it to a five-year-old boy with his arms wide spread, a big grin on his face. She tossed the ball and it bounced behind him. The young boy, despite a foot twisted awkwardly inward, turned around, and hobbled after the ball. She looked across to the other side of the playground where her son was playing in a pile of sand with two other children. *If only his father were still alive. If only Tae Woo had a father, life would be perfect.* She turned her head to see the five-year-old approaching her with the ball raising his arms to throw, and she put out her hands to receive his toss. Just as he drew his arm back, he dropped the ball and pointed behind her. "*Mikuk saram achumah (auntie, there's an American).*" She swiveled her head around to see Tom standing there with a bouquet of flowers in one hand and a bag in the other.

She clapped her hands to her face in surprise. "Tom! You came here. I wasn't expecting..."

He held out the flowers for her. "These are for you. I wrote to you to tell you I was coming. Didn't you get my letter?"

"No. I didn't receive anything," she said as she took the flowers and put them to her nose.

Tom took a deep breath. Now he knew why she hadn't replied. "I think the Korean postal service needs a new director," he joked. Lifting up the paper sack in his left hand, he said, "I have something here for Tae Woo. Is this Tae Woo?"

"No," she said. "He's over there." She called her son, and he came running over to her.

Tom drew a furry brown teddy bear from the sack and started to hand it to Tae Woo when Soon Hi stopped him. "No. He cannot have present for himself. Children here must share. He cannot accept."

Tom's first reaction was to feel hurt that she'd rejected the gift, but after considering what she'd said, he told her, "Hey, I was stupid to not think of that. What should I do with it?"

Soon Hi took the teddy bear and said, "I know you mean good, Tom. Don't feel bad. I give it to Miss Pang who takes care of children nursery."

Quickly changing the subject, Tom asked her about her mother. "Ah, she is in Seoul now living with my brother In Yong. He is married now and has child of his own. My mother is happy caring for him." Then after explaining briefly how she came to work at the orphanage, she said, "You like me show you around now? I take you to meet Pastor Millbrook."

Tom took Tae Woo's hand, and he and the boy followed Soon Hi to the pastor's office. After sitting and talking with the pastor for several minutes, his wife Sarah joined them and offered to show Tom around the buildings and grounds. He readily accepted the offer. Soon Hi watched Tom with her son as they went from building to building. To her surprise, the two of them seemed to hit it off amazingly well. She smiled approvingly when he pulled a coin from his pocket and made it disappear from his hand and reappear behind his ear, causing little Tae Woo to break out in gleeful laughter. The tour completed, Sarah excused herself and went into her office, leaving Tom and Soon Hi standing in an empty hallway with Tae Woo beside them trying to figure out how to operate a yoyo that Tom had handed him.

As they walked toward the compound gate, Soon Hi was somber over the thought that she might not see Tom again after this. At the gate, Tom turned to her and gave her a hug. Soon Hi, looked up at him, her eyes revealing her sadness. "Thank you for coming to see me, Tom. It means so much to me."

"This doesn't need to be the end of our friendship, Soon Hi. I was planning to spend the night here in Taegu. Would you let me take you to supper tonight?

Her eyes lit up and her heart started to flutter. With a strange sense of anticipation she hadn't felt since the last time she was with her husband, Soon Hi looked up at him. "Oh Tom, I like that very much."

"Great," said Tom, "and since I don't have to be in Pusan until Monday, perhaps the three of us could go to the city park tomorrow, and after that..."

AFTERWORD

Since first I visited Korea in 1964 I've wondered: What if President Truman had withdrawn American troops from Korea in the summer of 1950? How would the history of Korea and the United States be altered?

There are a number of scenarios that can be imagined had the Americans left Korea and allowed the peninsula to be unified under the Communist regime of Kim Il Sung. In this fictional account of the Korean War that I created Truman does withdraw from Korea, but conflict between the new Choson regime and Japan draws America into a renewed war to push back the Communists and reestablish a friendly non-Communist Republic of Korea. The fighting ends with the peninsula split north and south in a manner little changed from the real world situation today. This ending reflects my belief that American power to affect ultimate outcomes in foreign lands is limited.

After completing my final draft, I had an opportunity to meet my college academic advisor, Glenn Paige, who stimulated my interest in Korean studies long ago. At eighty-six-years-old, Dr. Paige remains active in pursuing his love of Asia and world affairs. As a young U.S. Army captain in 1950 he was attached to the ROK Army's 1st Division that captured and held Pyongyang for a month and a half before being driven back and nearly wiped out by massive Chinese assaults. Glenn survived the war to become a highly-respected professor of political science at the University of Hawaii. Late in his career, after witnessing first-hand the effects of war, he became an ardent peace activist, and founded the Center for Global Nonkilling. Sitting in a Korean restaurant in downtown Honolulu, Glenn shared with me a book he'd recently published under the title *Nonkilling Korea: Six Culture Exploration*. It is a collection of essays on the subject of non-violence written by scholars from around the world. I then shared with him a synopsis of my own novel of the Korean War.

After listening to my summation, Glenn, looking somewhat puzzled, said, "Your story ends essentially as the actual war ended. Is that right?"

I nodded my head and waited for his response.

"There's a sequel to this story. Don't you think?"

I pondered a moment as to what *he* was thinking. Then a light went on. There is a sequel that can still be told. It's one in which the two Korea's finally reach a peace settlement that ends the Korean War, a settlement that will introduce a new era in which Korea is at peace with itself and with the outside world, an era with no more killing and no more threats to kill others. A question still remains in my mind though. Will a writer of fiction or a historian be the first to write that sequel?

SELECTED BIBLIOGRAPHY

Acheson, Dean, *Present at the Creation: My Years in the State Department,* W. W. Norton & Co., New York, 1969.

Auer, James E., *The Postwar Rearmament of Japanese Maritime Forces, 1945-71,* Praeger Publishers, New York, 1973.

Brady, James, *The Coldest War: A Memoir of Korea,* St. Martin's Press, New York, 1990.

Cumings, Bruce, *The Korean War,* Modern Library, New York, 2010.

French, Thomas, *National Police Reserve: The Origin of Japan's Self Defense Forces,* Global Oriental Publishing, Boston, 2014.

Halberstam, David, *The Coldest Winter: America and the Korean War,* Hyperion, New York, 2007

Harvey, Robert, *American Shogun: General MacArthur, Emperor Hirohito, and the Drama of Modern Japan,* The Overlook Press, Woodstock, NY, 2006.

Hicks, George, *Japan's Hidden Apartheid,* Ashgate Publishing, Brookfield, VT, 1997.

Jager, Sheila Miyoshi, *Brothers at War: The Unending Conflict in Korea,* W. W. Norton & Co., New York, 2013.

Kinzer, Stephen, *The Brothers: John Foster Dulles, Allen Dulles, and their Secret World War,* Henry Holt and Co., New York, 2013.

Leckie, Robert, *Conflict: The History of the Korean War,* G. P. Putnam & Sons, New York, 1962.

Lee, Chong Sik, *The Korean Workers Party: A Short History*, Hoover Institution Press, Stanford, CA, 1978.

Lintner, Bertil, *Great Leader, Dear Leader: Demystifying North Korea under the Kim Clan*, Silkworm Books, Chiang Mai, Thailand, 2005.

Mitchell, Richard, *The Korean Minority in Japan*, University of California Press, Berkeley, 1967.

McCullough, David, *Truman*, Simon & Schuster, New York, 1992.

Miller, William Lee, *Two Americans: Truman, Eisenhower, and a Dangerous World*, Alfred A. Knopf, New York, 2012.

Miller, Merle, *Plain Speaking: An Oral Biography of Harry S. Truman*, Berkley Publishing Co, New York, 1974.

Paige, Glenn D., *The Korean Decision: June 24-30, 1950*, The Free Press, New York, 1968.
Park, Chung Shin, *Protestantism and Politics in Korea*, University of Washington Press, Seattle, 2003.

Perry, Mark, *The Most Dangerous Man in America: The Making of Douglas MacArthur*, Basic Books, New York, 2014

Ryang, Sonya, *North Koreans in Japan: Language, Ideology, and Identity*, Westview Press, Boulder, CO, 1997.

Smith, Jean Edward, *Eisenhower in War and Peace*, Random House, New York, 2012.

Spector, Ronald H., *In the Ruins of Empire: The Japanese Surrender and the Battle for Postwar Asia*, Random House, New York, 2007.

Wada, Haruki, *The Korean War: An International History*, Trans. By Frank Baldwin, Roman & Littlefield, Lanham, MD, 2014.

NOTES

[i] There was a fourteen hour time difference between Seoul and Washington, D.C..

[ii] A mudang is a Korean sorceress or exorcist relied on by many as a natural healer..

[iii] Supreme Commander for the Allied Powers

[iv] Zainichi is a Japanese term for ethnic Koreans resident in Japan

[v] U.S. Civil Administration of Ryukyus

[vi] Japanese Drum

[vii] Information on Prince Yi Un obtained from WikiPEDIA at https://en.wikipedia.org/wiki/Un_Yi

[viii] Zaibatsu refers to a specific oligarchic group of Japanese family-run businesses commanding major corporations with heavy political influence

[ix] Demonstrators did riot in Tokyo on May 1, 1952. This scene is based largely on eyewitness reports in the May 2, 1952 issue of the *New York Times*

[x] Yakuza is a Japanese crime syndicate similar to the Mafia

View other Black Rose Writing titles at <u>www.blackrosewriting.com/books</u>
and use promo code PRINT to receive a 20% discount when purchasing.

BLACK❀ROSE
writing™

www.ingramcontent.com/pod-product-compliance
Lightning Source LLC
Chambersburg PA
CBHW010442100726
47904CB00008B/2447